Welcome ***new dimensi...***

Life is the Teacher for
a college student named Emma,
as she struggles to resist her recently awakened
urges and her new life among the undead . . .

An immortal caught between two worlds
is a writer's *Demon Lover* in a blistering tale
of the ultimate seduction . . .

Music Hath Charms to bewitch a beautiful
talent agent when she falls under the spell
of two enigmatic and irresistible musicians
who guard a shocking, centuries-old secret . . .

It's a match *To Die For* when
a shape-shifting detective joins forces
with an alpha werewolf to track down
a missing person . . .

In *Brother's Keeper,* Selene is under
the protection of an intoxicating,
otherworldly male who holds the key
to her survival and her deepest desires—
as she battles an evil as seductive as a kiss . . .

HOTTER THAN HELL

Edited by Kim Harrison

HOTTER THAN HELL
HOLIDAYS ARE HELL
DATES FROM HELL

HOTTER THAN HELL

EDITED BY

KIM HARRISON

AND

MARTIN H. GREENBERG

HARPER

An Imprint of HarperCollinsPublishers

HARPER

An Imprint of HarperCollins*Publishers*
10 East 53rd Street
New York, New York 10022-5299

CONTENTS

INTRODUCTION

Short stories were where I fell in love with the power behind the printed word, a small little nugget of truth or observation, a "what if" of thought pared down to its simplest thought to make the complex easy. Those masters of the science fiction and fantasy field had created for me a gourmet meal, with its small portions elaborately presented to leave the participant impressed, knowing that they had taken in something out of the ordinary, even if it did leave them hungry for a burger on the way home.

So it was with great pleasure that I accepted Marty Greenberg's challenge to put together a short story collection of urban fantasy and paranormal romance: tastefully erotic tales of romance, love, and downright inescapable lust running the stylistic temperature from sweet to spicy to tantalizingly dangerous. With urban fantasy's goal of finding the reason behind the attraction and paranormal romance's open and honest explorations of love and lust, I found a refreshingly wide span of storytelling styles, but the common thread of an intelligent, strong-willed female protagonist in a little over her head rang true in every story.

I finished deciding that I hadn't helped prepare a gourmet meal in this case, but instead somehow created a cool, summer fruit salad: a bursting of sweet strawberries for romantic love, the twang of sour grapes for revenge and loss, chunks of apples and peaches—the stories from established worlds we have become familiar with, and the exotic flavor of kiwi and passion fruit—the tantalizing glimpses of something new we'd like to see more of, all mixed up with the sweet dressing of incomparable, good storytelling from some of the best authors in the paranormal romance and urban fantasy field today.

So please pull up a chair in the shade, prop up your feet on the cooler full of the icy beverage of your choice, set the phone on mute, and dig in. Enjoy! And if you're wondering what kind of fruit I think my work is? That would be the nuts. ;-)

Kim Harrison
July 2008

MUSIC HATH CHARMS

Tanya Huff

AS GLEN MANEUVERED HIS CAR OVER THE RUTTED field the sign insisted was the parking lot, Ali frowned out the tinted window at a line of teenagers dressed in white and leading enormous brown cows and wondered if her partner had lost his mind. Bands that played the county fair circuit might be a step above garage bands, but it was usually a small step. Bedford Entertainment needed to sign a group that could pull in some numbers, and she didn't think they'd find that here.

"What's up with the kids and the cows?" she wondered as they bounced to a stop next to an impressively rusted pickup.

Glancing past her as he shifted into park, Glen shrugged. "Different leash laws in the country, I guess. Come on, they're on in twenty minutes."

He'd brought her here to see a band named *NoMan*. Five-man, country-rock, fronted by two brothers, Brandon and Travis No-man. One sang lead, one played—well, in country-rock she supposed it was a fiddle, wasn't it? She wasn't sure about the name but names were easy enough to change. They were backed by guitar, bass, and drums but she had no information on the musicians.

When asked, Glen laughed. "Backup doesn't matter, Ali, it's the brothers you're here to see. You could back those two with . . . with boy-band leftovers and they'd still kick ass."

"A ringing endorsement."

He laughed again. "You'll see."

The stage had been set up at one end of the midway. It had a back and a roof of sorts and the ubiquitous three guys in black t-shirts screwing around with the sound system, but there was no disguising it was actually a hay wagon or that hay bales had been arranged in rows for the audience.

This explained Glen's instruction to wear jeans.

"How rustic," she murmured as they settled on a bale at the end of the fourth row.

"Trust me."

She closed her hand around his arm. "Please tell me you didn't sleep with them and you've dragged me out to the middle of nowhere to hear a thanks-for-the-fuck audition."

He laid his hand over hers, large and warm and calming. "I didn't and it isn't. Although I would have. Couldn't get close."

Leaning around him, Ali realized the bales were filling fast with an *interesting* cross section of humanity. She hadn't known baseball caps came in such a wide variety of colors. A closer look at the packed first three rows—the rows between her and the stage—and she realized no one sitting there could be considered either old or young and they all exuded a certain visceral anticipation as they waited for the show to start.

Evidently, NoMan had groupies. A decent enough showing for a Saturday afternoon gig at a county fair but not the kind of numbers that would have kept Glen away from the prize. Nor, more importantly, the kind of numbers that would make them the saviors Bedford Entertainment needed.

On the other hand, if they were as good as Glen said they were, she could build their numbers to the point where they'd become what she needed. And if they weren't . . . at least she'd got out of the city for the afternoon. There had to be some truth in what everyone said about fresh air.

"If you'd got to them, would they?" she wondered, determined to distract herself.

Mouth by her ear, he murmured, "I pegged them as enthusiastically nondiscriminating."

Well, she was all for enthusiasm. Settling her weight against Glen's shoulder, she found a certain amusement in noting the envious looks being sent her way. Six foot meant a lot of leg in tight jeans, the heavy white shirt emphasized the breadth of his shoulders, and the rolled-up sleeves exposed muscular forearms. It might have been gym muscle, not work muscle, but he didn't look out of place amid the surrounding country boys. The light dusting of freckles across his nose just added to the wholesome appeal.

"What are you smiling about?"

"The bottle redhead in the front row keeps turning to give you the eye."

He drew his tongue over a full lower lip, watched her squirm and said, "Her boyfriend's not bad."

"And that's why I was smiling."

"Bitch."

"And that's why you love me." Ali had a feeling she was attracting some attention herself, felt that prickling between her shoulder blades that said someone was staring. The feeling grew and, although she'd had every intention of ignoring it, she finally turned. No mistaking the familiar figure standing just behind the last row of hay bales.

He winked. He pushed back the curl of thick, dark hair that fell over his forehead and he unmistakably winked one brilliant blue eye when he caught her staring.

Bastard.

She tightened her grip on Glen's arm. "Tom Hartmore's here."

Muscle tensed but Glen didn't turn. "If Tom's here then Mike's interested."

"You think?" she snapped. There was nothing Michael Richter's Vital Music Group liked better than finding a band just on the verge of breaking out and thrusting them out onto the world stage. Vital made stars out of guts and raw talent—Ali had to give them that—and they were so good at it most of the musicians took years to realize they'd signed an iron-clad contract giving away rights to everything up to and including posthumous work. Michael Richter didn't believe in death cutting into his bottom line.

"Tom could be doing some preliminary scouting. Working on rumor. If he had actual word on the band . . ."

"Then Mike would be here himself, he wouldn't send Tom." The knot loosened in Ali's stomach. They were still one step ahead.

A squawk from the sound system drew her attention back to the stage. The guitar player was fiddling with his amp, the bass player looked stoned—although that was hardly unusual for bass players—and the drummer looked like he'd been borrowed from a thrash metal band. No sign of the brothers . . .

Almost before she finished the thought, they were on the stage. The matching black cowboy hats seemed to be the only affectation—given the blazing afternoon sun, she'd allow Travis's sunglasses as a necessity—otherwise they were both in jeans and worn boots. Brandon had on a black t-shirt with the band's name in red and Travis wore a black shirt tucked in over the biggest belt buckle Ali'd ever seen. The sun glinting off it kept drawing her gaze back to his crotch as he tuned up, not necessarily a bad thing, but she was after the larger picture. Brandon's dark blond hair just covered the back of his neck. Travis's was longer, lighter, and tied back.

As Brandon moved to the center microphone, the redhead bounced and squealed.

The redhead's boyfriend seemed close to doing the same. Another vote cast for enthusiastically nondiscriminating then.

While they wouldn't stop traffic, the brothers weren't unattractive. It was hard to get a handle on their height—given the stage and the hats—but she doubted either of them had hit six foot, although Travis looked a little taller. As far as she could tell, they were in good shape and both presented the overt masculinity that often came as a package deal with country singers. The way they moved made her think theirs came to them naturally. She was obviously missing something though, given Glen's reaction.

Well, Glen, the redhead, her boyfriend, a pair of busty blondes who waved wildly until Brandon acknowledged them with a smile, and pretty damned near everyone sitting in the first three rows.

"Glen . . ."

"Wait for it."

Then Travis drew his bow across the strings and Ali felt the note dance through blood and bone. It was the eeriest damned sound she'd ever heard.

The drummer counted them in as Brandon wrapped both hands around the microphone.

The first song was called *Sweet Southern Rain*, the second, *Wild Nights*, and by the third, Ali had lost track of the titles. She had to move, up on her feet like everyone else, the crowd growing with every song as men and women abandoned the midway and the show rings. She was unable to take her eyes off the way Brandon's mouth moved mere inches from a big, old-fashioned condenser mic—whiskey voice caressing, or screaming, or growling the words. All she could think of were those hands, cupping her face the way he held the microphone, fingers rough against her skin. When he started to sweat, she breathed deep, trying to catch his scent over the hay and the cotton candy wafting in from the midway. When he moved, she moved with him and imagined his skin slick and hot against hers.

Travis kept playing between songs, bow drawing out soft sighs and desperate moans, each sound the perfect counterpoint to Brandon's patter as he introduced songs and the band and flirted with the audience, the band, and occasionally, his brother.

They took two encores and finally left the stage, Travis playing one last note that hung over the fairground. As it faded, Ali took a deep breath and sagged against Glen's side, feeling like there wasn't enough oxygen left in the world.

"My God, I'm . . ."

"Wet?"

She was drenched, sweat molding her t-shirt to her sides, her hair damp and sticking to the back of her neck but as she smacked him on the arm, she knew that wasn't what he meant. "Enthralled." Her voice sounded raw. Wanting. Everything seemed . . . more. The sky seemed bluer. The grass seemed greener. The breeze didn't just blow past her bare arms, it caressed sun-warmed skin.

No need to look to understand why Glen had worn his shirt untucked. Although, given how tight his jeans were, that kind of pressure couldn't be fun.

The redhead sat straddling her boyfriend's lap, his face against her neck, one big hand buried in her hair, the other splayed over the patch of creamy skin between her jeans and the edge of her t-shirt. She rocked her hips slowly, the gentle rhythm suggesting the main event was already over and they were just riding out the aftershocks.

Unable to help herself, Ali rocked forward to the same rhythm, seeking the minimal friction her jeans could offer.

There were a few couples still in the first three rows but most of the bales were empty.

"NoMan has a very *hopeful* fanbase," Glen told her, shifting uncomfortably. "And backstage is probably one of the only private areas on the fairground. Even if you can't nail the band you'll still be able to take the edge off."

"Charming." She had control of her voice again and could only pray that her own need to take the edge off wasn't showing on her face. She turned, scanning the fairground. Tom Hartmore was nowhere to be seen. If they were lucky, he was on his way back to the city to report to the boss and they still had time. If they were *really* lucky, he was getting laid by some buxom farm girl and they'd picked up a little more time. If their luck truly sucked, he was already backstage. "Come on. We need to talk to the Noman brothers and we can't do that out here."

"So you want them?"

After the way she'd bitched and complained during the

drive out from the city she supposed he had grounds but she still gave his smug, smarmy tone the response it deserved. "Bite me."

"Yeah, I told you that you'd be . . ."

When his voice trailed off she turned, saw where he was looking, and smiled. Big guy, heavily built, mud on his boots and his jeans, straw cowboy hat, checked shirt, and eyes that tilted catlike up at the outer edges narrowed in a come-hither glare—as much challenge as invitation—directed right at Glen. Who made a noise low in his throat, kind of cross between a growl and a moan.

She couldn't say she blamed him. "Go ahead. Take the edge off." Her hand resting in the warm curve of the small of his back, she pushed him forward. "Save a horse."

"Ali . . ."

"Don't worry. I can convince a couple of rock-and-roll cowboys to come into the office and talk without you by my side."

"Not what I was worried about."

"Oh please." Her lip curled. "If Tom's back there, I can handle him. And if not, well, I like to think I can handle myself in a honky-tonk orgy. You go handle tall, dark, and country over there. Play safe," she added as Glen started across the trampled grass. "I'll meet you back at the car in half an hour."

"Forty-five minutes."

"Don't tell me you're going to talk to him too?"

He turned just far enough to flip her off.

She laughed and headed backstage. Competent musicians were a dime a dozen; to make it big a band needed to connect with its audience on a visceral level and NoMan could certainly do that. The brothers were exactly what she'd been looking for. Glen was right, she wanted them.

Backstage was a white canvas tent about twenty-five-feet long and maybe ten wide. It was a shelter for the sound board if the weather got bad, a place for the performers to pull it together before the show, and this far out in the country it could do double duty as a sheep pen for all Ali knew. It had the kind of sidewalls that could be tied up or staked down, depending. At the moment, these were staked down.

No big surprise if what Glen said about NoMan and how close they got to their fans was true.

She paused, one hand on the tent flap. The honky-tonk orgy crack had been a joke but if even half the NoMan fans who'd headed back here had been as turned on by the music as she'd been—as she still was—well, *orgy* might not be too strong a word for it. Not something she wanted to walk in on, mostly because the way she was feeling she wasn't entirely certain she could walk out again.

Still, the band wasn't signed and if she didn't want Michael Richter to grab them first . . .

And grabbing them sounded like a damned good idea.

Telling herself to focus, she slipped in under the tent flap . . .

. . . where things were almost anti-climactically low key.

Like the redhead and her boyfriend, the fans present seemed almost postcoital. They milled about in the front half of the tent looking dazed and a little like they were starting to come down off a very pleasant high. Eyes were half closed, smiles contented as hands lazily stroked bare arms, and cupped the backs of necks, and ran up under the edges of shirts and down under the edges of jeans but no one seemed to be taking things farther than they might late at a party with close friends.

At least not in the front of the tent. In the back, behind the sound board and a card table holding a box of NoMan CDs, a scrawled sign indicating they cost ten dollars, and an open cashbox, the drummer had his hand shoved in through the front of the bass player's open jeans and was slowly jacking him off. Without breaking his rhythm, he took a swallow from the bottle of beer in his other hand; leaned forward and pressed his lips to the other man's mouth. Ali watched mesmerized as a line of liquid escaped the kiss running along the bass player's jaw and down his throat. She wanted to move forward and catch it on her tongue, capturing the taste of the beer and sweat, licking her way back up past his tats until . . .

The edge of the sound board caught her in the thigh and the pain brought her back to herself. As she gasped, the guitarist, sprawled in an Adirondack chair, flashed her a satiated smile and waved a sloppy salute with his nearly empty bottle.

The Noman brothers were nowhere around. Nor was Tom Hartmore. If they were together . . .

Pleasantly startled by the images that evoked, she hastily dropped a ten in the cash box, shoved a CD in her purse, and slipped back through the crowd to the exit, ignoring the moments of warmth as bodies brushed against hers. Definitely past time to leave.

Once outside, she took a deep breath. The smell of grease and cotton candy wafting over from the midway combined with the odors of large farm animals and diesel fumes cleared her head and she felt like she was thinking clearly for the first time since Travis Noman had set bow to strings. Thinking back, the concert seemed wrapped in sensation, her memory of everything but the way it made her feel already fading.

It wasn't the strangest concert experience she'd ever had, but considering it had happened in a sunny field in the middle of the afternoon, it was in the top ten.

It shouldn't have been so hard to find the car. After all, it was parked in a field—a big, flat field full of lines of cars parked nose to nose that all seemed to look alike. After wandering around for nearly fifteen minutes, Ali spotted what she thought was the rusty pickup Glen had parked beside and headed toward it, skirting rear bumpers.

She spotted the cowboy hats first.

Realized who wore them as she moved closer, finding a path between two ancient Buicks.

Realized they weren't alone when she'd gotten too close to turn back.

Didn't actually think of turning back.

Brandon and Travis Noman leaned back against the hood of the pickup, side by side, shoulders touching. Kneeling at their feet in the strip of grass between the truck's bumper and the bumper of the car parked facing it were the pair of blondes from the front row. Although the car blocked all but the top of their heads, it was obvious what they were doing and from all the giggling, they certainly seemed to be having a good time doing it. Travis was still wearing his sunglasses and his head was back, exposing the long lean line of his throat. Brandon's head was tipped forward and Ali knew he was watching.

She shouldn't be watching.

She couldn't stop watching.

It wasn't like she could actually see anything . . .

Travis moaned—the sound broken, on the edge of shattering and his fingers, long and tanned, threaded through golden hair as his hips came up off the truck.

No, not a moan. Or not only a moan. Brandon was humming one of the songs from the show while Travis added a weirdly erotic bass line under it.

The girls' heads moved to the beat.

Hardly aware she was doing it, Ali slid her hand down into her jeans, past the edge of her underwear. Still aroused from the concert, she fell easily into the rhythm of Brandon's song, fingertips moving in unison with the quartet filling her vision. And then she had to bite her lip to keep from laughing because *quartet* made her think of chamber music and they weren't in a chamber, they were in a field and anyone could walk by just like she had and God, the memory of the music left her feeling stoned.

And close.

Really, really close.

Both men were breathing hard, the rhythm of the song beginning to stutter. The girls sped up and Ali sped up with them, linking her finish to theirs. Tension was building, low and sweet . . .

When it happened, it happened like flood waters finally breaching a levee. Brandon. Travis. Then both girls. A heartbeat behind them, Ali trembled on the brink until Brandon looked up—his pupils dilated, his irises reduced to a pale, narrow ring of blue—and the open, fucked-out expression on his face pushed her over the edge.

Riding the wave, Ali sagged against sun-warmed metal and concentrated on keeping her knees from buckling. The world went white around the edges and she closed her eyes, just for a moment. Just long enough to draw in a long, steadying breath. She opened them again as she eased her hand from her jeans and she may have made a noise because Travis raised his head and smiled at her over the honey-blond curls of the girl in his arms. Something in that smile said he—they—knew she'd been there all along. Still smiling, he slid his sunglasses forward . . .

A flash of gold.

And she was standing alone, facing the rusty pickup parked next to Glen's car. Power chords blared from the midway's speakers, nearly drowning out the screams of children riding the ancient Octopus and Scrambler. The world no longer wore the sheen given it by NoMan's music—the sky was more gray than blue and the grass underfoot dry and yellow. If not for the evidence of her own body, she'd have thought she'd imagined the whole thing.

Glen was right. If Bedford Entertainment could sign these guys, they were saved.

The CD wasn't bad but it was strangely flat.

"Not evoking much of a reaction," she murmured as they sped back to the city.

Glen laughed. "After that performance, I'd be amazed if you had a reaction left in you."

He had a point. And he hadn't seen the encore performance out in the parking lot.

NoMan had a barebones website that held a picture of the band, a headshot of the brothers—Travis had his sunglasses on—a song list, and an order form for the CD plus a link to their mailing list. There was no concert schedule and the mailing list was the only way to contact them. Ali added the email address for Bedford Entertainment, including in the body of the message their business number, the URL for the website, their MySpace address, and an assurance that Bedford Entertainment was definitely interested in representing them. Professional bases covered, she paused a moment, remembering, then typed *We nearly met in the parking lot.*

"They're twins."

She hit send before looking up to find Glen raising a brow in her direction. "What?"

"You're flushed."

"It's warm in here." It wasn't. "Who are twins?" Like she didn't know. Like she'd been thinking about anyone else for the last twenty-four hours.

Glen moved a stack of eight-by-ten glossies out of the way and perched on the edge of her desk. "Travis and Brandon Noman, twenty-seven, born in Tarpon Springs, Florida."

"So they're American."

"They're carrying American passports," Glen allowed. "Their mother was a Greek national named Thea Achelous. Travis is older by nine minutes."

When he paused, Ali frowned. "That's it?"

"That's it. And getting that much was like pulling teeth. They're living almost entirely off the grid."

"You said you heard about them from a friend . . ."

"And that's who told me what I just told you. He's a fan in the whole *fanatic* sense of the word and if he can't pull information on them, well, it's not there to be pulled. I've left messages with the people who booked them for that fair but we're talking volunteer labor and they haven't called me back."

"All right . . ." Staring at the exceedingly unhelpful webpage, Ali tucked a lock of hair back behind her ear. "The good news is, if we can't find them then Mike can't find them and . . ."

The intercom buzzed. Wondering what was up—she had nothing on the books until after lunch—she hit the connect.

"What is it, Brenda?"

"There's a Michael Richter to see you."

"Speak of the devil," Glen muttered.

"Don't even joke about that," Ali told him, more than half seriously.

She didn't get the chance to ask what Mike wanted before Brenda added, "He wants to speak with you but he has no appointment." Her tone, while polite, suggested she'd never heard of anyone named Michael Richter and couldn't imagine why he'd be dropping by. Mike had heard some of Brenda's voice work and wanted Vital to represent her until he discovered she weighed just over three hundred pounds. *Too much work to make presentable* had been his final judgment.

The position of office manager at Bedford Entertainment had been a part-time gig to fill in the corners around bookings but gradually the two jobs had evened out and, currently, office manager was slightly ahead. Unfortunately, it was also about to be made redundant unless they could find an act that actually paid the bills.

"You have an hour open Wednesday at nine," she announced. "Shall I schedule Mr. Richter for then?"

Glen mouthed an exaggerated, *"Burn!"* as Ali rolled her eyes. "I'll shuffle some things around and see him now, Brenda. We don't want him to have to come back."

"Alysha." Arms spread, Michael Richter walked into her office like he owned it. Given that he probably could have bought the building for the cost of his wardrobe and accessories, he had grounds and the shaved head only added to the whole Daddy Warbucks/Lex Luthor vibe. He was entirely unruffled by Brenda's little one-act play but that was hardly surprising—he had Tom Hartmore to be ruffled for him.

Ali came around her desk and moved into his embrace, skin crawling. Appearances were everything to Mike, and she knew she couldn't win if she declared war. Enveloped in a cloud of expensive cologne, she touched each cheek gently with her lips, felt his touch in return, and backed away, gesturing toward the more comfortable of the two chairs facing her desk. "To what do I owe this unexpected pleasure," she purred as he sat.

"Tom here . . ." A slight nod indicated the man who'd followed him into the room and now stood glaring behind him. ". . . says we want the same thing."

"Peace on earth? A little less David Hasselhoff? A really kick-ass pair of black ankle boots?"

"NoMan."

"Ah." Neutral expression locked on her face, Ali changed her mind about walking back around the desk and perched on the front edge instead. She crossed her bare legs, dangled one high-heeled sandal, and smiled down at the man who was trying to put her out of business. "It appears we both have excellent taste; but then . . ." Her smile flicked up to Tom and grew edged. ". . . I knew that."

"I'm not here to drag up old conflicts, Alysha." Mike's voice had always made her think of that velvet glove over the iron fist. "I'm here to offer you a proposition." To his credit he smiled when she raised both brows. "You flatter me, my dear."

He was eleven years older than she was, not nearly enough difference to be so damned patronizing.

"I want you to leave NoMan alone," he continued. "In return, I will open up a weekend at the Hazard. You know what that kind of exposure would do for one of your . . . acts."

The Hazard was currently *the* place to be seen, the place to build the kind of buzz that led to major recording deals and Vital had bookings locked down into the next decade. Mike was right; she had people signed who could turn a gig at the Hazard to a solid career, their success becoming the little engine that dragged Bedford Entertainment out of the red. Ali, a firm believer in the bird in the hand over two in the bush—no matter how extreme her reaction to the two birds in question—would have taken him up on the offer except for two things. The first was the disdain in the moment of silence before he said the word, *acts*.

The second . . .

"That's very generous of you, Mike, but I have no desire to become a subsidiary to Vital, living off scraps from your table." No matter how bad it got, she wouldn't sell her people out to a man who saw them as inferior product.

He spread his hands, the movement graceful and predetermined as though her response hadn't been entirely unexpected. "I respect your choice, of course, but perhaps you should take a moment to think about it. My scraps, to beat the metaphor vigorously about the head and shoulders, have more substance than any meal you can provide and I know you hate to see your people starve."

"No one's starving."

"Yet."

And there, in the single word Tom dropped into her office, was the stick to Mike's carrot. Ali waved Glen back and realized, almost as an afterthought, that she was standing. Tom looked down at her through narrowed eyes, daring her to react further. To move in closer.

Not going to happen. Except . . .

One of them had definitely moved, but Ali was sure it hadn't been her. They were less than an arm's length away now. She stared at the scar bisecting Tom's upper lip and remembered the night he'd got it.

The lip in question curled as if he could read her thoughts.

"Play nice, children."

The amusement in Mike's voice moved her back until the edge of her desk digging into her thighs stopped her. No way was she providing entertainment by fighting with her ex in front of his boss/lover/who the hell knew.

"I'm sorry you weren't able to accept my offer, Alysha." Mike stood as he spoke and gifted her with a benevolent smile. "It would have made everything so much easier."

"For you."

"For all concerned," he admonished, gently. "I can see myself out." He was at the door before he realized he was alone. He turned in the doorway and the velvet glove slipped. "Tom!"

"Your master's voice," Ali murmured. As Tom closed the distance between them, she raised her right hand and laid her palm over his heart, flat against his chest. She could feel the heat of his skin through the black silk shirt. It matched the heat of his breath against her cheek. The heat in his voice.

"You're going to lose this one, Ali," he growled, "and I'll be there to see you go down."

"You're going to pay for making Mike wait," she purred back, her breath moving the dark hair curling over his ear. "And I *wish* I could be there to see you go down."

He jerked away from her like he'd been hit, spun on one heel, and followed Mike out the door, slamming it closed behind him.

"Ali?"

Glen's voice dragged her back to the here and now and she realized her hand was still pressed up against the space Tom's chest had filled. Slowly, she closed her fingers and let it fall to her side. "That was interesting."

"I'll say." His tone was so totally neutral she knew he wasn't only referring to Mike's offer.

"Let it go, Glen."

His green eyes were worried as he watched her walk around her desk and drop into the chair. "Maybe you should take your own advice. It's been three years."

"I know."

"You and Tom bring out the worst in each other."

She thought about the scar. "I know."

Glen stared at her for a moment longer then spread his hands in surrender. "Fine. Why do you think Mike was trying to keep us away from NoMan? It's not like him to care if we're after the same band."

"No, it isn't." Usually he enjoyed the competition, secure in the knowledge that nine out of ten times, he'd win. Something about NoMan had made him try and tie up that tenth time. Try to buy her first, because that came with added benefits, and then threaten when she refused to be bought. It was a good thing he didn't know just how bad their situation was or he'd have merely waited for time to take care of it and not bothered tipping his hand. "He can't just be working off Tom's report and the CD. He has to know something about the Noman brothers we don't."

"We know almost nothing so that wouldn't be hard and I've tapped out my sources."

"Then go at it obliquely. You were right when you said it wouldn't matter who was backing them and, since they can't be making much money, I'm betting there's been a bit of a revolving door. Let's start by finding an ex member of the band."

Over the next ten days, a hundred small things went wrong. Not one of them could be definitively laid at Mike's door, not one of them big enough to confront him about, not one of them that would allow her to take any kind of legal recourse.

"It's like being nibbled to death by ducks *while* you're drowning," Ali muttered, hanging up as Glen came into the office. "An argument over a clause in a contract here, a sudden renovation of a venue there." She slumped down in her chair. "Do you know what I think? I think Mike has no more idea of how to contact the Noman brothers than we do and he's trying to distract us. I think that's why he tried to warn us off—there's a chance we'll luck out and find them first." Glancing up at her partner, she realized he was smiling. "Why are you looking so happy?"

"I found a bass player."

"When did you lose one?"

"I found a bass player who used to play for NoMan."

"Oh man, there was all the pussy you could ever want." Steve, the bass player, took a moment to grin at the memory. "We'd stop playing and the girls would meet us backstage, ready and willing. Boys too if that floats your boat. Me, not so much but Brandon and Travis, man, the two of them together, they could get anyone to do anything you know?"

Actually, Ali had a fairly good idea. She leaned forward, careful to keep her elbows out of the spilled beer. "Was it always the two of them together?"

"Always. When the two of them wanted something, they got it."

"They couldn't have always wanted the same thing," Glen protested.

Steve shrugged. "All I know is what I saw, dude."

"Was it always sex?" Ali wondered.

"Hell, no." Steve grinned again, broadly enough this time for a gold tooth to flash in the dim light of the bar. "Sometimes it was pie. But usually it was sex."

"Suppose they asked for money?"

"Long as they didn't ask me, man. Shit, I could never keep two bills together."

"I didn't mean they asked you," Ali sighed. "Suppose they asked the people who come to their concerts for money."

Steve's smile disappeared. "What part of if the two of them wanted something, they got it are you not understanding? But I never saw them ask for money, they didn't really give a shit about that kind of thing. They just wanted to sing and drink and have a good time."

Which made them pretty much the same as every other band that played the bottom of the market except . . .

"Were you their first bass player?"

"Hell, no. There were . . ." He stared off into the distance, lips moving as he counted back. ". . . seven, maybe eight before me. And a couple of them, they lasted twice as long. Me, two years was all I could handle. Just too much of a good thing."

A raised hand cut off whatever Glen was about to say. Ali had a feeling she knew what that was and didn't want to argue about it with an audience. "Why did you leave?"

"Leave?"

"The band."

Steve took a long swallow of beer and frowned down at the amber liquid still in his glass. "Well, there was . . . and it kinda . . . you know?"

"Not really," Ali told him while Glen rolled his eyes.

When Steve looked up, his expression was unreadable. "Sure you do."

Ali remembered the flash of gold as Travis lowered his glasses. Maybe she did. "Steve, did you ever see anything weird about Travis's eyes?"

"Nothing wrong with singing and drinking and having a good time but fuck, after a while it's exhausting." He took another long drink. "I do studio work now. Got an old lady. Got a life."

"Eyes," Ali prodded.

He grinned. "I got two."

Shaking his head, Glen leaned into his space. "Do you know how we can contact Brandon or Travis Noman?"

"Always Brandon *and* Travis, dude," Steve told him. "Never *or*. And I don't have a clue."

"That was ninety minutes we'll never get back," Glen snorted dropping into the car and reaching for his seatbelt. "Total waste of time."

"No, it wasn't. We learned a couple of things. We learned, based on the number of bass players, that the Noman brothers have been performing for at least twenty-four years—seven before Steve, Steve, and two after him averaging two years a piece with at least two of them hanging in for four—which would have made them three when they started and somehow I doubt that. I'm guessing that's what cued Mike in that there was something up, something about them he could exploit."

"He noticed they were lying about their age?"

"He noticed they've been around a lot longer than the evidence suggests."

"Ali, if you looked at the evidence the Rolling Stones should be dead and they're still performing."

"Yes, but Mick Jagger doesn't look twenty-seven. The Noman brothers have a power in their voices . . ." She could feel her heart speed up just remembering the way they'd held that crowd with their music, the way it lingered even after they stopped playing. ". . . and Mike wants to use it. The moment he gets them under contract they'll be singing for more than pie."

"Ali . . ."

"You heard what Steve said."

"He's got four functioning brain cells—one for each string and nothing extra. Brandon and Travis are good-looking guys with talent and stage presence; they know how to play the crowd. Of course they can get laid."

"Mike . . ."

"Mike wants them because he knows he can make money off them. It's why we want them. It's as simple as that."

Travis raised his head and smiled at her over the honey-blond curls of the girl in his arms. Something in that smile said he—they—knew she'd been there all along. Still smiling, he slid his sunglasses forward . . .

A flash of gold.

"No, it's not." She closed a hand over his forearm, willing him to believe her. "You didn't see what I saw."

Glen was out of the office, hand-holding a client through a recording session, when the email came. NoMan was playing at the Atlas on Friday night. Ali was pretty sure she'd have told Glen about it had he been around; he had been the one to bring the band to her attention after all, even if he continued to insist they were nothing more than they seemed.

The denim skirt was so short it barely required all five letters and the heels on her boots made her legs look at least three inches longer. A white shirt so she'd stand out in the dim light of the bar. Noticeable, Ali decided, checking the mirror as she picked up her black leather messenger bag, but practically business casual given the excesses of the music industry.

The Atlas was attached to a downtown hotel that had seen much better days. There was a pool table off in one corner, a heavy, dark wooden bar across one narrow end, and a decent-sized stage across the other. Ali arrived at eight for a nine-thirty start, but the redhead and her boyfriend were already at a table. Pulling a t-shirt from her bag, Ali arranged her face in her best *I can do things for you* smile and moved in to make her pitch.

By nine-twenty she had all six t-shirts in place. Tight and low cut, black on white and stretched over the redhead, the two blondes from the parking lot, and three brunettes with a similar advertising under-structure, the name *Bedford Entertainment* would be impossible for the brothers to miss. At fifty dollars a shirt, it would be three hundred dollars well spent.

By nine-thirty the press of bodies had raised the temperature in the bar just a little higher than comfortable. As far as Ali knew, anticipation had no actual scent but there was definitely something in the air besides sweat and scotch. Something that kept her shifting on her high stool at the bar, every movement bringing her into contact with the men and women packed around her, every contact making her nerves sing that much more.

Shadows moved across the stage, then one long note dropped the room into silence. As the stage lights came up, NoMan started to play.

The hats and boots hadn't changed, but above torn and battered jeans, Brandon wore a gray t-shirt with the sleeves ripped off that was so tight it looked painted onto his torso. Bare, muscular arms already glistened with sweat. Travis's jeans were in better shape, but his untucked white-and-pink-striped shirt was half unbuttoned and gold hair glinted between the wings of the shirt every time he pulled back the bow. Ali wasn't surprised to see he still wore his sunglasses.

The first two songs were the same as the last time but, just like the last time, by the third song Ali'd lost any hope of keeping coherent notes. All she could do was ride the sensation, intensified by the close quarters. Off her stool now, she moved with the music, with the crowd, touching, rubbing as

the notes from Travis's fiddle burned through her blood and
Brandon's voice licked at her skin.

Hands gripped her hips and dragged her back against a hard
body, hot breath lapped at her ear, and a familiar voice just
barely audible over the music growled, "You drive me crazy,
Ali. I look at you like this and I can't keep my hands off you."

She bit back the moan that possibility evoked and struggled to turn but Tom held her in place, his erection a line of
hard heat against her thigh.

"I could have you right now," he said, slipping one arm
around her waist and pulling her closer still as fingers
stroked up her bare leg under the edge of her skirt, blunt
nails digging lightly at her skin. "I could lift your skirt, drag
your panties aside, slip into you." Two fingers pushed under
the elastic. "I could fuck you in time to the music." The fingers slid down the wet line of her sex, teasing. Up on her
toes, Ali's head fell back against Tom's shoulder. "I bet
they'd notice—no one else would but Brandon and Travis,
they'd watch from the stage." Then the fingers were gone
and his grip was gone and there was only his voice at her
ear. "I want to, but I won't. Because I've moved on."

She managed to turn in time to see him push the fall of
thick dark hair back off his face and, eyes tracking the motion, she noticed there was something in his ear. By the time
she got all the way around, he was moving away, slipping
easily through the crowd, the only person in the room who
hadn't given control of his body over to the music.

Wax plugs in his ears to keep himself from being swept
away.

As heated bodies brushed rhythmically against her, and
the hands on her skin and the breath raising goosebumps on
her neck belonged to strangers, Ali looked to the stage where
Brandon held the microphone like a lover and sang of learning to touch and Travis danced the bow across the strings of
his violin spilling out notes in point and counterpoint . . .

. . . and she knew.

After, when the music ended, she slid back up onto the

stool, ordered a scotch, and waited. The crowd had thinned
and those who remained were moving around the room like
cats after a kill—slow, deliberate, sensual. The box of CDs
on the end of the bar had emptied as people paid for the
chance to take the sensation evoked by the music home.

Brandon stood just off the stage, brushing damp tendrils
of the redhead's hair back off her face while Travis stood
beside him, one hand gently kneading her boyfriend's broad
shoulder. All four of them glanced down at her chest, and
she half turned, pointing toward the bar.

As Brandon's eyes met hers, Ali raised her glass and
smiled.

Travis laughed, the sound falling into the room like peb-
bles into a pond, the ripple of reaction spreading. Someone
dropped a glass. Someone else moaned. Brandon leaned toward his brother, asked a question, and when Travis nodded,
led the way up onto the stage and toward the door at the
back. They paused at the door, standing close enough as
they turned that Ali knew they had to be touching shoulder
to hip. Still smiling, Travis beckoned.

Given the sunglasses it should have been impossible to
tell who he was beckoning to.

It wasn't.

His teeth were very white.

Backstage was nothing more than a long, narrow room between the rear wall of the stage and the brick, outside wall
of the Atlas. The air was cooler and smelled more like dust
than like sex and alcohol. Following the two men past
stacked chairs and empty boxes to where a small lounge had
been set up in the far corner, Ali wondered a little at her
willingness to throw caution to the winds. If the brothers
could make anyone do anything . . .

The possibility smoldered in the cradle of her hips, the
heat shifting and flaring as she walked.

"So, Alysha Bedford of Bedford Entertainment . . ." Travis dropped onto one corner of the disreputable-looking

couch, Brandon perching on the arm beside him. ". . . you've got our attention." His right hand rose to rest on his brother's thigh, long fingers absently stroking the faded denim. "What is it you want?"

Ali drew her tongue over dry lips. She wanted them to touch her. To drag rough fingers over her skin. To open her. To fill her. To feast off her. That was what she wanted but it wasn't why she was there. She was there because they had something she needed and she had to convince them that they in turn needed her. "I know what you are," she said.

Travis laughed but Brandon tossed his hat down on the other end of the couch and drew both hands back through damp hair, pale eyes never leaving her face. "I think she does."

"Do you?" Travis stretched out one long leg, the room narrow enough his boot ended up thrust between Ali's ankles. She looked down, saw the black leather and barely stopped her hips from rocking forward. "All right then," he murmured, "what are we?"

"Sirens."

In the silence that followed, her heartbeat sounded unnaturally loud.

"Well, I'll be damned," Brandon growled at last.

"Probably," his brother agreed. He beckoned and Ali found herself moving forward, straddling first the outstretched leg, then both legs, then his lap. It wasn't so much a compulsion as a mutual acknowledgement of the need to get closer that she knew had to be showing on her face. She was still standing but only because the couch was so low.

A little voice—a voice that sounded remarkably like Glen—reminded her this wasn't the business meeting she'd planned but she was too turned on to care. Besides, she'd always prided herself on being adaptable and nothing in the rules said business couldn't be discussed over friction.

"So . . ." Travis reached out and lightly stroked the inside of her leg with his thumb. ". . . you're half right."

His touch was distracting but then, she could see from his smile that his touch was supposed to be distracting.

"Momma was a siren," Brandon continued, shifting enough to watch his brother trace patterns up and down her leg. "And we split the power between us."

"Split . . . ?"

And then Brandon's hand curved around the inside of her other leg and her knees buckled from the rush of sensation. Travis's grip shifted up her leg, sliding up under the edge of her skirt to hold her hips, as she folded forward, knees going to the couch, her sex rubbing against the rough edge of denim over his erection.

"Takes both of us to make it work." Brandon's voice was a low, heated growl at her ear and she moaned as he dragged his tongue over her neck.

"Your name . . . it was the name Ulysses gave the Cyclops."

"Same story," Travis grinned. "Different chapter. Since Momma never said who our father was . . ."

"If it is no man, then it must be by the will of the gods."

"Good girl."

Brandon was behind her now, straddling his brother's legs, pressed up against her back, arms around her, hands working the buttons on her shirt.

This was where she could stop it. Should stop it. Should pull the business plan she'd drawn up out of her bag and . . .

She knocked Travis's hat off and bent to devour his mouth as he hiked her skirt higher with one hand and slid the other under the scrap of silk and lace. He tasted like honey and sunshine and she could feel him still smiling against her lips. When she pulled away, fingers buried in his hair, he murmured, "We never saw a lot of point in singing ships onto rocks."

Then Brandon took hold of her head and turned it. "This is a lot more fun," he breathed against her lips just before he claimed them. He was rougher than his brother, his tongue demanding entry. She opened for him and rocked down against Travis's fingers as Brandon fucked her mouth. When he finally moved along her jaw and scraped his teeth against the sensitive skin where her neck met her shoulders, she fought to bring at least one or two brain cells back on line, reminding herself this wasn't all she wanted.

"I'm not the only one who knows what you are." Her voice was husky, needy, desperate, and she was actually more than a little impressed she managed to complete the sentence.

So was Travis. He wrapped fingers wet with her own arousal around her wrist and stopped her from opening his fly. "Who else?"

"Michael Richter. He owns Vital Music Group . . . Oh God!"

"Brandon!"

Brandon snorted something unintelligible against the back of her neck and stopped rolling her nipples between his fingers.

"Go on, Alysha."

Go on where? Right. Mike. "One of Richter's people was here tonight, in the club, wearing ear plugs."

"Ear plugs?" Brandon straightened, his hands going from her breasts to her shoulders, lightly stroking the skin exposed when he'd pushed back her shirt, the motion somehow holding all three of them at that moment.

Held suspended between them, Ali dredged up a bit more of the myth. "If you sing and no one reacts then you have to throw yourself into the sea . . ."

"Metaphor." Travis's teeth flashed white. "If we sing and no one reacts then we surrender to an outside power. Mythically, the sea. As things stand right now, not so much."

"Surrender?"

"We give over control."

Ali frowned down at her reflection in Travis's glasses, the expression looking out of place sharing her face with swollen, spit-slicked lips and blown pupils. "That's what Mike wants. To control you. To make you sing up what he desires."

"Isn't that what you want, Alysha Bedford of Bedford Entertainment?"

"No. Not control, manage. It's not the same thing."

"A difference of degree," Brandon noted.

"I don't want to control you. I don't want to use you, Mike does. Some day, now he knows about you, I guarantee you'll do a gig where he controls the audience and then he'll control you."

"Good thing you showed up to protect us then." Travis's lip curled mockingly.

"We don't mind being courted," Brandon noted, fingers tightening on her shoulders, breath stirring her hair. "But we don't like being threatened."

"Threatened?"

"Someone else knows what we are. Someone else wants to control us. You saw a man in ear plugs and yet, we see only you." Travis's hand rose to his glasses. "Your timing sucks, Alysha Bedford. Should have waited until we finished to make your pitch."

That she wholeheartedly agreed with, but it didn't change the fact she had to convince them they were in danger.

"You can't . . ."

Travis slipped the glasses down and his eyes flared gold.

Ali came back to herself in a parking lot two blocks from the Atlas, standing beside her car, clothing more or less decently arranged over her body—the buttons on her shirt were off by one, but that was a minor point. She remembered everything up to the moment Travis lowered his glasses. Whatever mojo his eyes performed, its effect seemed limited. Twice now, he'd used it as a way to essentially say, *we're done here.*

She had a feeling the Noman brothers weren't cuddlers.

Teeth gritted, she pulled out her keys and unlocked the car. The bastards were mythical creatures and they didn't believe *her*? She had half a mind to let Mike have them. A few years under his beck and call, paranormal control issues added to his usual iron-clad contract, and they'd be sorry they hadn't listened. Fortunately, the other half of her mind was well aware that the brothers weren't the only ones who'd suffer.

Working together, Brandon and Travis could get whatever they wanted.

Working for Mike, they could get whatever Mike wanted. At the moment, Mike wanted to exercise his power in the music industry but he sure as hell wouldn't stop there.

She'd have to save NoMan in spite of itself. If she could save Bedford Entertainment at the same time, so much the better.

Mike wouldn't try his plugged-ear ploy at a concert, there'd be too many variables to control. It would have to be a private party. The brothers might not care much about money, according to Steve, but Mike could offer enough to tempt the significantly more saintly.

Tom had left the bar before the concert ended so he'd already accomplished what he'd had to do. Since he hadn't spoken to either brother, he'd probably left an envelope with the bartender to be handed over when they were paid. Mike wouldn't waste any time; his offer of a private venue where they could connect with the industry brass would be in the envelope. There'd be nothing about Vital Music Group, and, while he'd definitely be present at the concert, Mike Richter wouldn't be hosting. The number on the offer would be large enough that the other three members of the band would insist on accepting and the Noman brothers wouldn't see the harm. They'd been doing this for so long, they'd clearly gotten careless.

Too careless to listen to warnings.

She'd have to get invited to the party.

Tom's office was about the size of her office and Glen's office and Brenda's reception area combined. A plush, deep-blue carpet acted as a stage for ebony furniture—probably the color, not the wood, although given the depth of Mike's pockets, Ali wouldn't swear to that.

Head down, dark hair falling forward over his eyes, Tom kept working as she crossed to the desk, her sandals making no noise against the thick nap. As far as she was concerned, the whole *I told my secretary to let you in but I'm far too busy to actually pay any attention to you* was a childish power play but she wasn't going to call him on it. She needed him to feel superior if this was going to work.

Pushing a pile of paper out of her way, she perched on the edge of the desk, allowing her skirt to ride up just enough to be distracting. "So, you've invited the Noman brothers to play at a private party where you'll introduce them to everyone they'll need to know to make it big."

He looked up then, eyes narrowed.

"And, just to make sure they'll agree," Ali continued, "you've sweetened the pot with a big old wad of cash."

"They told you?"

She smiled. "You're obvious."

"And you're not?" He returned her smile then, leaning back in his chair, silk shirt pulling tight across his chest. "You didn't sign them last night or you wouldn't be here now." Frowning, he added, "Why are you here, Ali?"

"I came to warn you."

"Out of the goodness of your heart?"

Dropping her gaze to the hem of her skirt, Ali rolled a bit of the fabric between thumb and forefinger. "Believe it or not, I don't want to see you get hurt."

"Not."

"Okay fine." She looked up then, matching the challenge in his eyes. "I don't want to see you get hurt by anyone but me."

He looked startled, then he threw back his head and laughed.

White teeth. Long, lean line of throat. And his laugh still sent shivers down her spine. Ali stomped down hard on her reaction.

"All right," he said at last, "what did you want to warn me about?"

"I know what they are, what the Noman brothers are, and you can't control them. They're out of your league."

"*You* can't control them and they're out of *your* league." Tom's gesture covered the room, the gold records on the wall, and managed somehow to include all the resources the Vital Music Group could access. "What makes you think Mike can't bring a couple of good ol' boys to their knees?"

Because these aren't the kind of guys to take it up the ass for a fat paycheck and a chance to throw their weight around. But she trapped the words behind a smile because they had nothing to do with the Noman brothers and everything to do with Tom walking away. From Bedford Entertainment. From her.

Tom's smile tightened and she knew he could read her thoughts on her face. "You want proof, Ali?" he asked, pushing the chair back and standing. "You want proof we've won this round?" Leaning forward, he scrawled an address and a date on a piece of paper, straightened, and offered it with a mocking flourish. "Why don't you come see for yourself?"

She slid off the edge of the desk and just barely stopped herself from slapping the paper out of his hand. This was exactly what she'd expected him to do, exactly what she'd needed him to do if she was going to have any chance of stopping Mike from using the sirens' power to further his own agenda. If, to be completely honest, she was going to have any chance of signing the band herself. It was just . . . no matter how much she knew it had to happen, she hated being patronized. Hated it more when Tom acted as the extension of Mike's so very superior and entirely infuriating attitude.

"Mike will control the Noman brothers, Ali, and when he does you're going to want to be on his good side. I'm giving you that chance."

Fortunately, he'd know something was up if she made no protest. Her smile had edges. "So, out of the goodness of your heart, you're graciously allowing me to play the sycophant?"

"I am graciously not throwing you out of here on your ass," he growled, moving closer.

Too close.

And suddenly, it was that afternoon in her office all over again. But this time, there was no Mike to call him to heel and no Glen to tell her this was a bad idea.

Ali *knew* it was a bad idea and, from the way Tom's eyes narrowed, he knew it too.

One of them had to acknowledge that and back away.

"Ali . . ."

"Shut up." As memory replayed the sirens' song, she decided she'd had all she could take of wanting and not having. Wrapping her hands around his face, she rose up on her toes, and sucked the curve of scarred lip into her mouth, biting it none too gently, then lapping at with the tip of her tongue. He closed his hands around her wrists and pushed her away.

But he didn't let her go. His cheeks were flushed and he looked as though he was silently weighing alternatives.

Ali looked up at him from under her lashes and smiled. "Dare you," she said, just enough mockery in her voice to overrule any remaining remnants of his better nature.

He released her then, but only to shift his grip to her waist.

As he lifted her back onto the desk, she wrapped one leg around him and dragged him up against her—he wasn't starting something and then walking away. Not this time. Fingers buried in the thick, silken mass of his hair, she devoured his mouth, using her teeth as much as her lips, loving the low growls she evoked.

Tom wasn't about risk, he was about control, always had been, and Ali loved making him lose it. They'd been together for almost five years before Mike had lured him away with the promise of power and no matter how bad things had gotten during those five years, the sex had always been incredible.

He moved his mouth to her throat, licking and sucking at the curve where her neck met her shoulder, bringing the blood to the surface, his hands moving from her waist to her breasts, stroking her through the fabric of blouse and bra, strong fingers finding her nipples as they hardened and closing around them.

Ali fumbled with the buttons on his shirt, needing to feel his skin under her hands.

"You've been working out," she gasped, both hands brushing quick and rough over the hard, hot planes of his chest and stomach as he licked along her collarbone and down over the swell of her breasts. She'd been trying for glib and had a feeling she'd missed it entirely.

He laughed—at her, with her, at this point she didn't really care—and dropped his hands to her thighs, running them up under her skirt. "I don't have time . . ."

"I don't need time." Not with the siren song still playing in her head.

He took her at her word, reaching into the center drawer for a condom.

"Do I want to know why you keep condoms in your desk?" she asked, leaning back on her elbows, as he rolled it on.

Eyes dark, his lips curled. "Same reason I always did."

Same reason. Different partner.

Her lips curled in answer to his. "Be a nice change for you then, back on top."

"We don't have to do this, Ali."

She sat up, grabbed the wings of his shirt. "Yet we both know we're going to." She dragged his mouth back onto hers. He tasted like expensive coffee, the apple he always had for breakfast, and memories. The kiss got rougher, sloppier, wetter.

One hand splayed against the small of her back, Tom pulled her toward the edge of the desk. The other hand slid up under her skirt, trailing lines of want along her inner thighs.

Ali couldn't keep from crying out as he entered her, wasted a moment hoping his office was as soundproof as it looked or that his secretary was considerably more discreet, then wrapped her legs around him and matched him stroke for stroke.

Matching the rhythm of the music . . .

It felt like she'd been on the edge since the first time she'd heard NoMan play and it didn't take her long to fall.

After, as she paused at the office door to slip the piece of paper with the date and address of the private concert into her purse, she glanced back at Tom. Dark curl of hair falling down into his face, his cheeks flushed, he looked like a debauched angel. Buttoning his shirt, he frowned down at the glossy surface of his desk like he was trying to work out just what exactly had happened.

NoMan had happened.

That was one hell of a band and there was no way she was letting Michael Richter have them . . .

. . . too.

"How nice of you to join us, Alysha. Tom tells me you know what I'm hoping to accomplish here tonight."

Mike's smile was all dangerous edges and as he moved closer, Ali felt her heart begin to race. Behind him, Tom's smile suggested she was totally screwed, and not in a fun way. Not this time. The interlude in his office had been just that—when it came to choosing sides, Tom had made his decision three years ago and, to give credit where credit was due, regardless of any lingering heat between them, he stuck to it when it mattered.

From the hall where Mike had stopped her, she could see the backs of maybe two dozen well-coiffed heads. Heads belonging to the men and women who made the decisions—who recorded what, who got the promotion money, who'd be the new flavor of the month.

"Although," he continued thoughtfully, "I'm not sure just what exactly *you* hope to accomplish." A gesture toward the inner room. "Half of that lot thinks you and your little company that couldn't quite is on the way out. Make a fuss, run about shouting something about sirens like a crazy woman, and the other half will come to agree with them."

He had a point. A little screaming might save the band but ruin her.

"If you're planning on warning the brothers, well, they clearly haven't listened to you up to this point or you wouldn't be here."

Ali flashed him her brightest, falsest smile. "I'm here to witness your victory. Just ask Tom."

A muscle jumped in the toned line of his jaw. "Tom's judgment isn't exactly sound where you're concerned, Alysha, but I'm willing to give you the benefit of the doubt."

"Thank you." Her response was exactly as sincere as the statement that prompted it.

"Given the stakes, however, you will remain here only under certain conditions."

Before she had time to ask what those conditions were, Tom grabbed her arms, dragged them behind her, and Mike snapped a pair of handcuffs over her wrists.

"Kinky," she muttered, trying to get free.

"Just a precaution," Mike purred. The soft wax pressed into her ear didn't exactly take her by surprise.

"Very kinky."

With Tom's fingers digging into her jaw, angling her head toward his employer, Mike paused before sealing the second ear. "When the Noman brothers sing," he told her quietly, "no one will hear them and they'll be mine."

Ali pasted the false smile back on. "Isn't this where you're supposed to laugh maniacally?"

"If you like."

"One question before . . ." Her gaze flickered to his fingers and then back to his face. "How did you convince that lot to stuff wax in their ears? Tell them a story about Ulysses?"

His answering smile was entirely sincere. "They're industry executives. They don't actually like music."

The second piece of wax left her feeling as though she'd been cut off from the world. Ali fought the rising panic, kept her head high and her expression disdainful—a meltdown now would help no one. Not her. Not Brandon and Travis. Mike held her while Tom slid his own plugs in then kissed her fore-head gently, patronizingly, as he handed her back to her ex.

Who seemed to be overcompensating for their tryst in his office.

His hands wrapped around her arms above the elbows, his grip just on the edge of bruising, Tom held her about a foot out from his body. She struggled, just enough to know she couldn't get free, and then, together, they watched Mike make his way to the makeshift stage. Drummer, bass player, guitarist—they'd already taken their places back out of the light. They seemed to know what everyone else knew; they didn't matter.

When Brandon and Travis came on stage, Mike gestured and Ali saw the members of the audience clap politely—part of Mike's show, pre-arranged. Walking away, he plugged his own ears, then turned just behind the last row of chairs to face the band.

Although she could see both Travis and Brandon, the stage was angled in such a way that unless they turned spe-cifically to face the hall, they wouldn't see her. Tom's grip kept her from moving into their line of sight.

By the middle of the first song, the brothers knew some-thing was wrong; Ali could see it in the way they moved, their easy confidence replaced by the wariness of wild crea-tures sensing a trap. Trouble was, they'd sensed it a little late. She fought the urge to yell, *Still think you don't need me?* and concentrated instead on figuring out a way to get the wax out of her ears. Companies like Vital Music Group had the luxury of long-term planning; companies like Bed-ford Entertainment survived by improvising.

It wasn't a great metaphor but it was all she had.

First, Tom had to release her.

Ali stepped back, taking him by surprise. Reaching out with her cuffed hands, she cupped him through the fine wool of his dress pants. When he gave her a shake, she curled her fingers and gently squeezed. His grip tightened on her arms but she continued caressing him as he hardened. Let him think she wanted a replay of that morning in his office and, hopefully, let him remember what Mike's reaction to a replay would be.

She was starting to think she needed another plan when he jerked back and all but threw her against the nearest wall. Face flushed, he moved to block her view of the stage and silently snarled at her to stay put.

Fine with her.

The paintings hung along the hall had been illuminated by small halogen lights. Glad she'd worn the three-inch heels, Ali gritted her teeth and pressed the side of her head against the brass casing over the closest light.

She could feel blisters rising where casing touched her cheek and the back of her ear but she could also feel the wax softening so she thought about the smell of cotton candy and the wail of a fiddle on a warm summer afternoon.

. . . about bodies moving together, heated and wanting, packed into the dark anonymity of a downtown club.

. . . about Brandon's hands and Travis's mouth.

. . . about everything NoMan could do for her bottom line, and she forced herself not to move away.

When Tom turned to check on her, Ali managed a grimace he took for a smile. Or he assumed she was grimacing about the situation, not the pain. As long as he left her to it, he could make any assumption he wanted.

Finally, she felt a tiny dribble of warn liquid roll out of her ear. Tears sliding down both cheeks, she moved her scorched face away from the brass and tossed her head, once, twice. The softened wax shifted. Slid. Dropped out.

Brandon's voice slid in to fill the space, lifting the hair on the back of Ali's neck, the howl of Travis's fiddle coiling sleek and dangerous in her belly. Her body moved to the music as the familiar ache began to build.

They still couldn't see her, but somehow they knew. Travis drew one final note from his bow and Brandon stopped singing. Hands wrapped around the microphone, he smiled and said, "That was our last song, ladies and gentlemen."

She heard Mike growl, "Keep singing," although with the wax in he couldn't have heard himself.

"Not right now," Brandon told him, and Ali wished Mike could hear the threat in the singer's voice. It made every threat he'd ever uttered seem like posturing.

Tom grabbed her as she moved forward into the actual room, brought his face down to hers, and demanded to know what she'd done.

No point in answering since he couldn't hear her. So, she showed him.

Still handcuffed, she darted her head forward, caught his right ear between her teeth and, holding on as he tried to shake her free, plunged her tongue into his ear and worked the wax plug out. He'd always been impressed by what she could do with her tongue.

On the stage, while the rest of the band watched in confusion, Travis played a new note and Brandon sang the counterpoint. The two sounds rose and wound about each other as the *NoMan* brothers directed their full attention on the action in the hall.

Releasing her, Tom straightened, listened for a moment, and pulled the plug from his other ear.

Heads began to turn as more and more of the industry executives realized something new seemed to be happening. Expressions ranged from confusion to anger as hands rose and manicured fingers dug at the wax.

No matter what story Mike had spun to gain their initial cooperation, this was about to get messy. Ali turned to show the brothers her wrists. "Little help here, guys."

The note changed.

"Tom! What the hell are you doing?" Mike might as well have remained silent for all the notice Tom took as he pulled out the handcuff key.

Ali grinned as the cuffs dropped to the floor, steel ringing against the tile. "They're controlling him, Mike. Take my advice and cut your losses."

Unfortunately, he couldn't hear her.

When Tom wrapped one huge hand around his shoulder, crushing the elegant line of his suit, holding him effortlessly in place, he was too astonished even to shout. Demanding Tom listen to *him*, he grabbed the younger man's wrist with both hands. Tom ignored both the words and the grip and removed both of Mike's earplugs, one after the other.

As the music changed again, Ali scooped the wax plug she'd taken from Tom off the floor, scrubbed it against her dress, and shoved it into her empty ear.

Stepping back into sight of the stage, she raised a hand in farewell. *NoMan's* audience had begun to move to the music and while she had no idea just where they'd be moving to, it really wasn't something she needed to see.

"Apparently, Michael Richter is taking a well-earned vacation in an undisclosed location, no one knows where Tom Hartmore is, two recording companies have filed for bankruptcy, one high-placed executive has given everything to charity, two more have turned themselves in for tax fraud, and there are at least three messy divorces happening in the industry between people who'll be dividing acts with their assets." Glen set the paper down on her desk and shook his head. "If Brandon and Travis are responsible . . . Are you sure you can control them?"

"Not control, manage," Ali reminded him. "Besides, they owe me."

"Speaking of." He put one finger under her chin, and studied the burn across her cheek. "That looks like it's healing well."

"Still hurts."

Green eyes crinkled at the corners as he grinned. "You need something to take your mind off it. Just say the word and I'll break out the champers. Tell me that *NoMan's* finally decided to sign with us."

"I'll tell you tomorrow."

"Tomorrow? Why tomorrow?"

"Because once they sign, they're off limits and tonight I've been invited to a private concert." Ali leaned back, tucked her hair behind her ears, and smiled. "They've promised me an audition I'll never forget."

MINOTAUR IN STONE

Marjorie M. Liu

I DREAM OF THE MINOTAUR WHEN MY EYES ARE closed. I cannot see him, whole, just fragments: the cold hard sinew of his large hand, the corded muscle of a massive thigh. I glimpse, briefly, the line of a collarbone, the hollow of a straining throat; higher, the curve of a horn.

Minotaur. Son of a wayward queen and a god.

And he wants me to save his life.

The first time I dream of the Minotaur I am curled in a nook on the basement level of the library, the third lowest floor, part of the catacomb, the labyrinth. It is very quiet, deathly so, almost midnight. Security guards roam high above. I do not fear their discovery. At night, they are too uneasy to trawl for bottom-dwellers in the underground shadows of the library's belly. Spooks, ghosts, ax-murderers in the stacks; I have heard those men tell ridiculous stories.

There is nothing to fear. Books are my friends, have always been my friends, and when I lived homeless on the street I learned to hide in the tall stacks, live in the shadows of musty corners, hidden by the illusion of intellectual pre-occupation, studious charm. Now, barely in my twenties, it is a small thing in the evenings, after my tiny job at the library café, to make myself soft and invisible; to blend, to become, to live as an uninvited guest, quiet as a book—and as a book, a dull creature on the surface, but full of the raging wild dark inside the words of my heart.

The café closes at eight. The library doors at nine. By ten, all the stragglers have been rounded up. Thirty minutes later the lights switch off. I know this routine, though I have never seen it. Every night, as soon as I leave the café, munching on some snack I am allowed to take free from the pastry display, I meander down the broad marble stairs, flowing with the public. One more stranger, a slip of a girl, moving neither fast nor slow, sometimes with a book in my free hand. Going places.

People leave me. We part ways as I descend deep into the catacombs. Sometimes a crowd, then nothing at all. It is, I often think, like walking through a door no one else can see—a slipstream gate, from one world to the next—into a forest of stone and tile, where branches are straight as shelves, holding books and yellow brittle newspapers, aisles riding like paths into shadows, the illusion of endlessness, the maze, the winding circle.

Occasionally I find another reader in the labyrinth, but no one lingers. There is a cold air, a sense of oppression. Eyes in the dark. It bothered me once, long ago, but I did not run. I read out loud instead, in a whisper to the darkness, until the cold air turned warm and those eyes lost their power to scare. So that now I pretend I have a friend, one friend, someone who welcomes me home.

I hide my sleeping bag and backpack in the gap behind a row of crusty encyclopedias. The lights do not function in that particular aisle. I move by instinct and memory as I find my belongings and jiggle them free. There is a bathroom nearby. Ancient, also unlit, no door. The toilet works, as does the faucet. I keep a battery-operated lantern just inside, on the floor.

I undress, folding my clothes, putting them aside. I toss my underwear in the sink, and then, cold and naked and barefoot on the ancient tile, I clean up. Wash my short hair under the faucet with cheap shampoo, savoring the chemical scent of lavender and jasmine. Run wet hands over the rest of my body, soaping up, rinsing as best I can. A puddle spreads around me.

When I am done, I drape my wet body in a big floppy t-shirt. I wash and wring out my underwear. Hang the pair on the rim of a toilet stall, then take down another that has been drying there all day, and slip them on. It is an easy routine.

On the night I dream of the Minotaur, I turn off the bathroom lantern and in pure darkness walk back to my sleeping bag. Air dries my body. I lie down, cradle my head on my arm, and close my eyes.

I dream. I dream of a place I have never been, though in the way of dreams, it is familiar. There is sand underfoot and the air is warm and wet. I look up, searching for stars, but all I find is stone. Stone all around. I am in a box, and there is only one way out.

So I take it. I walk across the sand to a door made of bone, smooth and pale and grinning with skulls; a warning, a promise, an invitation. One touch and my hand burns. I flinch, but do not turn away.

I enter an oubliette. A place of forgetting, of never turning back. I know what that is. I know what it is to be forgotten.

I stand just within the doorway of the void, and for the first time in my dream, feel fear. A terrible urgent despair, the kind that begs sound—a wail or cry or quick breath—because sound is life, sound means presence, and I could forget myself in this place. I think I already have.

But just as I am about to retreat through the door of watching bones, I glimpse something in the void—a solid curving plane of gray. The round edge of a shoulder, perhaps, holding very still.

"Hello?" My voice is soft. There is no answer, but in the silence I sense another kind of weight, a longing, familiar as the unseen eyes that watch me nightly from the shadows of the basement labyrinth. I cannot turn from that presence; as though a hand wraps around my body, I am drawn across the sand.

I walk into darkness, blind. The shoulder I saw before disappears, but I continue on, helpless. *Just a dream*, I tell myself. *Only a dream.*

Except, I can feel the grains of sand digging between my toes, and the air in my lungs is heavy and hot. I feel very much awake, very much alive.

And suddenly I can see again. Not much, just that same sliver of gray; a shoulder, attached to a long muscular arm; higher still, the faint outline of a broad chest, a strong throat. All at a height much grander than my own. I am looking at a giant. A giant made of stone.

I stand very still, staring; then slowly, carefully, reach out. I cannot explain my action. I must touch and be touched, though it is only rock beneath my hands. But I hesitate, at the last moment. I fear, irrationally, that I might be burned—and indeed I flinch as though harmed, because what my fingers find is not cold or stone, but flesh and warm.

I stagger, falling. A hand catches my waist, then my arm; in that grip, profound strength. Terror flutters my heart, freezing my voice. I think, *dream*, but I cannot wake no matter how loud I scream inside my mind.

A rumble fills the darkness. I reach out. My palms press against yet more skin, a body trembling with sound. Like a thundercloud, sighing in the night. I try to see, but cannot. Try to free myself, and am held closer.

"Let go," I breathe, struggling.

"No time," whispers a low voice, rough and masculine. "Listen to me. Listen."

But he says nothing else and I gaze up and up, staring at shadows gathered around a curving line, hard and tipped and ridged. A horn. I can see nothing else. In the oubliette, where I should find only darkness, gasps of light are playing tricks.

Something grazes my cheek; fingers, perhaps.

"Tell me," says the voice, quiet. "Tell me what you hear."

"You," I whisper, my voice shaking on the word. "Only you."

I hear a sigh, another rumble that pushes through my body, settling around my heart. A sad sound, old and tired. Again, my cheek is touched. Fingers slide into my hair, warm and gentle. For a moment my breathing steadies and I can think again.

A dream, I tell myself. Then, softly, "You are a dream."

"A dream," murmurs the creature. "A dream, if I could so be. Your dream, better."

"My dream," I say. "But you are."

"No," breathes that low voice. "I am the Minotaur. And this is no dream."

The hand holding my arm slips away; the body beneath my palms follows. I am left standing alone in the darkness. I feel bereft, lost without that touch which so frightened me. I cannot explain it. I do not want to.

"Soon," rumbles the voice. "Soon, again."

"Wait," I say, but the world falls away, the oubliette spinning fast into a jolt, a gasp—

I wake up.

A week passes before the Minotaur returns to me. I think of him often. Dream or not, I cannot help myself. I feel his fingers on my cheek as I pour coffee. I feel his body beneath my hands as I wrap scones in wax paper. I hear his voice inside my body as I count change for an old man in a suit. Everywhere, the Minotaur.

And when I close my eyes for just one moment, I return to the oubliette, to the darkness filled with thunder, and feel him with me like a shadow pressed against my back, watching and waiting. The longer I wait, the more I want to be with him again. The more I want to understand.

Some dream. I wonder if that is all it is. If there is more, and whether, like Ariadne with her ball of golden thread, I will be able to find my way home again the next time the Minotaur comes for me. And I know he will. I feel it, fear it—am even eager for it—though it sows discontent, unease. For the first time in a long while, I think about my life. Not about the things I do not have, but the people who are gone. Parents. Friends. I had them once, I think, but at some distant time so far past, such people seem more dream than the Minotaur.

All I have is myself. All I need is myself.

Until now.

I follow my routine before bed. I must. Routine keeps me alive. But after stretching out inside my sleeping bag, I hesitate before closing my eyes. I can feel the library breathing around me; the labyrinth with its endless maze of books like a forest overhead. Wilderness bound, with my back against the ground. I search within my heart for the roots of the home I have made. Look deep inside, for comfort.

I close my eyes and fall into sleep. Fall some more, into the oubliette.

This time, there is no door of bones. Just the darkness and shreds of light, playing against muscles smooth and hard as stone. *A dream*, I tell myself, but this time I know it is a lie, though not how or why. Nor does it matter. I am here, standing in front of the Minotaur, and the air is hot and the sand is soft and I can feel sweat trickling between my breasts, above my pounding heart.

"You came back," says the Minotaur, as quiet as I remember, deep and rough and rumbling.

"I didn't think I had a choice." I remember his touch, and stand very still.

Shadows shift; light plays over a sinewy shoulder, the edge of a strong jaw. The Minotaur moves closer; a gliding motion, impossibly graceful. "There is always a choice. If you had fought me, in your heart, I would not have been strong enough to bring you here."

"Here," I echo. "Where is here?"

"It is a place with no name." Closer still he moves; I imagine a growing heat in the air between us. "No name, ever. Only, we are at the heart of a maze, a house of halls and riddles. One way in, no way out."

The Minotaur does not stop moving. I steady myself, refusing to back away. I glimpse only fragments of his body, but that is enough. He is very large. I can see his horns.

"What are you?" I whisper. The Minotaur stops, but not entirely. I stifle a gasp as he takes my hands, his fingers huge and strong. He gently, slowly, raises my arms. I almost resist, but I have been thinking of him all week—perhaps forever—and though I fear him, I have in my life feared more than the Minotaur, and I can suffer the unknown for my curiosity.

"I am a man," he says softly. "Though I have been made to live as a beast."

He places my hands upon his head. I close my eyes as he forces me to touch him, and I see with my palms a hard surface, unnatural.

A helmet. A mask, even. Made of bone and steel and hide. A terrible thing; terrifying. I feel straps run down the sides, behind, all around, holding it in place. I cannot imagine wearing such a device.

The Minotaur releases me, but I do not stop. I do not want to. My fingers explore and connect with flesh, a jaw, his lips. A flush steals through me. I pull away, but again the Minotaur catches my hands. His mouth moves against my fingers as he speaks. It feels like a kiss.

"A moment," he whispers, as his breath flows over my skin. "Just one moment, please."

I give him his moment. I cannot help myself. I feel in my own heart a pang of longing, a sympathetic echo, and it cuts. I live in my own oubliette, my own labyrinth. I am a forgotten woman, invisible as the Minotaur to eyes beyond this dream. I cannot remember being anything else. I cannot remember being held, ever.

I rest my forehead against his broad chest, pressing close to stand between his feet, seeing him with my body, feeling him lean and strong. I listen to his breath catch, and inhale a scent of sand and rock and something sharper still.

"I did not bring you here for this," whispers the Minotaur.

"I did not come here for this," I reply. "I do not know why I am here."

"A selfish reason." The Minotaur's fingers tighten, briefly. "To save my life."

"I don't save lives. I barely have my own."

"You live in darkness. Amongst the books. You go there in the night to hide."

"You've watched me."

"You know I have. You have felt me."

"Yes," I breathe. I have felt him for a long time. My watcher, my only friend in the catacomb darkness, who has always felt more real than imagination should allow. Now, here in the flesh. Perhaps.

The Minotaur loosens his hold, his hands sliding away even as my own fingers trail down his throat, soothing a path along his shoulders. His skin is warm. His hands are warm, as well. He touches me again, palms resting against my spine. I am wearing very little. As is he.

I open my eyes and tilt back my head, trying to see the Minotaur. I cannot. The fleeting light is gone. His face is lost. I am afraid that I am lost, as well.

"Why me?" I ask him. "Why?"

The Minotaur stands very still. "Because you know this. You know this pain. You know what it is to have no one. To be . . . no one."

My heart hurts. "And so? Because of that you think I can help you?"

"I hope," he says simply. "I hope you will understand. I hope you will have compassion."

"No. This is not real."

"It is real to me." The Minotaur pulls me tight against him. "And I think it is real to you. More real than the life you have left behind."

It is true, but I will not say that. "And this? Your life?"

"This is no life. Not here, in this place."

"You are confined?"

"A prisoner."

"Why?"

"For living. For breathing, for being. Much the same as you, I think."

"I'm not locked up."

"Are you not?" The Minotaur's hands tighten against my back. "I think we are the same, you and I."

I close my eyes. "I am alone, that's all."

"Alone," he echoes. "This place would be sufficient, if I was not alone."

"So you brought me here to stay with you?"

"No." The Minotaur's voice is rough. "No, I would not ask that of anyone. Only, there is a world beyond this darkness, and I would see it, find it, live within it."

"You might not like that world," I tell him. "You might want to come back to this place after you've seen what you want."

"Like you?" says the Minotaur softly. It is impossible to know his meaning, to dare divine those two words. All I know is that I wish to echo them, to say, *like you*, or to add another word: *I.*

I like you, I want to tell him. *I do not know why, but I do. And I am crazy for it. All of this, crazy.*

But the Minotaur is right. He has chosen well. I understand him. Or at least, part of him. The rest is mystery. The rest is insanity.

"I need to sit." I slide out of the Minotaur's arms to kneel unsteadily in the sand. The odd shadows of light are still gone; the darkness is profound. I cannot see myself. I am only voice, thought, sensation. But I feel the Minotaur crouch beside me, and savor the contact of his knee against my thigh, the heat of his sigh. Touch is a lifeline in this place. A reminder.

"How long have you been here?" I wonder if I could survive in the oubliette, alone.

The Minotaur rumbles. "Years. Centuries, even, though time moves more slowly in this place. I suppose millennia have passed in your world."

"And how do you live?"

"There is water and food. Magic sustains the rest."

I look toward the sound of his voice. "Magic."

"It is what brought you here." The Minotaur touches my hand. "The first time was the hardest. This time, easier."

I feel numb. "You have magic. You should be able to leave this place on your own, without me. There is nothing I can do for you."

"So you are an expert on such things now." His tone is light, but I protest anyway, embarrassed. The Minotaur touches my lips with his fingertips. The contact startles me into silence.

"I meant no harm," he says. "And if you do not trust me, if you still believe this is all a dream, so be it. I cannot force your heart to change."

The Minotaur pulls way. I reach out, blind, and catch his wrist. I feel bold and foolish.

"Dream or not," I whisper. "I don't want to be alone."

I hear his breath catch, and I listen for more, listen hard. There is nothing else beyond the two of us. A strong arm drapes over my shoulders. I do not flinch. The Minotaur surrounds; he lays me down against his broad smooth chest until we stretch close, entwined. I have never been held in such a way. Never been touched so gently. It startles me.

"You need to leave soon," he rumbles. I try again to see his face. Nothing. I reach for where his jaw should be, but I find the mask instead. My fingers glide along a curving horn, wicked and cruel.

"Why?" I ask, then forget my question as his large hands trail up my sides, beneath my shirt. I am surprised at the pleasure I feel; even more, when my own palms glide down his throat to his chest. There is cloth over his groin, but nothing else. So much skin.

He swallows hard. "You do not want to become trapped here."

No, I do not. But that does not stop me from inching up his

body, savoring his long lean muscles, touching him with my hands, gentle and curious. Curious about him, about myself.

"What are you doing?" whispers the Minotaur hoarsely.

"I don't know," I admit. "I don't know about any of this. Except, I am here . . . and I want to know *you*."

"Then know me," he murmurs. "Be the first to try."

I hesitate, listening to the echo of his words, his pain. Something comes over me—the darkness, a cocoon—and within it I find myself a stranger, as strange as this man who calls himself Minotaur.

Magic, I think. *Dreams and magic.*

I touch him. The pulse of his throat is quick, his hands raw and hot. When he turns us on our sides the sand is gritty and soft, climbing into my clothes, rubbing my skin. I am blind in the oubliette, but my fingers are not, and I find again his jaw, his lips, and press close enough to taste his breath, to taste him.

I kiss the corner of his mouth. I capture his sigh with another kiss, this time on his bottom lip. The edge of the mask rubs against my cheek and brow; bone and hide protrude over the Minotaur's nose. More wolf than bull, I imagine.

I stroke the hollow of his throat with my finger. "Who did this to you?"

His chest rumbles. "I am the child of a queen, but made out of wedlock and a bastard, still. To protect herself, my mother made a bargain with her lover to hide me away so that her husband, the king, would never know of her betrayal. It was done as she asked—the king was gone away to war. Though as such things happen, upon his return he discovered the truth. The king was a sorcerer, and my mother's choice to deceive him . . . poorly conceived."

I try to make sense of such a story. "So you were alone, then? No one cared for you?"

"I had a tutor, an old man who raised me. A nursemaid, too, though she was taken from me when I had no more practical use for her. A good woman. I learned not to miss her."

"And this?" I tug gently on a horn.

"An act of power," says the Minotaur grimly. "And fear."

He rolls me on my back before I ask another question. His mouth hovers over mine, hands cradling my face. He kisses me. It is a deeper kiss than what I gave him, and I am taken off guard by the slow heat of it, the pleasure. I am unfamiliar with intimacy, but my body responds as though born to it. I rise up against the Minotaur, clutching his back.

He tugs on my nightshirt—we part long enough for him to drag it over my head—and then I have no time for fear or regret as he strokes my breasts, fingers sliding over my nipples, at first tentative, then with more confidence. I moan against his mouth, hooking my leg around his waist, rubbing against him. I am wet between my thighs, pleasure clenching in my gut like a delicious fist.

The Minotaur overwhelms. I could not fight him off even if I wanted, and I do not. I have been alone too long, and this—no matter how strange—is an opportunity not to be lost. I might hide from the world, but I am a survivor—I take what I need, what I want, what I desire. Only, I have never desired this. Not until now.

His loincloth strains hard between my thighs. I writhe, savoring the luscious friction of his erection stroking my own wet heat. I reach down to touch him. His skin is soft and hot, throbbing, and he breaks off his kiss to push hard and long in my hand. I squeeze, gentle; a pulsing rhythm. The Minotaur groans and slams his fist in the sand. He pulls out of my grasp.

"You will finish me," he says, and then it is my turn to dig my hands into the sand as his fingers slide between my thighs, entering me deep. His mouth follows, tongue running swift as he sucks and licks, and a moan tears from my throat as I twist in his arms. He captures me. Hooks my legs over his shoulders.

And then, when I am almost on the brink, his mouth and hands disappear and I feel the heat of his body poise above me. He does not need to ask. I spread my legs wider. The Minotaur pushes inside, and though his size might have predicted discomfort, all I feel is delicious warmth so unexpected, so overwhelming, I am momentarily paralyzed with pleasure. Stiff with it, even as he is stiff, the both of us shaking. He is hard and hot; I feel mounted, pinned, like a puppet on the head of a spear, except this is flesh and blood and dream, and there are no strings attached to my body, no master controlling my actions.

One giant hand presses against my thighs, tugging them apart. The Minotaur slides deeper, but only just. And then his hands move again, but only to push my legs together, tight. Squeezing him inside me. Holding him like a vise, even as he begins to move, to draw out, just as slowly as he entered.

I shudder, a moan escaping from between my clenched teeth. The Minotaur's own breathing is harsh, though he is gentle as he thrusts, his large hands holding me close in a careful embrace. I wish I could see his eyes, and press my lips against his throat, feeling in my pounding heart a wild ache that reminds me of my first time in the library labyrinth, held safe within the darkness of a new home. I do not want that feeling to end.

"More," I whisper, and the Minotaur rumbles with pleasure. He sits up, holding my hips tight against him as he rises to his knees. I tip backward, head and arms resting against the sand, bound by flesh still large and hot.

The Minotaur is strong. He holds me flush against him and thrusts hard, driving into me with a strength that is both pain and pleasure. He is in complete control as he moves my body, rutting with a ferocity that makes me cry out, the tips of my toes digging into the sand. I try to move with him, but give up, letting him set the pace as he holds and pulls me with raw hungry strength. It is a punishing rhythm, but so is my desire, and the gathering pleasure inside my body is so devastating I lose myself when it breaks, arching violently, breath rattling in a silent scream as I come in his arms—as he comes in mine—sinking us down at the last moment to move against each other in the sand.

We keep thrusting, savoring the aftershocks, fighting for breath—so tangled that as the Minotaur turns us, I remain pressed against his body, one leg hooked over his waist, fingers digging into his hard shoulder. I do not want to let go. Neither does the Minotaur, if his hands are any indication. He cradles my body, holding me as I have never been held; as though I am wanted, needed, desired. His breath ruffles my hair; his lips trace a path down my flushed cheek.

"I did not dream," whispers the Minotaur. "I did not dare."

"You brought me here." I am still breathless, muscles limp and warm. "You must have thought something would happen."

The Minotaur touches my face. "Not this. Truly."

I close my eyes. "Not an optimist, then."

A short gasp of laughter escapes him. "No more than you, I think." He runs his fingers through my hair and I sigh at the simple pleasure of it, the warmth and strength of his fingers.

"There were others, long ago," he says quietly. "Women who came to me as a novelty, a freak to be bedded. But never for more. Not like this."

"You think this is more?" I press gently. The Minotaur shifts in my arms and places his hand over my heart. After a long moment, I do the same to him. I cannot help myself.

"Yes," he breathes. "I know it."

I try hard to think of a response, but before I can, the Minotaur stiffens and pulls away.

"What," I begin to ask, but his large hand claps over my mouth and my heart begins to pound all over again. The Minotaur is so very quiet, I would not know he was there if he did not touch me. I try to do the same, hardly breathing, and after a moment I hear a distant sound. It is a cracking note, like a whip—or a sail kicked by a sharp breeze.

Then, suddenly, a woman screams; a bloodcurdling howl that twists like a sour wind, so bitter the sound becomes a taste inside my mouth: like ice dragged over by filth, or candy doused in gasoline.

The Minotaur stands, dragging me with him. I do not resist. I stare blindly into the darkness, my fingers tight around the Minotaur's hand.

"You must go," he whispers.

I shake my head. "I thought you were alone. Who was that woman?"

"Not a woman. A harpy. More than one. And they have caught your scent." The Minotaur embraces me, an act that feel so desperate, so lost, fear cuts my heart, stealing my breath.

"I should not have brought you here," rasps the Minotaur. "Forget me when you leave this place. Please."

"No," I protest. "No, I won't."

But I hear that odd crack split the air—again and again—and in my head I imagine wings snapping, like bones breaking, and the taste of those rising howls makes me bend, gagging.

The Minotaur touches my hair, my cheek, and then slips away, leaving me alone and blind. I wipe my mouth with the back of my hand. I hear the harpies coming, but do not run. I do not know how, in this place.

"What about you?" I call into the darkness.

The Minotaur's voice drifts like a ghost. "They will not hurt me."

He is lying. I know it. And I see, suddenly, sparks of red in the darkness, glowing like the embers of hot coals. A deep fire, slow burning. It takes only a moment to realize I am looking at eyes.

The harpies scream. I flinch, stumbling backward, and for one brief instant glimpse against that hateful light the outline of a man. A man wearing the horns of a bull.

And then the harpies are there with us, the air stirring foul with the beat of their wings, and the Minotaur steps in front of the creatures with his arms outstretched, shielding me with his body. I watch, horrified, snatching glimpses of bulbous breasts, stringy hair, talons sharp as knives. The Minotaur bellows a word I do not understand, then staggers, grunting. I hear flesh rip, and something hot and wet spatters my face. I scream—and the world disappears. I bolt upright in my sleeping bag, skin slick with sweat. The sudden silence bears down upon me like anchors stuffed in my ears, and all I can do for one long moment is sit, staring, listening to my heart rage and rage. I lick my lips and taste something metallic. Touch my face. My fingers come away dark with blood.

My body is sore. My nightshirt is gone.

I throw back the sleeping bag and grab clothes. I dress quickly, heart pounding, staring into the darkness of the stacks, the labyrinth. *Not a dream*, I tell myself, fighting to hold on to that belief. It would be easy to forget, despite the blood and the aching. It would be easy to do as the Minotaur asked and pretend my time with him was nothing but fantasy. Everything about this, fast as a dream from beginning to end.

But I refuse. There is no explanation for what has happened, what I have allowed myself to become in so short a time—but I am changed now. I cannot turn back. Only, finding the Minotaur again will be difficult. Returning impossible if he does not want me, if he is hurt . . .

I stop myself from thinking. Stay simple. Crouch in my bedding and close my eyes, willing sleep. If that is what it takes.

Nothing happens. Worse, I cannot feel the Minotaur in the shadows. My watcher, who has been with me from the beginning of my time in this place, is gone.

I roll to my feet and stare into the unlit stacks, the endless aisles, the labyrinth. I listen with my heart, but still cannot find that quiet presence. Cannot find, inside my head as I close my eyes, that warm shadow pressed against my back. It makes me hurt. It makes me remember loss, something I have not felt in years. Abandoned once, abandoned again. Though the reasons, this time, are different.

I walk into the darkness, leaving behind my belongings, the evidence of my existence. In doing so, I abandon routine.

I do not care. I enter the labyrinth blind, hands stretched to trail across the spines of books, taking turns as they come, winding deeper and deeper into my own oubliette. The catacomb maze is endless, but so is my desire, and all I can think of is the Minotaur.

Somewhere distant, sound comes to my ears. I stop cold, listening, and from very far away catch the faint glimmer of a flashlight. Men, speaking. Entering my home.

"Heard a scream," says a low voice. "Like someone dying."

"Easy enough down here," replies another. "Goddamn, it's creepy."

I close my eyes, listening. I know they will find my belongings. Once they do, my life is over. My luck, the one time I am not careful.

Nothing to lose. Your life was already over. Over the moment you began believing in the Minotaur.

I search my heart for regret, but find none. Not yet, anyway. I turn and walk away, slipping deeper into the stacks, the labyrinth. The voices of the men fade quickly, as does the light they shine. I try not to think of them. I walk for a long time, each step a breath of memory—my childhood, my abandonment, my desperation—how afterward, the isolation and solitude of the library was a balm, sweetness.

All of that, my life, leading to this moment. Searching for a fantasy that should not exist. That perhaps does not exist. Not anywhere but my heart.

After a time, I stop. If the security guards are searching for me, I have not heard or seen them, and I must rest. Close my eyes, for just a moment. I sit on the tile floor, my back against the books, and think of the Minotaur. Remember him holding me, kissing me, moving inside my body. Warmth spreads through my muscles, making my eyelids heavy. I curl into a ball. Think of that low rumbling voice, and close my eyes.

Perhaps I fall asleep. Either way, when I open my eyes there is sand beneath me, darkness all around.

I sit up. I am not afraid. Not for myself.

"Hello?" I whisper.

"Hello," rumbles a familiar voice, soft and low and startling close. "Hello, again."

I close my eyes, fighting down a smile. "You're alive."

"Yes." I do not hear the Minotaur move, but his large warm palm suddenly presses against my cheek. "I heard you calling for me. I felt you. I could not say no."

"The harpies?"

"Gone. For now."

I touch his hand, holding it to my face. "I'm covered in blood. Your blood."

"A small injury," he says, and a moment later I find myself scooped off the ground, cradled in strong arms that hold me close against a broad hard chest. The Minotaur carries me. His presence feels like an old friend. My friend, if I allow myself to imagine him as such. And I do.

I kiss his collarbone. I kiss the smooth skin just below his shoulder. I run my tongue over the hard nipple near my cheek.

The Minotaur stops walking and hoists me higher in his arms. Bends his head and captures my mouth in a long hot kiss that makes me sigh. He sinks to his knees and sets me on the ground, still kissing me, his hands fumbling over my clothes. I brush him aside and curl close, reaching beneath his loincloth to touch him. The Minotaur shudders. I slide even closer. I take him in my mouth.

He is so thick I wonder how he ever fit inside my body, but I love the hot feel of him beneath my tongue—love even more giving him pleasure—because it makes me feel like part of him, and that is something I never imagined, not with anyone.

He touches my shoulders. He is shaking, but he does not tell me to stop, and I take the invitation, going further, deeper, using my hands and mouth, feeling him ignite as I push closer to some indefinable edge. His hips thrust, again and again, and a low shuddering moan escapes his throat, building as I suck hard.

The Minotaur pulls away from my mouth as he comes,

though I still hold him with my hands, savoring his violent release as though it is my own. His breathing is ragged, harsh, and when he grabs me up in his arms I feel a new weakness in his body; tremors in his muscles, in the breathlessness of his kiss, that makes me desire him even more.

"Why?" he murmurs. "Why do you want me? Why did you want to come back?"

"I don't want to be without you." The words slip free so easily it frightens me.

The Minotaur's breath catches. He cradles my face between his hands. I cannot see his eyes, but I am sure he can see mine. "Why? Of all men, why me?"

I wish I could see his eyes. I wish it so badly. "Why *me?*"

The Minotaur exhales slowly. His arms slide around my body. He holds me close and whispers in my ear. "Because I wanted you. Because I wanted your help, but I also wanted just . . . you. To touch you, once. I have watched you for so long."

I cannot speak. He stands and lifts me into his arms. "There is something I must show you."

He carries me through the darkness. I listen to his heartbeat and the shuffle of sand. The air becomes warmer, humid. Nothing of the harpies.

The Minotaur walks for a long time. The oubliette is larger than I expected, or else we have left that place and his entire home is made of darkness. He finally stops, though, and lowers me to my feet. I stay within the circle of his arms and he says, "In front of you."

I kneel. I reach out and touch water. Hot water. I lean closer and steam bathes my face.

"A natural spring," says the Minotaur. "Take off your clothes. I will wash away the blood."

"And you? It was your blood, after all. You're hurt."

"Then we will wash together." There is tension in his voice. He shows no hesitation, though, when he helps undress me. He holds my hands with care as I step blind into the hot water. It feels good, though I cannot help but think of the harpies. I mention them again as the Minotaur slides into the water beside me.

"There are always risks," he admits. "Risks for the unwary. It is the labyrinth, after all."

"I've always thought of the library as a labyrinth," I tell him, and the Minotaur makes a rumbling sound, splashing warm water over my arms and rubbing his wet thumbs across my cheeks.

"All places of paths and knowledge are part of the great maze," he says. "Some more so than others. Your library is one of them. The veil between worlds is weak there. Weak enough even for one as untalented as I to reach through."

"Why just reach? Why not step through entirely? Escape, if that is what you really want."

The Minotaur's hands still. "I am bound here."

"No." I think of all that has passed between us, what little he has told me. "No, not completely. You brought me here to save you. That's what you said."

The Minotaur remains silent for along time. Not until I press my fingertips against his cheek does he make a sound. His sigh is warm.

"I should not have brought you to this place," he murmurs. "Not the first time, not the second, and not now. Selfishness begged it. Despair and loneliness. But I know better, and better means keeping you safe. You must not free me."

"I must," I whisper. "You know I must."

Again, the Minotaur says nothing. He washes me and I do the same for him, discovering in the process a terrible slash across his shoulder.

"It is already healing," he says quietly. "I cannot die here. The king forbade it."

"He controls this place?"

The Minotaur's laugh is bitter. "No one controls the labyrinth. It is beyond spells and magic, beyond anything that can be controlled by mere men, or their counterparts. But that does not mean that those who come here are so free. The flesh is weak."

I kiss his shoulder. "Not so weak."

"Against you, powerless," he murmurs. "I never imagined such a thing. Not in any dream."

"Why?" I kiss him again, at the base of his throat. My breasts rub against his chest and his hands snake down to cup me tight against him. He is hard, and I feel a moment of astonishment at how ready I am for him. I hook my leg around his hip and he takes me in one long slow movement. I groan.

"Because I am a monster," whispers the Minotaur hoarsely, moving inside me with delicious strength. "I have always been so, since the beginning."

"No," I murmur, and cry out as he gently squeezes my breast.

"There is a legend native to your age and time," he says, breathless as he thrusts hard—once, twice—then slows his pace, drawing me out. "The Minotaur in the labyrinth, a beast of sacrifice and blood. Child of a queen and a God."

I have trouble speaking, thinking. The Minotaur leans against the edge of the hot spring; I move against him, riding his body, and manage with some difficulty to say, "I know that myth."

The Minotaur grabs my hips, thrusting up, dragging me down. Again and again he does this. I lean into him, wrapping my arms around his neck as we bury ourselves in each other with such force I feel stolen by pleasure, near death with it, as though my heart surely cannot beat one more moment at such a frantic rhythm.

I break first, my body clutching around the Minotaur in such brutal waves that all I can do is writhe, breath rattling with pleasure. I expect the Minotaur to follow, but before my body is done he turns me and thrusts again, still hard, hot, only now I am bent at the waist with nothing to hold on to but his hands on my hips as he pounds into my body with quick sharp strokes, faster and faster, frantic. I come again and again, helpless to stop him, unwilling to stop him even though the pleasure is too much. His hands move; he touches me, stroking, and I am rocked into one final climax that the Minotaur finally joins, his voice rumbling into a bellow.

We drift in the hot water—spent, exhausted—until, finally, the Minotaur pulls me to shore and we lean against each other, breathing hard in the silence of the labyrinth. For the first time in my life I feel truly satisfied—comfortable and safe—though those feelings do not last long. I turn my head, brushing my lips against the Minotaur's arm, and say, "You were telling me something."

He kisses the top of my head. "I was."

"And?"

"And you are not easily distracted," he rumbles, sighing. "So. You know the myth. You know what else is part of it."

"Death," I say. "The deaths of young men and women."

"That part, at least, is true." The Minotaur drags in a deep ragged breath. "The king thought to use me as a weapon against his enemies. So he made me a monster. Fitted me with the helmet, took away my name by magic so that I would know myself as nothing else, and then enchanted me into the labyrinth. He wanted fear and so he made it. In me."

"So you killed," I say carefully, because to utter those words feels almost as terrible as the crime. The Minotaur, though, makes a low sound—frustration, maybe—and I feel him shake his head.

"I did not," he says in a hard voice. "Or rather, I did not mean to. The young men who found me attacked with all their fear and fury, and I was forced to defend myself. The girls I did not touch, though I tried to help them. They ran from me. They ran into the darkness of the labyrinth and hurt themselves on the rocks, or were killed by the creatures who inhabit the maze."

"How long did that go on?"

"Years. Until the king was murdered by his enemies. His death sealed the gate into the labyrinth. At least, that particular gate."

"With you in it."

"Forever. Though the king, in a fit of humor before his death, left me one chance of escape."

"Ah," I say. "And is that where I come in?"

"If you wish," he says slowly. "But it will be dangerous."

"Harpies?"

"Worse." The Minotaur holds me close. "The king's own magic."

I close my eyes. I try to make sense of what he has told me, but it is no use; his words live like a fairy tale inside my head, indistinct, but full of simple truths—a prince, cursed, trapped in the heart of a tangle—and I, the poor woman lured to his aid. A golden goose will be next, I think; mice who talk, or a woman with hair as long as a river.

"Is there light here?" I ask the Minotaur. "Real light? Any at all?"

He hesitates. "There is. It is part of something I would have shown you later."

I frown. "Show me now."

The Minotaur sighs, and pulls himself from the water. I follow, stumbling in the dark. The air is cool on my wet skin. I shiver, and suddenly find myself draped in heavy furs, soft and warm. I hug the hides close to my body and listen to the Minotaur move through the darkness.

Then, light. A blue light, flickering and pure. It has been such a long time that I find myself momentarily blind, and I shield my eyes as I try to see the Minotaur. He stands before me, so very still, and I cannot look away from the hard lines of his body, covered in scars, or higher yet, his face.

What little I can see of it. The mask is as horrific as my fingers told me it would be, though it covers only the upper half of his head; the bridge of his nose and scalp. All bone and fur, with giant horns stretching like arms in the air. I can see the straps holding it in place, cutting into his skin.

I also see his eyes. I move close, staring. Blue, I think, though it is impossible to say. Just that there is a soul in them, a soul I have only heard and felt until now, and I want more of it, so much more. I want to look into his eyes and hear him speak. I want to know what he sees when he gazes at my face, what he feels when he touches me, when he is inside me.

The Minotaur moves, and that is enough to break the spell. I look down at the source of light in his hands, and find a round mirror, complete with silver frame and handle. Light flees the glass, flickering wildly, and when the Minotaur tilts it toward me I see another world—blue sky, trees, mountains bathed in snow and sun.

"I found it years ago," says the Minotaur softly. "I used it to see the worlds beyond the labyrinth. And there are many. Worlds upon worlds, gathered like beating hearts, warm and fine."

I stare at the mirror. "You left me in the dark on purpose."

The Minotaur glances away. "I thought you would fear me, otherwise."

"You could have tried."

"No. I did not dare."

I fight for words. "You thought I would be disgusted, didn't you?"

He goes very still. "And are you?"

"You can ask me that? After everything?"

He opens his mouth—stops—and his eyes turn somber. "Forgive me."

I sway close, but do not say what I feel—*you do not need to fear me, only trust me, please, before I lose my nerve in the light*—and instead point at the mirror. "Is that how you watched me?"

"Yes." The Minotaur tears his gaze from my face and holds up the mirror. An eagle soars; I hear music from beyond the glass. A flute, lilting and delicate. The image shifts; suddenly there is darkness again, cut with electric beams and men in uniforms standing over a sleeping bag. I watch them nudge my belongings with the tips of their shoes, and feel in my heart a pang.

"I could send you home again," says the Minotaur quietly.

"You are not of this place—not yet—and as such you are permitted to leave. The labyrinth does not hold every heart."

"Doesn't it?" I look him in the eyes. "How did you bring me here?"

"I willed it." He holds my gaze with a heat that reminds me of his hands on my body.

"To free you from the labyrinth? You could have found another."

"You and no other," he says firmly. "There was never any choice. Not for me, once I found you."

He has already said as much, but those are not words I tire of hearing. I touch his waist and slide close, until I must crane my neck to look at him. His jaw is strong, his skin smooth. And his eyes, caught behind the mask of bone, are most certainly blue.

I kiss the Minotaur. His arms wrap around my body, pulling me off the ground, and as my feet dangle and the furs drop away I realize something awful: I cannot imagine being without him. The Minotaur is part of me now. And I am part of him.

A scream cuts the air. We both flinch.

"Don't send me away," I say. "Promise."

He gives me a hard look. "If you are truly set on helping me, we must go now."

I say nothing—just nod—and the Minotaur presses his lips against my forehead—one quick hard kiss, full of something more than mere desire. He takes the mirror in one hand, grabs me with the other, and we run. I have no clothes, but forget to care as the air behind us cracks like a whip. Distant, but close enough. I remember how fast the harpies move.

"What do I have to do?" My voice is breathless. I almost trip and the Minotaur hauls me close. He says nothing and I ask again, tugging on his arm. His jaw tightens, and for a moment I see him as others might: the cruel mask, the horns, the giant body hard with muscle. Dangerous and powerful. A beast.

"I must have a champion," he rumbles, and his voice returns my heart and mind to its proper place. "I, who have slain so many."

"A champion," I say, but there is little time for more. The harpies grow louder, their shrieks violent and sickening. I fight the urge to gag, struggling to focus only on the Minotaur and myself.

He slows, and by the light of the mirror I see a familiar sight: the door of bones through which I entered the labyrinth, my first time summoned by the Minotaur. The skulls grin, bones polished and white, but as I near I see dark liquid trickle from the sockets of their eyes, and I know in my gut it is blood. The Minotaur's own eyes are hard as flint as he looks at the bones. His mouth tightens into a thin white line.

"Beyond that door is the site of the gate the old king used to usher in his sacrifices. It is the gate through which I entered, and it is the only gate through which I can leave."

"I thought you said it was sealed."

"Sealed, yes. But the labyrinth is not bound by doors. Nor would I be bound, if the curse upon me was lifted."

The harpies are nearing. I glance over my shoulder into the darkness and the Minotaur says, "Also trapped, put here by magic through the wiles of some ancient priest. Perhaps another legend, in your time."

"Can they be killed?"

The Minotaur shakes his head. "Harpies are immortal. So much in the labyrinth is."

I reach for the door. The Minotaur stops my hand. "One last chance. You could go, if you want. Back to your home."

"I have no home," I tell him, and haul open the door. Just in time; screams split the darkness and I glimpse red eyes, glowing like pincers left too long in flame. I dart into the room—the Minotaur follows—and together we close the door, leaning hard against it. Bodies slam into the barrier; my entire body shakes with the impact. Beneath my ear I hear faint laughter, more than one voice. The skulls on this side of the door are also leaking blood. My skin is smeared with it.

"So comes the Minotaur at last," they whisper; like ghosts, mouths unmoving. I back away, staring, and again hear laughter, faint voices drifting high and lilting.

"Oh," they whisper, and I feel the dead staring, staring so hard. "Oh, a woman now, heart so full. Not like the others, Minotaur. Not like *them*, those screaming butterflies in the oubliette."

"Enough," says the Minotaur. "You know why we are here."

"The king's gift," they murmur. "Ah, girl. You are dead as you stand. There is no heart full enough for this man. No woman brave enough to hold a Minotaur."

I do not understand. I glance at the Minotaur and find him pale, mouth drawn tight.

"No," I say, knowing well enough that look on his face, the defeat. "No, whatever it is I have to do, I am strong enough." I step up to the door and look straight into the eyes of a skull. "Tell me what I have to do to free him."

"You must hold him," they say.

"No," protests the Minotaur. "There is more."

But I cannot ask, because the Minotaur suddenly screams, back arching so deeply I hear his spine crack like the wings of a harpy. He falls to his knees and the skulls whisper, "Hold him. *Hold him tight.*"

I scramble to the Minotaur and crash into the sand, flinging my arms around his heaving chest. I press my cheek above his pounding heart and hold him with all my strength. He groans my name, but his voice—full of pain—shifts into a howl. I cry out with him, terrified, and then cry out for another reason entirely as the warm skin beneath my hands suddenly becomes fur. The Minotaur writhes; I glimpse his hands, long fingers shedding skin and nail to become claws. I almost forget myself—almost let go—but a voice inside my head whispers, *hold on, hold on,* and I do not loosen my arms.

The Minotaur fights me. He is large and strong, but I squeeze shut my eyes and dig my nails into his back, chanting his name, holding on with all my will. I am afraid of him—afraid for my life—but I think, *faith*, and do not waver.

The fur shifts, gliding into scales. A smaller chest; I almost lose him, but I regain my grip and hear a hiss, feel a tongue rasp against my cheek. The Minotaur struggles, flopping wildly, dragging me down into the sand and rolling on top of me. I cannot breathe, but I wrap my legs around the Minotaur—his entire body, one long tail—and hold my breath, screaming inside my mind.

Another shift—feathers—a body smaller, still—but I grapple and pull and hold—and then again—leather, tough—a beast as big as the room—but I take two handfuls of a mighty ear, shouting as my arms pull and my joints tear. Battered and bruised, I fight to keep him. Fight, too, for my life.

Again and again he shifts—an endless struggle of creatures I cannot name—until, suddenly, it is simply the Minotaur again, the man I know. He slumps within my arms. I do not let go. I am too afraid, and my fear is good. A moment later I feel another transformation steal over the Minotaur. This time, stone. Stone that takes me with him.

I do not understand at first. Only, my body feels heavy, as though gravity is pulling down and down. I hear a scraping sound, like rocks rubbing, and see from the corner of my eye the Minotaur's skin go gray and hard. I remember the first time seeing him, some ghost light playing tricks, the curve of his shoulder resembling stone. This time it is no illusion.

"Save yourself," whisper the skulls. "Let go."

Let go, my mind echoes, as I watch with horrified fascination as stone crawls up the Minotaur's body, over my own, encasing both our legs in a dull hard shell. I feel as though I am being dipped in concrete. I feel as though I am dying. I gaze into the Minotaur's face, looking for some sign of the man I am risking my life for. His eyes are closed. He is unconscious.

"Let go," whisper the skulls. "Let go and you will be free."

It is not too late. I could pull away. But I look again at the Minotaur and remember his voice, his touch, the feeling of home in his arms, and I cannot leave him. He is all I have, all I want, and to lose him, to lose that part of myself I have given him when for the first time in my life I *belong*—

The stone creeps. I press as close as I can, hooking my arms around the Minotaur's neck. I kiss him, hard, and after a moment I feel him stir and kiss me back. I smile against his mouth. Taste tears. Mine.

The Minotaur murmurs something I do not understand. I do not let go. I keep kissing him, even when he begins struggling, protesting, trying to push me away from the contagious gathering of stone. I hang tight, ignoring him. He has been betrayed by magic—both of us have—but I will be his champion to the end.

The stone rises. The Minotaur and I stop moving. We are locked together, and all I can do is tilt my head, to kiss him. I look into his eyes—blue like sky—blue with grief—and try to smile.

"Not what you expected?" I say, and the Minotaur makes a choking sound that I cut off with a kiss. One last kiss.

The stone covers my face. I go blind.

The next time I learn how to see again, I find myself cradled in strong arms. I am being carried. My feet dangle, my head lolls, and I feel sick to my stomach. I struggle to be put down. Just in time. I bend over, gagging, eyes streaming.

Then I remember. I fall to my knees.

A hand touches my shoulder. I turn. Find the Minotaur crouching beside me. He is not wearing the mask.

It startles me. For a moment I do not know him, but then I look into his eyes and they are the same soul, same heart. I touch his mouth with trembling fingertips, and he captures my wrist, holding me gently. His hands are the same, as well. Strong and warm.

"How?" I murmur. "I thought we were dead."

"We were," says the Minotaur, a hint of wonder in his voice. "You gave your life for mine."

I sag against him. We are still naked. I run my hands over his body, searching for injury. Explore his face, studying the unfamiliar lines, the dark curl of his hair. He is a handsome man. But then, I thought so before ever seeing his face. Before he was anything but a presence in the dark.

I trail my fingers down his neck, following the red imprint of the former straps. The Minotaur watches my eyes. There is such tenderness in his face I want to lower my head and weep. I think I might do so anyway.

"How?" I ask again.

"I was a monster," says the Minotaur, "and the king did not think it possible that anyone would ever care for me. Not enough to do what you did. The fact he even allowed one chance to lift the curse was meant more as punishment than hope. To break me with the futility of my existence. Because who . . . who would ever love a Minotaur?"

"I do," I say quietly, and he shuts his eyes, shuddering.

"You had faith," he whispers. "You believed in me, or else you would not have held me."

"It was difficult. I thought you would kill me in the process."

"I almost did." He opens his eyes. "I became the creatures I transformed into. Only your touch kept me centered. Only you. If you had let go . . ."

I stop him. I do not want to think about what might have been. I glance around, noticing for the first time that we are in some kind of building. The stones are dark and smooth with age, and there are pillars rising to a vaulted ceiling that is elegant in its massive simplicity. The silence is heavy. We are alone. But there is light—streams of it cutting through holes in the upper segments of the high walls.

I look at the Minotaur. "Where is the labyrinth? How did we escape?"

"The labyrinth is where it always is," he says gravely. "It

is everywhere and nowhere. But we were able to leave because you freed me. And as you know, I have . . . some skills of my own."

I shiver. The Minotaur helps me stand. "Come. There are clothes nearby."

"How do you know?"

"Because this is home."

I raise my eyebrows. "Home has been empty a long time. There won't be anything left to find."

The Minotaur smiles. "We shall see."

But before we begin walking, I lean in for a kiss. A soft kiss that becomes urgent, fierce. I remember fear, desperation, my decision to die, and such memories will never leave me. They are another darkness, another labyrinth, and I want the Minotaur to steal me away. To save me.

And he does, his own calm face breaking into a mask of grief and desperation. He pushes me up against a pillar, his breathing unsteady, tears shadowing his eyes. He kisses me so deeply I feel him in my soul.

The Minotaur takes me. He is hard and I am ready and he slides so easily into my body I wonder how two people could fit so well and still be separate hearts.

I say as much, later. Later, when my legs are still wrapped around him and we lie on the cold stone floor. The Minotaur smiles. I can still see the outline of the mask, the mighty horns resting like a crown. Fit for a prince, I think. A prince of the labyrinth.

"We are two pieces of a puzzle," says the Minotaur. "You and I."

"So where do we go now? What do we do?"

The Minotaur points. I narrow my eyes; a moment later I see the silver mirror resting close by on the stones. Set there earlier, no doubt, when I was ill.

"Anywhere," he says simply. "We go anywhere."

I think of my library, my home in the darkness, my routine. My old life, safe and quiet. I am not naïve; *anywhere* will not be easy. But I look at the Minotaur, curled around my body, staring at me with his shining eyes, and I know that he is not naïve, either.

And I would rather face a life with him, no matter the danger or difficulty, than rest easy by myself.

I take his hand. "Have we really left the labyrinth?"

"I think we are making our own," says the Minotaur. "It will be an adventure."

"I hope so," I reply.

And it is.

DEMON LOVER

Cheyenne McCray

CHAPTER 1

HE VANISHED IN A WHIRL OF MIST, LEAVING BEHIND scents of sandalwood and sex on a hot summer's night.

Ericka Roberts cried out and clenched her bedcovers in both fists as she woke. Perspiration coated her body and the sheets clung to her damp skin. Her breathing was harsh, her heart beating so hard it pounded inside her ears.

These dreams are killing me.

For the past week, since she'd arrived at the oceanside condo in San Diego, she'd woken sweating, body aching with need and frustration. In her dreams, her demon lover teased her with his tongue and tasted her until she was on the edge of a climax so powerful she knew it would rock her to her core.

The moment she reached that pinnacle, he would stop. He'd rise, spread her legs with his hips, a sensual expression on his strong features. He'd nudge his cock against her folds and she'd hold her breath in anticipation.

And he would vanish.

Goddamnit. He just disappears!

The dreams were so intense that each morning she woke up pleasantly sore from his rough attention.

How's that for a vivid imagination? She groaned and flung her arm over her eyes. "I've entered another dimension, where sane people don't exist."

Ericka moved her arm from her eyes and turned onto her side, facing the window. Shadows from palm trees and the first hint of morning sunlight winked through the glass as she faced reality.

Not too far away, the rush and pound of the surf matched the rush of blood in her ears and the pounding of her heart. The scent of sandalwood shifted into salt and brine mixed with the vanilla of candles she'd placed on every available surface of the room.

She attempted to grasp the power of the dream, but it faded through her fingers like tendrils of mist.

Yet *he* was there, never leaving her thoughts.

Ericka blew a strand of red hair out of her eyes and chewed on one of her nails. She slumped in the deck chair, her shorts hiking up her thighs. Her mind was anywhere but on the page on her laptop. Another planet, maybe.

It was nearing sunset. For most of the day she'd been sitting on the porch, trying to work on her nonfiction book that included people describing visits by beings from Otherworldly realms.

"The freaking book," she grumbled as images of her demon lover refused to leave her mind. "The damned dreams happen because you're *studying* and *writing* about similar paranormal occurrences." She glanced at the ocean. "Get a grip."

This hidden stretch of beach outskirting San Diego was a perfect place to "channel" her writing. The water called to her, calmed her, let her slip into a state of mind where her body no longer existed.

Usually.

"Okay, that's enough." She punched a few keys and exited her doc and her web browser before closing her laptop. "You sure better have a productive day tomorrow."

When she'd rented the condo in the past, her fingers always flew over the keys of her laptop as she wrote her nonfiction paranormal books. Everything about the supernatural attracted her, but she especially loved her current topic.

Hence the dreams.

The wind kicked up and pages of one open research book on mythology flipped one after another in a sudden cascade. She reached for the book as the pages stopped at the intro to Incubae and Succubae.

She drew the book closer and studied the picture she'd practically drooled over the first time she'd read the research book. A painting of the backside of a man. With her finger she traced his shoulder-length black hair, muscular back, and tight ass. Her imagination supplied the rest. No doubt he'd be as toned and fit *everywhere* if she could manage a peek at him from the front.

The corner of her mouth curved. When she first looked at the picture, she'd been intrigued by giving up one's soul for one's desires.

Ericka rolled her eyes. Between that fascination and the topic of her book, no wonder she'd been experiencing such intense nightly dreams. She'd been reading about Incubae and Succubae until her eyes damned near crossed, and now her imagination had brought a demon lover of her own.

She shook her head, snatched up her books and her laptop, and headed into the condo. After she put them away, she glanced at her cell phone. A tiny red light blinked, indicating she had a message.

Ericka checked the recent callers. *Mom, Mom, and Mom. And oh, Mom.* Being the youngest child of a huge Irish family, Ericka had to suffer through her mother's constant worrying over nothing and everything.

She smiled when she saw that Julia, her sister and closest friend, had also called. No one in the world knew Ericka like Julia did.

For a moment, Ericka thought about calling her sister and talking about her dreams, but shook her head and set the phone aside. Despite Ericka being well known for her books on paranormal occurrences, Julia refused to believe in anything she couldn't see for herself. A real skeptic.

Ericka slipped outside of the condo into the wavering

sunlight and trotted barefoot down a rocky, sandy path. The cool ocean breeze lifted Ericka's hair from her shoulders. She sucked in a deep lungful of salty air.

Ericka's thoughts wandered as she looked out at the beauty of the ocean. The water was relatively calm, only making a deep sucking sound before the onrush of a wave. Sand squished between Ericka's toes as she walked closer to the water.

"Could a dream man manifest himself as real?" she said out loud, then shook her head. Julia would be catching the next flight from Seattle before Ericka could blink if she started talking about a man coming into her condo at night—even if he was a dream man.

Ericka reached the firm wet sand just as a wave receded, and she wiggled her toes. Water rushed back and the small wave slapped her bare calves and ankles with a salty sting before drawing away again.

"You should be writing fiction, Ericka," she mumbled. "He's a freaking *dream*."

Another small wave splashed against Ericka, this time high enough to reach the hems of her shorts. She looked out at the soft swells of the ocean and the reflection of the oranges and pinks of the sunset rippling on the waves.

Her heart rate kicked up a notch—it was almost dark. Anticipation fluttered in her belly.

Almost time for sleep.

And her dream lover.

Aedan studied the winking stars above his quarters. The constellations were so different in his realm than in Ericka's.

Ericka.

Just the thought of her hardened his cock so that it tented his toga. His skin felt tight beneath the material, as if he were being stretched from his bedchamber to Ericka's bedroom in the Earth Otherworld.

He took a deep breath before he lowered his gaze from the glittering sky to several pools of exotic fish he had collected from places he had visited over the centuries. His mother Belisma found it amusing that he, an Incubus, had a sort of hobby. He had to admit she was probably right.

Demons didn't have hobbies. Demons had missions.

And I have friggin' fish.

He sighed.

The swimming blurs of the colorful fish were likely proof that his mind—and demonic mission—was slowly unraveling.

His chamber was carved from rock and in one corner a waterfall rushed over stones into a bathing pond. Moisture dampened the walls, moss growing on the surfaces, and the floor was soft grass—his own private paradise. Every Incubae or Succubae had a different type of chamber, depending on whether they were of fire, earth, air, or water.

A water Incubus, Aedan was the offspring of the water goddess herself.

Which probably explained his fascination with fish.

Sort of.

His bed commanded the center of the chamber and had a mattress of soft leaves in a carved-out stone shell. He wondered what Ericka would think of his world, never mind the fish. What it would be like to bring her here. To take her in his bed.

He pressed his fingertips to his forehead.

First the fish, and now dangerous thoughts. Way past dangerous. Why after centuries of fulfilling women's desires, was he thinking of such abominations?

That was never done—bringing the human through the veil. Only souls could travel with the Incubae or Succubae to where the souls were stored until the human's shell died. Soul after soul he'd collected without a second thought.

But Ericka . . . Over the past month he had watched her as he prepared to go to her and work toward winning her soul. He had witnessed her strength, her beauty, her commitment to family and friends, her sense of fairness, her intelligence, as well as her love of writing. Which, ironically enough, involved researching his kind. Something he found both amusing and intriguing.

For some reason she made him feel more real, alive. Made him want things he had never wanted before. Made him look at who and what he was, and long for something different than he had always known.

Like wishing he was human so he could spend his life with her.

Aedan scowled. An idiotic thought. Why was the woman affecting him like this?

When a Succubus or an Incubus was sent to a human, the person had projected a powerful desire. Perhaps a wish for the fulfillment of a fantasy, or a longing that included the phrase, "I'd give anything for . . ." The human usually exchanged his or her soul in payment, often unaware of the magnitude of what they'd done.

And that was the key.

Unaware.

I will take her soul, and she might not even realize what she has surrendered—if I don't tell her.

He pictured Ericka's beautiful body as he prepared to take everything from her. He imagined the way she would look at him when he finally thrust into her core. She was already wild in his arms when he went to her—the way she whimpered and moaned, trying to seek the completion he denied her.

It was his job to drive her insane with need nightly until she reached the point she would tell him anything, anything he wanted to hear—including giving up her soul.

But . . . *damnation.* Something about Ericka made him feel as if he were a part of her and she a part of him. An irrational thought that had him grinding his teeth. The idea of taking Ericka's soul tore at him like a piranha eating his gut.

Piranha.

Hmmm.

Maybe I should get a piranha for my collection.

Godsdamn, I'm losing my mind.

Centuries of fucking women, yet this one drove him to thoughts of piranha. He had to shake off his madness. It was time. No matter how he felt, he had to claim the woman's soul.

It was either that, or he would face eternity in the fires of the Realm of the Dead.

Aedan ground his teeth and left his bedchamber. It was time to go to the woman.

His thoughts churned as he strode down the Hall of the Lost. When he reached the Chamber of Veils, he walked to the archway that would take him to Ericka. He crossed his arms over his chest and watched her through the veil for a long moment.

Her eyelids were closed, hiding her startling blue eyes. Her lips parted as she shifted in her sleep, the sheets rumpling beneath her naked body. Her red hair was a wild mass against the white of her pillowcase, her nipples high and puckered with arousal. Around the room, several candles burned within their holders and the soft light danced upon her skin.

Gods and goddesses, he could already smell her woman's musk and her warm vanilla scent.

Yes, there was something about this one. Something innocent, yet wild at the same time.

Something . . . perfect.

His groin tightened, his cock aching. He wanted to be inside her. So many times he had come close to pushing her over the edge when she neared climax. The thought of pleasuring her for the sake of pleasuring her made his lust spiral and his erection harder.

His muscles tensed and he swallowed the feelings of rebellion rising within him. Feelings he shouldn't be having—that contradicted everything an Incubus was.

Ericka was his last assignment before he made the Great Transition to Annwn, that special place in Underworld reserved for those who pleased the gods and goddesses. Aedan had been successful with every assignment and had earned his place, earned the right to live in such peace and beauty. He was looking forward to it. He had lost his taste for his work years ago. It was time for a change.

More importantly, he had earned his reprieve from the flaming depths of the Realm of the Dead, where most demons and the soulless were sent.

He rubbed his forehead with his thumb and forefingers.

If he took Ericka's soul, she would go to the Realm of the Dead when her human shell died.

The mere thought made him grind his teeth.

If he did *not* take Ericka's soul . . . That was unthinkable for an Incubus or a Succubus. To fail in the last assignment, to be moments from salvation from the Realm of the Dead, then feel the fire's hideous, terrible bite for all eternity. Sweat broke out on his skin at thoughts of the endless labor he would be forced to do as liquid heat splashed against his body.

Aedan returned his gaze to Ericka, to that beauty and innocence that called to his being like no other had before.

"You want her." Jeff appeared at his side, bringing him out of his thoughts. The Succubus stroked his arm. "More than anyone you have taken in their dreams. This one is important to you."

Aedan forced himself to tear his gaze from the erotic sight of Ericka Roberts. "She is naught but another human."

"Hmmm . . ." The black-haired beauty at his side looked at him with her brilliant gold gaze. Her toga sparkled, the same color as her eyes. "This assignment is taking longer than normal." She curled her fingers around his biceps that flexed beneath her touch. "Another Incubus, Kyne perhaps, should accompany you."

A low rumble rose in Aedan's chest. His jaw tightened at the thought of another Incubus touching Ericka.

That was irrational. Aedan had played out this drama with countless women over the centuries, fulfilling their needs and desires in exchange for their souls. What Incubae and Succubae performed had been twisted into something considered evil. When in fact what they did only served to pleasure men and women and bring their fantasies to life. So what did their souls matter if they could have every wish granted?

Jett gathered her long hair and pulled it over one of her shoulders. "Perhaps you have become too close to this human. Maybe you should have Kyne take your place completely, before you get into trouble."

"No." The word came out sharper than Aedan intended. "Ericka Roberts is my assignment and I shall deal with her."

Aedan caressed Jett's back at the base of her spine with his palm. Touching her in that location always served to distract her, and she released his biceps when he moved away.

As he watched Ericka his cock ached enough to drive him senseless. He hadn't allowed himself an orgasm, just as he refused to let Ericka climax.

He vanished his toga with a thought as he prepared to walk through the veil.

Tonight . . . would Ericka be ready to offer up her soul?

Was he ready to take it?

CHAPTER 2

WHEN THE BED SANK BENEATH THE WEIGHT OF someone easing onto the mattress beside her, Ericka wasn't surprised. She opened her eyes and smiled at her dark lover.

Shadows still hid his gaze from her, but because she had left several candles lit, this time she could make out his angular jaw, a cleft in his chin, and his straight nose. Dark hair skimmed his shoulders and his smile was so sensual it made her squirm.

His naked body was a work of art. If she wrote fiction, she couldn't have created a character to rival him. Broad shoulders, carved biceps, a muscled chest, well-defined abs—definite hero material. And his cock—wow.

Ericka reached up to touch his face and he captured her hand in his. He held it to his heart and she felt his flesh, so warm and real against her palm.

"Who are you?" she asked as his mouth neared hers. "What are you?"

"Aedan." His accent sounded old-world, as if he came from another time, another place. "I am here to fulfill your fantasies."

"That doesn't include leaving me hanging like you have been, right?" His breath teased her lips as she spoke. She should have been irritated, but somehow she wasn't. "I certainly haven't fantasized about that."

Aedan stroked her naked body with his fingers as he kissed her. It was sweet, incredible, and she hungered for more. She grasped his cock and began stroking his erection as their tongues met and she tasted his unique flavor.

He hissed against her lips before drawing away. Moonlight spilled through her window and when he moved she saw his face clearly for the first time.

The man was gorgeous. And he had gold eyes. Not brown or amber or any shade in between. They were gold.

In a powerful sweep of his arms, he caught her in his embrace, forcing her to release his erection. She gasped and wrapped her arms around his neck as he stood.

She couldn't tear her gaze from his golden eyes as he carried her to the braided rug and laid her on her back in front of the lifeless fireplace. Additional candles flickered to life around them and she widened her eyes in surprise. Yet at the same time it seemed as natural as the way he came to her every night.

Candlelight touched his features, casting dark shadows on the planes of his face. He settled beside her and she caught her breath as he trailed his finger over one of her nipples that tingled beneath his touch.

In her heart and soul, she knew it had been him all week. It had never been just a dream.

He was here, now, and real.

Hell, she *did* write about paranormal events. Anything could happen.

He started to lower his head to slip one of her nipples inside his warm mouth. It was all she could do to make herself stop him.

"Aedan." She captured his face in her palms and it surprised her how smooth his skin was, no roughness from stubble. He paused and his golden eyes met hers and so many questions rose within her. She wanted to know more about the man who came to her each night.

He caught her wrists in one of his large hands, pulling her palms away from his cheeks. "What, sweet one?"

She squeezed her eyes shut then opened them to stare at him. "We need to talk."

For a second he furrowed his brows and then his features relaxed. He gave her a dark, sexy look that made her want to forget about questions and answers and just melt into him. "I can think of much better things to do," he said as he lowered his head and slipped her nipple into his warm mouth. At the same time he moved one of his thighs across hers and pressed his cock against her hip.

Something between a sigh and a moan escaped her before she tried to draw her wrists away from his grip. "I'm serious—" She cried out as he bit her nipple then whimpered when he moved his mouth to her other taut bud. "I can't think—*stop.*"

Aedan raised his head and studied her. She felt his body heat, the firmness of his grip around her wrists, his thigh pinning hers. "What do you wish to discuss?"

She tugged her wrists and he released them. "You."

Something dark flickered in his eyes and for a moment his sensual expression slipped away. But then he smiled again. He placed his hand on her belly, and his warmth seeped into her skin and spread throughout her.

Ericka took a deep breath. "How do you come here? How do you get into my condo?"

"You believe in the unbelievable, Ericka Roberts." He traced her navel with his fingertip. "You tell me."

She frowned. "That's not an answer."

With a casual shrug of one shoulder, he said, "I am who I am."

This was going nowhere in a hurry. "Are you real?"

He pressed his erection tighter against her hip and brushed her brow with his lips as his scent of sandalwood and male swept over her. She wanted him to roll her onto her back and feel his body weighing hers down.

"Do you think I am real?" he murmured.

"Yes—I think so. Yes." She tried to focus as he moved his mouth to her earlobe and gently nipped it. "But I need to know more."

He bit her earlobe again before trailing his lips down her jawline. "And that would be?"

"Where you come from. Things about *you*." She brought one of her hands up and placed her palm on his chest, forcing him to raise his head and meet her eyes. "Do you have any brothers or sisters? What about your mother, your father?"

Again that dark look flickered in his eyes, but vanished when he smiled. "I have many brothers and sisters. And my mother . . . she is *different*."

He gave a low groan as she scraped her fingernails from his chest to his abs. "Different, how?"

"In ways I find difficult to explain." He sighed. "She has much to attend to and I do not see her often."

"Oh." Her fingers neared his cock as she skimmed past his abs toward his groin. "At home in Seattle, my family is constantly around and my mother fusses over all of us. Sometimes I need to get away, you know?"

A soft look came over his features. "Yes."

Her hand reached his erection and she wrapped her fingers around it, causing him to suck in his breath. Ericka smiled at the desire and strength rising within her. Power. She felt so much power over him and his desires. It was her turn to drive him crazy.

She pushed harder at his shoulder and he rolled onto his back at the same time he removed his thigh from where it had rested on hers.

Ericka moved off the braided rug and straddled him. "You *will* tell me more." She gave him her naughtiest grin. "But not now."

Before he could speak, she eased down his body so that she was between his thighs, her mouth brushing the soft skin of his erection.

Aedan groaned and tangled his fingers in her wavy hair. After all the teasing he had done, she was tempted to draw out his torture as long as possible. She ran her tongue along the length of his cock and cupped his balls with her free hand.

He gripped her hair tighter and raised his hips as she slipped her mouth over the head of his erection. He was so big and thick, and tasted salty and delicious.

Tenderness filled his voice when he said, "I want to see your beautiful eyes."

Immediately she looked up and she wanted to melt right into that wonderful golden gaze.

Damnation, but the feel of Ericka's mouth was incredible around him. She sucked as he raised his hips and slowly thrust in and out of her mouth. She gave just the right pressure that would please any man.

The thought enraged him. He clenched his fist tighter in her soft red hair and she whimpered. He wanted to be the only man to please her.

But then he realized once again that he wasn't a man, that he would never be a human male. He was an Incubus, here to take this woman's soul.

Only he found himself not wanting her soul—but her heart. Her innocence, her intelligence—everything that drew him to her again and again made him want her for so much more.

Gods, what am I thinking. Her heart?

His look must have been fierce because Ericka widened her eyes. He calmed his expression but gritted his teeth as he felt an orgasm rushing toward him with the power of an Underworld storm.

He thrust in and out a few more times and then jerked his cock out of her mouth just as he was about to reach orgasm. He held Ericka still, his hand fisted in her hair. Her lips were moist and his cock wet from her mouth.

He wanted to take her now, to fuck her hard and fast until they both reached climax.

But his nightly visits had been to prepare her for this moment.

Time to take her . . . and take her soul.

Aedan shifted beside Ericka on the braided rug as he drew her up from between his thighs so that she lay beside him.

She sighed as he kissed her and slipped his tongue into her mouth. She tasted his wild male flavor, and his scent of sandalwood and sex filled her senses.

When he drew away he smiled and her heart nearly stopped beating. "Your beauty is beyond compare, Ericka Roberts."

She started to return his smile but instead frowned as a thought occurred to her. "How do you know my name?"

"I know much about you, sweet one." He brought one of his hands between them and drew a line from between her breasts to her belly button. "You have a large family whom you love very much. You write about Otherworldly realms and all that is paranormal." Aedan pressed a kiss to her forehead before he moved his lips to her ear and whispered, "What less would you expect of your dream lover?"

He had her there.

Any other thoughts she might have had escaped her as he cupped her mound with one hand while skimming the curve of her neck with his lips and tongue. He slipped his finger into her slick folds and she whimpered.

Slowly, so slowly, he eased down her body, licking, tasting, sucking. His tongue left a wet path over her collarbone then up the rise of her breast to her nipple. When he latched onto the taut nub, Ericka cried out and arched her back. His long dark hair brushed her skin in a silken caress as he moved his mouth to her other nipple.

Ericka's mind spun and she was beyond words as he thrust two fingers into her core and pumped them at the same time. She clenched her hands in his hair and squirmed as she rode his fingers while he pounded them in and out of her.

When he had eased himself down her body so that his head was between her thighs, Ericka could barely breathe. Blood rushed in her ears as his breath stirred the curls of her mound.

Ericka let out a cry as he swiped his tongue from the sensitive place between her anus and folds, all the way up. His hair felt silken between her thighs as he moved his head and drove his fingers in and out of her.

The intensity of his licking and sucking was almost too much to bear. So much, so much, so much! She had to climax. She was so close to orgasm she could almost scream.

She parted her lips with a louder moan while he continued to delve into her folds. Tingling sensations ran rampant in her body, and her mind spun with desire.

Just when she thought she was going to lose control, he stopped.

"Aedan!" she shouted and looked down at him. She felt dizzy, lightheaded, and had to have an orgasm so badly she was almost insane with it. "Don't stop. *Please.*"

Tears stung the backs of her eyes from the incredible need to climax. Aedan raised his head at the same time she looked down and she saw a spark in his gold eyes. He was so good-looking, so masculine, so powerful, his muscles flexing with every movement he made. Her breathing grew harsher and her heart thundered as she stared at Aedan's starkly handsome face. Her dark lover.

Always she'd thought of him as her demon lover, the way he came in the night and left her sweating and wanting. Was he going to leave her aching for fulfillment—even more so than before?

Not this time! Not this time. He can't do it to me again.

Aedan smiled, an incredibly sexy smile that caused more tingling and wetness between her thighs.

He lowered his head and swiped her folds again with his tongue. She gasped as he began pounding his fingers in and out of her core again.

This time it seemed like her head was going to float away and only the heat and ache in her body kept her grounded. What he was doing to her was more than she could bear. Her body trembled. She was so close to losing total control.

She couldn't think past what she was feeling. The edge of an orgasm so powerful rushed toward her—it was like she was burning in white-hot fire.

Oh, God, she needed to climax and climax *now.*

He stopped.

For a moment Ericka was disoriented, ripped away from the peak she had almost fallen over.

"Don't stop," she begged again. Perspiration coated her skin and her hair was damp against her scalp. She squirmed as he slipped his fingers out of her core. "Don't do this to me."

A predatory smile crept over his face. He rose up between her thighs and placed his cock at the opening of her core and nudged it enough to make her gasp. She held her breath, waiting for that moment of penetration that would bring her fulfillment. For days she'd prepared for this. He would finally be inside of her.

Aedan's gaze caught hers and for a moment it was like he had cast a spell over her. Ericka's body was still on fire but suddenly she felt suspended in time. Waiting. Wanting.

He opened his mouth as if to say something, then stopped. Again he started, then closed his mouth.

His expression changed to one of anger. "She's not ready yet," he growled, like he was talking to himself.

The spell fell away. "I'm ready!" Ericka squirmed, wondering what in the hell he meant.

He shook his head. "Not yet." Ericka cried out as he moved away and rested on his haunches.

Tears flowed freely down her face. She rose so that she was sitting up and pounded her fists on his rock-hard chest. "You can't do this to me!"

He leaned down and kissed her forehead. "I am sorry."

Frustration and fury tore through Ericka. "You bastard." She slapped him as hard as she could.

Aedan's head snapped to the side, and then he looked directly at her. She flinched when he put his fingers to her forehead.

Relaxation flowed through her, taking the edge off her need to climax. Not entirely, but enough that she didn't think she was going to die if she didn't have an orgasm.

Aedan drew Ericka into his embrace. She collapsed against his chest, her arms around his neck. And she cried. She couldn't move, couldn't speak as Aedan rose to his feet and carried her toward her bed.

He laid her gently on the mattress and she stared up at him. The bedsprings creaked beneath his weight as he sat next to her. He stroked her hair from her face and he wore an odd expression. Regret? Sadness? Longing?

She didn't care. This time she was *pissed.*

"Damn you." She pushed herself up in her bed and shoved him away. "Why are you doing this to me?"

He shook his head. "It is difficult to explain."

"What?" Ericka nearly smacked him again. "How can it be difficult for *you* to not give me a damn orgasm?"

"It is time for me to go." He cupped her face and ran his thumb across her cheek. "I am sorry."

She knocked his hands away and stared into his eyes. "Tell me who you really are. Tell me what's going on."

"Nothing, sweet one." He brushed his fingertips over her forehead and closed his eyes, the gold of them lost to her for a moment. "Be at ease."

He opened his eyes and Ericka felt a little dizzy as he lowered her fully onto her back and drew a quilt to her shoulders. She needed to climax, she *knew* it. Yet the intensity she'd experienced moments ago faded a bit.

He kissed her cheek. "Sleep. I will return."

Ericka's eyelids drooped. She didn't have the strength to fight off his kiss or tell him to go to hell. She was too limp, too exhausted.

She tumbled into a world of crazy, crazy dreams.

CHAPTER 3

AEDAN NARROWED HIS BROWS AS HE TURNED AWAY from Ericka, walked through the veil and the archway. What in the Underworlds had he been thinking? At that moment, when she'd been so close to orgasm, when he could have taken her, she would have given him anything. Even though she wouldn't have realized what she was giving up, she would have said the words. He had sensed it, known it.

And he hadn't asked her for her soul.

He half expected the guides to the Realm of the Dead to be waiting for him.

Instead, Kyne and Jett were.

"What the fuck was that about?" Kyne shouted, his gold eyes blazing. His muscles tightened as he clenched his fists at his sides. "You had her. She would have turned over her soul without thinking twice."

"She wasn't ready." With a thought, Aedan dressed himself in a toga then tried to shoulder his way past Kyne and Jett, but both stepped in front of him.

"Are you out of your mind?" Jett was as loud as Kyne had been. She tossed her long black hair over her shoulder. "By all that crawls the Realm of the Dead, she *was* ready."

"You are much too close to this one." Kyne folded his arms across his chest, his look fierce. "Errol or I should finish it."

"You hold no power over me." Heat washed over Aedan and he scowled at Kyne. "This is my assignment and I will complete it. Neither you nor Errol will touch her."

I will save her from you, whispered his mind. *And from myself, too.*

"You are coming with us." Jett took him by his upper arm and tugged, her fingers pressing into his flesh.

He stood firm. "I am retiring to my quarters."

"No," Kyne said. "First we have something you must see."

A low rumble rose within Aedan. "If it will get you to leave me in peace."

Jett studied him. "That will be for you to decide."

Aedan growled again, but walked between Jett and Kyne from the Chamber of Veils into the Hall of the Lost. The floor was cool and smooth beneath his bare feet, the silence thick and heavy between the three of them.

The vast hall stretched endlessly, yet it wasn't long before they reached a chamber that Aedan had always avoided. It was the Chamber of Futures, and he had never desired to see what lay in store for him. His future would be whatever he made of it. He merely had to make the choice.

To pacify his companions, he allowed Kyne and Jett to shove him into the room. They could not enter, as only the being who wished to see his or her future was allowed.

His throat tightened as he walked into the darkened passageway of a cave. Rough rock walls surrounded him, sharp stones pricked his soles, and smells of dust and age filled his nostrils. It was akin to a holy place, had they not been demons.

He turned a corner and came to a stop in the doorway of a small, round chamber. The walls were white and as smooth as polished marble. On the floor at the center of the room was a circular mosaic depicting the gods and goddesses of the four elements—fire, wind, earth, water.

Four figures intertwined. The god of earth was at the top of the circle, north, and he bore a green seedling in his palms.

The goddess of wind was to the east, her red hair flowing in a breeze and a bird perched on her shoulder.

At the base of the circle, south, was the god of fire. He held both hands up to either side of him, a flame in each palm.

And then on the west side of the circle was the likeness of the goddess of water, who tipped her head back as rain fell upon her face. Belisma, his mother.

Aedan sucked in his breath and stepped into the center of the mosaic. Immediately, sensations of cool earth beneath his feet warred with sudden heat warming his legs. A breeze raised his hair from his shoulders and flattened his tunic to his body. It felt as if the welcome caress of water wrapped around him.

His skin tingled as he stared at the smooth, white wall. He forced himself to breathe as he waited for his future to be shown to him.

For a moment, nothing. Then the entire room vanished.

He stood on a sandy beach looking out at the ocean. Sunshine warmed his body—a strange sensation. He was an Incubus, never allowed in the sunlight, always relegated to the dark.

Annwn. I must be in the afterlife where my kind go if the gods and goddesses are pleased.

The tightness in his throat increased and his heart pounded in time with the waves against the sand. Of course he would be sent to a place near water. But this . . . he had not expected such beauty, such vastness.

A cry from a sea bird mingled with the roar of the ocean. The scent of salt was heavy enough that he even tasted it on his tongue. To either side of him grew thick green foliage that hugged the small cove.

For the first time in all his centuries of being, he felt alive and free. Free of the constraints of serving the gods and goddesses, and alive with possibilities.

In one moment, he felt joy.

In the next, terror.

Light and joy vanished.

Aedan shouted as he was enveloped in flame, the pain so deep and constant it was as if the flesh was charred from his bones. Bursts of fire lit the darkness while bubbling pools of lava lapped at his feet like the ocean waves had when he had stood on the shore.

With every splash of lava against his ankles and calves, Aedan wanted to cry out. But he ground his teeth and held it in as he searched for some way out of this version of the human hell—

The Realm of the Dead.

Sweat rolled down his face and arms but quickly dried in the searing heat. Shrieks, cries, and sobs of other beings in the realm echoed from sharp and sheer volcanic rock. He could make out figures now. Men, women. No doubt some he had sent here himself.

Dear gods and goddesses.

A wave of heat slammed into him, forcing him to drop to his knees in a lava pool. Aedan gave another shout.

Everything vanished.

He was in the Chamber of Futures again, but on his knees.

Aedan's breathing came hard and fast and in his mind's eye he could still see the flames and the tortured souls. His tunic was now damp with his sweat and clung to his body.

When the beating of his heart slowed and his breathing calmed, he stood and straightened to his full height.

His choices had been laid out before him.

Annwn, or the Realm of the Dead.

His choice.

Robbing Ericka Roberts of her soul was the key.

Aedan clenched his fists at his sides and strode from the chamber, nearly running into Jett and Kyne when he entered the Hall of the Lost.

Without speaking to either of them, he turned and headed away from the pair who remained silent.

He needed . . . he needed his quarters. The stone, the water. He needed to think.

When he reached his quarters, he slammed the door, raked his fingers through his hair again, and looked up at the starry sky. "Gods and goddesses, what is happening?"

A sigh and a breeze whirled through his chamber and he turned to face the direction it came from. Like the reflection of water on a pond, his mother, Belisma, appeared before him along with her scent of fresh water and moss. The goddess of water was as beautiful as a crystal waterfall tumbling into the River of Life.

Surprise sent a jolt down his spine that Belisma had answered his cry. He knelt before the blond, golden-eyed goddess, and kept his head lowered.

"Rise, Aedan of the Incubae." Her voice even sounded like water trickling over rocks.

When his eyes met hers, the beautiful goddess did not smile. "This has never been a battle for the human's soul, my son. It is a battle for yours."

Aedan's mouth wouldn't open as he stared at the water goddess. Before he had a chance for her response to register and to ask her what in the Underworlds she meant, Belisma wavered like the ripples from a stone tossed in a pond, and then she was gone.

"What the fuck?" This time he scrubbed both hands through his hair. "What the fuck did she mean, *my* soul?"

He was Incubae. He was a creation of the gods and goddesses. He didn't have a soul.

He had heard stories in childhood, of demons granted reprieve from their soulless state, usually at the whim of some god—but he had never known that to happen in modern times.

Aedan shook his head and stared around his room. It was no surprise Belisma had been the one to answer his cry since she was his mother. But why the cryptic message?

My soul?

He stalked from one end of his large chamber to the other. The sound of the waterfall in the corner made a rushing sound like the blood in his ears.

It was well past his time of resting before he could lie down and attempt sleep.

Utterly exhausted, Ericka rolled out of bed, got to her feet, and stretched. Cool morning air drifted from the window over her bare skin.

Vivid images flashed through Ericka's mind and crashed down on her. Her knees gave out and the bedsprings creaked as she dropped onto the bed. She blinked and rubbed her eyes with her fingertips. The dream rushed toward her—only it didn't feel like a dream.

It felt like a memory.

Everything tumbled through her at once. She sucked in a deep breath and gripped her sheets in her fists.

Aedan. His name was Aedan. With every fiber of her being she knew he was real, a dream lover brought to life. He'd truly been coming to her every night.

But he'd done it again. He'd brought her to the peak and hadn't let her climax.

She ground her teeth and clenched her fists tighter.

Bastard.

Would he come back tonight? If he did, she'd give him a piece of her mind. And she'd let him have it with her fists, this time. Or a well-placed knee to the balls.

Until last night she hadn't thought he was real. Not truly. *Well, maybe.* He'd been a phantom, there but not there.

But he's oh-so-real.

Ericka rubbed her temples with the heels of her palms. He was real. Real. But where did he come from? What about the disappearing act? Was she going crazy?

She pushed to her feet even though her legs trembled. She headed for the shower and wondered how the hell she was going to get any writing done today.

With a sigh, Ericka plopped on the bright patchwork couch in her living room, a heavy book in her lap. The book contained extensive accounts of people who believed they had been visited by Incubae or Succubae.

It was twilight, so she flicked on the antique lamp on the end table beside the couch. As the day had passed, Ericka felt like she was caught in a dream. Everything was so surreal, as if she was experiencing life outside her body. No matter what she tried, her mind wouldn't stray from last night, and every other night Aedan had come to her.

She'd finally given up trying to write and put away her laptop and research books, with the exception of the book spread open in her lap now.

Ericka crossed her legs on the couch as she began to read. At first, her focus wasn't so hot, but as she read, she fell deeper into the stories of countless people.

Some were nothing like what she'd experienced. But when she ran across one by a woman in Idaho, her heart started pounding against her breastbone. *A man visited me,* the woman had said. *He had a perfect, muscular body, long dark hair . . . and gold eyes.*

A wash of heat flowed over Ericka at the thought of another woman being with Aedan. The rush of jealousy surprised her and made her grind her teeth.

It had to be him.

The sex. Dear God. The woman, Betty something, claimed the man denied her an orgasm each night and would vanish before she climaxed.

Finally, when she made the promise he demanded, he brought her to completion.

He never returned.

What had Betty promised?

Ericka's hands shook as she held the book, her gaze slowly moving down to the end of the woman's story. Her heart lodged in her throat.

My soul, Betty said in the interview. *I promised him my soul.*

Ericka's heart dropped from her throat to the pit of her

stomach and she almost doubled over, feeling as if she might throw up. Sweat broke out on her skin and her body went from hot to cold, hot to cold.

It took long moments, but the sickness in her belly finally eased and her heartbeat slowed. When she collected herself, she took a deep breath and straightened, resting her back against the couch.

Aedan truly was a demon. An Incubus who had come to take her soul.

What he said last night suddenly made sense.

She's not ready yet.

But she would have done it. That sick feeling weighted her belly again. All he'd had to do was ask, and she would have said yes without realizing what she was doing.

Ericka closed the book and set it aside on the couch as she stared at the window across the living room. The sheer curtains stirred. It was already dark and soon it would be time to go to bed.

Did she dare? Or should she pack her belongings into her SUV and drive through the night back to Seattle?

She rubbed her sweaty palms on her shorts and swallowed hard. No, she wasn't going to run. She was prepared, armed with the truth. She and Aedan had some unfinished business.

And no way in hell was he getting her soul.

Aedan stood at the veil between him and the Earth Otherworld. He watched Ericka pace as she glanced at her bed every now and then. Candlelight from the many candleholders around her room flickered and caused shadows to dance along the walls. A fat blue candle burned on her nightstand and he caught the scent of blueberries along with her vanilla scent.

She chewed on one of her nails while carrying a glass of red wine in her other. Every so often she would take a sip, before returning to pacing and chewing on her fingernail.

Instead of being naked, she wore a short, sheer gown. It didn't hide a lot, but the meaning was clear. She was placing a barrier between them. No doubt because he had denied her again last night.

At the thought, his heart ached. He didn't want anything between them.

It was well into the night when Ericka settled on her bed and put the now-empty wine glass on the nightstand. She remained sitting, her back propped against the pillows she'd stacked in front of the headboard. Her eyelids drooped despite her obvious efforts to keep her eyes wide open. She jerked awake a couple of times, then slid into an exhausted sleep.

Aedan almost hated to wake Ericka, but the need to be near her was so great he couldn't stay away.

He wished away his tunic with his magic, then stepped through the veil.

CHAPTER 4

WALKING THROUGH THE VEIL WAS LIKE STEPPING inside gel, a sticky, gooey sensation. Aedan's feet met the bedroom's carpet and he was free of the veil. It was always behind him, but was not something a human could see.

When he reached Ericka, he watched her sleep. What did she have to do with Belisma's baffling message about *his* soul? His body tightened with frustration. Then he forced himself to relax, to push thoughts of Belisma away, and concentrate on Ericka.

She took deep, even breaths but her forehead was crinkled as if concerned. As always, her red hair fell in a mass about her face, down to her slim shoulders.

The almost-sheer blue nightgown allowed him glimpses of her nipples and areolas. Seeing her nipples along with the hint of the patch of hair on her mound caused his cock to harden even more than it had while he watched her through the veil.

Aedan settled beside her on the bed, trying to ease down slowly enough that the springs didn't whine. With the back of his hand, he brushed a curl from her cheek and she made a soft sound and turned her face toward his touch.

He slipped his fingers from her cheek into her hair as he lowered his mouth to hers. He heard her soft breathing and even the pounding of her heart.

Gods and goddesses, when his lips touched hers, fire raced through his body and straight toward his erection. She sighed and he slipped his tongue into her mouth and tasted her sweet womanly flavor along with the hint of the wine she'd been drinking.

Ericka moaned and returned his kiss. He didn't know if she was awake yet, but her body responded to him. The scent of her musk grew stronger the deeper their kiss became.

Aedan placed his palm over one of her breasts, feeling the hard nipple poking through the fabric. He squeezed and she moaned louder then slipped her arms around his neck and nibbled at his bottom lip.

It was his turn to groan. He drew away to see her beautiful blue eyes open. Her lips were parted and moist, and she ran her tongue along her bottom lip.

"I knew you'd come." Her voice was husky, yet had a slight edge to it. "But I didn't know if I wanted you to."

"Why not?" He began rolling her nipple between his thumb and forefinger, and she groaned.

Ericka looked into his eyes. Something flickered in her gaze, but she said nothing. He tried not to frown at not being able to read her expression.

Instead, he let it pass, slid onto the bed, and she scooted over to let him recline beside her. She moved so that they were both lying down, facing one another. He traced the line of her body with his fingers, from her shoulder, to her waist, to her hip. Her warm vanilla scent and her woman's musk filled his senses.

As an Incubus, he didn't need light to see in darkness. But the candlelight touching her features made her seem softer and more vulnerable.

An Incubus. Why couldn't he be a man? At this moment, more than anything he wished he could stay with her forever. To wake with her when the first rays of sunlight peeked through the windows, and to walk with her in the sunshine. By the gods and goddesses, if he did have a spirit-essence, he would offer it to her.

His gut twisted and ached as he thought about his vision of Annwn and the beach that would be his home, as long as he took Ericka's soul.

The alternative—the constant feeling of being burned alive in the Realm of the Dead. If he didn't take her soul that would be his future.

If he did take her soul, the Realm of the Dead would be Ericka's fate.

Ericka didn't pull away when Aedan touched her face with his hand. How could he make her feel this way, make her want him even more, when she knew exactly what he was?

This very moment she should push him away, tell him to not come back. Giving away her soul was not an option.

God, he was good. Playing the part so well that she could almost believe he cared. Becky, Betty, whoever she was, hadn't mentioned that. Just the incredible sex, and then his vanishing act when she gave him what he wanted.

Her soul.

Ericka shivered as Aedan trailed his thumb over her lips and across her cheek. A thrill stirred in her belly and between her thighs, and her nipples pressed against the sheer nightgown. His eyes darkened to a deeper gold and his jaw tightened as he slipped his fingers into her hair and started to draw her to him at the same time he moved his lips toward hers.

What was wrong with playing along and getting what *she* wanted from *him*?

And wouldn't this go over well in one of my books? My own experiences with an Incubus?

His lips brushed hers. She groaned and wrapped her arms around his neck. She couldn't stop herself. His kiss was so exquisite she could think of nothing but him.

Aedan moved his lips from hers, licking a path to her ear. He nipped at her earlobe, causing her to squirm with desire. "What can I do for you, Ericka?"

Her face screwed in a frown. "I'm not having sex with you

in any way if you're going to leave before I climax." She drew away and darkened her frown. "I mean it."

He raised his head and grinned. "Perhaps I should tie you up and—"

Ericka slugged him in the shoulder. "You're getting *nothing* unless I get an iron-clad promise from you. Sex with an orgasm to end all orgasms."

He smiled, an almost sad, wistful smile.

With the aid of the candlelight, she studied his strong features and body. He was fit, not an ounce of fat on him. She loved his muscular thighs and tight ass, not to mention his good-sized erection—she wanted to push him on his back and straddle him. He was breathtaking with his long dark hair and golden gaze.

She reached between them and stroked his cock. "You have amazing eyes."

He grasped the bottom of her nightgown. "All my people have eyes of gold or silver."

Yeah. I know.

Any thoughts of further conversation vanished as he pushed up her sheer nightgown. It was the only one she had brought with her to the condo. She'd intended on refusing Aedan tonight. But she couldn't refuse him. Anything.

Dear God, she was falling for an Incubus.

Am I losing my mind?

Ericka pushed away the thoughts and wriggled to help him pull the nightgown over her head and drop it on the floor.

Aedan hooked his thigh over her hip, and in a thoroughly possessive movement he brought her tight to him, flattening her breasts, and making her nipples ache more.

He rained kisses over her face. "I want to see you spread out wide for me. Only me."

Ericka's breath caught and her belly fluttered.

His gaze fixed on hers. "For this night you will have everything I can give you."

A lump rose in her throat at the thought that he probably

wouldn't be back after she told him what she knew . . . and that he would never get her soul.

"What would *you* give *me*?" She swallowed back thoughts of him never returning. "Would you give me anything I asked of you?"

Aedan jerked back a little as if surprised at the way she'd turned the tables on him.

"Anything," he said softly. "If you wanted my very soul, I would give it to you."

"Your soul," she repeated. But he was an Incubus. He didn't have a soul, so his promise was empty. He stirred against her, the heat of his body making her mind spin with lust. She let her body take over her thought process again. "How about an orgasm instead?"

A slow, sensual smile curved the corners of his mouth. "I will make certain of it."

She touched the side of his face and stroked his black hair. "*Promise* to let me climax this time."

"You have my word." He kissed the corner of her mouth and palmed one of her breasts. "You will have an orgasm like you've never had before." He brushed his lips over hers and she sighed into his mouth.

"Yes," she whispered, almost without thought. She craved him. Her body craved him. Everything about her *needed* him.

When he drew away his smile was devastating.

Ericka's heart beat faster.

He trailed his fingertips over her breasts, and her nipples tightened and ached. "Do you know how beautiful you are?"

"You are." She stared into his golden eyes. "No wonder women can't refuse you."

At first Aedan frowned, but then appeared to ignore what she'd said about other women. He moved and spread her thighs wide with his palms as he knelt between them. A yellow scarf appeared in his hand.

"Er, what do you intend to do with that?" She fixed her gaze on the scarf.

His grin was absolutely wicked.

He trailed the yellow scarf up one of her thighs and then through her folds. Intense sensations swirled through her. He continued to make his way up her body until he reached her face. She caught the scent of her musk on the scarf.

The bed dipped as he moved and he brushed his lips over her cheekbone. "Gods and goddesses you look so perfect," he murmured.

He took the scarf and continued to trail it over her body in a feather-light caress. Goosebumps rose on her skin and she shivered.

Every caress made her want to shout out in ecstasy. In his unusual accent, he spoke softly in a language she didn't understand, which made her hotter yet.

She needed him inside her so bad she wanted to scream.

"Soon, love," he murmured, as if hearing her thoughts. "I will fuck you. Hard. Fast. Deep. The way you beg me for it."

Aedan began licking her body, from her toes to the arch of her foot and the inside of her ankle. She trembled as he licked and sucked his way up her calf and made her shudder with desire when he flicked his tongue against the skin at the back of her knee. So damn slow, he made his path up to that sensitive spot between her folds and her thigh and she arched her back.

He blew his warm breath on her, then the bastard moved down to her opposite foot and began taking a lazy trail up that leg, just like he'd done with her other.

Ericka thought she'd die or go crazy. The man was driving her mad. She trembled, needing him to do something. Lick her or take her—right now she didn't care. She just needed to climax.

When he reached her folds again, she held her breath. But no, he moved up her belly. He dipped his tongue into her navel and it sent shockwaves straight to her core. He continued higher until he reached the spot between her breasts. He had to feel how hard her heart was beating.

She made a combination sigh and groan when his mouth latched onto her nipple. It was still sensitive from last night when he'd pinched it, and that made his attention to it all the more erotic. He sucked her other nipple and the wetness of his tongue made her squirm.

"So anxious." He moved so that his chest brushed her nipples. "Do you wish for me to take you now?"

"Yes!" Ericka nodded in fast, jerky movements. She was so wet. So ready. And she wanted him so bad.

Aedan groaned and he teased the entrance to her core with his erection. He brushed his lips across her cheek. "I do not think I can wait any longer either, my love."

My love? repeated in Ericka's mind a second before he slammed his cock inside her.

This time Ericka did scream. She tossed her head from side to side as he drove in and out of her like he'd promised. Hard. Fast. Deep.

His balls slapped against her, and his chest rubbed her nipples. Her whole body was alive. On fire. She was burning. His sweat-slicked skin moved against hers and she smelled sandalwood and sex.

The way he filled her—she couldn't begin to describe it. He stretched her, reached deep inside her.

A climax built and built until it spiraled and spiraled, like she was spinning toward some distant peak in her mind.

If he left her hanging now, she'd kill him.

Could a person kill an Incubus?

She'd sure as hell find out if he left her hanging.

The thoughts vanished as he kept thrusting into her, taking her like she'd never been taken before.

Her body shook as his hips pistoned between her thighs. His chest rubbed her nipples even harder. She'd give *anything* to finally have an orgasm with Aedan.

Not her soul, though, not her soul.

He jerked and fell out of rhythm and paused, his breathing harsh.

Ericka cried out with anger and frustration.

Then he started driving into her harder than ever. Hard, hard, *harder*!

Oh, God, she was almost there, almost there, almost there—

"Come for me, Ericka," was all Aedan said.

Behind her eyelids, Ericka saw pure white as if her world had just gone supernova.

She screamed.

She couldn't think past what she was feeling. White-hot fire exploded from inside her. Aedan continued to slam into her. Tears rolled down her cheeks from the exquisite sensations.

Ericka soared to places she hadn't been to, ever. He kept driving into her relentlessly.

His golden eyes glowed and the sight made her core clamp down on his cock even more.

"Aedan," she cried. "Please. God, please."

She didn't even know what she was begging for. He'd given her the most powerful orgasm of her life. What did she want now?

His look was intense, sweat dripping down the side of his face.

Her spasms went on until they faded, then started to build up again. "Come, Ericka," he said. "I want to see your eyes when you climax again."

She hadn't thought another orgasm could be even more intense than the last one. But it was. It was almost too intense. Her whole body shook and she cried his name over and over again.

A few more thrusts and he shouted as he climaxed. The throb of his cock inside her made her contractions continue on way past the point she was certain she couldn't take anymore.

Apparently she could.

Aedan rolled her in his arms and held her tight. "I wish I never had to let you go," he said, his voice shaking. "I never want to let you go."

CHAPTER 5

THE PAIN IN AEDAN'S VOICE AND WHAT HE'D SAID sent Ericka's mind reeling. She stiffened in his arms.

Something was wrong. Had he taken her soul without her permission? Her heart beat faster and her throat grew too dry to speak.

He lifted his head and fear rose in a heated rush when she saw his tortured expression. He pressed his lips to her forehead, then rolled onto his side so they faced each other and she was in his arms.

He didn't. He couldn't have stolen my soul.

Ericka forced herself to take a deep breath. *Don't panic. Don't panic.*

"Most likely you will hate me when I tell you the truth." Aedan brushed her hair from her forehead as her heart pounded harder. "I am not what you think I am." His golden gaze was so intense she couldn't say anything. "I am Incubae, and I was sent to take your soul."

More heat prickled her skin and a slight dizziness overcame her. She opened her mouth, but he placed two fingers over her lips, not allowing her to speak.

"However, I will not take anything from you." His features relaxed and he gave her a sad smile. "Your soul is your own. I only wish I could share your life. That would be my greatest dream."

Relief whooshed through her and she relaxed against her pillow. He hadn't taken her soul.

Then she realized what he'd said about sharing his life with her and a strange feeling settled in her belly.

"Aedan," she tried to say behind his fingers, but he pressed them harder to her lips. Smells of sandalwood and sex mingled with the vanilla-scented candles.

"I must go." He sighed. "I cannot return."

Ericka's eyes widened. "What—you have to come back."

He moved his fingers and pressed his lips to hers. "I hope you will remember and think well of me."

He started to move away from her when she grabbed hold of his hand. "Wait." She clenched his fingers tight. "I already figured out you're an Incubus. I won't give you my soul, but I don't want you to stop coming." An ache grew tighter in her chest. "Please."

Aedan gave another melancholy smile. "It is not my choice. I answer to the gods and goddesses and I must face my destiny."

"What is it?" Her hand started to tremble, but she didn't let go of his. "Your destiny."

He stared at her for a long time and she tried to imagine never looking into his golden eyes again. "The Realm of the Dead."

Ericka caught her breath. In her research books that place was a version of Hell. Where one burned for eternity. "No." She shook her head as she tried to unscramble her thoughts, attempting to remember more of her research. "Isn't there another place, a good place? An—An—"

"Annwn." He gently took her hand from his and eased off the bed as she sat and faced him. "But I have failed in my last mission and my fate does not lie there any longer."

"Stay, Aedan." Her whole body felt like she was going to shatter. "Stay with me." She knew her words were crazy. He was a demon. *A demon.*

"I have grown to love you." He stroked her cheek with his fingertips. "Thoughts of you will carry me through my destiny."

Tears burned in her eyes and she felt like she had already started breaking apart. He moved away from her and she scrambled out of bed and tried to follow him. "Wait!" Panic laced her voice. "Isn't there something we can do?"

Aedan gave her an intense look of longing before cupping her cheeks with his hands and brushing his lips over hers. He whispered, "I love you, Ericka."

The unreality of it all made her mind spin. "Aedan, please!" She tried to grab his arm to stop him.

He vanished.

"No, no, no." She held her palm over her mouth as tears burned her eyes and her body shook. "That can't be it," she said as she let her hand drop away. "I won't let it!"

Ericka grabbed her robe that was draped over a chair. She wrapped herself in it before running to the living room straight for her mountain of research books. There had to be a way to save him.

Aedan knew the escorts would be waiting. Hideous demons wearing cloaks that rippled like fire. Aedan didn't bother dressing himself with his thoughts. The clothing would simply burn away even though he would not.

Jett and Kyne stood to the side. Jett's eyes were wide and fear was on her features. Kyne clenched his fist so tightly his muscles bunched. "Give him another chance." Kyne's voice had a rough edge to it as the guards took Aedan by his upper arms.

"I will miss you," Aedan said to Jett and Kyne as the guards started to take him away. "May you find much happiness in Annwn when you should go."

Jett choked back a sob. "Aedan, why? Why throw your life to the fires for a human?"

Aedan shook his head then stared forward as the guards escorted him from the Chamber of Veils.

During the long walk down the Hall of the Lost, Aedan's

heart grew heavier. He pushed aside his fear with thoughts of Ericka and smiled knowing she would be safe.

When they reached the doorway to the Realm of the Dead, heat blasted Aedan. He closed his eyes for a moment. He opened them before he and the demons stepped through the rock entryway and down steps leading to another archway. Flames singed his cheeks even before the guards pushed him into fire and lava.

Hours flew as Ericka flipped through pages of book after book after book that she had piled beside the couch. Something had to be here. Hadn't she read or heard that an Incubus could be kept from facing such a horrible fate? Or was it merely her desperate desire to save him that made her imagine things that couldn't be?

After Aedan left, she put on a pot of coffee and even had to brew another batch as she pored over the books. Her eyes burned, her vision swam, and she was so jittery she spilled a few drops of coffee onto her robe.

She set the cup down and picked up another book, held it in her palms, and stared at the worn cover. It was merely a book of very old tales of faeries, elves, demons, and other fables.

As she opened the book to the table of contents, she blinked the tiredness from her eyes. She glanced at the table of contents and noted the section on demon fables before rifling through the pages until she reached the first tale. Disappointment tore at her gut as she saw a picture of a stereotypical demon with a hideous face, horns, and a forked tail.

Ericka bit the inside of her cheek, trying for control. She didn't have time for tears. She flipped the next page and the next. She came to an abrupt stop when a few words caught her eyes.

Annwn. Realm of the Dead.

Butterflies batted her belly and she forced herself to slow

down and read the passages. Annwn a place of beauty, almost Heaven, but not quite. The Realm of the Dead—it was Hell.

The butterflies dropped like lead as she read descriptions of each place in the afterlife.

A section brought her to a complete stop.

> *Stolen souls are taken to the Realm of the Dead where they serve the god of Death.*
> *Surprisingly, Incubae and Succubae do not face the fate of the Realm of the Dead unless they fail in the tasks set forth to them by the gods and goddesses.*
> *The only known way for a demon to escape the Realm is for a human to voluntarily release half of his or her soul and offer it to the demon. By doing so, the human will bind himself or herself to the demon. Because the demon shares the human's spiritual essence, the demon neither fails nor completes his assignment.*

Ericka's heart raced and she could barely breathe. Half of her soul. Was she willing to give that much to save Aedan?

She closed her eyes tight. Imagined all the times he'd come to her and the bond she'd felt between them. He had sacrificed his own future for hers.

Am I willing to do it for him?

Yes. Yes!

Ericka sucked in another breath and released it, her skin tingling from the magnitude of her decision. She slowed and read the ritual carefully. She no longer felt tired. Instead, her body buzzed with energy, and it wasn't just the caffeine.

She'd need three white candles, a lock of her hair, and three flat, water-smoothed rocks. After she gathered all of her supplies, she'd need to make up some kind of rhyming chant that expressed her desire to share her soul with Aedan. That would be the hard part.

Still in her robe, she dashed out of the condo to the beach

and combed the line of kelp for smooth rocks. The salty air was moist and humid and wind tugged at her robe as waves slapped the shore. Over and over in her mind she worked on the words for a chant.

The sun peeked over the horizon, the faint morning light just enough to see by. When she'd found the rocks, she hurried back into the condo and grabbed three candles from her bedroom, along with a black marker, a lighter, and a pair of scissors. Slightly out of breath from rushing, she knelt on the kitchen's tiled floor as she snipped a lock of her hair, then lit the candles. She tossed the scissors aside, along with the lighter and they clattered across the floor.

She grabbed the marker. Her hand shook as she drew a circle on the kitchen tile, around herself and the items beside her.

Ericka eased onto her haunches and stared at the candles. The flames danced, almost mesmerizing her. She swallowed then picked up the lock of hair.

God, she hoped the chant would work.

As she draped a third of her hair over each flame, the strands hissed and curled as they caught fire. The smell of burning hair overpowered scents of the vanilla candles.

Her heart pounded in a harsh rhythm and she chanted as she placed the hair on the candle flames.

> *All my love and half my soul,*
> *I give to Aedan the Incubae.*
> *With that gift, I demand his return this day.*
> *Free him now, to find his true fate.*
> *Gods and goddesses, I claim him as my mate.*
> *Forever halved, twins sharing a soul,*
> *Heart to heart, we will both be whole.*

Tears stung Ericka's eyes as she placed the three smooth, flat stones, one at a time over each flame. She snuffed them with the rocks, pressing the wick into the melted wax and burned hair.

When she finished, a breeze immediately swept the room, lifting her hair from her shoulders. Goosebumps prickled her skin and butterflies skipped in her belly.

Everything around her wavered like she was looking through a window of water.

Ericka's lips parted and her heart thundered as she got to her feet. A stone archway appeared and she couldn't see the condo's kitchen anymore. On the other side of the wavering air was an enormous room with lots of other archways.

She raised her hand. Instead of air, she touched a rubbery surface. She pushed—

And tumbled through the archway.

Ericka screamed when the sucking sensation grabbed hold of her and the condo vanished. The sensation of being engulfed in goo surrounded her before she stumbled out of it and dropped to her hands and knees on a polished marble floor.

If her heart didn't stop beating so hard it was going to explode.

"What the hell?" she said as cool marble chilled her knees and hands.

She glanced up from the floor.

Someone was in front of her.

Ericka's gaze slowly traveled up the blue-robed form until she met the golden eyes of a gorgeous blond woman. Her beauty was marred only by her hard expression.

"Rise." The woman motioned with her hand for Ericka to stand. "I wish to see the woman who cost my son his future."

Ericka's cheeks burned as she got to her feet and stood eye-to-eye with the woman. "I never wanted Aedan to go to the Realm of the Dead." She spoke so fast she stumbled over her words. "Don't let him be taken. *Please*." When she finished speaking she was clenching her hands so hard her nails dug into her palms.

"It is . . . too late." The woman's voice softened. "My son has been banished to the flames."

"No." Ericka shook her head as her mind began to reel. "No, he can't be." Heat flushed her as if she was in the fire as a vivid image of him burning alive seared her mind.

Something the woman had said clicked. "You're Aedan's mother?"

She inclined her head. "I am Belisma, the water goddess."

"A-a goddess?" Ericka's brain stuttered at Belisma's statement. But she managed to grasp one obvious thread. "If you're a goddess, can't you save him?"

Belisma stepped closer to Ericka and raised her hand. The goddess's fingertips were cool as she brushed them along Ericka's cheek.

The goddess stared thoughtfully at Ericka as she stroked her fingers through Ericka's wild red hair.

She wanted to scream and stomp her feet but instead she felt the power of the goddess's hold and didn't move.

Belisma let her hand fall away. "You have offered a great gift to my son. Perhaps only half your soul, but you have also given of your love." The goddess nodded as if to herself.

She continued. "I believe my son has earned his peace and his reward. His choice to spare you and love you is a powerful thing. In the eyes of the universe he should be free of the Realm of the Dead by right and fairness."

Ericka swallowed, hope welling up within her, but she said nothing.

The goddess now had a faraway look in her eyes. "I will call for a Council session." Her gaze met Ericka's again. "They may disagree. Nothing is certain. You both may be saved, or both condemned."

"Condemned?" Ericka whispered.

"If the Council does not make this exception for Aedan, you could be forced to join him in the Realm of the Dead—if you indeed choose freely to give him half of your soul." Belisma's expression hardened again. "Are you willing to take that risk, as he was willing to send himself to the Realm to spare you such a fate?"

Ericka hesitated and closed her eyes. Would she choose an

eternity of being burned alive and never seeing her family or friends again? Would she risk all of that to save Aedan?

The right and true answer came from deep within as she opened her eyes. "I will take that risk."

The goddess inclined her head. "Wait in Aedan's quarters while the Council makes its determination."

"Thank you," Ericka said just before her stomach dropped to her toes and the room spun.

She no longer stood on the marble floor.

Her feet touched down on grass. The dizziness vanished as she caught her balance and took in the chamber she'd been sent to. Aedan's room.

The sense of the surreal accompanied her as she explored the chamber. A waterfall tumbled over stones in one corner of the room, adding the clean scent of water to the smells of grass and moss covering the rock walls.

She stepped past the large bed carved from rock that had a mattress in it.

Aedan sleeps here. This is where he comes when he leaves me.

No. Where he slept before . . .

She couldn't even finish the thought. Only positive thoughts from here on out. The Council *would* rule in her and Aedan's favor. She didn't know what would happen next, but she wasn't going to give up hope.

Ericka stopped in front of one of several pools around the room. Colorful fish glimmered in the water—some she was familiar with, like angelfish and Japanese koi. But others she didn't remember seeing before. At the Rainforest Café, they had the coolest aquariums—

"I don't believe it." She tipped her head back to see a star-filled night sky above her. "Aedan's burning alive *right now*, I'm in some strange Otherworld, and I'm thinking about *fish*."

Ericka bit the inside of her cheek and glanced at the bed. Heart and soul heavy, she moved to the bed and perched on the edge of a straw-filled mattress. She stared at the wall across from her, tracing cracks in the stone with her gaze.

She'd made the right decision. No doubt about it. No matter what happened.

Right?

CHAPTER 6

AEDAN HAD NEVER KNOWN SUCH PAIN EXISTED. He could barely choke back screams from the never-ending sensation of his flesh burning away.

The demons had chained him to jagged volcanic rock. The iron manacles seared his flesh. He ground his teeth as boiling lava splashed his legs and blasts of flame singed his chest and face. Sweat immediately dried in the beyond-terrifying heat.

Screams, shrieks, and sobs echoed from every direction. His gut twisted at the thought that *he* was responsible for so many of the people who now spent an eternity here. Mafia bosses and gang leaders, murderers, psychopaths, rapists, thieves—those he didn't regret as much as he did the innocents.

Had he ever been given a choice to do anything but take souls? No. He was what he was created to be, an Incubus who served the gods. Choice never entered his mind.

He had never given a second thought to what happened to the souls once he retrieved them—until Ericka.

Her name echoed in his mind and he tried to focus on her instead of the blistering pain. The fall of her red hair against her pillow, the intense blue of her eyes, the perfect feel of her thighs around his hips.

But more than that was all he had witnessed when he studied her before he began visiting her each night. Her love for her family, her dedication, her tenacity, her kindness, her joy.

Aedan couldn't help fighting against his searing bonds, even though it did no good. Even the air he breathed burned his lungs as he kept his thoughts on Ericka.

He had never understood why he had been sent to her until now. It had been a test. A test he had failed.

Two demons appeared in front of Aedan. They unshackled him, grabbed him under his arms, and dragged him through great pools of lava. He couldn't help a shout from the excruciating pain.

Surprise shot through him as the demons took him to the entrance to the Realm of the Dead and tossed him out of the flames and into the cool tunnel. His head struck rock and his mind spun, but relief from no longer being in the Realm was immediate. The memory of the pain still caused him to feel like his skin was burning, but it was slowly fading.

He stumbled as the demons took him under his arms again and forced him to his feet before prodding him to walk. "What—what is going on?"

No one *ever* left the Realm of the Dead.

The demons ignored Aedan and caught him when his legs gave out. They pulled him through the passageway and into the Hall of the Lost that now seemed chilly. He could barely focus as they dragged him along the cool marble floor.

His vision wavered and time lost meaning. Then the demons arrived at his chamber. More shock prickled his skin when the demons pushed open the door and shoved him into his quarters.

Aedan landed on his knees on the thick grass and rested his forehead in his palms. Trying to catch his breath as the demons slammed the door, he breathed in the sweet scent of grass and water and . . . vanilla?

"Aedan!"

He jerked his head up.

Ericka.

His mind could not process what he was seeing—Ericka rushing across the chamber to him. *A hallucination*, he thought until she reached him, dropped to her knees, and flung her arms around him.

He almost toppled from the force of her throwing herself against him, but he recovered enough to hold her tight.

"Oh, God." Tears trickled down her cheeks and slid onto his chest. "Or gods or goddesses. Whoever brought you to me."

Ericka's words shocked him to his senses and he grabbed her by her upper arms. "What are you doing here?" he growled as he stared at her beautiful face. "Have they taken you? What have they done?"

"I'm okay." She caressed his cheek as her blue eyes met his. "I came for you."

"No." He gripped her arms so tight she winced and he immediately relaxed his hold. "You will return. Where you will be safe."

"I-I have something to tell you." Ericka cleared her throat then words spilled from her lips. "I've told your gods and goddesses that I'm giving you half of my soul. And all my love."

"Half of your soul?" Aedan's whole body tensed. He could not have heard right. "*Are you daft?*"

"I realized you mean too much to me to let you go. And I couldn't let you be sent there." She hurried before he could say anything else. "Your Council . . . Belisma went to them to determine what will happen to both of us."

"No. I will not allow you to suffer in any way." He shook his head. "You *will* go home."

Belisma appeared like the crest of a wave.

She spun into Aedan's quarters with the grace and power of the rapids of a river.

Aedan refused to release Ericka to bow to the goddess.

"Rise, Aedan of the Incubae." Belisma's voice was surprisingly soft.

He eased to his feet, holding Ericka tight to him.

"The Council made its decision on your fate and Ericka's,"

Belisma said, no expression revealing whatever emotions she might have.

"Because a mortal has offered half of her soul to you, and because you have earned her unconditional love, you are spared the fate of the Realm of the Dead." She smiled and added, "You will return to Ericka's world and you will live as a mortal. You may walk in the daylight, take a wife, and reproduce."

"He can come back with me?" Ericka's voice was one of both disbelief and excitement.

"It is so." Belisma's gaze returned to meet Aedan's. "You will be given what papers and human things you need to live in the mortal world. You will age and you will die and you will forget your life as an Incubus.

"Or," Belisma continued, "you may go to Annwn and continue to live as an immortal. The choice is yours."

Aedan had difficulty finding the right words as he looked at the beautiful woman still cradled against him. "If she will have me, I would choose to live a mortal's life with Ericka."

"What do you mean, if I'd have you?" Ericka turned and threw her arms around his neck. "I love you, Aedan. I'll have you any way I can get you."

She kissed him hard and hungry and he returned the kiss just as passionately. So much so that his thoughts spun and he heard only the pounding of their hearts.

Aedan jerked his eyes open and his head up when his feet no longer touched grass but smooth tile. It took a moment for him to realize they were in Ericka's home. He almost laughed when he saw glass tanks now lining one wall—tanks filled with water and his collections of fish.

When he looked at Ericka, she was grinning and his smile widened.

"Your eyes are brown now, not gold." Ericka stroked his cheek. "They're beautiful."

Aedan had nearly forgotten Belisma. He turned to see if she had accompanied them, but she hadn't. Even the ever-present veil was gone.

For a moment he felt lightheaded and stumbled forward.

Ericka caught him by his shoulders, her expression concerned. "What's wrong?"

He looked at her and this time he did laugh. "I think I'm feeling . . . human."

"Wow," she murmured. "My own demon lover."

Aedan settled his hands on her hips. "Your human lover, you mean."

Her expression grew serious. "I love you."

Aedan took her face in his hands and kissed her hard. He separated his mouth from hers and whispered against her lips, "I love you, Ericka Roberts. For all of our years. I love you."

EQUINOX

L.A. Banks

CHAPTER 1

SHE OPENED HER EYES, LISTENING TO THE OTHER goddess murmurs in the moonlight. It took a moment to adjust her thoughts and her understanding to the new era, to the new languages being spoken, to the new weapons available for her use. She sat up slowly, quietly, as a deep sadness claimed her and then shuddered in horror as she became aware of all that had been done.

Silent tears cascaded down her high, regal cheekbones. She tossed a thicket of dark, brunette hair over her caramel shoulders and stood wide-legged, naked and majestic, in a warrior's stance. Her bow in a tight grip, her quiver filled with deadly arrows, she peered down into the still mountain pool that shimmered like glass.

"I, daughter of the Nubian queen, Leto, a Titan revered in all of Greece, and begat by the Greek god, Zeus, stand I the twin and sister of Apollo—Artemis—and *vow* by my bow and arrows created by the great Hephaestus and the Cyclopes to avenge this injustice against the wilderness! What have they done?"

Vancouver, Canada . . .

Vincent D'Jardin rubbed his palms down his face in weary agitation. How the hell his commanding officer had found him at his favorite bar way out here made every muscle coil in his body with tension. But that's what they did in their profession—find people who didn't want to be found. Still, it wasn't right. They'd said after the Delta job in Miami, he'd have some time off. Vincent locked gazes with Major Harcourt for a moment before returning his angry glare to his bourbon. This was bullshit.

"I know," the major said, sliding onto a barstool next to Vincent and hailing the bartender for a beer. "That's why I came myself."

"What's the job and for how long?" Vincent didn't look at the man beside him, just took a surly sip from his drink.

The major slid an arrow tip across the bar toward Vincent. "I figured with your background, you might be able to shed some light on this." He sat back eyeing him. "You've heard about them, I'm sure."

Vincent let out an agitated breath. He'd been undercover in Miami, not under a rock. Who hadn't heard about the kooks who were abducting CEOs of major mining and lumber firms without a trace and simply leaving dead stags shot up with bronze arrows? From Wall Street to the Amazon, work sites had been disrupted and dead stags had been left everywhere.

It was a seriously vexing puzzle—who could get a twelve-point stag into Wall Street office buildings, past security cameras, without a trace, and then butcher it? To his way of thinking, that ruled out environmentalists. They wouldn't sacrifice the animal. Had to be terrorists trying to leave some coded message.

But he took grave offense at the assumption that, because the perpetrators worked with arrows as their calling card, he should have some insider knowledge. Vincent stared at the unfamiliar shape that was a three-dimensional cone that was designed to leave a gaping hole in the victim, as well as briefly studied the strange etchings on the sides, then took a slow sip of his bourbon, considering how he would answer.

"You run the markings by the foreign languages boys?" he asked, looking at the arrowhead again but not touching it. Vincent glanced up into his CO's impassive blue eyes. "Or the guys that specialize in antiquities—or did you think the Owiqwidicciat would have some special Native American insight through his maternal DNA about freakin' arrows?" He narrowed his glare on the major, becoming more pissed off as he thought about it. "Or, maybe, it would be because my father was French Haitian . . . perhaps I could check with a voodoo priest and get back to you?"

Major Harcourt sighed and took a swig of beer to wet his dry throat. "Gimme a break, D'Jardin, and drop the chip on your shoulder while you're at it. I know you're pissed off about us recalling you so soon for another job, but it doesn't have anything to do with heritage. You're the best man for the situation, given where these Artemis bastards are tracking." He leaned in closer. "Yeah, we decoded it off the arrowheads, and it's ancient Greek—so we've got some Mediterranean assassins, go figure."

"I'd rather not," Vincent said, coolly assessing his CO. "I'm on leave, remember? You promised me a month."

Dismissing the comment, Harcourt pressed on. "You ever heard of this terrorist group, D'Jardin? We can't figure out if they're a splinter cell, an individual cell, a gang, bandits just out for financial gain by kidnapping the wealthy, or what. But they're cutting a swath through Yukon country, crossing international boundaries from the U.S. to Canada and back again using the wilderness as camouflage, and headed—we think—toward pipeline outposts up in Alaska. It hasn't been publicized yet for obvious reasons, and we were able to cite the Wall Street incident as an isolated, possibly organized-crime-related event . . . just like we could clean up the other situations that happened on foreign soil, keeping certain details out of the media and on a need-to-know basis. However, they've abducted an oil baron . . . that got presidential attention. Now the powers that be, who are much higher than you or I, want this problem to go away very quickly and very quietly, with a good group to pin it on. No matter what, terrorists did it. That's the only reason I came to you. We clear?"

Vincent looked at the major and clenched his jaw with a nod. "Clear. Just as long as I don't have to cut my hair."

The major smiled and accepted Vincent's surly peace offering in good humor. "No, you can leave the mane—will probably help you blend in on the job up there, anyway." He took another swig of his beer and stared at the French barmaids with appreciation. "I'd be mad at me, too, you ornery SOB. But duty calls."

"It's not a mane, they're dreadlocks," Vincent corrected with a mutter, but the major's attention was slow to return.

What else was there to say? The man had always been fair and wasn't a bigot he'd give him that. But after living underground, hustling through the damned Everglades after drug dealers, the last thing he felt like was a wilderness job. His nerves were raw and the accusation leapt from disappointment. Not to mention, oil fat cats, mining and logging robber barons were the antithesis of victims to his mind's eye. They had been the enemy as far as he was concerned. The things they did to the environment, and their ever-present threat to it, made him sick to his stomach. As it was, he'd come home to help vote on the proposed water quality standards for Neah Bay for submission to the Environmental Protection Agency. But now he couldn't even do that and he'd have to chuck his personal philosophies to get the job done.

"What do you need in terms of resources, Vince?" The major finally looked at him, the tension relaxing from his weathered, bronze face as he put the arrow tip back in his pants pocket.

"Top squad, Bravo commandos," Vincent grumbled, his gaze on his drink. "Five men."

All his dreams of going back home to the Makah Nation where he grew up were evaporating as he sat, his mood darkening by the second. All he wanted was a few weeks to return to the Olympic Peninsula in Washington State . . . the small town of Neah Bay was calling his name . . . so was home cooking, and the beaches flanked with red cedar and pristine wildlife. He wanted to find a place of solitude that the people who lived by the rocks and sea gulls had known for thousands of years before invasion . . . to sit in the wilderness to stare across the Straight of Juan de Fuca to Vancouver Island. All he'd wanted to do when he walked in this bar was to relax, finally tie one on, and get laid—now this. "And a brunette."

The major gave a start and then caught the joke and laughed. He downed his beer and slapped Vincent on the back. "You always get me, D'Jardin. I can never tell when your surly ass is serious or not. I'll see you at o-eight-hundred in Anchorage. There's a Black Hawk waiting for you at the military hangars here." He shook his head and ran his fingers through his close cut hair as he slapped down a twenty-dollar bill on the bar and stood to leave. "You kill me, D'Jardin—I swear."

Vincent watched his CO thread his way through the bar toward the exit. "Who was joking?" he said, polishing off his drink as he stood.

At least he didn't have to go through a bunch of crap with rookies. The squad that assembled were familiar faces, and slow smiles crept across each one as recognition was made.

Lou, short for Lu Chen, everybody respected as a fighting machine despite his wiry, compact size. It was good to have him on the team, and his explosives expertise was undeniable. He offered Vince a slow, confident nod and Vince nodded back, feeling much improved as he quickly assessed the group. Dutch, the crazy Swede, was six feet, six inches, of blond destroyer. Having a solid artillery man was a must. Good. Jermaine, an insane brother from Brooklyn who was an unparalleled communications whiz, stood with sinew-cut arms folded over his cinder-block chest, attitude raw, and cornrows glistening. Cool.

Vincent laughed to himself as Donovan walked up and gave him a Cuban brotherhood embrace. Like him, Rodriguez could track anybody and find the wings of a fly in the middle of a hurricane, if he had to. They'd both survived Miami.

Jesse, one of the best snipers in the unit, stood back, chewing on a toothpick, his shock of red hair blowing from the force of the chopper blades as he pushed his lanky frame off the side of the craft. "Howdy, all," he said with a wide grin and a distinctive Midwest drawl. "Good day for huntin', ain't it?"

Indeed it was.

CHAPTER 2

SHE SPIED THEM FROM THE TOWERING TREE TOPS, she and her nymphs blending into the thick canopy watching, their eyes keened like hawks to each male form that walked through the wilderness. These hunters carried weapons that no animal would stand a chance of survival against. Even their method of hunting was unbalanced, unfair. They made war against the innocent—her forests.

If they came in search of their missing generals of destruction, they would be trapped by their own folly. Those decimators of green places had been turned into stags as her great legends prophesized—*he who befouled Artemis's wilderness would be transformed and then hunted to his death.* Was the edict not clear? Had they forgotten over the eons? The thought of such disrespect enraged her. She only wished she could deliver to them the fate that had befallen Actaeon, whom she'd turned into a stag and beset his own hounds upon!

Seething, Artemis followed the men with soundless footsteps, her nymphs taking strategic positions. They had employed mercenary Titans against her! These men were of no mere mortal proportions. Their height and stature, like her own, was surely a Titan blend, if not of pure blood.

Closely studying them, she keened her eyes, taking each in as she steadied her bow. One had hair like a flame and loped as he strode, another was thick and tall, his hair like sunburned wheat. Another was clearly of Nubian origin, perhaps Ethiopian, she couldn't be sure. One had hair as dark as Egyptian onyx, his frame smaller, but his agile speed noteworthy. Another was hard to judge . . . Persian, Asiatic?

The most magnificent one in the lead had a mane like a lion's . . . he walked with a royal cat's agility, his aura almost stroking the trees with uncommon reverence as he passed them. Splinters of sunlight glinted off his tawny hue. His eyes were intense, that of a seasoned hunter . . . his shoulders broad and sure. He was at least two hands higher than her, and she stood as a goddess at six feet tall. Her bow lowered slightly, but then she reset her stance. She would not be tricked. This was no immortal, and certainly not one with reverence to her pristine lands.

Yet their mission intrigued her and she almost laughed aloud. Were they so foolish as to be searching for the missing? They already had them, the dead stags, that was the laughable thing. She had no real interest in slaughtering soldiers who simply followed orders—she had gotten to the generals who gave the orders. Once she'd conquered them all, no more orders would be given to harm the dear land. However, there was so much to learn . . .

Strange customs, strange palaces, buildings with lights that rendered no flame. Odd lifts that carried people away in fast-moving boxes higher than the tallest trees she'd ever witnessed. Chariots without horses . . . throngs of pedestrians more dense than all of Rome's populace it seemed, and underground dragons that roared so loudly they shook the ground. All of this she'd seen quickly in her mind as she'd acclimated to the new time . . . some of it she'd seen as she'd dropped an errant stag in the high palaces. But the roaring, wide-tooth monsters that ate at land and trees had broken her heart. She had to understand this assault against the beloved earth, for it seemed to be everywhere, even against the seas. If there was one source to negotiate with, one king of all these lands, she'd have his head. Otherwise it could take years of battle to bring it all to an end, and she feared most deeply within her very being that time was running out for the wild.

"It's like they're ghosts," Vincent said, shaking his head as he stooped with Donovan to study the ground. "There was a recent encampment here," he added, feeling the heat off the small, charred remains of a campfire and hunting through the leaves to find where tents could have been pitched. "This is the only viable hiking path to the main pipeline outpost buildings, and all roads leading to it have roadblocks checking IDs, reporting nothing . . . no helicopter—"

His words were cut off by the whoosh of an arrow that tore through his fatigue jacket at the bicep, grazing his arm and then lodged deeply in the trunk of a tree. The squad immediately fell back, took cover behind trees, and open fired in the direction of the arrow.

Automatic weapon report rent the air. Flashes of bullets sprayed the terrain blasting away ground cover, bark, setting birds in flight, the stench of spent ammunition eclipsing the fresh forest air.

Completely appalled by the woodland destruction, Artemis gave a hand signal for her nymph warriors to wait. The Titans had harnessed the lightening of Zeus? How could they have? These were strange Titans indeed. Infuriated, she dropped down from the top of a tree landing in a crouch in the center of the glen, so startling the soldiers before her they began squeezing lightening from their weapons before she could speak.

But she was immortal.

Her flips defied the bolts that took down trees, and she heard one yelling, the magnificent one shouting for the others to hold their fire. Winded, she stood erect, and leveled her bow at his forehead. He had the expression of awe on his face that was sufficient enough to possibly spare his handsome life.

"Who dare penetrate my forests and defile them so!" she demanded.

Six stunned pairs of male eyes looked at her.

"Are you deaf? Mute? Speak and you shall live. Who is your general?"

For a moment, no words came to Vincent's dry throat. He had watched a woman back flip through dead-aim AK-47 gunfire, miss M16 rounds, and the shells from a Glock nine millimeter pass through her, all after dropping from a seventy-foot-high branch above. But there she stood, un-marked . . . not a scratch on her radiant, caramel skin. She didn't even have leaves or refuse from the tumbles in her thick, velvety hair.

He locked gazes with her dark eyes, witnessing how fury seemed to actually cause them to smolder in a hypnotic way. Rage and adrenaline made the bow she gripped slightly tremble, and his line of vision ran the length of her athletic arm to capture her breathtaking face and full, lush mouth. Six feet tall, built like an Amazon, half naked except for a gossamer of sheer white silk, everything male in him couldn't help but appreciate her firm, round breasts, or the way her flat waist cinched in only to give rise to a slim swell of hips . . . and man, oh, man, the broad was all legs.

In a standoff, he stared at her, she at him. Even if she had guns behind her, if she let the arrow go—he'd dodge it and she'd be dog meat. If not him, one of his men would put her down, single shot. Lou already had a grenade on standby, pin in his teeth, to lob behind her toward her soldiers.

"What do you want with the hostages?" Vincent said, his tone even and controlled as he began to negotiate. "No de-mands have been made. State your purpose. Who are we dealing with?"

"You are not in a position to question the great Artemis!" she said through her teeth. "You are their leader?"

"I'm the one talking, sis," he said. "Put down your weapon and we won't fire."

"No one dares presume to tell me when to disarm." Without even blinking she let her arrow go.

Then everything seemed to happen in slow motion. Vincent dodged the tip of the spiraling arrow; Lou pulled the pin on the grenade and lobbed it over the crazy chick's shoulder. The blast felled several trees as more women rained to the forest floor. The arrow that was destined for Vince hit Dutch dead in the chest, knocking his shot that would have entered the female attacker's forehead off center. But instead of the huge Swede dying, he fell and began screaming as his clothes burned away and his body contorted. The men beside him tried to quickly grab him to pull him to safety behind a tree, but fell back in horror as he began to change into an animal.

Running forward, Vince heard the panic-laden shouts of his men, but he was not about to let the terrorist suspect get away. He couldn't understand what they were screaming—something about a stag. Then all of a sudden as he neared her, nine millimeter drawn, something grabbed his feet and his world snapped upside down.

She slowed down as he bobbed from a vine, and then smiled. But he hadn't lost his grip on his weapon, and he held it with both hands and fired at her.

Dodging the wicked things that flung from his lightning rod like hornets, she watched in amazement as he cursed, steadied himself, and did a sit-up, then had enough upper-body strength to grab the vine, extract a huge knife from his boot, and cut himself down.

"Who the hell are you people!" he bellowed, whirling around in a bull's rage.

Admiration tried to thread itself through her, but she fought it as she stepped out from behind a tall tree. "Well done, Titan. But your weapons are no match for immortals, even if you did steal Zeus's lightening rods."

He blinked as she sashayed forward and placed one graceful hand on her hip. The fact that there was no more weapon report behind him, but he could hear his men yelling, made him take aim at the center of her forehead. An eerie chill slid down his spine and he spoke through his teeth.

"What do you people want, where are the hostages, and what the fuck are the terms?"

She cocked her head to the side, growing amused. His fear was beginning to become palpable, yet his courage was starting to awaken something else within that had been dormant for centuries. She lifted her chin in an attempt to make the coiling flame in her belly recede.

"We want peace. We want your people to stop pillaging the forests, to stop desecrating the land, to stop poisoning the lakes and streams. This demand is non-negotiable. The terms are simple—do what I ask, or die."

The urge to pull the trigger was so great that his arm bounced from repressed emotion. "The hostages . . . where are they?"

"Stags," she said calmly, moving closer to him and studying his body from head to toe. "And you have them already."

"Stop playing games, lady." He fingered the trigger, but was disturbed by her unusual, almost otherworldly calm. "If you return them alive, all you and your environmental terrorist organization face are kidnapping charges and federal property damage, and if you tell us who's behind all of this, you might even get close to a plea bargain. But if you take this bull too far, you're going down and might get the chair. So, don't lie—where—"

"I never lie," she said, taken aback by the charge. "See for yourself!" Unafraid of his weapon, she brushed past him, still clutching her bow, and walked into the glen where the firefight had erupted.

He stood there, mouth agape, watching his men bobbing upside down from vines that had ensnared them. But the thing that paralyzed him was the sheer terror on their faces as they looked from each beautiful maiden to the huge, blond-coat, twelve-point buck that snorted and pranced, seeming bewildered and trapped between the women that had arrows trained on it.

Something very crazy, extremely implausible slithered through Vince as he stared into the eyes of the trapped animal . . . it had Dutch's eyes, but that was impossible!

"Where's my soldier?" Vince shouted, beginning to panic, too.

Female laughter filled the glen.

He locked gazes with Donovan, who had tears sliding down his nose . . . Donovan? Oh, shit. If he had broken this fast, after dealing with all the madness they'd seen in Miami and in South America, what had the man witnessed? Jermaine's eyes were closed and his mouth was moving as though he was praying. Lou and Jesse wouldn't take their eyes off the buck, and stared at it wide-eyed, upside down, not blinking.

"Cut one of them down and show him where his soldier is," the woman who was clearly the leader said.

Jesse swung a punch that missed as a tall, lithe maiden with flaxen hair approached him and nicked his cheek with an arrow tip. Instantly, Vince reached out and grabbed the leader's arm, pressing the nine millimeter to her skull. "If he dies, you die. What'd you do, poison him? What kind?"

She coolly regarded Vince as his man began to convulse. "Cut him down before he hurts himself. He'll be a magnificent creature like the other one, I'm sure."

Vince's vocal cords seized as he watched them carefully lie Jesse down on the forest floor. How his clothes began burning, he didn't know—but the way they burned was from a weird, cobalt blue flame that didn't seem to harm his skin. The other men were shouting, and the huge, trapped stag was rearing on his hind legs. But Vince could barely hold his gun as he watched a man slowly, painfully, change shape, his bones snapping and body elongating as a wail ripped from his throat.

The sound of Jesse's skull cracking to bear antlers cut through the forest with a horrifying echo. Red hair from Jesse's head and beard turned into a thick coat that swallowed his skin, and the sound of a whimper fled his lips when his nose became a snout. As though growing out from his elbows and knees, his limbs extended and fingers fused together. Vince backed away as he watched his squad sniper roll over and struggle to stand like a newborn fawn.

"What the hell is this," he whispered, blinking hard and touching the place where an arrow had grazed him. He knew there were all sorts of psychotropic drugs out there, but he'd never known of one that could produce an effect like this.

A red stag pranced hysterically in the clearing, making the blond one become even more skittish. Vince looked around. They were outnumbered three terrorists to one. They'd all obviously been drugged somehow . . . his face was hot, and he felt like he was moving forward against his own will.

"Can we keep these?" one of the terrorists asked, her gaze pleading with the leader. She walked up to the massive blond stag and tried to gentle the frightened creature. Oddly, it bobbed its head, stopped its agitated prancing and nuzzled her as she stroked it. The half-nude women looked back at their commander. "Please, Artemis," she whispered. "I don't think they were with the others."

Another joined the willowy brunette that had spoken, pushing her long onyx braids over her shoulder. "He's magnificent," she murmured, going to the animal to lay her cheek against his neck.

"He's not old like the generals, yes?" a wheat-haired captor said, producing an apple from thin air and feeding it to the animal with a flat palm.

Then three more female warriors moved forward, slowly approached the other large stag, attending to it gently and staring at their leader.

"It's been thousands of years, Artemis," the tallest one among the women gathered beside the red stag said, her voice strained and her expressive brown eyes seeming to beseech reason from their leader. "We all took the vow with you . . . but . . . in this new era the things we've—"

"It does not matter what temptations you've seen or felt in this new era! I care not. You will all keep your vow, as will I—a vow that I made when I was three years old." The beautiful warrior folded her arms over her ample breasts and glared at her warriors.

Vince watched the one they called Artemis straighten her back as the female expressions became crestfallen. He blinked hard trying to get past the drugs they had obviously given him just so he could see straight. Something in his system was making him short of breath, making him stagger forward, had made his hand too heavy to hold a weapon. He was weaving where he stood, beginning to sweat. It was as though heat radiated off the leader and even though it went against all of his training, he stepped away from her to keep from passing out.

Regardless, during their standoff he was beginning to figure out their strange coded language—if it was a thousand-year-old vow, or so, then it had to be a Middle Eastern group, since that was the only reference point in his quickly fogging mind which had disputes that lasted that long . . . Greek or thereabouts in the Mediterranean, was close enough. Maybe leaders of each cell were called Artemis, a fake name, likely to denote who was in control of a specific engagement. That was plausible.

His mind scrambled for a rational explanation as an eerie silence folded over the glen. It was almost as though they'd become sealed away in a soundless envelope. It had to be the drugs, whatever was on the tip of the arrows—but what they didn't know was that he and his men were the tip of the spear! Be strong. Maybe all this talk about the environment was bullshit, and fearing reprisal, the men behind some of the deadliest terrorist activity in the world had sent females out front to do their bidding . . . that would make sense, given the way the U.S. had been leaning on their resources. They'd abducted millionaires and billionaires, a ransom demand would have to come soon—who would waste such an opportunity. Dead stags his ass!

Obviously it was some grudge that went back before anyone could remember, and loyalists of the group were beginning to mutiny—not having the stomach, maybe, to kill off a bunch of military for whatever environmental cause they had. No. But it wasn't an environmental cause. Vince shook his head, trying to clear it, feeling woozy, and hating the calm, smug expression on the one called Artemis's face. Somewhere between them, one of the members of the group had to have figured out they were in deep shit and perhaps wanted a way out. But drugged, outgunned, outnumbered or not, his mission was clear; bring back the hostages alive, if possible, and find out the source of this terrorist cell to take it down.

"You don't care about the environment," he said, slurring his words, and trying to continue standing upright. "You blow up cars and innocent women and children, so stop the charade and tell us how much money you want for the CEOs."

"Are you mad, barbarian?" she said with a gasp that cut through his skeleton.

On the verge of passing out, he slapped his chest, needing something to fracture the group, something to cause dissention to buy them time, searching for anything that would give him more information while the drugs wore off.

"I am Owiqwidicciat! My mother's people are from the Makah Nation—what gives you the right to invade my forest, my trees, destroy my land? Huh? We walked here for thousands of years, and you come with death and destruction talking about peace? That's bull! You're no different to me than the first wave of invaders!"

The leader recoiled from his charges and suddenly he could breathe, his mind felt clear, and he straightened.

"Your forest?" she said as the women with her covered their hearts with their hands.

"That's right, lady, you heard me! My people are from the Olympic Peninsula, as far north as you can go. This is our country, not yours!"

Discernable murmurs filtered through the trees.

"You are from Olympus?" Pure shock entered the one called Artemis's eyes.

"Damned straight I am!"

She opened her mouth and closed it, her eyes raking him for the truth. "Your weapons—you stole them from—"

"We stole nothing, unlike you!"

"I stole nothing; we took back what was ours by rights."

"Zeus gave them the thunder bolts and lightning rods?" one woman whispered.

"I must know who sent you," Artemis demanded.

"I want the same information, so I guess that makes it a standoff. I wanna know who's poaching on my land." Vincent walked away and touched a badly damaged tree with clear disgust. "How many years would it take to replace just one? After all the wildfires," he added, shaking his head and looking at the blaze that had been started from the grenade.

He watched the female leader cover her heart with her hand, briefly close her eyes, and the blaze quieted. Vince rubbed his eyes with his fist.

"Cut my men down before they pass out. Tie 'em up if you have to, but get 'em right side up."

He'd said it just to see how far they'd go, not expecting them to comply, and he was shocked when she nodded and wrists got tied then vines got hacked. His men fell into female arms and the stags reared. He couldn't tell what was happening as the women gathered behind the two animals.

"Oh, all right! But you do not break your vow unless I break mine. Bring their belongings and weapons. Extract what we must know without harming them, if possible," their leader yelled, and then she raised her bow, withdrew two arrows from her quiver, and threaded and released them both before Vince's hand could rise with a gun. Her arrows found their marks and the great stags dropped to their knees.

"Come," she ordered. "Your men will befall no harm. That is no longer the objective of my nymphs, it seems. The ones transformed will return to the human forms. We should speak freely in my tent. I have much to ask you about this new world, Titan."

CHAPTER 3

THEY HIKED HARD FOR WHAT FELT LIKE CLOSE TO
an hour, going further into heavily forested terrain until they
reached a grouping of nearly inconspicuous tents. The semi-
circle of crude dwellings surrounded a small charred plot of
ground where a campfire had recently been.

Vince kept his senses keened, looking for signs of more
terrorists, looking for the males, and each man exchanged a
glance as they were separated off from one another and
forced into a tent with several female captors. Oddly, though,
he noted, Jesse and Dutch still looked dazed, if not drugged.
But he was counting on Lou, of any of them, to be able to get
away. Lou was so damned flexible and double jointed, he
could escape from almost anywhere like Houdini. He didn't
need his hands free to kill you, just had to get close enough.

Then Vince looked at the gun in his hand. Bizarre. They
hadn't bound him or stripped his weapon. And although Artemis's female soldiers had an indefinable but palpable sense
of anticipation sweeping their group, their leader trudged
ahead of him unconcerned. There was almost a weary resig-
nation about her, a sadness that worried him, despite the fact
that he was still armed . . . and all the chick had on her was a
bow and poisoned arrows. After what he'd seen so far, he'd
come to the conclusion that that was enough.

It was all surreal, but he was sure that he was drugged

once he stepped inside the leader's tent. Firstly, it took him a moment to orient himself to the size. Outside it seemed about the height and width of a small military pop, but when he stepped inside, it loomed frighteningly large as though he'd walked into a forty-by-sixty palace chamber. Everything was draped in white satin and sheer gauze interspersed with finely woven Moroccan rugs, ornately decorated Mediterranean urns, and lama hides. Vince pushed the heel of his hand against his eyes to recapture reality.

"Wine or water?" Artemis said on a weary exhale, and then dropped her weapon against a white alpaca fleece by the far tent wall. When he didn't answer, she turned to stare at him. "If you are not thirsty, barbarian, then I offer grapes . . . olives, goat cheese, bread? Surely by this point you do not think my goal is to poison you?"

She ignored him as she briefly lifted her hair off her lovely neck and stretched, and then helped herself to the bounty that graced her table. She settled herself in one lithe move and continued her solitary meal unfazed.

"I have many questions, many things I do not understand that I must know if I am to be the protectress of the wilderness. Sit, Titan, and talk genuinely, or draw my wrath . . . I grow weary of rage, so let us find an accord." She popped a grape into her mouth and cocked an eyebrow. "Why do your people behave as they do—don't they realize that if you hurt the beloved forest, you will also starve?"

He watched her eat and take a careful sip of dark mulberry-hued wine, and despite the incomprehensible circumstances, found himself drawn to the stain it left on her mouth. Tentatively he approached her table and sat on an ornately carved wooden stool across from her. As though reading his mind, she handed him her challis, and then poured wine into the empty one that he didn't remember being there earlier. Yes, he'd drink only what she drank and eat only what she'd eaten, breaking bread with the enemy to better understand, but would not subject himself to be drugged or poisoned again.

"My people used everything the bounty of the wilderness offered," he said quietly, taking a sip of wine and studying her eyes very carefully. "We wasted nothing, never hunted more than we could use. We respected the wilderness."

An eerie tingling began in his chest and fanned out to slowly consume his body as she stared at him. Then she nodded.

"I believe you," she said quietly. "My search of your soul agrees with your words. Continue . . . worthy warrior. Know that in all my years of battle, you are the only one I have allowed to enter my tent."

Her bizarre statement was accompanied by a rosy flush on her high, regal cheeks, and she looked away as though somehow embarrassed. He couldn't fathom why or what had happened and he glanced into his challis for answers. Albeit he knew his people worked with some pretty potent hallucinogens, but whatever these chicks were plying—*man*. He just wondered what she'd spiked the arrow with because not only was he seeing strange things but he also had the irrational urge to tell this woman the truth . . . not that such a thing was allowed. But if telling her beliefs from his people could give her something to identify with, and maybe save a hostage's life, make her drop her guard, then it was a tactic he'd employ.

He searched her gorgeous face, trying not to become hypnotized by the subtle beauty of her eyes or the strange innocence that seemed to hide just beneath the surface of her placid expression. Her sad, philosophical tone washed through him, reminiscent of the elders he'd listened to as a boy on the reservation when they'd orally recite the history of lands lost and treaties broken.

"You can't win this fight," he murmured, not meaning to allow his voice to drop the way it had. "At least not through these methods."

He watched tears rise and shimmer in her luminous dark eyes. "I know," she whispered. "My nymphs do not yet understand that, however. I have seen the new weapons of this era . . . the suns that explode against the ground and burn all that is alive for eons."

"Nuclear bombs, daisy-cutters, napalm," he said flatly, for some reason wanting to reach across the table and hold her hands so badly his ached. Every fiber in him knew this tone of defeat; he'd heard it all his life spoken on the reservation, spoken in French by his Haitian father, spoken by people whose history would be distorted by the conquerors.

The tears in her eyes fell. "Yes," she said nodding. "I am not the enemy."

"Then who is?" he asked quietly, unable to forebear reaching across the table to clasp her hands. He set his gun aside and stared at her. But it was impossible to touch her satin hands and stare into her eyes at the same time without feeling her thread throughout his system.

"You do not believe in the cause you fight, do you?" she whispered. "You know they are wrong. You know who desecrates the land."

He nodded. "But I can't let you execute them. There are courts, other ways . . . laws . . ."

"The words are hollow even to your own ears," she said, squeezing his hands. "Your people heard those words and laws, too, and were betrayed by failed treaties."

He looked away, but could not remain out of the gravitational pull of her dark irises except briefly. "Who are you?" His voice came out as a hoarse, broken whisper. The tingle that began in his chest and spread throughout his body had become a dull ache centered in his groin.

"I am Artemis," she said, her gaze rambling over his face. "Goddess . . . and I have never in my existence wanted to break my vow so thoroughly. Therefore, the true question that besets me is who are you, Titan? Of what hidden Olympus do you herald? I have never felt honor as pure as yours enter my ethereal body and lay siege to it."

He couldn't answer that—not because his actual hometown was classified data, which it was, but simply because as she touched his jaw and allowed her fingers to gingerly explore his lips, his voice failed. "You are definitely a goddess," he finally managed. "And I wish the world was different . . . wished they understood your heartbreak and mine, but they don't."

"Are you displaced, too?" she asked, leaning forward. "A being greater than mere mortal trapped by the disbelief of the era?"

Her question made him smile. "I am trapped by the disbelief of this era, yes, and therefore, I guess displaced."

She sat back quickly and laid her hand over her heart, gaping at him for a moment. "I felt the earth people in your aura. I felt the reverence of the trees toward you as you passed them—the forest welcomes you, and you understand it . . . honor it. That is why I didn't . . ." Her words trailed off as her gaze slid away. "That is why you are still standing."

Her admission snapped him out of the haze. He had to remember that she was an adversary. Was he crazy! But, *damn*, she'd turned him on. "You felt the trees, too?" he asked, unable to hold back the question. "They hold the spirits of the ancestors, you know."

"Yes . . ." She closed her eyes and he almost leaned across the table to take her mouth, but thought better of it.

"I honor the wilderness. It's a part of me, how I was raised. Artemis, I . . ."

"You never looked at me like the others long ago," she added, her voice both sad and filled with wonder. "You saw me as a hunter, an equal. You didn't try to molest me—why not?"

"Because you had a bow and arrow, a serious squad, and obviously we're evenly matched in a firefight. But, that wasn't why I came here, anyway. We came for the hostages." He had to wrest his mind back to the mission!

She nodded, her exotic eyes smoldering with something he didn't want to acknowledge. "Your words again ring true. You saw me as an equal . . . none of the others did before, that is why they sealed their own fates—but that was a very long and bitter time ago."

He stared at this beauty, a black widow that could most assuredly take lives, wondering how a gorgeous woman like this ended up as an assassin. "How many bodies?"

"If I ask you the same, could you answer?" she said evenly, no apology or defensiveness in her tone.

"Touché. We're both soldiers."

"Warriors," she corrected. "To be a soldier is to take orders, hence why I rarely execute soldiers. They are only doing the bidding of those who control them. A warrior, however, is under his or her own command."

He nodded but looked away for a moment, wishing that the times were different and that he could be a warrior.

"You may be conscripted into service by them, but you still have the presence of a warrior," she said quietly. "I did not mean to offend."

"No offense taken. You spoke the truth." Again his gaze searched her face. There was something magnetic about her, something almost supernatural, like she claimed. "And you are definitely a goddess with a sound mind and decent heart . . . you know that no good end will come of this if you persist. Why don't you let the hostages go or tell me your demands for them? Give us a chance to work something out before you have blood on your hands and a murder rap you can't shake."

She sighed. "Their bodies will return and they will not be dead. In this era of disbelief nothing I do holds together for long. The temples are now for tourists, true believers are too few against the world gone awry with carnal distractions. I just wanted them to feel the terror of being hunted for no purpose. That will stay with them forever, even as all else fades. My goal was to humble, that was all."

The melancholy tone of her voice, the new shimmer of tears in her eyes, and the way her fingers traced his open palms was mesmerizing. Relief also wafted through him—she'd promised not to kill the hostages. Progress . . . even though she'd given him ridiculous wood.

"What do you want in exchange for their release?"

She looked away, and he slowly closed his hand around hers, almost swearing that he could hear his own heartbeat pounding in his ears when he did.

"To break my vow. It is no longer of use. I have fought the good fight and now wish to take my place with the others as a distant memory."

He wanted to tell her not to commit suicide, that she didn't have to become a distant memory, but what promises for a good life beyond prison walls could he offer? A free spirit like this would surely die behind bars. Once she turned over the hostages, the authorities would hunt her down to the ends of the earth. He could offer her no assurances; he was in no position to cut a deal. That was the stuff of lawyers. He was just Special Forces, a soldier, and all of this was well outside his realm of expertise and comprehension. But people's lives were at stake, so he had to set aside any personal concerns about this abductress.

"Break your vow with me, Artemis," he said, not even sure what her vow was. "Trust me. I—"

The sound of one of his men's tortured moans made him stand and grab his weapon. Artemis was also on her feet in a flash, but staring at the tent wall, rather than down the barrel of a gun.

"If any of my men are violated—"

She covered her heart for a moment and grabbed her bow. "Never! That was not supposed to happen. If it has, then my own have betrayed and shamed me!"

"Take me to them now!" he shouted, all previous negotiations vanished.

"As you wish," she said, unafraid and seeming to do so from some personal sense of integrity, not from any threat he imposed.

Running in tandem, they followed the sound of the cries, barging into a very small tent that expanded inside into a huge space with floors covered in white pelts and pillows. Artemis and Vincent stood at the entrance and became very, very still. He opened his mouth and then closed it. She tried to look away, but couldn't.

Artemis felt her face flame hot. She did not believe her eyes. Never in her existence had humiliation singed her so completely. There was no way to blame this on the barbarian; he was bound.

Deep shame made her simply give her bow over to the Titan beside her. The nymphs of her sacred grove had desecrated a body. The reign of the goddesses was surely at an end, if it had come to this.

The soldier with long onyx hair who had the likeness of a Persian barbarian was lashed to a tent post with his hands over his head, his body drawn flat against the floor pelts. His legs were splayed, each ankle bound by heavy silk cords . . . his manhood naked and rigid, that is, as much as one could see beyond the homage her most loyal nymphs paid to it. She didn't need to investigate further, knowing full well the extent of the so-called torture being delivered to her captive's men. So engrossed in their love play, the nymphs never looked up and the captive never opened his eyes.

Artemis thrust her bow at Vince and turned away. "Shoot them all," she said, her voice thick with emotion. "It is your right. I would have done no less if three of your men ravished one of my maidens. Your soldier probably wants to die from this humiliation as well."

The room went still. Nymphs shrieked and scurried away from Donovan's body. Vincent looked at the bow in one hand, the Glock nine in the other. Confusion tore at him as he stared at Artemis's back and then the plea on Donovan's face. He frowned at his man for a moment—these chicks could claim they were raped in the capture, would have DNA evidence on his man, and all of this bull could compromise a case and military careers. Shit!

"Let's, uh . . . let this matter go under the banner of détente and not kill anybody. There's been enough bloodshed and I don't think these ladies meant him too much harm while trying to extract vital information," Vince said, returning Artemis's bow. Without arrows what good was the partial weapon? Besides, he needed to understand what freaky trap they were laying.

"That was our only desire, goddess," one of the nymphs

said, covering her nudity with her hands as she knelt on the floor. "Throughout the ages we have remained celibate in your honor—but we were instructed not to hurt them and to extract vital information . . . that was our quest."

Vince looked at Donovan and tried not to crack a smile, despite the compromising position. The man could barely catch his breath, and since Donovan was still tied up, it wasn't like he savaged them . . . maybe a lie detector test would save the man if the madness ever came out.

"Can I check on my other men . . . just to be sure they're not, uhmmm, being molested? And, maybe, let this one be untied so he can defend himself against further ravishment? Again, all in the spirit of dètente." He shot Donovan a glance and his man silently acknowledged the look while trying to steady his breathing.

"What is dètente spirit? I don't know this word. I have never heard of this entity." Artemis stared at Vincent for a second and then looked away, appearing horrified and flushed by what she'd witnessed. She wouldn't even dignify her nymph's entreaties.

"It means relaxing the hostilities between warring nations, I believe."

Artemis nodded. "In dètente, then, release that prisoner and feed and clothe him."

She stormed out of the tent with her head held high and her back rigid. Cool forest air from the chilly spring slapped her cheeks and the sudden temperature drop was welcomed. A troubling heat had unleashed itself between her thighs . . . along with a thawed river that dampened her hotly swollen valley. She could barely take a step without a stab of need piercing her as though one of her arrows, and her breasts suddenly felt heavy, the very tips aching like bees had stung them. When the barbarian stood next to her, it seemed as though all the air had left the clearing, even taking the smallest amount that remained in her lungs with it. What was this magic he owned?

Not sure where to begin, and for the first time in her life feeling shaky, she glanced at the semi-circle of tents. Pointing toward one at random, she sucked in a deep breath, set her shoulders, and forged ahead. She didn't care that the barbarian found this amusing. His customs were clearly very different from hers.

Closing her eyes briefly, she peeked in a tent, and then dipped her head out before the large warrior beside her could enter. She stopped him with both hands against his chest.

"Don't," she said, her voice a raw whisper. "I . . . I don't know what has become of my followers." She covered her mouth and then turned away.

"Allow me to inspect my men," Vincent insisted, hoping that nothing crazy like a butchering would meet his eyes. If they all went out like Donovan, fine. But crazy people had a way of turning fun and games into something deadly.

Still on guard, he pulled back the flap a bit and peered in.

After a long pause, he let the flap fall very slowly and straightened himself, rolling his shoulders. He needed to walk away for a minute to get his mind together and to shake off the hot shard of desire that had filled his shaft. The image of what he'd witnessed replayed itself a few times like a CD with a skip in it before he could get the visual out of his mind.

"Horrible, wasn't it?" Artemis said quietly, touching his shoulders. "Virgins since longer than I can remember and now it has come to this." She looked up and swallowed hard. "I wish they would have never called me back here."

For a moment, he just stared at her. Virgins? They were all virgins? What kinda insane environmental cult was this?

"Can I check on my remaining soldiers?" he asked, forcing his voice to be rough, forcing his mind to remain focused on the very real dangers these women presented . . . trying to get the hard-on to die down.

Artemis nodded but didn't move. He could tell that she was giving him permission to go look, but that she didn't want to see any more for herself. In a way he couldn't blame her and was glad that she'd simply be staring at his back as he took a glimpse inside each tent.

"It is bad, is it not?" Artemis asked as he slowly returned to her side.

He nodded, mouth dry, and kept his gaze on the horizon. "Yeah." That was all he could say before turning so that she couldn't see his arousal. "I have one more man to check."

Artemis graciously nodded as he strode away, peeped into the tent that held Jesse captive and winced. He quickly dropped the tent flap, inhaled a deep breath through his nose and tried to do math in his head to regain focus on the mission.

"The offense is grave," Artemis murmured when Vince returned to stand before her.

"Yeah," he said quietly. "So, how do we resolve this?"

"My nymphs are in the wrong, therefore, by rights, as has always been; you may decide the punishment . . . even though I am a goddess. There are still laws."

"All I want," he said quietly, "is for the hostages to be returned unharmed, and for me and my men to be able to walk out of here alive."

She frowned. "That you would doubt my word when I said they would be unharmed is troubling." She turned away and headed toward her tent.

"You also said they would be unmolested, and they have been." There was amusement in his tone as she stiffened and dipped inside her tent.

He put the safety back on his gun and watched her pour water from an urn into a basin to splash her face. "Mind if I do the same?" he said calmly, watching her from across the expanse.

"Yes, I mean no—you are more than welcome to wash the stain of humiliation from your face."

"I am not embarrassed," he said in a low rumble. "It's spring."

She dabbed her damp cheeks with a thick towel and then wound her hair up into a knot atop her head, applying the wet side of the towel against the nape of her neck. A deep rosy hue stained her cheeks and small beads of perspiration kissed her cleavage. He couldn't help allowing his eyes to travel down her breasts and over her erect peaks, knowing that if she felt anything near what he was feeling, she was also wet.

Against his better judgment, he neared her and gently removed the towel from her hands, dipping it in the cool basin water and then dabbing her collarbone with it.

"What was the vow?" he murmured, staring at her.

"That I would remain a virgin always until the end of time . . . as would my nymphs."

Her breathing had become shallow from his attention, and it had the effect of stilting his too.

"Why?" he asked hoarsely. "To what end?"

She licked her lips as they parted and the pink tip of her tongue darted out. "Because rutting males are barbarians that pillage the wilderness," she whispered.

"But what about marriages to honorable men, and then having children?" he asked, stepping in closer. "You need us barbarians for that, right?" Then again, he thought about the advances of technology and realized that that wasn't a given.

"I don't understand what has happened . . . why this time when we were called it was so different . . . why they would break a vow held for so long?" Her voice was an exhausted lament as she stared up at him. "Unless they felt the decency in each of you that I felt?"

"I don't know," he admitted, finding it very hard to keep up any ruse with her or even to think of her as the enemy. There was something completely disorienting about her the moment he stood physically close to her. It also dredged the truth, this magnetic pulse and he fought with himself not to ask, but caved to the need to. "*What* is it about you that the moment I'm close like this, I . . ."

"My aura," she murmured in a near rasp, her eyes now heavy-lidded and her breathing shallow. "I've never let any male being get this close—you have one, too . . . an aura field that is . . . spectacular."

"Really?" he asked quietly, his groin throbbing so hard that he could barely breathe. "Your nymphs, they have this, too . . . is that what seduced my men or were they drugged?"

"We don't use drugs; only Aphrodite does . . . it is their auras, which is why we stay in the wilderness and away from humans . . . normally."

He didn't know if it was complete hocus pocus or what, but the rational side of his brain was oozing out of his ears as she began to slightly pant. Her dewy skin made his fingertips burn to touch it, but he didn't want to take liberties that could get anybody killed, so he kept wetting the towel and slowly bringing it over the swell of her breasts and down her bare arms, teasing her neck as they spoke in dètente.

"I am not against marriage," she gasped, "and I am the protectress of women in labor . . . during childbirth."

"Then why do you shun one of the most fundamental rites of spring . . . mating, making love, and becoming one from two?" He couldn't deny it; he wanted this woman—bad guy or not.

Her answer was a quick gasp and a shudder as his thumbs finally grazed the swell of her breasts and he dropped the towel, standing inches from her. "I cannot remember."

CHAPTER 4

A YEAR OF ABSTINENCE WHILE UNDERCOVER
imploded in his groin as he took her mouth and summarily
drowned in the sweetest kiss he'd ever tasted. He couldn't
help it; it was an involuntary reaction to stimuli too great to
ignore. Her smooth hands fought with his jacket and stripped
away the heavy outer layer, and she pulled back, her eyes
glittering with pure fascination as her fingertips gently outlined the definition of his chest, making him suck in air
quickly between his teeth.

"Your bodies are so different from ours," she murmured,
her gaze following her hands.

He didn't breathe for a moment as she explored, then
gasped as her fingertips left his abdomen and settled on his
groin.

She drew away confused and concerned. "I'm sorry I hurt
you, I—"

He stopped her apology with a kiss and sought her ear.
"No, it doesn't hurt . . . but aches like this," he murmured
and then kissed down her neck to spill the attention down
her collarbone to bring a distended nipple between his lips
through the sheer fabric she wore. When she gasped and
arched, he gently thumbed the other nipple and then kissed
her earlobe. "It hurts like that."

"Oh . . ." she whispered on a rush of breath, sealing the space between them. "Then it is normal for every place else to hurt, too?"

He gently cradled her face with both hands and kissed her forehead, her eyelids, the bridge of her nose, and then softly swept her mouth. "Yes . . . you tell me where it hurts, and I'll kiss it till it stops aching."

She closed her eyes and turned her face away.

"Especially there," he murmured, gently bringing her face back to his with a finger beneath her chin and then slowly taking her mouth.

He lifted her with care, knowing he was wrong, knowing he was out of order, was so far off mission he couldn't get back on track—but another more primal mission had taken priority. At least for the moment. Right now there was only right now, and the goddess draped in his arms clung to his neck with complete faith in her eyes.

When he deposited her on the bed amid the silk and pelts he studied her, taking his time to pull his t-shirt over head, slowly, cautiously, removing his weapon, unlacing his boots, wondering if he'd lost his mind . . . but her agonized stare wasn't something that could be feigned. He unzipped his pants; she licked her dry lips and slid off her sheath. That was when he was sure it was safe. If she knifed him in bed . . . well . . . that was a risk he was willing to take. Never in his life had he been so drawn to a woman so fast, who was this beautiful, and so very off limits.

Thousands of years came to a central ache of need between her legs, so strong that she almost cried out with no shame when he freed himself from his clothes. Definitely a Titan, his body was pure chiseled symmetry, his mane a gorgeous rival to the most majestic of creatures on earth. Her hands throbbed to touch him, the center of her palms burning, her fingertips tingling. Unable to restrain herself, she reached out, and his burning body covered hers. The sound that rushed from her came up from her diaphragm, forced out of her by the sheer weight of him covering her. She arched and writhed against him, not exactly knowing what her body craved but sure that he owned it.

Torturous kisses flowed over her shoulders and breasts, his body heat receding like a hard tide, pulling down her abdomen, over the swell of her hips, sweeping over her thighs, opening them, plundering the very sensitive ache that throbbed between them until her body spasmed with sobs.

Limp, gasping, set adrift on her own sea, she never knew a kiss or a gentle tip of a tongue could cause then release such a building floodwall of pain. Yet before she could summon her wits, the hot tide of him flattened her, and she clung to his back, wrapping her legs around his waist, holding on as he kissed her deeply, making her taste her own salty sweet essence.

A strong hand flat-palmed the small of her back. Agonized eyes met hers. His dark bronze skin was damp with a glistening sheen. The scent of him was the very wilderness itself. She breathed him in with tears of appreciation in her eyes as her fingers twined in his luscious, textured hair.

He didn't speak, but stared at her, easing himself inside her by infinitesimal degrees, holding her still by his weight and his firm grip that now captured her buttock, his eyes making her trust him, his grimace making her know how difficult his slow advance was . . . until she couldn't watch him any longer, the pain-pleasure too great a beast to contain. Each brick of his defined abdomen pressed against hers, his pelvis locked into her pelvic cradle, his thick, muscular thighs trembling, holding back . . . her hands swept down his spine trying to gain purchase on his sensual, tight rise of haunches that were the source of his locomotion and power. He had to let whatever he held back go.

She was going mad, needed to hunt it, needed to let it run wild and free and had to chase it with her body lunging. Her quick breaths must have told him that. His breathing grew shallow as he lodged deeper within her, a groan forced from them both in unison.

Then he moved . . . beginning as a slow rolling motion that clenched every muscle in her body, his long, thick shaft a spear of pure pleasure each time it slid in and out of her. The exquisite sensation made her need to run hard, nearly gallop after what he'd loosed. But he held her firm, refusing to let her go until she arched and begged him, "Let me hunt you!"

He let go of her hip, kissed her hard, threw back his head, and ran. Tears stung her eyes as he thundered against her soft ground, her nails digging into his shoulders, her body lunging with his, against his, at times outpacing him and making him holler. Sweat slicked skin, air scorched lungs, muscles strained, veins standing in necks, they caught up to each other, the capture complete, total, bedlam—a battle of flesh and searing bodies, their mutual deaths coming in waves of convulsions, blinding ecstasy, and then they dropped twitching.

Heaving in air, sweat dripping off the bridge of his nose, eyes shut tightly, he slowly gathered her in his arms and rolled over so she could breathe.

She laid her cheek against his chest, eyes shut, listening to his heart thud, gasping, hair wet, wild, a massive spill across his chest and shoulders. His warm caress up and down her back offered reassurance. What had she done on the vernal equinox? The power of this Titan's pull was so strong that she shuddered. And, yet, she could feel panic rising within him as his haze of passion abated. She also understood why.

He kissed the crown of her head. "This . . ."

"Yes. I know. Even though it wasn't supposed to happen, it was . . . supernatural."

She felt his body relax.

"I'm just a soldier, Artemis. I have to eventually report back . . . I have to tell the authorities something . . . have to take back the hostages."

She nodded. "Shush, I know. At least wait until your heart stops beating so hard."

He smiled; she could feel it against the crown of her head. "That might be hours from now," he whispered.

That, too, she knew.

"What are we gonna tell the major, Vince?" Donovan glanced around the glen where they'd originally been ambushed as the men gathered into a tight huddle surrounded by beautiful nymphs.

"We were drugged," Dutch said, nervously glancing around, but a mellow smile cascading across his face as the women from his tent waved coyly at him.

"Yeah, uh, the fight broke out here," Vincent whispered, indicating with a nod. "A firefight ensued. Several grenades got lobbed . . . we were running, got hit with arrows that had the hallucinogen, couple of us were caught in the vines . . . uh, then, we staggered in that direction and found an encampment after freeing our own men. More fire power got unleashed, and the abductors fled. We dropped from the effects of the drug—but the other side had already pulled back—we hit one or two, but they dragged their own to safety. But we got all the hostages that were stashed."

"I don't know, brother," Jermaine said nervously. "Some of us left a lot of DNA evidence back there."

"Ballistics won't match up unless we go back through and act it out," Lou said, glancing around and wiping his palms down his face. "For bigwigs that important, they'll raze the forest looking for a trail."

"I know, but what else can we say?" Dutch said, raking his finger through his hair.

"They didn't kill nobody, didn't ransom them like they could have," Jesse said, glancing around the group, "and seriously made up for the inconvenience, if you ask me."

"That's the thing, dude," Lou fussed under his breath, "nobody's gonna ask you what *you think*. You'd better get this story tight and right, or all our asses are gonna spend a very long time in the brink."

"Damned straight," Vincent said. He looked around. "We go

back to the original glen, anything we say we're gonna do, we do. If we say we blew it up—we gotta blow it up. If we say we sprayed an area—we gotta spray the area. If . . ." his voice trailed off as he watched a goddess walk toward him.

Artemis sauntered over to the group and the small circle of men opened to allow her in. She touched Vincent's face with trembling fingers and then lifted up to take his mouth. "Don't worry," she whispered. "I'm a goddess . . . it will all work out. Men will see what they need to, the hostages will remember what they should, and you will each be honored for your courage."

He couldn't take his eyes off hers, wondering if this very insane woman really did have something supernatural about her. He wanted to tell her he was going to miss her, one very long afternoon with her wasn't enough. But with his men standing there, each with the same expression on their faces as they stared at their temporary captors, he couldn't. Contact with her after this would have vast repercussions.

Her sad gaze told him that she understood as she touched his face one last time. "Goodbye, gentle Titan . . . if you ever want to see me, visit my temple in Crete and call me by name . . . or simply go to your Olympus and find a meadow beneath the crescent moon . . . and whisper my name. I will come to you there."

His ranks splintered, the men in his squad walked over to the respective nymphs trying to get their names, the method to contact them, and all pandemonium broke loose. Artemis shook her head and smiled with a quiet chuckle. Vincent raked his fingers through his locks, hoping all would be well. Then he watched sadly as Artemis began running, her long tresses sweeping her back, and her nymphs waving goodbye.

Somehow going into a tent to collect bound and gagged old men with tears running down their faces seemed completely anticlimactic. But as the squad opened the tents, they backed away in pure horror leaving the flaps flung up. Each tent was tiny, the size it appeared on the outside. What happened to the sumptuous love dens? Where were the bound and gagged hostages they'd been shown?

A buck was bound and gagged in each tent now. The animals had congealed blood on their coats exactly where the original mortal injuries had been. Glassy, dead, animal eyes stared at Vincent and his men. The poor creatures had been dead so long that rigor mortis had set in and each animal was washboard stiff.

"Oh, shit—we got played, partner," Donovan whispered.

A cold sweat made Vincent's t-shirt cling to him. The twitching of one deer freaked everybody out.

"What the fuck do we do now?" Jermaine yelled, beginning to walk in a circle.

Then another deer twitched, and still another, until the fragile nervous systems around Vince snapped, frayed, and popped, and guns got drawn toward the carcasses.

"No!" Vince shouted, not sure why. "Don't screw with any more evidence. Leave it. Let's put our heads together, we have to think through this, pick up the trail, we gotta . . ."

His voice trailed off as a human cough riveted everyone's attention to one of the tents. A pudgy CEO lay naked, shivering, and bound by vines, leaves stuffed in his mouth. Terror-stricken, they watched each dead animal reanimate and then transform into a hostage. Jesse and Dutch stared at each other, voices choked.

"We weren't drugged," Jesse whispered.

"It happened." Dutch wheezed, grappling at his chest as though having a heart attack, and then stumbled away and puked.

Nervous glances passed around the squad.

"Gotta still be the crap that's in our systems," Lou said, his voice quavering.

Vincent looked at the tents and then out into the vast wilderness, knowing. "Yeah," he said. "That's all it is."

EPILOGUE

ARTEMIS KEPT HER WORD. THINGS WORKED OUT, more than he could have imagined. Since the glen, every man on the squad retired. Donovan got a boat as an unspoken and untold gesture of appreciation from the CEO he helped half carry to the rendezvous point. He headed down to the Caribbean and disappeared. Last anyone heard, Donovan regularly had three gorgeous, out-of-this world babes on his yacht.

Jermaine went back to Brooklyn, and then moved to Harlem to buy a brownstone in the up-and-coming section . . . the squad quietly heard tell that some appreciation dollars fell off the table. Now Jermaine is tracing his family genealogy after a nymph mentioned something about him being a dead-ringer for an ancient king. Jesse went to Wyoming, and somehow some cattle land got ceded to him, mysteriously enough, along with a hundred head of healthy beef. He's a happy man who only takes a harmonica into the woods these days. His hunting days are over.

Dutch was traveling abroad, last anyone heard, and getting VIP treatment wherever he goes—no expense spared—all financed from a nice, quiet Swiss account. Lou moved to southern California, joined Greenpeace, and became a New Age guru. Some say that a nice investment portfolio that changed hands as a private thank you allows him to pursue his environmental platform with gusto.

Major Harcourt still knows something about the whole story wasn't right. There were no hallucinogens found in anyone's systems, but all insisted on such bizarre occurrences that mind control or a new, experimental substance that leaves no trace could be the culprit. He is still searching for that drug or method of group hypnosis.

That day in the glen changed each and every man—both those who were captives and those who were hostages. Vince . . . well . . . he went back on home to Neah Bay on the Olympic Peninsula and is using his quiet, unspoken gift from the appreciative wealthy to help build up the town and rebuild the traditions of his people . . . preserving, especially, the culture and the oral stories called by some legends and myths.

He spends a lot of his days contemplating the universe and the wisdom of the ancestors as he burns incense and waits for the crescent moon in a quiet glen . . . from where he sits he can see across the Strait of Juan de Fuca to Vancouver Island. The equinox is their anniversary. She comes so swiftly that he doesn't mind waiting to be hunted, knowing soon he'll be felled by a true goddess.

He loves her, plain and simple. She finally learned his name and has visited his people, unbeknownst to them what she really is. She still thinks he's a Titan, and cannot believe him to be a mere mortal . . . because she hasn't been so adored since the times of old, and never, ever, quite so personally.

RIDE A DARK HORSE

Susan Krinard

WHEN SHE WAS THIRTEEN, SHE DREAMED OF horses.

Most of the girls her age were horse-mad, and Catalina was no exception. That alone would have explained the dreams. But Abuelita, after whom she'd been named, had different ideas.

"It is a sign," Grandmother had told her. "The women of my line have often been blessed with such omens. You must not forget this, but watch for its tokens in the future."

Mom had laughed; she'd grown up with Abuelita's stories, but she had never believed. And Dad had merely rolled his eyes. The Irish, he said, had the same kinds of superstitions. None of it was real.

Catalina believed. She saw the black horse when she slept, his glossy neck arched, his eyes shining with invitation. But she never got close enough to climb up on his broad, powerful back. He ran, and though she chased him she never caught him.

In time she almost forgot about the dreams. There was no room for real horses in Bel Air. Catalina went to law school just as Dad wanted. She married an attorney from the top law firm in Los Angeles, a man of ambition and little imagination.

Life was busy and successful and very ordinary until she began having the dreams again.

Then it all fell apart.

Catalina O'Roarke, formerly Mrs. Neal Kirkland, Jr., jumped out of the battered Chevy truck, her new boots raising little puffs from the dusty ground. The ranch house was small and rustic, surrounded by empty corrals and a few scrawny cottonwoods. The prairie stretched all the way to the foot of the mountains; the countryside seemed almost desolate, mile upon mile of nothing but sage, chamisa, and open sky.

It was exactly what she wanted.

"Can I do anything else for you, miss?" the aging cowboy asked.

Cat managed a smile. "I'll be fine, thanks."

"Then I'll be headed back to Taos. Turk and Pilar will look after you right and proper."

He got back into his truck and drove away on the rutted track that passed for a road. Cat picked up her bags and walked to the porch. The boards creaked under her feet. The smell of cooking beans wafted out one of the windows.

She closed her eyes and let the tension drain from her shoulders. "It doesn't look like much," Heather had said, "but the place always seems to help me get my head on straight when I can't take L.A. one minute longer. Just give it a chance."

Give it a chance. She didn't have anything to lose.

With a rueful shrug, Cat stepped through the door.

Turk adjusted the buckle under the saddle's fender and stepped back. "That'll do ya," he said. "Perfect fit. And you don't have to worry about ol' Kelpie here . . . he's the gentlest horse we got. He's Miss Heather's favorite."

Cat shifted in the saddle, already anticipating the sore muscles to come. Seventeen years ago she would have given anything to be where she was now: mounted on a handsome buckskin with the prospect of a long, solitary ride ahead of her.

But she wasn't thirteen anymore. If she'd had any sense, she would have admitted to Turk that she hadn't been on a horse in well over a decade. But she didn't want to admit weakness to any man, even one as inoffensive as Turk. She wanted to be left alone, even if it meant taking a few small risks.

God knew she'd almost forgotten what it was like to take a chance on anything outside the courtroom.

"Like I told you, Mrs. Kirkland—"

"Cat. Call me Cat."

Turk cleared his throat. "Cat. Like I told you, just stick close to the river gorge and you can't get lost. Kelpie knows his way home even in the dark." He scratched his chin. "Still think you ought to take someone along . . ."

"I'll be back by nightfall." Cat pulled on the reins, turning Kelpie toward the barn door. "Please tell Pilar not to wait dinner for me."

Turk touched one grizzled hand to the brim of his hat, a faintly worried look on his leathery face. Cat pretended not to see.

She started out along the rutted road and then cut across the plain. The sense of vastness she'd felt when she'd first arrived redoubled. The sky was a landscape in itself. She knew the Rio Grande gorge was nearby, winding its way south from Colorado until it became the broad brown river that bordered Mexico and Texas, but there seemed to be hardly any other landmarks except for the Sangre de Cristo mountains rising sharply from the prairie like skyscrapers built of earth and stone.

For most of the day she let Kelpie wander at will, basking in the late summer sun that warmed her face and shoulders. She stopped for lunch in the shade of an abandoned cabin, listening to the wind rattling in the rabbit-brush while she ate her sandwich. A hawk circled in the sky, but aside from him she was completely alone.

She was glad. A good dose of solitude, even loneliness, was

just the cure for what ailed her. No more of Neal's hypocritical lies. No more strict and unvarying routines. Just a sense of freedom she hadn't felt since childhood.

By late afternoon she was ready to return to the ranch. Kelpie, looking forward to his ration of hay, broke into a trot as soon as she reined him south. Neither he nor Cat noticed the prairie dog town until his hoof plunged down into an unexpected hole.

He staggered. Cat lurched in the saddle and grabbed at Kelpie's coarse mane. Immediately she knew the gelding was injured. She dismounted and bent to study his near foreleg.

It didn't seem to be broken, but Kelpie's limp told Cat that his fetlock had suffered some damage. He wouldn't be carrying a rider anytime soon. The only thing Cat could do was lead him home as slowly as possible and hope she didn't get lost in the dark.

Night fell with surprising swiftness. Cat buttoned her coat against an unexpected chill. Kelpie snorted and bobbed his head.

"I'm sorry, boy," she murmured. "I should have taken Turk's advice." She paused to let Kelpie rest. "It isn't his fault that I've had my fill of the male sex."

Kelpie lifted his head, ears pricked as if he'd heard a sound that had escaped Cat's ears.

"You'll tell me I was stupid to trust him, that I should have seen it coming. All the signs were there." She clenched her fists. "He used me, and then when he got what he wanted . . ."

Kelpie stretched his neck and nickered. Cat cocked her head, listening. The earth vibrated under her feet. A low rumble beat the air. A blast of wind, warmed by the heat of a dozen bodies, swept over Cat an instant before the horses leapt out of the darkness.

They were every color men had named: buckskin and Appaloosa, chestnut and bay, pinto and sorrel, white and gray. Their eyes glittered with starlight; their hooves flashed like dark jewels. Cat's heart surged into her throat. She clung to Kelpie's reins and closed her eyes. The herd rushed on, implacable, parting at the last moment to flow around woman and horse in a swift and savage tide.

An incredible feeling claimed Cat's body. Her breath came in sharp bursts. She flung back her head, surrendering to sensation. Her legs buckled and she dropped to her knees, dizzy and stunned.

"Are you well, *señorita*?"

The voice was soft, but it carried through the darkness like a roll of thunder. Cat tried to stand, but her legs refused to obey her commands.

"Hello?" she said, using her courtroom voice. "Who's there?"

The man seemed to appear little by little, as if the shadows gave him up with only the greatest reluctance. Cat's first impression was of dark hair and broad shoulders, a lithe and muscular figure that moved with the grace of the horses that had preceded him. He wore the typical uniform of a working cowboy: battered leather boots, scuffed jeans, long-sleeved shirt, sweat-stained Stetson. The jeans fit him like a glove, molding strong thighs and an imposing package.

Cat shivered and looked up. He wasn't particularly tall. His face was a little too angular to be handsome, but no one could have denied that it was striking. The long, thick hair that trailed from beneath his Stetson was jet-black. His lips were sensuous and slightly curved, his nose a little arched, his eyes . . .

Oh, his eyes. They welcomed the moonlight like a lover. Pale they were, though she couldn't make out the color. They stripped Cat naked and left her utterly defenseless.

"*Señorita*," he said, touching the brim of his hat. "How may I assist you?"

Cat grabbed Kelpie's stirrup and pulled herself to her feet, half afraid she might fall without the gelding to support her. The stranger spoke only the simplest of phrases, and yet his faintly accented voice raised goosebumps on her skin.

"It's nothing," she said thickly. "My horse . . . he stepped in a prairie dog hole. I'm taking him back to the ranch."

"Indeed. Would that be the Blue Moon, *señorita*?"

His tone was mild and courteous, but the steadiness of his gaze unnerved her. She tried to calculate how much farther she and Kelpie had to go . . . how far she was from any help at all. She'd never thought to bring her pepper spray. She'd fight, of course, but he was all whipcord muscle and supple strength. She wouldn't last long . . . .

What in hell's wrong with you? He'd offered no threat whatsoever. He wasn't armed. He didn't even have a horse that she could see.

"The Blue Moon, yes," she said. "They'll be waiting up for me."

He smiled as if he fully recognized the false bravado in her words. "I have no doubt," he said. He reached for Kelpie's head. The gelding stood very still. Cat held her breath.

"So, *querido*." The man stroked Kelpie's muzzle, but his gaze remained on Cat. "Shall we see what ails you?" He knelt to examine the gelding's leg, murmuring in Spanish all the while. "It is not so bad, *mi amigo*. A poultice, a few weeks' rest . . ." He rose slowly. Cat felt as though he were running his hands over her body. "I will guide you back to the ranch, *señorita*," he said.

"Thanks, but that won't be necessary."

"But you are traveling in the wrong direction," he said. "Those who wait for you will surely worry."

Was he mocking her? She drew up, all her anger against men spilling into her chest. "I'll be all right."

"Will you?" He moved closer. "It is not wise to travel alone, even in a place like this."

He smelled, she thought, of sagebrush and horses and a unique, completely masculine scent that threatened to overwhelm her senses.

He was dangerous, but not in the way she'd feared.

"If you'll point me in the right direction," she said, "I'm sure I can make it the rest of the way."

His dark brows lifted and his nostrils flared. Cat began to feel hot . . . hot in the face, in her belly, in between her legs. She could almost feel the pressure of those sensuous lips on hers, the thrust of his tongue, his hands slipping beneath her shirt to caress her nipples . . . .

She swallowed hard. "Thank you, but no. I prefer to travel alone."

For a moment his pale eyes flashed with something that might have been anger. Then he touched the brim of his hat again and gave a slight, ironic bow.

"As you wish." He leaned toward Kelpie's ear and whispered words Cat couldn't hear. Kelpie nickered and nibbled at the stranger's sleeve as he withdrew.

"*Adiós*," he said, fading into the night the same way he had come. "We shall meet again, *señorita*."

The silence was absolute. Even the wind had stilled. Cat pressed her hand to her chest, trying to quiet her racing heart. Remembering the man's advice, she turned Kelpie around and started in the opposite direction. Two hours later she saw the lights of the ranch house. Turk ran out to meet her.

"Miss Cat! Are you all right?"

"I'm fine. It's Kelpie who's hurt."

Immediately Turk lifted the gelding's leg. "Don't look too bad." He glanced up at Cat. "I'll take care of Kelpie. You'd better get yourself into the house. Pilar's worried sick over you."

Cat gladly obeyed. Her mouth was dry as a desert, and she felt more than a little weak at the knees. The housekeeper greeted her with relief and good-natured scolding, which Cat accepted as her just due. She drank the cocoa Pilar set down in front of her and meekly retreated to the guest room.

No bed, no matter how luxurious, had ever looked so welcome. Cat stripped out of her dusty clothes, threw them across a chair, and climbed naked between the sheets. The plain cotton felt incredibly soft against her skin. Every movement awakened strong sensations, as if her nerves had been lit on fire. Her imagination conjured up vivid images of the stranger, spawning pictures of sleek muscle and a strong, angular face.

A face that looked at her out of the darkness, eyes burning with unreserved lust.

Cat tried to close her eyes, fighting the images and the reaction of her body. Finally exhaustion claimed her, and she slid gratefully into sleep.

She had never seen men like these before.

They came boldly into the village, sitting on great beasts with long necks and sweeping tails, the metal on their heads and chests gleaming in the sun. They smiled as they leaped from the backs of their mounts, speaking a tongue she had never heard.

The village headman welcomed them with courtesy and care, for he, too, had no knowledge of this tribe of pale-skinned warriors with their sharp-edged weapons. It was best to be safe until more was known about them.

For her, it was enough to know that a new excitement had come to the village. She watched the men with fascination as they removed the leather chairs from the great beasts' backs and brushed the creatures' coats until they gleamed. She stared in fascination as they shed their heavy clothing to reveal skin that surely had never been touched by the sun. She spied on the elders as they spoke with the strangers, and always her gaze was drawn to one among the foreign warriors.

He was tall compared to the villagers, though his hair was as black as that of the people. The shape of his face was different, but she found it handsome in its own way. His eyes drew her most, for they were the color of the first light of dawn.

One day he caught her watching him, though she had done her best not to let him see. He spoke to her in his stranger's tongue, gently and with admiration in those pale eyes. Sometimes his companions seemed crude and loud, but he was not. She began to teach him the peoples' language. He was a swift learner, and at last he began to speak the words she had longed to hear.

Too soon it was time for him and his companions to leave the village, to rejoin their tribe. She could not wait for him to return and for the marriage to take place. When he asked her to come with him into the forest, she went eagerly, knowing that what they were about to do would change her life forever. . . .

Cat woke to the glory of an orgasm.

At first she wasn't sure exactly what she was feeling. She'd almost forgotten what it was like; Neal hadn't bothered to satisfy her in years. But she felt between her thighs and her fingers came away wet.

Panic sent her heart into overdrive. She sprang up and stood in the center of the room, searching every corner.

He wasn't there. How could he be? He had been a dream, in a time and place that had seemed alien and yet utterly familiar.

A dream who had walked out of the shadows and into reality.

Cat sank into the chair and began to laugh. There was no reason for the levity except that she felt more than a little loco, and laughter seemed the best medicine for her ailment.

"Señora?"

Pilar was knocking on the door, undoubtedly alarmed by the racket. Cat put on her thick chenille robe and opened the door.

"I'm sorry to have disturbed you," she said. "I'm all right. I just had a crazy dream."

The older woman's brown eyes were skeptical. "You should rest today, *Señora* Catalina. I will make you a good breakfast . . ."

"I'm not very hungry. I'll take a little fruit, if you have any."

"Si." Pilar continued to regard Cat in a way that made her

feel like a naughty little girl. "You say nothing happened to you last night?"

"Nothing." Nothing that really mattered, anyway. "I think I'll go for another ride this morning."

Pilar sighed and walked back toward the kitchen. Cat showered, dressed in jeans and denim shirt, and grabbed a slice of melon and an apple on her way out the door. Turk wasn't in the stables. Cat leaned on the corral fence, wondering if she ought to try saddling one of the horses herself. She'd done it a few times when she'd gone to riding camp as a teenager, but that had been a lifetime ago.

As she kicked at the dirt and debated her course of action, she looked up and saw the black horse.

He . . . and she had no doubt that it was indeed a "he" . . . stood outside the fence on the opposite side of the corral, unburdened by either saddle or bridle. His coat was a true black, not burned brown like so many dark horses. His mane was a luxurious ebon wave that fell almost to the bottom of his neck, and his tail was held high as a flag. A white star in the shape of a cross blazed his face.

Cat shivered, remembering how a horse exactly like this one had haunted her childhood dreams. He had been so far away then, impossible to catch. Now he stood no more than twenty yards distant, and his eyes—his strangely pale eyes—gazed at her with uncanny intensity.

She never knew why she did what she did then. Without a moment's thought, she circled the corral and approached the horse, walking slowly and carefully. She still had the apple in her jacket pocket. Her fingers closed around the smooth, polished surface and pulled it out.

The stallion watched her come with elegant ears swiveled forward and nostrils flared. He arched his neck and shifted from foot to foot as if to display his strength and elegance. Cat felt no fear at all. She offered the apple in her extended hand.

He took it with remarkable gentleness, his lips sliding across her fingertips.

"You're a beautiful boy," she said, patting his silky neck. "Where did you come from?"

The stallion finished the apple, watching her all the while. He made a low, coaxing sound deep in his throat.

"You must be valuable," she said. "Maybe I should go ask Turk who—"

The stallion reared, ears flat. Cat stepped back, suddenly aware of his sharp hooves and sheer size. It was almost as if he'd understood her.

"Okay," she murmured. "I'm not going anywhere."

The stallion danced, tossing his head and eying Cat with suspicion. After a moment he approached her again, stretching his neck and nibbling her shoulder.

"I sure wish I knew what was going on in that head of yours," she said. "Are you hungry? I can bring some oats . . ."

He snorted with contemptuous eloquence. His blue eyes seemed virtually human, the pupil more round than oblong. Cat was eerily convinced that he really did understand every word she said.

"What do you want?" she asked softly. "How can I help you?"

Drawing back his head, the stallion dropped to his knees. There was nothing in the least humble in his posture. He nickered an invitation.

Surely his odd behavior couldn't mean what it seemed to mean. Cat moved to his side and laid her hand on his back. He rumbled approvingly.

"You want me to ride you?"

He nodded. There was no other word for his reaction. Cautiously Cat leaned across him, enchanted by the muscular curve of his withers and hindquarters. He remained quiet. Cat swung her leg over his back, looking toward the house to make sure no one was watching.

The instant she was settled, the stallion surged to his feet. Cat grabbed for his mane as he wheeled about and began to run.

The horse was kidnapping her. And she had absolutely no way to stop him.

For several minutes all she could do was hang on. The air was crip and cool. The sun was just beginning to peek above the mountains to the east. The stallion galloped straight north, his tail streaming behind him.

Cat caught her breath. The stallion's gait was so smooth that she felt in not the slightest danger of falling off, even though she had no reins, stirrups, or handy saddle horn. Her initial concern had passed. In fact, she felt an undeniable exhilaration at the feel of her mount's muscles flexing between her thighs, the snap of her hair, the sense of flying over the earth.

This was true freedom. *This* was what she'd been seeking ever since those dreams fifteen years ago. She flung back her head and laughed aloud. The stallion twitched his ears to listen and stretched his legs in an even faster pace.

Miles passed in a blur. Cat hardly noticed when the stallion slowed. His coat gleamed with sweat, but his neck was still arched and his sheer magnificence claimed obeisance from every creature that shared his world.

A small grove of cottonwoods crouched over an unexpected green jewel nestled in the brown setting of the plain. Cat thought gratefully of water, even if it wasn't sterilized and out of a tap.

Another dozen yards revealed a tiny pool and the bubbling of a spring. A pair of pronghorn antelope sprang away from the bank, white rumps flashing. The stallion ignored them and paced to the water's edge. He twisted his head back to look at Cat.

His message was clear enough. Cat slid from his back, staggered a little as she got her land legs again, and sat down under the shade of a cottonwood. The stallion dipped his muzzle into the pool and drank.

"I can't just keep calling you 'the stallion,' you know," Cat said. "You're black as a storm cloud. Let me see if I can remember . . ." She snapped her fingers. "I've got it. What about *trueno*? That's 'thunder.' Nice and succinct."

Trueno bobbed his head. Cat chuckled and stretched out on the green grass. It was well into mid-morning and not by any means hot, but Cat keenly felt the confinement of her clothing. She removed her jacket and scarf, undid the top several buttons of her shirt and kicked off her boots.

She should have been thinking about where she was and how she'd get back to the ranch. She should have asked herself a few more questions about why the stallion had behaved as he had, why she'd climbed onto his back with a complete lack of the most basic common sense.

But she didn't. She closed her eyes, blissfully relaxed, and dozed while Trueno grazed nearby. Once or twice she woke, noted vaguely that the sun had moved again, and sank back into sleep.

The forest closed in around them, a perfect bower for secret lovers. Firm lips pressed against hers, demanding entrance. She opened her mouth in a cry of surprise and a warm, insistent tongue thrust into her mouth, hungry and caressing. She felt calloused fingers inside her blouse, circling her nipples. She gloried in the heat of a hard, lean body stretched out beside her. Wetness pooled between her legs.

"*Sí*, my beautiful one," he said, running his tongue over her lips. With long, lean fingers he pushed her blouse above her breasts. "*Muy linda*," he murmured.

She gasped as he bent and took her nipple in his mouth. Dark, unruly hair brushed against her face and shoulders. She whimpered while he suckled her, licking and kissing and grazing her breasts with his teeth.

She was so close, so close to something wonderful. Somehow she knew that if she opened her eyes, the pleasure would stop. If she dared to question, even for a moment, it would all go away . . . .

Cat opened her eyes. The sky was dark and studded with stars. The branches of the cottonwood shivered overhead. And she remembered.

The man didn't resist as she pushed him away. In one fluid motion he detached himself and settled into a crouch, pale eyes catching moonlight.

Oh, God. She'd seen him before. He was the cowboy she'd met last night. And he had been . . . doing things to her. While she slept. And in her dreams.

With trembling fingers she buttoned her shirt. Her nipples were wet from his kisses. Her mouth throbbed. She nearly groaned with the intensity of her arousal. She stared at the stranger's lips and slowly raised her eyes to his.

"*Señorita,*" he said, his voice husky and low.

Cat scooted away. "I warn you. I can fight. If you try anything—"

He shook his head. "Oh, no, *señorita*. I will not do anything you do not wish me to do."

His long hair drifted across his face, softening the angles of his cheekbones and jaw. Cat's heart was beating hard enough to be heard in California. She had been lying there, doing nothing, believing it was all another dream. But *he* was real. And she'd wanted him to keep on doing what he was doing, both in the dream and in reality. She still did.

"Where is my horse?" she demanded, her voice cracking.

He stood up. Her eyes were level with his hips. There was no mistaking his impressive erection.

"Don't worry, *querida*. He is here."

Cat glanced around. If the stallion were more than a few feet away, she wouldn't be able to see his black coat in the darkness.

"Who are you?" Cat demanded. "What are you doing here?"

He tilted his head. She saw that he wore the same shirt as he had last night, but it was unbuttoned almost to his waist. Sleek black hair dusted his chest. His pecs were beautifully developed, his stomach ridged with muscle.

"My name," he said, "is Andrés. And you are Catalina."

The sound of her name on his tongue left her shaken. God, he was beautiful. All she had to do was hold out her arms, and he would take her. Just like that. A stranger she wanted with every fiber of her being.

Not a stranger, her heart insisted. You know him. You *know* him . . . .

"You aren't afraid," he said. "You will never be afraid of me."

"I . . ." She swallowed. "I'm going to find my horse and leave."

"It would be far wiser for you to remain here until sunrise."

He was right, damn him. She couldn't risk letting Trueno hurt himself as Kelpie had, presuming she could get the stallion to come to her in the first place.

Andrés dropped back into a crouch, his arms draped over his knees. "You will suffer no harm from me, *señorita*," he said. "Or is it *señora*?"

Cat couldn't quite believe that he was asking her such questions after what he'd been doing. "That's none of your business," she snapped.

His smile was devastating. "You are no virgin, Catalina. Your response was . . . most satisfactory."

Satisfactory. Cat suppressed a moan. "You . . . you don't know anything about me."

"I know that you deny your own passions, *mi gatita*."

"I don't deny anyth—" Cat stopped, stung with outrage. "Gatita"—kitten—was what her grandmother had called her when she was a child. Andrés whoever-he-was had no right to use that nickname. No right.

"I don't generally welcome the advances of total strangers," she said.

"And if I were not a stranger?"

His question compelled her to relive the dream in all its astonishing detail. Why did it seem almost like a memory? Why was part of her so convinced that she had lain in Andrés's arms in another life?

Cat dug her fingers into the bark of the tree trunk. This was ridiculous. The dream didn't mean a thing, except that her fantasy life had become a little too vivid. Vivid enough to make her lose her hard-won control. Here she was, holding a normal conversation with a stranger who was clearly crazy and possibly dangerous.

Except he hadn't hurt her. He'd backed off when she told him to. For all her legal expertise, she couldn't define the man who crouched before her.

The best thing you can do now is be completely objective. Treat him as a hostile witness.

"Why did you follow me?" she asked.

"Follow you, *señorita?* But I did not."

"Are you saying you've been here all along?"

"No."

"How did you get here?"

"On my own feet."

Hostile, indeed. "Where do you live?"

"I call no place home."

No horse, no home, apparently no vehicle or significant belongings. But if he were truly an indigent, he'd probably be in much worse shape than he was. No one could claim he was anything but hardy, healthy, and unmistakably virile.

He could still be certifiably insane.

And what's so sane about the way you felt when he touched you, Catalina O'Roarke?

She folded her arms tightly across her chest. She'd slept through most of the afternoon and a good portion of the night, and yet her legs were growing heavy and her thoughts were sluggish. She was very much afraid that she'd begin to ramble if she tried to keep the conversation going much longer.

"You are tired," Andrés said. "Sleep, *gatita.* No harm will come to you."

Laughter bubbled out of her throat before she could stop it. "I think I'll stay awake, thank you very much."

Andrés stretched out where he was and made himself

comfortable, resting on his elbow. "You were not always so frightened," he said.

Cat straightened. "What the hell does that mean?"

"You are from *la ciudad*, are you not?"

"I'm from Los Angeles. What of it?"

"I have heard that your great cities have no soul, that those who live in them have forgotten the look of the sky and the feel of the earth."

"That's crazy." *Careful.* "Haven't you been to a city before?"

"*Sí.* Long ago, in another place." His gaze turned inward, remembering. "I had no love for them, even then. It is why I came to this continent."

"You're not from Mexico?"

His eyes cleared. "Did your own people not come from *Méjico*?"

"My grandmother was born there. She journeyed alone to the United States when she was sixteen."

"Was it she who named you?"

"Catalina was her name."

"Ah." He plucked a blade of dry, fringed grass from a clump near his shoulder. "Do you know its meaning?" He twirled the grass between his fingers. "Pure. Innocent. When did you lose your innocence, *mi gatita*? What is the name of the man who hurt you?"

"No one hurt me."

"Your eyes betray you, *querida*. Was he your *esposo*?"

"The subject is private."

He got to his feet with that same feral grace and approached her, hands loose at his sides. "He was not the man for you. He mistreated you. He gave you no pleasure."

Cat blinked, startled to realize that she was on the brink of tears. "He didn't . . . It had nothing to do with—"

"You would blame yourself?" He stopped with the tips of his boots touching hers, such gentleness in his expression that she could hardly bear it.

"No. I should never have . . . I thought I knew what I wanted."

"And still you do not know." He lifted his hand, his fingers lightly touching her cheek. "I could teach you."

Her mind told her to jerk away, but her body held her captive to his caresses. "I came here . . . to be alone."

"So alone." He leaned into her, lips parted. His body pressed her thighs and hip and breast. His mouth closed over hers, tongue seeking.

Cat plunged into a maelstrom of desire. She returned the kiss, panting with excitement. She had no defense when he seized both of her wrists and pulled them up above her head, trapping them against the cottonwood's trunk. He held her easily with one hand while his other stroked her face, trailed over her breasts and paused to unfasten the button of her jeans.

The rational part of Cat's brain knew how simple it would be for him to complete what he'd begun while she slept. How easy it would be to give in.

You want it. You want it more than you've ever wanted anything in your life.

His fingers slipped under her panties, teasing hot and swollen flesh.

"So wet," he murmured into her ear. "So ready for me."

"I . . . I don't . . ."

He traced her lips with his tongue while his fingers circled. "You do," he said. "Tell me, *gatita*. Tell me what you want."

She tried to answer, but he didn't wait. He withdrew his hand and began to push her jeans down her thighs, working her panties off as he cupped her bottom. He released her hands and held her with the weight of his body while he unzipped his jeans. The heat of his cock caressed her inner thigh, eased over slick flesh, thrust aggressively against her damp curls.

Sanity returned like a blast of icy wind. Panic gave Cat strength she didn't know she had. A sharp shove was enough to throw Andrés off balance. Cat stumbled away from the cottonwood and stopped, frozen by emotions that demanded more of her than she could ever give.

Andrés turned to face her, his expression unreadable. Slowly he bent and picked up her jeans. He tossed them toward her, and she caught them reflexively.

"I see that the time is not yet right," he said. "But it will come, Catalina. It will come."

Without another word he walked into the darkness. Cat pulled on her jeans, fingers numb and trembling. She could think of nothing but getting far away from this place, even if she had to walk all the way back to the ranch. It wasn't fear of Andrés that drove her. It was fear of herself.

With only the vaguest idea of direction, she began to run, her ears straining for sounds of pursuit. Andrés didn't follow. After ten minutes Cat's legs were aching and her lungs burned for air. She slowed to a jog and then a fast walk. The vast sky had paled to sapphire, the stars flickering out one by one.

She estimated that she'd gone about two miles when Trueno reappeared. He trotted up alongside her, neck arched and hooves dancing as if he had nothing for which to be ashamed.

Cat stopped, chilled by the sweat cooling on her body. "Where have you been?" she asked, more weary than angry. "You couldn't have picked a worse time to disappear."

Trueno gazed at her without the slightest hint of shame. Cat laughed. "Of course not. You're only an animal. I was the stupid one."

The stallion shook his head with broad movements of his neck and shoulders.

"Yes. Stupid. I guess I've learned my lesson." She began walking again, already contemplating what Turk and Pilar would say when she finally appeared at the ranch, windblown and limping from a bootful of blisters. Trueno slowed his walk to keep pace with her, occasionally lipping her collar or nickering in her ear. She pushed his head away.

"Someone must be missing you," she said. "Go home, horse."

He cut in front of her, pivoted around and butted her in the chest.

"Sorry. I'd rather walk this time."

Trueno fell back, pawing at her dusty footprints. She thought he'd finally gone, and an immense weight of sadness collected in the space beneath her ribs. But then the soft clop of his hooves resumed, and she found a little extra energy to keep walking. She spotted the dark band of exposed basalt that marked the deep gorge of the Rio Grande and set her course beside it.

Turk and another cowboy met her around midmorning. The old hand dismounted and hurried toward her, his face long with concern.

"Miss Cat! Are you all right?"

Her skin went hot. "I'm fine." She shoved her hands in her pockets. "Have you been looking for me?"

"Just about all night." He tipped his hat back on his head and subjected her to a thorough examination. She was almost certain that he knew exactly what she'd been doing . . . how close she'd come to making a very bad mistake.

"I'm really sorry," she said, staring at the toes of her boots. "It was very foolish of me to ride a horse I knew nothing about."

Turk frowned. "What horse?"

She turned around. Trueno was gone.

"It's a long story," she said. "I promise I won't let anything like this happen again."

Even Turk's unfailing courtesy couldn't quite conceal his skepticism. "You'll ride with me, Miss Cat." He addressed the other cowboy. "Thanks for the help, John. I'll take it from here."

The cowboy waved and rode off. Turk held out his hand, pulling Cat up behind him.

Pilar met them at the house, tight-lipped with concern.

Cat found it impossible to meet the older woman's gaze. She retreated to her room, still trying to make sense of the nonsensical.

It was almost as if her mysterious encounters with Andrés were about much more than just sex. She'd never before been in the least bit tempted to make love with a complete stranger; she couldn't dismiss the idea that her uncharacteristically wanton behavior had some rational basis.

Dreams aren't rational. There's no excuse for you, Catalina O'Roarke.

Night was slow in coming. Cat tossed and turned, imagining she felt invisible hands stroking her body. She got up, threw on her robe and went to the kitchen for a glass of milk.

Someone scratched on the front door.

Cat nearly dropped her glass. She set it down on the kitchen table, crept to the door, and checked the lock.

"Who is it?"

There was no answer. *Just your imagination.* But she was struck by the uncanny certainty that someone was waiting outside. Waiting for her.

Andrés.

Fear and anticipation held her paralyzed for a dozen heartbeats. She unlocked the door, holding her arm firm against the shaking of her fingers.

The porch was empty. Cat flipped on the light. A small, cloaked figure stood several yards away, dark eyes deeply set in a nut-brown face.

Cat released her breath. *"Buenos noches,"* she said. "Can I help you?"

The woman only stared. Cat stepped onto the porch, pulling her robe close around her throat. *"Necesitas ayuda?"*

Gnarled fingers shaped the sign of the cross. *"Bruja,"* the old woman whispered.

Witch. Cat remembered the word from the childhood stories

Abuelita had so delighted in telling her. "I don't understand," she said.

"*Cuidado conel caballo oscuro.*"

"*Qué?*"

"*Ha venido a jugar contigo.*" The woman backed away, clutching the crucifix about her neck. "*Cuidado. Cuidado!*"

"Wait!"

"What is it, Catalina?"

Pilar stood in the doorway behind her, peering sleepily over Cat's shoulder. "Who were you talking to?"

Cat drew Pilar back inside the house. "An old woman," she said. "I've never seen her before. She came out of nowhere, gave some kind of warning, and then disappeared."

"What did she say?"

"I didn't understand all of it. First she called me a witch, and then she said something about a horse. At least I think she did." Cat repeated the words the old woman had spoken.

"Beware the dark horse," Pilar translated. "He has come to deceive you."

All the warmth drained from Cat's body. *The dark horse.* "What . . . what do you think she meant?"

Pilar sat down at the table. "I have heard stories about a black horse that wanders the *meseta*, a great stallion who has never been caught. Some say he is a ghost, others a demon." She shook her head. "I myself have never seen the beast, but there is always talk, especially among the old."

"Why would the old woman come to warn *me*?"

"I don't know." Pilar met Cat's gaze. "This means nothing to you? Nothing at all?"

"I . . . may have seen this horse."

"Ah. Then perhaps you should heed the old woman's warning."

"You don't really believe it's a ghost or a demon?"

"No. But it does no harm to be careful."

Pilar returned to her room, preoccupied with her own musings. Cat made another attempt to sleep. Half-formed images of black horses and pale-eyed strangers flickered in and out of her consciousness. They seemed to blend together, hurling her into a dark space suspended between vision and nightmare.

The day of his return was the happiest in her life. His face was darker than she remembered, carved with deeper lines of sorrow, yet the joy came back into his eyes when he saw her. He shed his heavy armor and tight-fitting clothing, putting on the proper garments of the people.

The marriage was arranged as quickly as possible, taking into account the most auspicious days and the advice of the *tonalpouhqui*. The headman and elders were convinced that Andrés brought good luck with him; they provided him with a house, to which she went when the ceremonies were complete. They lay together on the reed mat, and once again she knew the ecstasy of his touch. . . .

The shout sent Cat bolting from her bed, scattering pillows across the polished hardwood floor. Several moments passed before she realized that the noise had come from her own throat.

The dreams were getting stronger. Cat didn't know how to stop them. She was beginning to believe they were something more than dreams. But what did they mean? What was that alien world where Andrés wore armor and rode a horse, and who was the girl?

Who am I?

Anxious to banish the alien memories, Cat plunged into the shower and stood under the spray until the hot water was gone. Then she dressed, snatched a piece of freshly baked bread from the kitchen, and looked desperately for a distraction.

It was Turk who provided one. "Morning, Miss Cat," he said, looking up from the tack he was mending. "Don't know if it would interest you, but there's a music festival going on in Taos this weekend. Mostly local stuff . . . folk and something called 'world music.' You're welcome to take the Dakota into town for a couple days."

Cat closed her eyes. "Bless you, Turk." She went back into the house, throwing a few pairs of shirts and jeans into her duffel. After a brief exchange with Pilar—during which neither one of them mentioned last night's peculiar visitation—Cat settled behind the wheel of the Dakota and drove south on the dirt road leading to State Route Sixty-Four.

Taos was a colorful village, vivid with Hispanic and Native American influence, a little rustic in spite of the thriving arts community that revealed itself in numerous studios and gift shops around the Plaza. The majority of the buildings were adobe or mock-adobe, painted in tones of terra-cotta, turquoise, and gold. Hollyhocks and blanket flowers graced neatly fenced gardens.

The narrow streets were busier than usual, clogged with out-of-towners arriving for the music festival. Cat found a room in a modest motel at the southern edge of town, tossed her duffel on the bed and headed out to explore.

Though Cat had spent most of her life in the dynamic world of urban Los Angeles, she found Taos no less stimulating. The locals were easygoing and sometimes eccentric, reminding her of people she'd met in Berkeley and San Francisco. The mood was both peaceful and inspiring.

She felt remarkably free as she rambled about the town, stopping as the mood struck her, listening to a Mariachi band in Kit Carson Park and Finnish folk music at an eclectic coffee house. She had a sandwich and iced tea for lunch, browsed shops on the plaza for several hours and then decided to have a drink at a bar off Paseo del Pueblo. She found music there as well; a young, long-haired man perched on a stool in the corner and played melancholy airs on a Native American flute.

Cat claimed an empty bar stool and sat, feeling in great good charity with the world. Though she seldom enjoyed beer, she tried a pale ale from a local microbrewery and found it quite congenial. She'd just started on the second glass when the young flautist stepped down and another musician took his place. She didn't pay much attention until she heard the first golden strains of the guitar, beginning a melody rich with the distant and exotic sounds of another age.

The voice that accompanied the music sang in liquid Spanish, a voice she recognized even before she turned to see the man who owned it.

Even from his corner, Andrés dominated the room. He sat with one knee drawn up, cradling the guitar like a lover while his fingers danced over the strings. He sang with such intensity and sorrow that every eye in the room was drawn to him, yet he never glanced up from his intricate finger work. The melody curled around Cat like a silken rope, binding her limbs and her loins and her heart.

"Do you understand the song?"

She started, turning toward the bar. The bartender, a man of middle years and a slight Spanish accent, leaned on the scarred wood and nodded toward the singer.

"It is a very old song," he said. "The words he sings are from an ancient form of Spanish . . . one only scholars would know today."

"Really?" Cat said, feeling stupid and confused. "Is he a scholar?"

"He doesn't look like one, does he? But looks can deceive." He smiled. "I was a teacher myself, once. Shall I translate?"

"Please."

The bartender began to recite.

> " 'I don't know how I can reveal to you
> the ardent fire
> that burns me to the bone
> and I can't see any time or place;
> alas, I'm burning in the fire
> without any comfort.' "

Cat shivered. She could almost imagine that Andrés was singing directly to her. But surely he hadn't even noticed her. Surely the fact that they were together in this bar was the sheerest coincidence. . . .

Andrés looked up. His gaze met hers.

"Do you know him?" the bartender asked.

"No." She heard her own trepidation and deliberately turned her back on Andrés. "Do you?"

"I've never seen him here before. Would you like me to ask around?"

"No. No, that's all right, thanks." She placed several small bills on the bar and headed for the door.

"Where're you going so fast, beautiful?"

The man at the table caught Cat's arm and held on, stopping her in her tracks. He was blond, muscular, and handsome; plenty of women would have been flattered by his attention. Cat wasn't.

"Excuse me," she said, shaking him off.

"Hey. No need to be so unfriendly." He gave her a dazzling grin and patted the chair beside him. "Have a seat. I'll get you whatever you want."

"Sorry. I've got . . . things to do."

"It can't be all that urgent. Come on." He grabbed the hem of her jacket and tugged. She lost her balance and banged her hip on the table. The blond looped his arm around her waist and pulled her against him. Cat could smell the alcohol on his breath.

"I'd advise you to let me go," she said.

"Advise?" He laughed. "You a lawyer or something?"

"As a matter of fact, I am."

He rolled his eyes. "Oooh. I'm seared." He pushed her into the chair. "You need some loosening up, princess. And I'm just the man to do it."

"You will unhand the lady, *cabrón*, or you will regret it."

The jerk looked up into Andrés's face with blank incomprehension. "What did you call me?"

"Do you require a translation, *pajero?*" Andrés glanced at Cat. "Are you hurt, *señorita?*"

"No." She scrambled up and backed away. "It's all right. I was just leaving."

All her hopes of defusing the situation were shattered when the blond stood up, toppling his chair behind him. He towered over Andrés by a good six inches, and he was nearly twice as wide. "You shouldn't have stuck your nose where it don't belong," he said, flexing his muscles.

"The lady is with me," Andrés said.

"That so?" He turned to Cat. "This is what you like? Some pansy musician pretending to be a man?"

Andrés met Cat's gaze. "Go outside, *mi gatita.*"

"Only if you come with me."

"When this is finished."

"That won't take long," the blond said. He beckoned to Andrés. "Go ahead, faggot. Just be careful not to hurt your pretty little fingers."

He had barely lifted his own massive fists when Andrés struck, hitting the blond with a series of punches that snapped his head from side to side as if it were made of rubber. The bigger man crashed into the table and collapsed to the floor, sprawling in an ungainly heap.

The bartender appeared beside Cat. "You'd better get him out of here," he said, nodding toward Andrés. "I know this guy, and he's trouble. I don't want a brawl."

"Of course. I'll pay for any damages." Cat took Andrés's arm, feeling the muscles bunched beneath his shirt sleeve. "Please, Andrés. Let's go."

He regarded her with a wild look and suddenly relaxed. "As you wish, *mi gatita.*"

Together they left the bar. It had grown dark; the plaza twinkled with lights that rivaled the stars. Cat paused to get her bearings.

"Where shall we go?" Andrés said close to her ear. "Have you a bed, *querida?*"

Prickles of excitement raced from the back of Cat's neck to the base of her spine. "Thanks for your attempt to help back there, but it really wasn't necessary."

"That *cabrón* was mistreating you."

"I could have handled it."

"Few men are to be trusted by a woman alone."

She turned to stare at him, challenging her own unease. "Does that include you?"

"Is that not for you to decide, *amada?*"

The very sound of his voice was a caress. Cat retreated several steps. "I don't know why you just happened to be here in Taos, but I came to spend some time alone. That's what I intend to do."

Andrés searched her eyes. "If that is what you truly wish."

"It is. Good-bye." She began to walk away, feeling his gaze like fire licking between her shoulder blades. Only when she was in the parking lot of her motel did she let down her guard. She ran up the stairs to her room on the second floor, went inside and leaned against the door, her breath coming fast and shallow.

It wasn't a coincidence. She was certain of that. Andrés hadn't been here just to join the music festival. Either he'd followed her, or he'd known somehow. . . .

And that's ridiculous. He couldn't have.

Cat flung herself down on the bed, grabbed a pillow and hugged it to her chest. No matter where she went, she couldn't escape: not Andrés, not this feeling that made her wish she'd invited him up to her room and let him have his way with her. She could imagine his lean, muscular body naked beside her, his cock hard and high, his eyes blazing with lust the way Neal's never had. She saw herself lying on a reed mat beside him, enjoying the pleasures of their wedding night. . . .

She pounded the pillow with her fists. She was wet again, desperate for release that wouldn't come. It was too early to sleep. She jumped up, paced the small room for a quarter of an hour, turned on the television to some abominable made-for-TV movie, and finally decided on a nice, long, hot shower.

The bathtub was hardly luxurious . . . one of those featureless molded plastic stalls that was about as welcoming as a tombstone in a graveyard. Cat was too muddled to care. She turned on the spray to its hottest, shed her clothes and stepped in with a sigh of relief.

But her mind would not be still. The water cascading over her breasts and hips made her shiver. Her body was transformed, as if she had become a creature of pure sensuality. She stroked her stomach, suddenly fascinated by the slight mound that had never matched the washboard ideal but now seemed a proclamation of her womanhood. She cupped her breasts, circling her nipples until they rose to firm peaks. She turned her face up into the water and let it cascade over her face while her fingers skimmed down her thighs and came to rest on warm, plump flesh.

Andrés. Oh, God, Andrés.

Her imagination was so vivid that she could almost hear the shower curtain sliding aside, feel the heat of a body behind her, masculine hands resting on her waist and massaging her hips. She could feel his tongue licking moisture from her neck as his cock worked between her parted thighs.

"Mi gatita," he whispered.

She turned, eyes tightly closed. He put his hands on her shoulders and kissed her urgently, tangling his tongue with hers. After an eternity of such kisses he bent his head, following the slope of her chest lower, lower, until his tongue found her breast.

"You want more, *querida?"* he murmured.

"God. Oh, God. Yes."

He flicked the tip of her nipple and then took her into his mouth. The cool plastic of the shower stall supported Cat's weight as he suckled, first one breast and then the other, demanding, devouring. He wedged his hands behind her bottom, squeezing, lifting. His cock was trapped between them, hot and heavy. He withdrew to reposition himself and worked her thighs apart. She made no attempt to resist. He rubbed against her, the head of his cock caressing her swollen lips.

"What do you want?" he asked. "Tell me."

"I . . ." She gasped as he pushed a little deeper and then pulled back. "Please . . ." Someone knocked on the door.

Cat came crashing back to reality. She staggered and clutched at the shower curtain to keep her balance. There was no one else in the shower. She was alone, silently screaming for deliverance.

The knock sounded again. Cat half stumbled out of the tub and reached for the towels folded on the rack above the toilet. They were barely big enough to cover her from breast to upper thigh.

The door seemed a million miles away. She leaned against it and looked through the peephole.

"Who is it?"

But she knew even before he answered, his voice all seductive music.

She hesitated for a second, two. Then she opened the door. She didn't ask how he'd found her, or why he had come. She grabbed his hand, dragged him into the room, and kissed him.

His reaction was everything it had been in her dream. He thrust with his tongue as he stripped the towel from her body and tossed it aside, leading her to the bed. She went willingly, expecting him to shed his clothes and take her then and there. Instead, he knelt at the foot of the bed, pulled her toward him, and spread her thighs. His lips pressed against her vulva, then his tongue stroked over the moist folds of her labia. She couldn't remember the last time she had experienced such a sensation or wanted it so much.

Andrés licked upward and found her clitoris, already distended and burning with something very near pain. But he didn't touch it. He kissed her mons, driving her crazy with need.

"You taste of wine and honey," he purred.

Cat groaned. "Don't stop."

He bent and drew her into his mouth. She arched up, demanding more. His teeth grazed her, his tongue fluttered and teased, bringing closer, ever closer to the release she had so desperately craved. He thrust his tongue deep inside her. She spiraled toward climax, higher and higher.

And once again Andrés denied her. He stood and began to unbutton his shirt, revealing his beautifully developed pecs. Cat couldn't take her eyes from him. He removed the shirt, folded it and draped it over the chair by the window. Then he unbuttoned his jeans. The zipper slid down with a sensual hiss. He wore nothing underneath. His cock sprang free, bigger than even Cat's fantasies had predicted.

His jeans fell to the floor and he kicked them away. His cock arced high against his stomach, ridged below and capped with the silky-smooth head. Cat's thighs slackened in anticipation. Andrés knelt on the bed and positioned himself between her legs. He worked his fingers inside her. She bucked and moaned. He stretched out atop her, his cock gliding easily over the slickness of her sex. She strained against him, urging him to end her torment.

Deliberately he rubbed himself over her, glazing his cock in her wetness. His lips closed over her nipple just as they had in her shower dream, circling her breast while he flicked at the aching tip with his tongue.

Cat was delirious with pleasure and pain. She felt a vast, searing emptiness that only Andrés could fill. She lifted her legs higher, praying that his next move would send him thrusting into her. But he held his body still and kissed her mouth with the greatest tenderness.

"Andrés," she whispered.

He licked her chin. "I told you once that I would not do anything you did not wish me to do," he said, his voice husky with lust. "Tell me what you want."

But Cat didn't speak. She pushed him away and kept

pushing until he was forced off the bed. He stood there, uncertain for the first time, his eyes reflecting much more than disappointment.

Cat moved to the foot of the bed, sat on the edge and took Andrés's cock into her mouth. He gasped in surprise and pleasure. He laced his fingers through her hair and held on as she sucked and licked and tugged, moving his hips as his breathing quickened.

Within a few minutes he was rigid and ready to come. But he drew back, panting hoarsely. He lifted her to her feet, turned her around and laid her face-down on the bed. Strong, calloused hands raised her hips and buttocks, holding her in place.

"Are you ready?" he asked softly.

"Yes. Oh, God . . ."

He hesitated, and for a shattering moment she thought he was going to leave her. But then, without warning, he drove into her from behind. She moaned his name. He withdrew, taking a firmer grip on her hips, and thrust again. His movements slowed. He pulled out, waited, and then slid inside with astonishing gentleness. He was massaging her to orgasm, but she didn't want it soft. She'd gone too far.

"Harder," she begged.

He continued to move with steady strokes. "We have waited so long," he said. "We can wait a little longer."

Just when Cat believed she could tolerate no more Andrés began to pump more urgently, rocking her forward with each thrust. She gasped as he reached beneath their joining and rubbed her in time to his driving rhythm. The climax was so overwhelming that she cried aloud, her body glorying in sensations she'd never known before.

Andrés remained inside her. She expected him to soften, but his cock was still firm and full. Somehow he'd brought her to orgasm without enjoying one himself.

"Andrés," she said, her voice shaking with reaction. "You didn't . . . you need to . . ."

He brushed damp hair from the back of her neck. "I will,

mi gatita." He wrapped his arms around her waist and turned her to face him, adjusting her legs so that she was sitting on his lap with his cock trapped between them.

Cat touched his face from the angle of his cheekbone to the straight line of his dark brows. "I never thought it could be like this."

"It is not over, *querida."*

She found his erection with her fingertips, caressing the velvety head. "Tell me what *you* want."

A shudder ran through him. "Forgive me."

"For what?" She leaned her cheek against his chest. "You've given me something . . . I didn't even know could exist. Neal . . ." She bit down hard on her lip, cursing herself for even mentioning her ex-husband's name.

But Andrés was untroubled. "You have never had a real man before. This I knew when we first met."

She drew back and met his gaze. "But why me? Why did you seek me out? Who *are* you, Andrés?"

He put his finger to her lips, lifted her and eased her down onto his cock. She was so wet that there was no discomfort; she felt a tingle as if she might come all over again. But when she began to move, sliding up and down, he stopped her.

With casual strength he rose from the bed, holding her impaled, and carried her to the wall. He clasped his hands around her cheeks and supported her as if she weighed no more than cottonwood down. He held her tight as he entered her, and she recognized with disbelief that she was on the edge of another incredible orgasm. She clasped her legs around his waist, moving with him. He closed his eyes and worked until beads of sweat stood out on his forehead, plunging, grinding, pounding. The glorious pulsing started in the pit of Cat's belly.

"Let it go," she whispered. "Come to me."

For a moment he gazed right into her eyes, and she saw pain and desperation and centuries of suffering.

"Forgive me," he said hoarsely.

"Yes. Yes. I forgive—"

He stiffened, the muscles of his stomach standing out in

harsh relief, his hips slamming against hers. He finished with a cry of triumph, gathering her against him as his shuddering came to an end.

Cat dropped her chin on to his shoulder, breathless and exultant. Andrés kissed her mouth and forehead and carried her back to the bed. He laid her down with her head on the pillow and smoothed the tangled sheets over her, tucking the edges under her chin as if she were a child. Then he backed away, his eyes still full of sorrow.

"Don't go," she said, reaching for his hand.

He glanced toward the window. "There is little time."

"Time for what?" She tried to push the sheets away, but he pressed her back and sat on the edge of the bed with a sigh.

"Perhaps it is over," he said. "Perhaps there will be no change."

"What change?"

Instead of answering he stretched out beside her and tucked her head into the curve of his arm. "Rest now, *mi gatita.*"

Cat realized that she was exhausted, not only by the vigorous sex but also by emotions she couldn't quite comprehend. A minute ago Andrés had been dominant, guiding and controlling their lovemaking with her full cooperation. But now he was something else entirely: tender, solicitous, and melancholy in a way that made her want to take him in her arms and tell him everything was going to be all right.

"You won't go?" she asked sleepily.

He kissed her forehead and brushed his fingers over her eyelids. "Sleep."

The *caballos* charged into the village, nostrils flared and teeth bared like the fangs of the jaguar ready to slaughter its prey. Their riders were gods of destruction and malice, helmets and weapons flashing as they trampled the villagers who came to meet them.

Itzel stood at the door of her house, mouth open to cry out. No sound would come. Men she had known all her life collapsed into the dust, great gaping wounds spilling blood bright as forest flowers. Women screamed and fled, some falling under the horses' hooves, others dragged by their hair to be violated and cast aside. Children wept. And yet the conquerors slew on, laughing and merciless.

Filled with despair, she turned to the one who stood behind her. She begged Andrés to stop those with whom he had once ridden, to save the village from their murderous rampage.

But Andrés didn't move. He stared, his skin the color of bleached bone, his eyes no longer the hue of clear water but swallowed up in obsidian black. He had become like some forgotten stone idol, unable or unwilling to interfere in the fates of men. Only when one of the *conquistadores*, his hair golden as the sun, drove his huge mount toward the house and reached for Itzel did Andrés act. He pushed her behind him and looked up at the man on the horse. He spoke words in the enemy tongue. Hair-of-the-Sun laughed again, spun his beast about and rode away, his followers behind him.

Itzel staggered from the doorway, her eyes glazed with horror. She knelt beside the lifeless body of her brother and stroked the matted hair from the terrible gash across his forehead. There were a few others left alive; they, like her, wandered from one body to the next, searching for those they had loved.

Much time passed before Itzel turned back to the house. Andrés still waited there, empty as one whose heart had been given in sacrifice to the gods.

She had loved him. She had made the others see that he was not like those he had abandoned. But she had been wrong. He was no different.

"Itzel," he whispered, his voice a broken husk. But she felt no pity. She came to stand before him, fists clenched at her sides.

"You have betrayed us," she said.

"No. I . . ."

"You did not stop them. For this . . ." She closed her eyes. "For this you must pay."

For the first time in many suns she drew upon the powers her grandmother and mother had passed to her, powers bestowed by the earth and the sky. "You will suffer as you have watched the people suffer," she said. "Your kind are bound to the great beasts you call *caballos*. Now you shall run as such a beast for all the days of your life, walking as a man only at night. But you shall not die. You shall have no relief until one of my blood forgives you for your cowardice this day."

Andrés heard her, but he did not believe. She saw that in his eyes. But a few minutes of daylight remained; he grew taut, the curse beginning to work its way through his body.

Itzel turned her back on him and walked away, ignoring the wordless cries of agony and terror as Andrés lost his ability to speak with a human voice. The last she heard of him was the drumming of his hooves as he fled into the forest.

Cat shot up in the bed, her heart hammering and her breath locked in her throat. It took several moments before she recognized the room around her.

Andrés stood by the window, his shoulder propped against the wall as he gazed outside. Tension had turned the muscle of torso and buttock and thigh to sculpted stone. He still looked exactly the same as he had in that other, ancient world. Not even his name was different.

He had begged her forgiveness. She had given it, unthinking, never questioning why he had asked. From the very beginning he'd tried to seduce her while revealing as little about himself as he could get away with. Suddenly she had a reason for his behavior.

Incredulous laughter roiled in Cat's stomach like an over-rich meal. *It isn't possible.* But Andrés had appeared only when Trueno had vanished. And the black stallion hadn't returned until daylight.

Coincidence, no more. Yet the anger from the dream was a bleak knot in Cat's chest. She felt Itzel's despair, the agony she had experienced when she'd placed the spell on the man she loved.

If it were true—if, in spite of every rule of logic, Andrés and the black horse were one—then he had deceived her from the first moment they'd met. The only reason he'd have asked her to forgive him was if he'd believed that Itzel's "blood" ran in her veins. He'd arrogantly assumed that the way to control a female was to give her a good banging. He'd made her so helpless with passion that she'd hand him anything he asked.

Even her love.

She got out of bed, dragging the top sheet from the mattress and wrapping it around her body.

"Trueno," she said. "It's almost daylight."

Andrés looked at her . . . only for an instant, barely long enough for her to see the flash of shock in his eyes when he recognized the trap she had set. He smiled, though it was too late.

"Mi gatita," he said. "You have been dreaming."

"Yes." She walked toward him, righteous fury flowing through her body. "Very vivid dreams. Dreams of a man who would not defend those who had welcomed him."

The color drained from Andrés's face. "Catalina . . ."

"Don't lie to me." She stopped inches away, holding his gaze. "I saw it all. I saw *her.*"

"Itzel," he whispered.

"Yes." She let her heart become a block of ice. *"You* are Trueno."

He must have known then that denial would do him no good. "Yes," he said, despair weighting the word like an anchor thrown to a drowning man.

Cat didn't falter. "You must have been looking for centuries . . . looking for someone who could lift the curse. Then you discovered me. Somehow you knew that Itzel was my distant kin. You needed to win my forgiveness by any means necessary."

"No. It is not so simple, *queri*—"

"*Do* you have an excuse, Andrés? She loved you, and you let them destroy everything she cared about."

"Have I not paid enough?" He reached out to touch her face. "Listen to me. It was five hundred years—"

She jerked free. "Maybe if you'd been honest, if you'd really tried to atone . . . but you set out to use me instead."

"No. When I first saw you . . . your grace, your strength . . . I could not help . . . could not help but—"

"It's too late, Andrés. I won't play."

"Catalina. I beg of you . . ." His voice thinned, and he grabbed at his throat. His skin began to ripple as if every muscle and tendon beneath were attempting to assume a new shape. He fell against the wall, pushed away violently and staggered toward the door, his hands extended before him.

Cat rushed after him, ready to take back every word she'd spoken. But Andrés flung open the door and rushed onto the landing. He stumbled downstairs into the parking lot. Cat dashed back into the room and threw on jeans and a shirt. She practically fell down the stairs. The black stallion stood trembling among the trucks and SUVs, his coat shining with sweat.

"Andrés!"

He looked toward her, ears flat against his head, and spun on his hind legs. Before she'd taken another step he'd set off at a wild gallop toward the weedy field that backed the smattering of motels, fast-food joints and garages to the west. Dawn had just broken; cars on the road were sparse, and only a few early-rising souls noticed the saddleless horse charging across the street.

Cat slumped, cursing her pride and the implacable judgment that had driven him away. Even if she got right into

Turk's truck and drove as fast as she could, she knew she'd never catch up with him. He could cover terrain no vehicle could manage. And he had every reason to run and keep running until sunset found him human again, friendless and alone.

There was no reason in the world for him to come back. She'd given him not a shred of hope.

And all her hope had gone with him.

She checked out quickly, tossed her duffel in the truck and drove back to the ranch by a circuitous route, indifferent about when she arrived or what she'd do once she got there. She pulled up in front of the ranch house well after noon, as weary as if she'd walked all the way from Taos.

Turk tapped on the window. She rolled it down and summoned a smile.

"Back so soon?" he asked. "Thought you might be spending the weekend in town."

"I had a good time, but I think I may be coming down with something. If I have to be sick, I'd rather be sick in my own room."

"Sorry to hear it, Miss Cat. I'll put the truck away." He opened the door for her and took her place in the driver's seat. Cat looped the duffel over her shoulder and plodded toward the house. Pilar met her in the kitchen, the housekeeper's hands and lower arms coated with flour. A ball of pie dough sat on a wooden board beside the sink.

"Catalina!" Pilar hastily washed her hands and dried them on a thick cotton towel. "How was the festival?"

"It was fine." Cat dropped into a chair and stared at the pretty bouquet of wildflowers Pilar had set on the table. "I just . . . got a little lonely."

"Ah?" Pilar rubbed at a patch of flour left on a fingernail. "Did you find no one to keep you company?"

The inevitable blush burned Cat's cheeks. Pilar nodded gravely. "I saw the change in you the night Kelpie came back lame. I see it even more strongly now. Who is he?"

Cat found that she had no desire to pretend any longer. "I met him that night. He helped with Kelpie, and—" She broke off, unable to describe how she'd felt that first time. "He was . . . is . . . unlike any man I've ever known."

"What is his name? Where does he live?"

All of Pilar's questions were logical, but the answers would tell her nothing. "His name is Andrés," she said. "I don't think he has a home."

"Yet he has won your heart."

Pilar's words, so simple and blunt, stopped the air in Cat's lungs. She tried to stand and fell back again, her muscles gone weak and useless.

She'd known Andrés all of three days. It just wasn't possible to fall in love so quickly. But she'd never believed in curses or men who could change into horses, either.

"He was not what you expect to find when you came to us," Pilar said.

"No."

"Your mind tells you to stay away, yet you cannot." The older woman placed a plump hand on Cat's shoulder. "Has he done you some wrong, this Andrés? A wrong you can't forgive?"

How could Pilar possibly have guessed? Andrés had betrayed Itzel. He'd let her people die while he stood by, refusing to intervene. His punishment had been no less than he deserved.

But that isn't why you turned on him. It isn't what happened hundreds of years ago that matters, is it? It's what he did to you, how he deceived and manipulated you. . . .

"Perhaps you came to us for a reason," Pilar said. "Not only to find love, but to free yourself from your own past."

And to free Andrés as well.

Cat jumped to her feet. "I have to go out, Pilar. Don't expect me back before dawn."

The housekeeper nodded, smiled, and returned to her pie crust. Cat grabbed several bottles of water and a chunk of cheese from the refrigerator, fetched a blanket from her room and ran outside to look for Turk. When she didn't find him, she saddled a mare and placed the blanket, food and a supply of oats in a pair of saddlebags she hung over the mare's hindquarters.

Rosie was more than ready to cooperate with Cat's eagerness to be gone. Cat rode north toward the Colorado border, certain that Andrés would head away from civilization. She paused at five to drink and eat and rest the mare, refusing to give up hope.

By eight the sun was beginning to set. Cat had no idea how far she'd gone; the countryside had hardly changed, and she'd encountered only cattle, horses, and a few pronghorn antelope. Her legs ached, and Rosie was beginning to droop.

Cat dismounted at the foot of a small hill, stretched, and left Rosie to graze while she finished off the last bottle of water. Her heart was a leaden weight in her chest. She couldn't continue with only the supplies remaining in the saddlebags; when morning came she'd have to turn around. The chances that she'd find Andrés were growing smaller by the moment.

Wearily she spread the blanket on the brown grass and lay down. She had just closed her eyes when Rosie nickered softly. Half afraid to hope, Cat opened her eyes again.

The stallion stood at the top of the hill, the plume of his tail stirring in the evening breeze. Cat rose, adrenaline rushing through her body.

Come, she begged silently. *Come to me.*

For a handful of minutes it seemed he would turn and flee. But slowly, hesitantly, he started down the hill, head lowered and ears pressed flat. He stopped several yards away, his eyes filled with that very human sadness.

"Andrés," Cat whispered.

His ears flickered, but he came no nearer. Cat offered her upturned hands.

"I was wrong," she said. "You've paid enough. It's time you had a second chance."

The stallion lifted his head. An eldritch light sprang up around him, gilding his coat and crackling the grass under his hooves.

Cat was never sure what she saw then. Andrés changed; four legs became two, and the ebon mane became a shock of thick, dark hair. He stood naked before her, still silent, still waiting.

Love and desire tangled in Cat's mind, one inseparable from the other. She, too, had been transformed.

"We forgive you," she said. "I forgive you, Andrés. Be free."

He began to shake, and she realized he was laughing. His voice boomed in a cry of triumph and joy. He opened his arms and she walked into them, breathing in the sharp, clean scent of his body.

"*Mi gatita*," he said, taking her face between his hands. "*Gracias. Gracias desde el fondó de mi corazón.*" He searched her eyes. "How may I repay you?"

In answer she kissed him, her hand wandering between them to stroke his erect cock. "If you really want to repay me," she murmured, "don't make me wait a second longer."

She took his hand and led him to the blanket. He removed her clothing with something like reverence, worshiping her body with lips and tongue. But when he parted her thighs to enter, she rolled over and pushed him onto his back.

"It's my turn now," she said, and mounted him with a groan of pleasure.

That night she had the ride of her life. And when it was over and they lay together gazing up at the fading stars, she knew Itzel was at peace.

"Stay with me," she said. "Stay with me forever."

He traced her lips with his fingertip. "Forever is a long time."

"Not nearly long enough."

"You hardly know me. How can you be sure—"

"Let me show you just how sure I am."

And they rode together, bound as one, until they could ride no farther.

TO DIE FOR

Keri Arthur

CHAPTER 1

THE WORST THING ABOUT WORKING FOR AN INVES-
tigative agency specializing in paranormal and psychic
events was the long, often irregular, hours.

My field of expertise might be missing persons rather
than things that went bump in the night, but it still involved
late nights and long shifts. Monsters mostly preferred the
cover of darkness, it seemed.

But the second worst thing about working for the afore-
mentioned agency was having a boss who had no respect for
the "eight hours between shifts" rule, made law years ago.

So when Frank's phone call woke me up after I'd barely been
asleep for three hours, I was neither happy nor surprised.

"Rioli?" he said, his voice more gravelly than usual.
Meaning he'd either been up all night or he'd hit the smokes
again. "Need you in here ASAP."

"Frank, I only just got home from the Harbor case—"

"This one's important, Grace. Be here by seven."

I glared blearily at the clock. He'd given me a whole
thirty minutes. How generous of him. I hung up, dragged
myself out of bed, and threw on some clothes. Luckily for us
both, the traffic at that hour of a Sunday morning was practically nonexistent, and I found a parking spot right out in
front of the agency's multistory building.

It turns out I wasn't the only investigator Frank had called in early. And when I heard the rapid tattoo of footsteps coming up behind me, I barely restrained a groan. There was only one man in this building who could make the mere act of walking sound so sexy, and I really wasn't in the mood to cope with his banter this morning.

"Hey, Ravioli, wait up."

"Ravioli is a food," I said tartly, not breaking stride as I headed for the elevator. "And my name is Rioli. I'd appreciate it if you'd actually remember that."

"Are you always this touchy in the mornings?" he asked, his voice so warm, so rich, that shivers of delight ran down my spine.

But then, I'd been supersensitive to this man's presence from the moment he'd walked elegantly—and oh-so sexily—into the Preternatural Investigations offices eighteen months ago. Luckily for me, I was not alone in my admiration, and Ethan had wasted no time dipping into the pool, so to speak. The man was a werewolf who knew how to work both his aura and his lean, powerful body. He was sex on a stick, as one of my cubicle mates had noted. Right before she'd taken him home and enjoyed his stick.

Thankfully, I'd been spared the grittier details of their activities the following morning. I had imagination enough when it came to Ethan.

Which wasn't to say I'd never been tempted to do *more* than imagine, but I often worked with the man on missing persons investigations. Unless you were very lucky, mixing business and pleasure always got messy.

Not that I'd actually *mind* a little of Ethan's mess every now and again.

I blew out a breath and punched the elevator button. Control. I needed control. Ethan would smell the merest hint of arousal, and that would only stir his interest more. And I needed that like I needed a hole in the head. Especially when it had been so damn long since I'd had anything decent in the way of sex.

Weres of any breed might be free and easy when it came to sex, but I was a wolf *shifter*, and my parents were depressingly old-fashioned when it came to the whole mating act. Though I was pretty sure I could shake their overly strict sensibilities if the right man and moment came along. Ethan certainly *wasn't* that man, hence the cobwebs and me feeling hornier than a bitch in heat whenever he got within hormonal radar distance.

I punched the button again. As usual, the damn elevator was taking its freaking time getting here.

"Or is it just me that brings out the worst in you?" he continued, from right behind me.

I took a breath that was filled with the warm, spicy scent of him, then slowly turned to meet the vivid blue of his gaze. A gaze that was too bright, and saw too much. A gaze that never gave much away, no matter what the situation.

But Ethan Garrison wasn't just sex on a stick, he was ex-military, and a dangerous man despite his to-die-for smile. He was dressed in black this morning, his roughly rolled up shirtsleeves emphasizing the strength of his shoulders and upper arms, while his close-fitting jeans paid homage to the long, lean length of his legs. Even his boots and baseball cap were black. With his golden hair and skin, it was a potent combination.

"Going for the bad boy look today, are we?" I said, more to break the tension that always seemed to build between us than from any real need to talk to the man.

"Heard you liked a bit of bad. Thought it worth a shot." His grin was pure cheek, and crinkles of amusement touched the corners of his bright, watchful eyes.

A combination that had my hormones doing happy little cartwheels.

"The bad boy is getting no closer to me than the other incarnations you've dreamt up," I said, and wished my words would come out less breathy. "You and I work together. That's enough."

One dark eyebrow rose as he stepped a little closer. "Care to take a bet on that, Ravioli?"

The sheer heat of him slid across my senses like a caress. A caress I *so* wanted. My heart was doing a triple-time dance and desire not only swirled through me, but around me. His nose flared and a lusty spark ignited deep in his eyes. Damn, I was in trouble now.

Still, I raised my chin. Defiant to the end, that was me. "I don't bet." Especially when I was likely to lose.

"Shame that. I enjoy a challenge."

"Then I challenge you to take a flying leap out of a twentieth-floor window and make like a bird."

He smiled, and my breath caught somewhere in my throat and refused to budge. Smiles like that should be declared lethal weapons.

"You'd miss me if I did."

"Yeah," I said, forcing a note of dryness into my voice. "Like I'd miss a proverbial pain in the butt."

His gaze slid downwards. "And a very nice butt it is, too."

The chime of the elevator arriving saved me from answering. I gave a silent sigh of relief—then wondered why as the doors opened, revealing the empty interior. Confined elevator spaces and Ethan were not a wise combination right now.

"Are you going to stand there gawking all day?" he asked, voice dry and a knowing smile touching his lips.

It was a thought. Not a practical one but a thought all the same.

I stepped inside and punched the tenth-floor button. "What floor you going to?"

"Tenth, same as you."

He stopped beside me, so close he made me burn.

Damn, damn, damn.

I stepped back, trying to get some space between us, trying to cool my overheated body. "So Frank *has* called you in?"

"Yes. Something urgent has come up."

Oh, I had *no* doubt about that, I thought, my gaze detouring briefly down his long, lean length. Man, what I wouldn't give to be able . . . I wrenched my mind away from *that* particular direction and tried to think of boring things in an effort to calm my pulse.

Only nothing boring would come to mind.

The doors slid closed and the elevator began to rise at what seemed like a snail's pace. Ethan took a step towards me. I couldn't help taking another one back—though there weren't many places I could go in such a confined space. I pressed my back against the cool steel wall and watched him almost breathlessly. Anticipating his touch, even though common sense suggested he was only teasing. After all, there wasn't much he could do in an elevator in the space of ten floors.

Was there?

He moved closer. My breath stuttered to a brief stop. Like a rabbit caught in a spotlight, I watched as he bracketed his hands on either side of my head. Then he leaned forward, sending my senses into a spiral of delight. My nipples hardened, as if reaching out to brush his body. Which they couldn't, because he wasn't *that* close.

Part of me wished he was. Wished I could just melt against all that warm, hard flesh and allow my fingers the freedom to roam. But that would only be asking for more than I could probably handle.

So I raised a hand and simply pressed it against his chest, stopping him from coming closer. Even through the soft silk of his shirt, his muscles felt like iron under my fingertips, and my skin itched with the need to feel, to caress.

"Don't," I said. Unfortunately, my voice came out husky and that only ignited the spark in his eyes all the more.

"Don't what?" he said, his breath a whisper across my cheeks. "Do this?"

His weight pressed against my hand, a gentle force I suddenly couldn't stop and couldn't resist. My aching nipples finally came in contact with the softness of his shirt, and something akin to electricity shot through my body. Lord, it felt good. And he was so close, so tempting, and his lips there, right there, right within tasting distance.

Oh, how I wanted to taste them.

And he knew it, damn him.

"Or this?" he added, then brushed his mouth across mine.

It felt like the touch of fire. Or maybe it was only me who burned, not him. Not his delicious lips.

"You want me, Ravioli," he murmured. His lips moved from my mouth to my chin then my neck, tasting, teasing, arousing. I closed my eyes, savoring the heat zinging across every fiber of my being.

"Go on, admit it."

I didn't have to admit anything, especially when the scent of my arousal was so damn obvious.

"How can I want a man who can't even remember my name?" I somehow managed to say.

His lips brushed the pulse point at the base of my neck, sending a tremor through my limbs, then continued down, following the V of my shirt. I closed my eyes, torn between the sweet desire of his kisses, and the knowledge that I needed to push him away before this got out of hand.

And it *would* get out of hand. He was a werewolf *and* an alpha, and the wolf within me just couldn't help reacting to the power and masculinity of his presence. Not to mention his sheer, must-have-you-now sexiness.

"Ravioli suits you," he murmured. His teeth grazed a nipple. I shuddered, and barely resisted the urge to arch into him. To offer myself to that tantalizing, tempting touch.

"So does my name." My voice sounded as liquid as I felt. "Which is Grace Rioli, in case you've forgotten."

"I haven't." His lips trailed fire back up my neck. When his tongue flirted with my ear, my knees threatened to buckle. "But ravioli is my favorite food, and this particular dish is one I've longed to taste more fully."

If he kept this up, he'd be able to drink me, because I'd be little more than a puddle at his feet.

"So basically, you're saying I remind you of a small square pasta?"

His chuckle vibrated against my neck, and my toes curled in delight.

"You may be small in height and waist, Grace, but you're sure not small in other departments."

His tongue alternated with his teeth against my ear, teasing the exact right spot, and my body vibrated with the force of pleasure shooting through me. God, why was the elevator taking so damn long to climb ten floors?

This had to stop. Not the elevator—*him*. Or I wouldn't want to. I squeezed my other hand between us, and pushed with both. Not too much, just enough to remove the heat of his lips from my neck. "So now you're saying I've got a fat ass? Charming."

His gaze scorched mine, blue eyes rich with amusement and lust. It was the same sort of lust that pounded through me—the hot, let's get down and dirty, right here, right now, type of lust.

Damn it, why couldn't I find that sort of intensity with someone I *didn't* work with?

"You're determined to twist everything I say, aren't you?" he said, deep voice edged with amusement.

"Yes." Because sarcasm was my only line of safety. I was far too susceptible to this man's charms otherwise.

I ducked under his arms as the elevator finally halted and the doors opened. The simple act of walking was an effort, because my heart still raced a million miles an hour and my legs were all fluid and wobbly. It was just as well Frank's office was down the far end of the hall—at least it gave me time to gather some sort of composure.

Ethan reappeared by my side, his long strides curtailed to match my shorter ones.

"Why?" he said. I was still so attuned to him his voice seemed to flow over my skin as sensually as a warm summer breeze. "The attraction between us is getting stronger, and you can't keep denying it exists."

I could, and I would. For as long as we had to work together, and maybe even after that. "There has to be hundreds of women working in this building. Why don't you go try your luck with the half you haven't sampled?"

Something flashed in his eyes. Something that looked an awful lot like annoyance. "Because I'm attracted to you, not them."

Attracted to the challenge more than the person, I suspected. "Yeah, well, I have no intention of becoming another notch on your bedpost." As much as my hormones danced excitedly at the very idea.

"What if I promise to make that notch worthwhile?"

His grin was pure cheek, and I couldn't help responding in kind. The man might be a dangerous rogue, but he was undoubtedly a sexy one. "Not even then."

He stopped to open Frank's door then ushered me through, his fingers searing my spine though his touch was feather light.

"The more you challenge me, the more determined I get," he murmured.

His words sent another tremor racing across my skin. Lord, if what he was doing now wasn't determination, what was? And how was I going to survive it?

Janet, Frank's secretary, glanced up as we both walked in. "Go straight through," she said, her gaze lingering appreciably on Ethan.

"Thanks, Janet," he said, voice so intimate the older woman blushed.

I shook my head, and continued on through the second door. Like most werewolves, the man just couldn't help flirting—and that was part of the problem. If I'd had any reason to believe he was after anything more serious than a quick roll in the sack, then maybe I'd reconsider—

I scratched the rest of that thought from my mind as Frank, our semi-bald boss, glanced up.

"Sit down," he said.

"What's the problem?" I crossed my legs so that my feet pointed away from Ethan. Even an accidental touch could be deadly given the aroused state he'd so easily worked me into.

"We've got a couple of missing kids I want you to look for."

"When and where?" Ethan asked, voice becoming cool and businesslike.

Something inside me relaxed. *This* Ethan I could handle. It was the flirty, oh-so-sexy version of his personality that got me all flustered and out-of-sorts.

"The first was three nights ago." Frank shoved several files across the desk. Ethan leaned forward and picked one up, quickly scanning it before handing it across to me.

I was careful not to touch his fingers and amusement flared briefly across his lush lips. The basic details were all there—name, location, and the particulars of where and how he'd gone missing.

I looked up. "Were there any threats? Ransom demands? Anything to suggest this was a standard crime?"

Frank shook his head. "The kid disappeared from his bedroom in the middle of the night. No evidence of a break-in, and all the doors and windows were still locked in the morning."

"From the inside?"

He flicked a glance my way. "Yeah."

Meaning someone had a key. Ghosts might be able to get past locked doors and windows, but humans—large or small—couldn't.

"Why were we called in?" Ethan asked. "The official investigation would still be underway. We usually don't get pulled in until after the dust has settled."

"A second teenager went missing last night under the same circumstances." Frank pushed the other file closer. "That teenager is my nephew."

"Ah." Ethan's voice was neutral, and yet as attuned as I currently was to the man, I sensed his distaste. He hated jobs that involved personal connections—though he'd never actually said why.

"I want answers," Frank said, "and I want them fast."

And that was probably why Ethan hated personal connections. Hard to do your job properly when someone closely connected rode your back.

I glanced at the file in my hand. The teenagers had gone missing from Wild Dog Creek, a small beachside town about ten minutes beyond the popular Apollo Bay. "Getting accommodations at the height of summer holidays is going to be a problem."

"My sister-in-law has a guest house. She's putting you up there."

I glanced briefly at Ethan. He still wasn't giving much away, but the taste of his displeasure was thicker in the air. "Do you think that's wise?"

"Mari won't get in the way of the investigation."

The problem wasn't so much his sister-in-law or the investigation. It was more me staying with a man I was only barely resisting.

"Why the two of us?" I asked. "I can handle a missing person case by myself. I don't need Ethan to babysit."

Frank raised his eyebrows at that. "Do you have a problem with Ethan?"

Yeah, he was too damn sexy for *my* own good. I had a hard enough time resisting the man in the few minutes our paths crossed each day—how much more difficult was it going to be if I had to spend all day *and* all night with him?

Spending *that* much time together could only have one result—us in bed, getting hot and heavy. My sex drive was perfectly normal, even if the works were a little rusty, and there was no denying the fact I *did* want him. I just didn't want to end up getting hurt. Thanks to my parents, I wasn't very good at the casual stuff, and Ethan was the sort of man I could fall for. Except he didn't seem to want a relationship of *any* kind.

"I just think it's a waste of resources," I said, then realized just what I'd said the minute Frank's expression darkened.

"It's my company and my people, and I'll send who I damn well please to find my nephew." He glared at me for several seconds, then said, "Now get going."

I got. Outside the door, I said, "This is going to suck big time."

"The job, or the fact that I'm going with you?"

I glanced at him, saw the amusement playing about the mouth I so wanted to kiss again. "What do you think?"

"I think your psi abilities mesh extremely well with my pragmatism and innate ability to track a killer, which is why Frank put us on this one."

"Probably." I punched the elevator button and crossed my arms. And tried not to think about constricted space and what had happened not so long ago. "It still sucks."

He leaned casually against the wall. And managed to look so damn hot my hormones started their crazy cartwheels again.

"Why are you so afraid of being alone with me?"

"I'm not afraid of being alone with you."

He smiled. A long, slow, dangerous smile. "Then it's game on, Ravioli."

I knew in that moment my resolution to keep him at arm's length was in big, *big* trouble.

CHAPTER 2

THE SO-CALLED GUEST HOUSE TURNED OUT TO BE A tiny little cabin barely big enough to contain the ancient old brass bed that dominated the main room. A creaky-looking wooden table and several chairs were squeezed into one corner, and in the other, a small kitchenette. The door leading to the bathroom was at the other end of the tiny house, on the left side of the bed.

Which was my side. Heaven only knew I'd need plenty of cold showers to get through the night without giving in to the delicious temptation that would be lying beside me.

"What can you tell me about the night your son disappeared, Mrs. Symmonds?" Ethan said, throwing his sports bag on the bed beside my case.

He'd packed light. I'd packed heavy. Lots of layers was now my motto, whatever the actual temperature.

Mari took a shuddery breath, and exhaled it softly. She was a small, pale woman with even paler hair. Not an albino, because her eyes were brown, but she still possessed that almost ethereal delicateness albinos often had. It was rare for a cat shifter to give off that sort of vibe, because they were usually the independent, don't-you-worry-about-me types, but maybe it was simply the stress of the situation.

"He went to bed at ten, as usual. His light was still on at eleven, so he was probably online, chatting." She shrugged. "He does that most nights."

"And you went to bed when?" Ethan asked, his voice all business, all matter-of-fact.

Which should have put me at ease, but didn't. After the long, close-quarters drive down here, I was still far too aware of the man. I blew out a breath, and tried to concentrate on her voice, listening for anything out of place in her answers that might help find the missing teenagers.

"Midnight," she answered. "I said goodnight, and he answered."

"And you heard nothing all night?"

"Nothing at all. The dogs didn't even bark."

And they certainly had at us. But then, we were wolves, and basically invading their turf.

"What time did you notice he was missing?" I asked softly.

She looked at me. "As soon as I got up at seven. His door was open and the bed empty."

"What did you do then?"

"Looked for him, of course. But he was nowhere." She stopped and gulped, then looked back at Ethan. "Frank said you'd find him. He promised."

Frank was a freaking fool who *should* have known better than that. Ethan touched the woman's frail shoulder and squeezed it lightly. "We'll do our best, Mrs. Symmonds."

"Thank you."

Ethan looked briefly my way. The dangerous spark still glittered bright in his eyes, but I wasn't entirely sure if it was anger or desire. "We should go to his room and look around. Mrs. Symmonds?"

She led the way along the daisy-strewn stone path to the main house—a rambling, two-story affair so often found on older farms. Which this had once been, before Mari and her now-dead hubby had sold it off to developers.

As we neared the back door, Ethan pressed a hand to my

back, guiding me inside. Even that slightest of touches had my system going into meltdown.

This *wasn't* good. Not when the lives of a couple kids might well depend on my ability to concentrate. I stepped away from him, but the air between us still seemed so very heated.

"If you don't mind," I said, touching Mari's arm gently. "I'll get you to wait here. The less interfering vibrations up there, the better."

She didn't ask what I meant, simply nodded. Ethan and I moved up the stairs. We knew the layout of the house—it had been included in the files Frank had given us.

Ethan stopped in the doorway while I continued on. We'd worked together enough now that this side of our relationship had almost become routine. Lord how I wished the other part, the part I kept denying, had the same, easygoing feel.

"Sense anything?" he asked.

I stopped near the bed and drew in a deep breath, tasting the flavors in the air, feeling for the emotions and shadows that rode underneath.

The world was filled with such things. I'd learned to leash and control the senses that detected them, but had never truly been able to explain it. Especially since I come from a very long line of mundane, normal wolves that wouldn't know a psychic skill if they fell over it.

But for me, the very air I breathed was alive, and sometimes, that *wasn't* a good thing. There were the standard, everyday emotions that everyone could see and feel and sometimes taste, but there were just as many that ran underneath normal sensory lines. Many of these were the darker, more destructive emotions and aromas, and they lingered like a cancer in the air, polluting and destroying any sweeter scent.

This room was filled with such a darkness.

"It feels like a vampire," I said, the chill running across

my flesh making me suddenly glad of the multiple layers of clothing.

"Vampires can't cross thresholds uninvited." Ethan's footsteps echoed on the wooden boards as he walked across to the window.

"There's no saying Jon didn't invite it in."

"Except the cops reported that all windows and doors had still been locked from the inside." He paused, looking out the sea-salt blasted pane of glass. "Besides, we're on the second floor, and there are no nearby trees. Vampires can't fly."

"But they can climb ladders."

"Soft soil. They would have found ladder imprints."

I sucked in the air again, felt the foulness of it swirl through me. "It's definitely a vampire. Or at least something along those lines. It has that same dead feeling."

"And there's nothing else?"

I sifted through the undercurrents and deeper threads of lingering emotions. "No fear. Whatever took him, he wasn't afraid. Not at first, anyway."

He glanced at me. "Not at first?"

I crossed my arms, and frowned. "No. I have a feeling that fear might have come later, but at the very beginning, he was a dreamer caught in a dream." I paused, finding a hint of arousal and excitement—and neither emotion had anything to do with Ethan or me. "He was chasing sexual completion."

Ethan raised his eyebrows. "He's run off with a girlfriend?"

I shrugged. "It would explain the locked doors and windows. Most teenagers his age have keys."

He studied me for a moment, then walked over to the rumbled sheets, his nostrils flaring as he breathed deep. "There's no lingering scent of sex."

I raised my eyebrows. "Would you have sex with your girlfriend when your mom was in the room next door?"

His sudden smile was decidedly roguish, and had my pulse doing one of those excited little quicksteps.

"You'd be surprised what I got away with when my mom was in the next room."

"Actually, no, I *wouldn't*."

He picked up a photograph and stared at the image. "Going off with a girlfriend doesn't explain why you smell vampire."

"It would if the girlfriend was some sort of succubus." Succubae—or energy vamps, as they were sometimes called—sucked life force rather than life blood and, unlike true vamps, they had fewer restrictions. Like being able to cross thresholds.

"They're rare—especially in a small, out-of-the-way place like this."

"Rare doesn't mean can't exist."

"True." He put the photo frame back down. "You up to visiting the other kid's room?"

Part of me wanted to say no. Tasting shadows and darkness was never a pleasant thing, and usually I avoided doing it more than once a day. "It's doubtful any useful scents will remain after a week."

"But are you up to trying?"

I rubbed my arms. "Yeah. I guess."

But only because time was of the essence if we were dealing with a succubus. Unlike regular suckers, they didn't drain their victims in one hit, but rather over a couple of days. We still had a chance of finding Jon alive if we hurried.

Hope had all but faded when it came to the first boy, though. Succubae rarely went after another victim until they'd finished with the first.

"Did it say anywhere in the file whether the two boys hung out together?"

He shook his head. "But in a town this size, they probably would." He paused. "Why?"

"Because it just seems odd an energy vamp would go after

two teenage boys. I always thought they went after older, stronger life forces."

"Normally, yeah." He looked down at the bed for a moment, then walked around it and lightly touched my elbow. "Come on, let's get you out of here."

Warmth flared where he touched, spreading like a wildfire up my arm and across my body, washing the chill and the thick feeling of darkness from my skin.

Normally I would have pulled away but right then, I needed that warmth. Needed the reminder of life and healthy, normal emotions to erase the last remainders of evil from my soul.

We walked down the stairs and back into the kitchen. Mari turned around as we entered, her hands gripped around a steaming mug of coffee and hope in her eyes. "Anything?"

"Perhaps," I said cautiously, not wanting to feed the hope, but unwilling to crush it, either. "Tell me, did Jon have a girlfriend?"

She smiled. "No. He preferred hanging out with his mates."

"Could you write out their names and addresses, and give it to us when we come back this afternoon? We'll need to talk to them, just in case they know or saw something."

She nodded. "I think the police already talked to them."

"We'd still like to double-check," Ethan said, and lightly squeezed the elbow he still held.

We continued on outside, and I took a deep breath of the warm, summery air. Felt it brush the last vestiges of darkness from my lungs.

"Now you look a little healthier," Ethan said, his gaze sweeping my face.

I pulled free of his grip and got some space between us again. "It always feels like the darkness is invading my soul, eating away at my very self." A shudder ran through me. "And I always fear that one day, there won't be any *me* left, just a memory and the sweeping strands of darkness."

Which is something I'd told so very few people. Maybe my brush with evil had left me feeling more vulnerable than normal.

Though you'd think I'd be used to such brushes by now.

He frowned. "Then why do it? Why take that risk?"

"Because I have a gift, and it can sometimes save lives." I shrugged. "My parents were the type who ingrained the ideology that if we have a skill, we should use it."

"Even at the risk of your very self?"

"Even at." I rubbed my arms again as we made our way towards Ethan's car. "Can we talk about something else?"

"How about sex?"

"Other than that," I said dryly.

He opened the car door and ushered me inside. "I don't believe my topics of conversations contain anything else."

"Why am I not surprised?"

"Because I'm a werewolf, and werewolves only talk about two things, don't they? Sex, and how to get sex."

He slammed the door shut and walked around to the driver's side of the car, leaving me wondering about the slight edge in his voice. It wasn't like I'd actually brought the damn subject up. Far from it.

He climbed into the driver's seat, started the car, then accelerated down the driveway and onto the Great Ocean Road. Three streets and a quick left, and we were outside the second boy's house. Like Ethan had said, this town wasn't very big.

A woman waited out in front, her arms crossed over massive bosoms and an anxious expression on her fleshy face. "Mari rang and explained why you were coming," she said, voice filled with strain and tiredness. "Do you really think you can help?"

"We can only try," I said, then held out my hand and introduced myself. Ethan did the same. "What can you tell us about your son's activities in the days before his disappearance?"

She shrugged. "He was out with his mates, most days."

"Was one of those mates Jon?"

She nodded, then gave us an anxious sort of look. "Are the two connected? The police won't say whether they are or aren't."

Maybe the police weren't, but the local papers sure as hell were. Which undoubtedly was making life even harder for the parents of the other teenagers in Brad and Jon's "gang." "We don't know as yet." I paused, looking past her. "Can we go inside and look at his room?"

She nodded and led us inside. Brad's room was at the rear of the house, and had easy access to the back door and the garden beyond. It would have been a simple task for a determined teenager armed with a key to get out of the house without his parents knowing.

I stepped into the room, gaze sweeping walls hung with pictures of semi-naked women. Jon had football stars. Maybe Brad was more sexually advanced than his mate—and perhaps that was a factor of him going first. If, indeed, we were dealing with an energy vamp.

"Anything?" Ethan asked.

I shook my head and stepped further into the room. Scents and emotions swirled around me, fading wisps of teenage hopes and dreams. But no darkness, no shadows.

I turned and looked at Ethan. His gaze roamed the pictures.

"The energy vamp didn't enter this room," I said, a touch sharper than I should have. Not that I actually *cared* if he ogled pictures of other women, I just wanted a little attention on the job. Damn it, if I could find the strength to resist base emotions and concentrate, then so could he.

Amusement briefly flared in his bright eyes. "She might have called him out. It looks like Brad was more sexually motivated than Jon."

I picked my way through the clothing-strewn mess on the floor to the window. "I still don't understand why this vamp would be going after teenagers. If it's sexual energy she wants, older men would be more viable and strong, wouldn't they?"

Ethan followed my steps, a heat I could feel more than see. He stopped just behind me, his breath brushing warmth across my neck, sending little flash fires of desire skittering across my too aware, too hot skin.

"It would depend on whether she prefers innocence or experience."

"I didn't think vamps of *any* kind were picky when it came to sustenance."

"All creatures do what they must to survive. Doesn't mean they aren't picky when they have a choice."

I looked over my shoulder and raised an eyebrow. "Even werewolves?"

His bright gaze was still aware, still watchful. For what, I wasn't entirely sure. "A werewolf has to have sex during the week leading up to the full moon, but that doesn't mean we aren't more choosy beyond those times."

"And yet werewolves have a reputation for wanting sex twenty-four-seven, and for not being particularly caring about who their partner is."

He reached out, and lightly brushed a hair from my cheek. His fingers barely even touched my skin, but I was a moth to his flame, and a shudder of sheer delight ran through me.

"Enjoying sex is not a crime. And I, like most werewolves I know, am more choosy than you seem to believe."

It didn't matter, I wanted to say, because *we* weren't going to happen, and whatever I might think or feel wasn't important. But I couldn't force my tongue around the words.

Because probably sooner rather than later, we *would* happen.

I knew it, he knew it. All my protests to date were merely delaying the inevitable. He might not be the right man, this might not be the right situation, but it just didn't seem so important any more. Not to hormones that had hungered for so long. I might not be a creature whose needs were swayed by the blooming of the moon, but I was still a wolf, still a woman, and I still needed the touch of another every now and again.

I stepped sideways. Fighting the inevitable just that little bit longer. "What next?"

He shoved his hands in his pockets. It didn't do much to hide the bulge of his erection. It was good to know I wasn't the only one aching.

"We need to talk to the other kids. In the meantime, we'll get Frank to check the database and see if there's any records of an energy vamp being active in this area."

I raised my eyebrows. "Would there be records?"

"Vampires tend to be territorial, so maybe." He shrugged. "Come on, let's get out of here."

He didn't touch me this time. Perhaps his control was as tenuous as mine.

I followed him out, and let him answer the mother's questions with his usual charm and reassurance. He was better at that sort of stuff than me. The werewolf aura and all that.

We got into the car and headed back to Mari's to collect the list of Jon's friends. There were four other teenagers in his gang, and after interviewing three of them, one thing became clear.

They were all lying.

"But why?" I asked, as we climbed back into the car after interviewing the third kid. "It just doesn't make sense. They were all scared that what had happened to Jon and Brad would happen to them, so why wouldn't they want to do everything they can to protect themselves?"

"We're talking about teenage boys here."

I frowned at him. "So?"

"So," he said, starting the car. "Teenage boys don't tattle on their friends, especially if they were doing something illegal."

"And you think they were?"

He shrugged. "Logical reason for the lies. You want to grab some dinner before we interview the last kid?"

I looked at my watch and nodded. "We've got an hour or so before he's home."

"Time enough."

There was something in the way he said those words that had my pulse skipping. "Time enough for what?"

He gave me one of those to-die-for smiles. "Time enough to eat. What else do you think I meant?"

"I have absolutely no idea," I muttered, looking away from his knowing gaze.

He laughed softly. I continued to ignore him.

We grabbed a couple of burgers and some chips, and headed on down to the beach. Ethan parked, then grabbed a blanket from the back seat and climbed out. I followed with the food and drinks.

"So," I said, once the blanket was spread over the sand and we were munching our burgers. "What sort of illegal activities do you think the boys were up to?"

He shrugged. "It could be anything, from peeking into bedroom windows to breaking into houses. Whatever it is, they've obviously made a pact not to talk about it."

"Boys are weird."

He raised an eyebrow, amusement playing around his lips. "And girls aren't?"

"It's a well-known fact girls are the sensible species. You boys are just all hormones and need."

"Meaning girls don't need?"

"Meaning girls aren't a prisoner to their needs." And this was a conversation I should *not* be having. Not with this man.

"Oh, really?" That gleam was back in his eyes, stronger, lustier, than before. "Want to bet on that, Ravioli?"

I finished my burger and brushed the crumbs from my hands. All the while avoiding his heated, steady gaze. "I told you before, I don't bet."

"And why is that? Afraid you'll lose?"

My gaze rose to his. "Yes."

He somehow seemed closer, though he hadn't actually moved. Maybe it was merely a sharpening in my awareness of him. Maybe it was simply the erotic and sensual heat of him wrapping around me, cradling me like a lover.

"Afraid of me?" he asked softly.

"No," I answered. "Afraid of me." Afraid of wanting more than would ever be offered.

"Ah."

If one single word could say many things, then that one word did. He understood what I meant. But as I stared into bright gaze, I realized understanding did not equate to backing away or backing down. That it had, in fact, only hardened resolve.

"Don't," I said, my words a bare whisper quickly whisked away by the wind, "play with me."

He rose on all fours and moved toward me. I watched him warily, knowing I should move and yet not wanting to. He straddled my legs and stared at me eye to eye.

"I have never played with you, Grace."

The delicious scent of man and musk and spices swept around me, sending my hormones into another wild dance. He raised an eyebrow, as if daring me to retreat.

I couldn't. Wouldn't. Not this time.

"Only because I've never given you the chance."

"Then *you* have one chance now." He lowered his mouth toward mine, but didn't quite kiss me, his breath a delicious whisper on my lips as he added, "Yes or no?"

For one second, the sane half of me raised a reminder that getting physically involved with this man was utter madness. That he was after a good time, not a long time, and I was the one who'd be left feeling awkward and uncomfortable long after the brief affair had ended. That he would go on just fine, pretending nothing had ever happened and that we could just be casual friends and sometimes partners. But the part that had gone hungry for well over two years shouted the reminders down and said, "Yes. If you can avoid sand in bits."

"No sand," he promised, then kissed me.

It was an urgent, hungry thing, that kiss, and so very, very thorough. He kissed me until my head was spinning and my heart was pounding so loudly it seemed to drown out the sound of crashing surf. Kissed me until the thick scent of desire filled the air, until it felt like a blanket that burned and suffocated. Kissed me until I wanted him as I'd never wanted another man.

All with a kiss. I couldn't wait to see what he could do once his hands and body were involved.

"Why don't we strip," he said, after a long, long while.

"Sounds like a plan," I murmured, and began to do just that.

He removed his clothes more slowly, a master of control and a man who knew how to work a strip-tease. I smiled when we were both naked, and ran a hand across the warm hard planes of his abs. In the sunshine, his golden skin glowed with an almost unearthly fire. It was beautiful, as he was beautiful.

He caught my hand, brought it up to his lips, and kissed it gently. Then he tugged on my fingers lightly, dragging me down, until we were both kneeling on the rug again.

"Let the games begin," I murmured softly.

"It's never been a game, Grace. It's all been foreplay building to this moment."

His hand gently touched my cheek then slid slowly, sensually, down my neck and onto my shoulders. His mouth followed his caress, kissing and nipping my flesh, making me shudder and squirm in pleasure.

When his tongue circled the dark ring of one nipple, teasing but not touching the oversensitive center, I moaned, wanting more, wanting it now, but at the same time, not wanting to rush. Every inch of me trembled—ached—with expectation. And waiting that moment when he did more than circle was a part of that. I closed my eyes and pushed my breasts forward, offering them fully to the delight that was his tongue. He nipped lightly, then drew one aching nipple deep into his mouth, sucking on it hard. The unexpected rush of pleasure had me gasping.

As he suckled and nipped my breasts, his caress moved, with agonizing slowness, down my belly, touching, teasing, exploring. Drawing ever closer to the one place I wanted him most. Goosebumps scurried across my sweat-beaded skin, and my heart hammered so loudly its beat seemed to echo across the evening.

When his fingers finally brushed my clit, I could only shudder and press harder into his touch. Then his caress delved deeper, sliding through wetness, one finger plunging inside, then two, but neither staying long enough. Longing flowed like a fire through my veins, until my whole body quivered and throbbed to the tune of that gentle yet insistent caress. A caress that quickly created a tide threatening to overload my senses.

And as much as I wanted the rush his touch was building, I wanted *him* more. Wanted to caress and stroke and taste *him*.

So I pulled away and began my own explorations, allowing my fingers the freedom to roam his beautiful body, reveling in the feeling of power that seemed barely contained under skin.

I kissed him, nipped him, licked the salty taste of sweat and desire from his skin. All the while my hand slid ever further down, until I was stroking the long, glorious length of him. I watched his eyes, watched the lust grow. Felt the power of it roll through me, pooling deep, so very deep, until I was barely resisting the urge to simply mount him, to thrust his thick erection inside, and ride him until we both came hard and fast.

I pushed him back, until he was forced to brace his body with his arms to stop from falling over, then bent and ran my tongue across the tip of his cock. His groan was thick and filled with pleasure.

I swirled my tongue around the tip of him for a while, then moved to his shaft and balls, enjoying his reaction, the tremble that ran through his body. The way his cock leapt and throbbed with eagerness with every careful stroke of my tongue. He groaned again, stronger, more urgent. I smiled and took him fully into my mouth.

He thrust in response, his body shaking with the effort of

restraint as I drew him deep, sucking and tasting and teasing him, until his movements became desperate and the salty taste of pre cum began seeping into my mouth.

Only then did I release him, kissing my way back up his body until my lips found his. It was a desperate thing, that kiss, filled with the urgency that fueled our bodies.

"On your hands and knees, Grace," he murmured against my mouth.

I obeyed and a second later he took me from behind, thrusting hard and deep. God, it felt *good*. He stretched me, filled me, in a way no man ever had, and all I could do was groan in pleasure. For several seconds neither of us moved, enjoying the sensation of oneness, enjoying the tension and the pulsing heat of need that swirled through and around us.

Then he began to thrust, sliding through my slickness with ease, claiming me fully, deeply, and so very thoroughly. The feel of him penetrated every fiber, enveloping me with a heat that was so basic, so powerful, and so very wonderful. His hands were on my hips, holding me steady as he rocked deep. It was a touch that seemed to brand my skin as his thrusts gradually became more urgent. Jolts shuddered through me, and desire raged, flaring across my body like an out-of-control wildfire, building quickly to the final crescendo.

"Come with me, Grace. I want to hear it. I want to hear you."

His words were hoarse, urgent, his breath hot as it whispered across my skin. His powerful body pumped fast and deep, driving me insane with pleasure. I pressed back harder against him, urging him deeper still, wanting, needing every inch of him. He groaned, thrusting harder, faster, and it felt so good I cried out. Still he stroked, and the sweet pressure built, and built, until it felt like I was going to explode. And then everything did.

"Oh God, *yes*!"

He came with me, his roar echoing across the silence, his body slamming mine so hard my hands were sliding in the sand. I clawed at it, trying to gain some purchase as I shuddered and groaned and drowned in a myriad of delicious sensations and the thick feeling of repletion.

And when it was over one thought echoed through my mind.

It would be all too easy to become addicted to Ethan's style of loving.

CHAPTER 3

"ONCE WE GET DRESSED AND PACK UP, IT'LL BE TIME to go see the other kid," he said, sitting back on his heels and looking at his watch.

Not a man for after-fucking small talk, obviously. Not that *that* entirely surprised me. Weres were notorious for not caring about that sort of stuff. "You pack up. I need to clean up."

I rose and walked down to the beach, rinsing the scent of man and sex from my skin in the gentle waves. Maybe now that the cobwebs had been cleared, I could get back on an even keel and act a little more sensibly around the damn man. But given the ripple of pleasure that ran across my body as I watched him dress, perhaps *that* was a faint hope. Seems my hormones weren't finished with him yet.

I walked out of the waves and grabbed my t-shirt, using that to dry myself off before getting dressed. The salty scent of sea clung to my skin, and I could feel the grit of sand in places that were just damn uncomfortable. So much for being careful.

"Ready?" Ethan asked, once I was dressed.

"Yeah," I said, keeping my tone as matter-of-fact as his. Something flickered in his eyes, but he'd turned before I could pin it down.

We walked in single file up the beach and back to the car. The kid was home from football practice by the time we arrived at his house, and like the other teenagers, he was nervous, moving restlessly on the old kitchen chair and not meeting either of our gazes when his mom introduced us.

In fact, he was so nervous I could taste it on the air. "This one you can push," I murmured. "He'll tell."

Ethan nodded briefly, then squatted down in front of the kid. "Jimmy, you know what's happened to Brad and Jon, don't you?"

He shook his head, sending long, blond strands flying. "I don't know anything."

"But you *do* know what Brad and Jon were doing just before they disappeared?"

"No." He said it too quickly, then looked up at his mom. "Can I go now?"

I squeezed Ethan's shoulder to stop him answering, then said, "Jimmy, telling us the truth might mean the difference between saving Jon's life and killing him."

His eyes widened. "The papers lied? Jon's not dead?"

"Maybe not yet. Which is why we need all the help we can get."

"I don't know—"

"Do you want to save your friend or not?" It was horrible to lump that sort of guilt onto the kid, but we weren't only trying to save Jon's life here.

He swallowed heavily. "Okay."

"What were you doing last week that you shouldn't have?" Ethan asked immediately.

"We were over at the Manton house." The kid looked at his mom. "It was a dare."

"Jimmy, how many times do we have to tell you that damn place is danger—"

"Mrs. Jenkins, that's not helping right now," Ethan cut in, voice curt, then added, "What did you do there, Jimmy?"

"Went to the cellars. Dead things live in the cellars."

I shared a glance with Ethan. "What sort of dead things?"

He shrugged. "Never seen them. But there's bones and stuff. And a coffin. It's neat."

Only a teenage boy would classify finding a coffin as a "neat" thing. "Was there anyone in the coffin?"

"Nah. But it was moved around a lot."

Other teenage boys, or something more sinister? "Did you ever see anything or anyone else out there?"

He snorted. "Like a vampire? Get real. Vampires don't live in Wild Dog Creek. The place is too boring."

"Says the authority of youth," Ethan muttered as he rose. "Where's the Manton house, Mrs. Jenkins?"

"Just follow this road to the top of the hill. You can't miss the place."

"Thanks." He half turned, then hesitated. "Can I suggest you take any house keys off Jimmy and keep an eye on him for the next few days? We don't think someone's breaking in to grab the boys, we think the boys are willingly walking out with her."

"What?" Jimmy said, obviously horrified at the prospect of losing his freedom. "No way am I giving up my keys. How will I get back into the house if I go out?"

"That's the whole point," his mom said, with a grim sort of relish. "You aren't going out for a while."

The kid groaned. I restrained my smile and followed Ethan out to the car. Once we were on our way again, I asked, "Why would a vampire—even an energy vampire—need a coffin?"

"They don't. But some vamps do enjoy living up to human expectations." He shrugged.

"But if this vamp is trying to remain under the wire, why leave a coffin laying around?"

"Until we know the history of the house and whatever is in it, that's not a question I can answer."

I looked upwards as the car started climbing. All there was to see on the horizon was an oddly leaning chimney reaching for the sky past a line of pines.

"Maybe we should call Frank and get in some specialists." Werewolves and shifters were fast and strong, but vampires outdid us in both areas, and had the advantage of being able to disappear into shadows. We might be able to track her with scent, but we might never get near enough to kill her. And I wasn't entirely sure I was up to the whole killing bit anyway. That wasn't my field of expertise.

But it was Ethan's.

And he seemed more than a little put out by my suggestion. "We don't need help to deal with one lone vampire."

I raised an eyebrow. "You have the equipment here?"

He gave me a grin that had my toes curling. "I always come equipped, Ravioli."

"Heard that about you." I looked up at the pines we were rapidly approaching. Dusk was settling in, and the sky above the chimney was streaked with pink. "Not sure it's a wise move to be entering a vamp's lair on the cusp of night."

"If we want to save that kid, then we have to move now."

I knew all that. I just didn't like the sensations that were already beginning to crawl across my skin the nearer we got to that house.

The road ended. We drove through an old wooden gate and up the winding drive. The house revealed itself slowly, a long, two-story building that was all angles and windows, wrapped in shadows and age.

Goosebumps tripped across my skin, and I couldn't help shivering. This place just felt *wrong*, and I hadn't even gone inside it yet.

"I can see why teenagers would enjoy this place," Ethan commented, as he parked the car out front. "It's kinda spooky-looking, isn't it?"

"Understatement of the year," I muttered, and climbed out of the car. The breeze that swayed the pine tops merely whispered across the old building, as if reluctant to stir the house to life. The air was thick and filled with a gloom that felt heavy on my tongue. Traces of darkness and evil teased my psychic senses, taunting indications of what was to come once I entered the house.

Ethan had raided the trunk, and handed me a flashlight and several stakes. They weren't particularly large, those stakes, but thick and sharp. I shoved them into my pocket, pointy end down so they didn't stab me in the back as I moved, and watched while he strapped on a gun.

"A bullet won't stop a vampire," I said eventually.

"It will if you shoot their fucking brains out." He slammed the trunk closed. "You ready?"

No, I thought, then blew out a breath and nodded. As one, we walked up the old steps and approached the front door. Paint peeled from its battered surface like old skin, and another tremor ran through me.

Ethan raised a hand and with his fingertips pushed open the door. It didn't creak, nor did the dying sunlight seem to penetrate very far past the threshold. The inside of the house was all shadows and gloom, just like the outside.

He took a step, then stopped, his nostrils flaring. "I can smell the dead." He looked at me. "And not vampire-type dead."

I drew in a breath, tasting the flavors that ran with the air. Shadows of evil and darkness ran across my psychic senses, an evil that felt old and yet young at the same time. But underneath that, the aroma of decay. Of rotting flesh and putridity.

"It can't be the boys. It tastes older than that."

He nodded, then motioned me to follow. We stepped into the shadows. It felt like we were stepping into another world. It was still, this house, so still and yet somehow so watchful. Though there were broken windows in the rooms that we passed as we made our way down the hall, neither sunshine nor wind seemed to go beyond their threshold. The musty smell of decay and age lay thick on the air, and yet these scents were almost pleasant when compared to the deeper, darker aromas that ran underneath.

Whatever used this house for a sanctuary, it had been here a long time. So long the house seemed a part of it, rather than merely a refuge.

We walked past some worse-for-wear stairs, the beams of the flashlight highlighting long, dust-covered webs that trailed like a curtain from the ceiling high above. The scent of dead flesh led us to the rear of the house. Ethan pressed open another door, took the flashlight, and had a quick look around.

"Kitchen," he said. "There's a cellar door to the right."

Dead things lived in the cellars, Jimmy had said. I shuddered and had to fight the urge to run, to just get out of this house and away from the evil it sheltered. But if teenagers had the courage to go down those stairs, then I damn well could.

He directed the flashlight's beam into the cellar door, illuminating the well-worn stairs and the boarded-up walls. The air drifting up was damp, musty, and the scent of flesh and decay stronger. I swallowed heavily and started breathing through my mouth. It only helped a little.

The stairs creaked as we went down them, the sound jarring sharply against the thick silence. The watchfulness of the house seemed to increase the further we descended into the cellar's darkness and yet I couldn't pinpoint it to the presence of a vampire. Which didn't mean it wasn't near, just that I couldn't sense it in the stinking air.

The stairs finally met floor. Ethan swept the light across the black, the bright beam pinpointing corners, cobwebs, and shelving stocked with cans and other goods that looked as old as the house. No bones or coffins, though. I wasn't sure whether to be relieved or not.

"There's another door over here." He pointed the light to a right corner, then he reached back with his free hand and wrapped his fingers around mine. "Are you all right?"

For a moment I clung to him, needing the warmth and the strength that flowed from his grip to battle the chill beginning to invade my soul. "Just."

"You can go upstairs—"

"No," I cut in. "We both need to confront this evil."

He didn't question the certainty in my voice, just squeezed

my fingers again then released me. The room seemed darker, more depressing, without his touch.

We went through the second door. Our footsteps echoed and the boards creaked under our weight. It was here we found Jimmy's bones and coffin.

"These are years old," Ethan said, picking up what looked like a femur and studying it.

I shuddered. It was bad enough feeling the wisps of agony stirring the air. Touching the bones of the dead would only intensify that connection, and that I *didn't* need. I walked over to the coffin sitting against the wall with the lid open. It was squat and fat, and far wider than a normal coffin. And it was made of hardwood that had hastily been banged together and then lined on the inside with what looked like an old blanket. Homemade rather than professional.

"This isn't the coffin of an adult," I said, squatting down next to it. Strands of eagerness and darkness rose from the inside of the box, as if the emotions had soaked through the wood over time. "And it belongs to our vampire. But why would a vamp use it when they don't need to?"

"Maybe she gets off on scaring the crap out of visiting teenagers." He shrugged and rose. "None of these things is the source of our smell. We need to find that."

We may have needed to, but I didn't particularly *want* to. I might not be able to talk to souls, but I could hear them. Could feel their hopes, their dreams and their deaths lingering on the air, and these particular deaths already felt bad enough. I didn't know if I could face the pain that waited where their bodies lay.

We walked on. The creaking in the boards increased, until the whole floor seemed to vibrate under each step.

"This doesn't feel particularly safe," I muttered.

Ethan stopped again and held out one hand. I wrapped my fingers in his gratefully. It might not be any safer, but damn if I didn't feel more secure.

A large crack ran across the silence as we moved on. I paused, but Ethan tugged me forward. "I doubt we'd fall very far, even if the flooring gave away," he said. "There are probably only a couple of inches between the boards and the earth, just for ventilation."

The words were barely out of his mouth when there was an almighty snap, and the flooring underneath us fell away.

And we were falling, tumbling into deeper darkness.

CHAPTER 4

I HIT EARTH WITH A CRUNCH THAT JARRED EVERY
bone from toes to neck, and fell sideways with a gasp. Wood
and dust rained around me, and something sharp speared
into my leg. I yelped, and scrambled to my hands and feet,
moving into the deeper darkness, desperate to get out of the
path of the still-falling wood.

"Grace?" Ethan said, his voice little more than a hiss of
air. "You okay?"

"Yeah. Just gotta stop a cut from bleeding." I called to my
wolf shape, felt the surge of magic roll my body, shifting,
changing, and in the process, healing. To my wolf nose, the
scents in the air sharpened dramatically, and I knew without
even seeing it that bloody death awaited discovery a hairs-
breadth away. I shifted shape again and said, "Point the flashlight my way."

There were several clicks, then light flared across the utter black. I turned. Bodies lay before me. Bodies in various
stages of disintegration, some fully fleshed, some not, but all
rotting.

And the smell . . .

My stomach turned and bile rose thick and fast up my
throat. I gagged and quickly backed away, not wanting to
puke over those who already suffered enough. Not that
they'd know, but their ghosts might.

And their ghosts were here, in this room, filling the shadows with their pain and confusion and horror. The sheer force of it flooded my senses, making my whole body shudder and my heart ache.

"My God," Ethan said softly. "There have to be at least twenty of them."

The ghosts were stirring, whispering. Warning. I gulped down air, trying to keep calm, trying to keep their shadows and pain at arm's length.

And then something else stirred out there in the blackness. There was no sound, no shifting of air, nothing to indicate movement. But I felt it all the same.

Evil had woken.

I backed away until I reached Ethan, and slowly reached for the flashlight, directing the bright beam toward the distant shadows ahead.

There was a quick gleam, like the sparkle of a cat's eyes caught in moonlight, then it was gone.

Evil was on the move.

Ethan swore softly. "Keep behind me," he said, taking his gun from the holster. The click of the safety being released echoed across the heavy silence. I reached back, freeing the stakes and gripping them tightly.

"Can you smell it?" I asked.

He shook his head. "The reek of decay is so strong it's overwhelming everything else. You?"

I flared my nostrils, sucking in the foul air, letting it run across my other senses. Even against the thick stink of rotting flesh, the taste of evil could not hide. "It's to our right, near the wall. Waiting, watching."

He swept the light in that direction. Again, eyes sparkled briefly before disappearing. "It's retreating," I said softly.

"Then let's follow it to its lair."

Let's not, I thought, but followed him onwards anyway. The utter blackness seemed to close in on us, as thick and as heavy as a blanket. The vampire was out there, but it wasn't running, wasn't scared. Just moving away, trying to avoid us. Like a kid who knows she shouldn't be out, I thought, as a chill ran across my skin.

If there was a kid, could there be a parent? Was this evil swirling through the air the sum of two vampires, not one?

The room ended in a shored-up wall. Ethan swept the light left, then right, until the bright beam highlighted a break in the wall. A break that led into stone and dirt and the chill of deeper underground.

"I didn't know there were any caverns in this area," I said, wincing a little as my voice echoed across the heavy silence.

"It's not natural. There are pick marks. Could be part of an old mine that the house was built over."

An old mine that a vampire had labeled home . . . I stilled suddenly, and raised my nose, sucking in the foul air. There, entwined in darkness and old evil, was another, familiar scent.

"Jon's here," I whispered. "To the left."

"I smell him. I can't hear him, though."

Though I strained my ears, I couldn't hear anything either. No breathing, no scent of life. Nothing that would indicate anything else lived in this foul place.

We moved into the cavern. Ethan swept the light across dank walls, until it finally came to rest on the body of a boy.

There was no sign of life because Jon was dead. His face gaunt and pale, his neck torn open, his mouth red from bloody kisses. Kisses that had sucked his life force after it had sucked his blood.

"Shit," Ethan said, and moved forward.

In that moment, evil attacked.

"Look out," I yelled, a heartbeat before the vampire hit Ethan. He leapt aside, but not fast enough. A whirlwind of evil swamped him, scrawny arms and legs all force, all power. The gun and light went flying, and for an instant, we plunged into darkness. Then the flashlight flickered back to life, and for several heartbeats I could only watch—heart in my mouth—as Ethan battled the thin but far-from-frail vampire.

He blocked more blows than a werewolf should have been able to, but the vampire's speed still allowed many others to get through.

I gripped the stakes so hard my knuckles were practically glowing, and ran at the pair of them. The vampire spun and hissed, sharp teeth gleaming and green eyes glowing with unearthly fire in the dark. I propped and stabbed with the stake, aiming for her heart. The vamp twisted away, then dropped and lashed out with a bare foot. I jumped the blow, saw Ethan dive forward, tackling the vampire at waist height in an obvious attempt to drag her down.

Wolves were strong, but vamps were stronger, and this one had the power of a fresh feed behind her. He barely even moved her. She hissed again, then twisted around and smashed Ethan in the head, throwing him down and back. And then she lunged at me.

I dropped to the ground. Her shadow soared over my head, and the stench of blood and death and sheer evil was so bad I gagged. The soft thump of her landing told me where she was, even if her scent was too overwhelming to pinpoint it exactly. I spun, and lashed out with a booted foot. The blow connected with solid darkness and she grunted. But it didn't stop her. I twisted, whipping the stake across the darkness. Felt it scrape across flesh, saw sparks flicker like fireflies. She howled and lashed out with a clenched fist. I leaned back, felt the breeze of the blow brush past my chin. I didn't even see her other fist. It caught the side of my face with enough force to knock me off my feet. I hit the floorboards with a grunt, the stakes flying from my hands as I battled to catch my breath.

Then her weight hit me, her body covering my length, pinning me to the floor. Her stench flooded my senses, making it hard to breathe, to think, to feel anything but darkness and evil.

"Grace, thrust up!" Ethan yelled.

I bucked with my body, dislodging her grip on me slightly.

Then I shoved my arms between us and thrust her back with every ounce of strength I had. It was enough to push her up and away from me.

A gunshot rang out, and the vampire's head exploded. Blood and flesh and God knows what else sprayed across the wall as the vampire's body slumped to the floor. I scrambled to my hands and feet, sweeping the floor with my fingers, looking for the stakes. And finding them.

"Let me," Ethan said, taking one from me and moving with grim resolution to the vampire. In one smooth, clean motion, he drove the stake through her sternum, into her heart.

Fire flared where wood met flesh, quickly becoming an inferno that consumed what remained of the vampire. I released a shuddery breath, and closed my eyes. At least she could no longer threaten anyone.

So why did it feel as if evil still resided in this house?

"Are you okay?" Ethan's voice was filled with concern as he dropped to his knees in front of me.

I nodded. "It doesn't feel like it's over though. It still feels like this house has secrets."

"Yeah, and that secret is just how many people have found their deaths at that vampire's hands."

"No, it's more than that."

He looked past me, nostrils flaring as his gaze swept the darkness. "I can't smell anything beyond old death and new blood. Can your psychic senses pick anything up?"

"Just a continuing sense of evil."

"If this vamp was a fosterling, then its creator would have appeared the minute we attacked her."

"I know, I know." It still didn't ease the feeling we were missing something. Or someone.

But maybe that was merely nerves. A leftover of the evil that had been entrenched in this house for generations.

"Let's go back to the guest house and write up a report for Frank," he said, taking my hand and tugging me to my feet. "We'll let him and the cops deal with the rest of this mess."

With that I couldn't argue.

CHAPTER 5

"WRITING THE REPORT" TURNED OUT TO BE A euphemism for getting back and having sex. Not that I minded. After all the death and decay of that house, I needed to feel life and heat and healthy emotions. Needed it to sweep away the remaining strands of darkness latched to my soul.

The minute the door slammed shut, he grabbed my hand and drew me into his arms. His body was warm and hard against mine, his gaze fierce.

"I'm so glad you weren't seriously hurt," he muttered, "And I have so needed to do this."

"This" was his mouth on mine, plundering hard, our tongues tangling, tasting, the kiss urgent and hungry.

He pushed me back until I hit the wall. The thunder of his heart matched mine, and the heat of him warmed every pore. But the hard length of him, pressed firmly against my belly, was nowhere near close enough.

His hands were on me, his fingers scorching my flesh as he ripped off my clothes. I unbuttoned his pants, tore off his shirt. Then he was in me, filling me, liquefying me. His thick groan of pleasure was a sound I echoed. He began to move, and there was nothing gentle about it. His body plundered as his lips had plundered, his movements hard and fast and urgent. The rich ache grew, becoming a kaleidoscope of sensations that washed through every corner of my mind. Then the shuddering took hold and I gasped, grabbing his shoulders, clambering up his body to wrap my legs around his waist and push him deeper still. Pleasure exploded between us as he thrust and thrust and thrust.

When the tremors finally eased, he laughed softly and rested his forehead against mine. "I could get addicted to this."

"What? Sex? I thought all werewolves were anyway."

"Trust me, there's sex, and then there's *sex*." He kissed me gently. "But it's you, Grace, that's addictive."

"An addiction cannot be gained after only two nibbles," I refuted, not wanting to give any credence to the tiny spark of hope that flared deep inside. The flare that dared to think this could be more than just another brief fling.

"I said *you*, Grace, not the sex."

"You don't know me well enough to get addicted." I let my legs slide to the ground and pushed him back a little. "Coffee?"

"When are you going to learn that pushing me away only makes me more determined?" he asked, voice hinting at frustration though there was little enough to be seen in his expression. Perhaps that's why I wasn't willing to trust his words.

"I told you before, it's self-preservation."

"And I have never given you a reason to distrust me. Nor do I intend to."

What could I say to that? That I didn't trust the fact a werewolf could stay with one partner for more than a couple of days? That my heart wasn't willing to give him the chance of proving me wrong, simply because I was afraid of him breaking it? How could I win what I wanted if I wasn't willing to put anything more than my body on the line? That was a coward's way, and up until now, I'd never been a coward.

I turned on the coffee machine and looked out the window as I reached for the coffee mugs.

And saw the thin, pale face that was almost the spitting image of the vampire we'd killed.

Felt the sudden thickening in the air, the charge of darkness and evil across my senses.

I barely had time to open my mouth and she was through that window and at me. She was thin and weedy and stinking of blood and sex and grief, and I knew I'd been right before, that it hadn't been just one vampire who was killing the boys, but two. They were twins of darkness, one a blood vampire, the other an energy vamp.

She hit me in a rush, pushing me back and down. The back of my head cracked against the floorboards and the shock of it left me gasping for air. The vamp snarled, her breath fetid as it washed across my face. I looked up, saw fangs gleaming brightly in the pale kitchen light, saw them slash down toward my neck. I shoved my arms between us, felt her teeth slice into skin. Not to feed, but to mutilate, and maim, and kill. She twisted her head, dragging her teeth through muscle and flesh, slicing through both as cleanly as a knife through butter. Pain rolled through me, and I screamed. She sucked in the sound and an excited gleam flared in the dead, dark depths of her eyes.

This one was the energy vamp, not the other.

And then she was gone, thrown across the room like so much rubbish, and Ethan was hauling me up, thrusting me behind him.

"We have no weapons," I gasped, cradling my wounded arm. Blood dripped between my fingertips, dropping to the floor, filling the room with its sweet metallic scent.

"Run for the car," he said, "I'll keep it occupied."

He lunged for the vampire, but it moved so fast it literally blurred, swinging and kicking in one fluid movement. Ethan dodged, sucking in his gut, somehow avoiding the blow and landing one of his own. The vamp staggered back, then caught her balance and threw a punch. It landed in Ethan's side, so hard I heard bone snap. He grunted, but didn't back away, hitting the vamp a second time, his fist smashing into the vamp's face and mashing her nose back against his face. Blood spurted, and she snarled in fury.

As much as I didn't want to, I turned from the fight and ran for the door. We needed weapons and we needed them fast. But suddenly the vampire was there, her fist flying. I ducked, but not fast enough, and the blow hit my chin and sent me reeling backwards. I crashed into the table, felt it give underneath me, and fell to the floor amongst the ruins of wood.

Dimly, I saw Ethan and the vampire struggling, fighting, against the door frame. Saw Ethan being flung back, the vampire coming at me yet again.

I scrambled backwards, desperate to get out of her way. The jagged remains of the table speared into my butt and scattered across the floor.

Wood, I thought, and grabbed the nearest, sharpest bit, gripping it tight and thrusting it with all the force I could muster at the vampire.

The needle-sharp point arrowed through flesh and bone, straight into her heart. Fire flared where wood met flesh, and spread quickly across her body, the heat of it burning me, setting my clothes alight. She screamed, I screamed, and the smell of burning flesh and material rent the air. I struggled against her weight, trying to push her off me, but she wouldn't move, wouldn't budge, and I was panicking, burning . . .

And then she was gone, and Ethan was there yet again, tearing off my shirt and stamping out the flames before dragging me into his arms. He kissed my cheeks, my nose, my lips, and he was shuddering, shaking, as much as I was.

"Next time I ignore your instincts, feel free to knock me over the head with a baseball bat," he said, after a while.

I laughed shakily, and pulled back. "I need to shift shape to stop the bleeding."

He nodded and sat back. I shifted to wolf form, healing the wound enough to stop the bleeding, then shifted back to my human shape. "Well, at least that's over with."

"You sure?"

I nodded. "I only felt one other presence. How long do you think they were living in that house?"

"Probably as long as the house has been around, if the bodies and bones are anything to go by."

"But how could so many deaths go unreported?"

"I'm betting they mostly snatched tourists, or teenagers who were on their own."

I guess as towns like this got built up, there were fewer drifters and farmhands that could be taken unnoticed—and that only left the unwary. "But why go after kids with families? Especially if they were trying to avoid notice?"

"Who knows? Maybe the lone tourists have been scarce and they had no other choice. Maybe the boys were simply easy prey."

He shrugged and reached out, cupping my cheek with his palm, letting his thumb brush my lips. Heat slithered through me, an aching that was mind and body. And as I stared into his bright, watchful eyes, I knew that whatever the consequences to my heart, I had to see this thing through. Had to see where we went.

"Ethan—"

"I'm not asking for commitment, Grace," he cut in. "I just want you to stop running and give me some time."

I smiled and kissed his fingertips. "Time I can give."

"Good," he said, as that dangerously sexy light came back into his eyes. "So now, we can get back to our report making."

I grinned. "Is this going to become a standard feature of our working together?"

"Totally." His breath washed heat across my lips, sending anticipation and desire racing through my limbs. "Can't think of a better way to get over the tedium of writing a report."

Neither could I.

CURSE OF
THE DRAGON'S TEARS

Heidi Betts

CHAPTER 1

HE WATCHED HER FROM THE SHADOWS, HIS BREATH
speeding up, the blood pumping hard through his veins.

It had been years since anyone had set foot inside the
walls of his refuge. Anyone other than juveniles up to no
good, daring each other to cross the threshold of the eerie
and reportedly haunted Castle MacKay.

But this one . . . this woman . . . was no adolescent bent
on mischief. She was up to something.

He could tell by the way she glanced around, slowly and
with great interest. And by the bags she was carrying, one
thrown over her shoulder, the other clutched in her hand at
knee level.

Long shafts of evening sunlight shone through the tall,
thin windows, illuminating the specks of dust in the air and
sending wavering slivers of blue and violet through the
woman's otherwise inky black hair.

She wore a loose pink top with some type of picture and
writing on it, and a small golden cross that hung to just between her full, rounded breasts. Her legs were covered in
denim, a thin black belt at her slim waist and sturdy brown
hiking boots on her feet.

With a sigh, she let the duffle in her hand fall to the dirt
floor, lowering the bag on her shoulder much more gently.

"This should be fun," she muttered.

She twisted around, looking for a moment in his direction, and he jerked back, standing even tighter against the wall.

From the corner of his eye, he could still see her, but he didn't think she'd seen him. If she had, she wouldn't even now be walking back outside at a leisurely pace.

No, if she'd seen him, she would be running. And screaming in fear.

Only a few minutes after she'd disappeared through the castle's main, if crumbling, entrance, she returned with a rolled-up sleeping bag, a worn leather satchel, and a large silver thermos.

His heart thrummed in his ears, pounding hard against his ribcage as she began spreading out the sleeping bag and he realized she meant to stay. Here. Overnight. In his secret lair.

Fists clenching at his sides, he watched her, torn between fury at having his private sanctuary invaded and acute interest at being so close to another human being—a woman—for the first time in a hundred years.

Stifling a yawn, Laura Tomescu finished spreading out her things and creating a space on the ground to both sleep and work. Though she wasn't entirely sure where to begin, she was itching to get started on the undertaking that had brought her here in the first place, and to explore Castle MacKay, which had apparently been abandoned nearly a century ago.

From the dirt on the floor and the cobwebs coating the ceiling, she could believe it. She shuddered at the thought of what was likely crawling around in this shadowed room. But she knew in her bones that this would be where she'd find the answers to all of her questions, and so she was ready to face almost anything . . . even the creepy crawlies living in this abandoned keep.

But it was late, and she'd already had a long day of traveling and talking with townspeople from the village below. It seemed that everyone in this part of Scotland knew of the half-man, half-beast who was said to haunt the area.

Whether he truly lived in Castle MacKay, no one could say

for sure. What they would say, depending on who she'd asked, was that he was either a saint or a monster. Some claimed that he butchered sheep or stole children from their beds. Others swore that he left gifts of food or clothing on their doorsteps, or had saved them from harm in one way or another.

Laura didn't know what to believe, and she wasn't sure it mattered. She was here because of her family's part in the legend of Dougal MacKay . . . or perhaps she should say her family's part in the curse.

And because of the dreams she'd been having about him for the past several years. Dreams that were growing stronger and more vivid with each passing day.

So she would bunk down here for the night, then wake up early to begin her exploration. As eager as she was to solve the mystery eating up such a large chunk of her life, she wasn't quite as enthusiastic about poking around a dark, dingy, supposedly haunted castle by herself, with nothing to light her way but a flashlight.

Better to wait until morning when she could see, and maybe, if she was lucky, when there would be less chance of running into things that went bump in the night.

Kicking off her boots and jeans, she shook out the hem of her t-shirt until it fell to mid-thigh. As sleepwear went, it was sorely lacking, but it would do for a single night, alone on a dirt floor.

Shoving her feet into the opening of her sleeping bag, she scrunched down and made herself as comfortable as possible. She closed her eyes and yawned again, a faint trace of uneasiness skittering down her spine.

Not for the first time, she felt as though she was being watched, and if her dreams and research could be believed, she had a pretty good idea what—or rather, *who*—her observer might be. The good news was, she didn't think it—or he—would hurt her.

But since she couldn't be positive, that was one more reason to put off her search until tomorrow. Confrontations of this sort were better left for the bright light of day.

Screwing her eyes tightly shut, she gave a slight shiver and snuggled deeper beneath the folds of her sleeping bag. If she started thinking about *him*, and rats, and all the other creepy-crawly things that might be sneaking around this place, she'd never get any rest.

And the sooner she fell asleep, the sooner it would be morning, so she could wake up and get started on her quest for—literally—the man of her dreams.

She'd been asleep only a few minutes when the dream began. And she knew it was a dream, knew it was one of *those* dreams, even as she drifted through that delicate space between slumber and reality.

She was in Castle MacKay, curled up in her sleeping bag, but she wasn't alone. It was no rat or spider keeping her company, either, but a man.

Dougal.

He stepped out of the shadows, all six-plus-feet of him, and walked toward her.

He moved slowly, making no sound as he crossed the earthen floor, giving her a chance to study him. He was bare-chested, wearing nothing more than a kilt and soft-soled, worn leather boots. His hair was black, tousled, and long enough to brush his broad, well-formed shoulders. His green eyes glowed, looking serpentine in the dark, with their thin, vertical pupils.

And his flesh . . . every inch of that strong, impressive chest that she could see . . . was covered with a beautiful, almost iridescent sort of tattoo. But not of any picture or form she could make out. Instead, it looked like layer after layer of lovely, colorful . . . scales.

That might have seemed odd to her, probably had in the beginning, but after so many dreams of this man, she was not only used to the unique markings, but found them attractive and erotic to the extreme.

Even as that thought flitted through her brain, he was upon her, kneeling down and flipping back the top fold of the sleeping bag. Heat radiated from every pore of his body as he stared down at her, taking in her pale pink t-shirt with its hibiscus flowers and hula girl, advertising Hawaii as "a great place to get leied." The hem had ridden up around her hips, leaving her stark white, French-cut bikini panties in full view.

He murmured a single word, low and emphatic, but in a language she didn't understand, had never heard before she'd begun having these dreams. And then he was loosening the wide belt at his waist, kicking off his calf-high boots, and letting the blue, black, and green fabric of his family tartan fall to the floor. A second later, he was stretched out full length on top of her.

His mouth covered hers, furnace hot, sending flickering flames down her throat and to her very center. He bit, licked, sucked, devoured her like a starving man at an all-you-can-eat buffet. The firm contours of his muscled chest and arms pressed in on her, his legs straddling her own, the rigid length of his arousal rubbing against the soft material at the apex of her thighs.

She had been wet long before he touched her. One glance at his rippling, masculine body towering over her, and she'd turned liquid with fiery lust. Her nipples were puckered and jutting beneath the cotton of her top as she writhed beneath him.

His lips and teeth burned her flesh, tugged at her lips, skimming her cheek, trailing down the line of her throat. He lifted up only long enough to grab the bottom of her shirt in his large, long-fingered hands and strip it off over her head. Then he lowered his head again and feasted at her breast.

Her back arched on a moan, her fingers threading through his black hair as his tongue circled her areola, the budded tip, and then drew her fully into his mouth.

"Yes, please." She scratched at his back with her nails, lifting, reaching for more.

The heat of his long, seeking member brushing between her legs made her want him inside her now. Hard, hot, fast.

She rotated her hips, trying to hurry him, trying to take him in, even before she was fully naked.

And—thank you, Jesus—he took the hint. His rough, callused fingers traced her waist, and then her legs, taking her underwear with them. Without ceremony, he shoved her legs apart, settled himself between them, and thrust home.

Laura gasped at the feel of him embedded so deeply and stretching her to accommodate his incredible size. She took a moment to concentrate on her breathing, and before she knew it, her body relaxed, going soft and loose around him.

He gave her only a moment to recover before lifting her legs over the crooks of his elbows, growling low in his throat, and beginning to pump.

Her back arched at the intensity of sensations racing through her blood. He was a demon, pounding into her like a jackhammer, harder, faster. And she responded, rising to meet his rapid movements, raking his back with her nails, emitting high-pitched keens of delight from the back of her throat that she'd never heard herself make before.

Almost without warning, the orgasm ripped over her, sharp and powerful. She screamed her pleasure, clutching at him more tightly as he continued to thrust frantically.

And then he stopped, going still above her as he came with a roar, spilling inside her.

As quickly as the dream had begun, it faded away, and she drifted more deeply into sleep. She was exhausted, and now—thanks to one of the most violent orgasms of her life—thoroughly sated.

Long after the woman had crawled under the blankets and gone to sleep, Dougal watched her. Watched her chest rise and fall with her deep, even breathing. Watched her mouth drift open and her eyelids flutter as she slipped further into slumber.

He wished that he could show himself, go to her and coax her slowly awake with passionate kisses and a slow caress. He imagined stripping her of blankets and that fitted shirt, devouring her as he hadn't had the chance to devour a woman in a century or more.

When she moaned and rolled to her back, he straightened away from the wall, afraid she may have sensed his presence. He shouldn't have to hide in his own castle, but nor could he risk discovery.

A moment later, it became obvious she was still asleep, but the moans continued. Perhaps she was dreaming. Of monsters and ghouls and other things that went bump in the night, he was sure. Any woman spending the night alone in an abandoned Scottish castle was likely to be skittish.

His brows crossed, though, when she threw off half of the thick red sleeping bag as he'd pictured himself doing, revealing her torso and the tops of her smooth, shapely legs. And then his brows arched, shooting high up on his forehead as one hand, with its softly painted nails, lifted to cup her own breast through the material of her form-fitting top. The other slid over her waist and under the small wisp of material that covered her private areas.

His erection, which had already been at half-mast simply from observing her for the past few hours, shot to full attention. In his mind, he pictured where he wanted her hands to go, the areas he wished his own hands could explore, and to his amazement, she seemed to follow his silent commands.

She continued to touch herself, making tiny mewling sounds of need, and arching up as though meeting a lover's caress. The hand at her breast moved beneath the shirt to tease bare flesh. Her nipples hardened to swollen, pointing peaks, sending a lightning bolt of lust straight to his groin.

Clenching his teeth to keep from groaning aloud, he lifted his kilt and wrapped his hand firmly around his shaft. It had been a hundred years since he'd touched a woman, and though he wasn't shy about relieving his own pent-up desires when the need grew too great, he hadn't had the luxury of watching a woman in the throes of passion to help himself along for a hundred years, either.

He was hot and heavy, his erection pointing skyward with an arousal he hadn't felt in recent—or extended—memory. Several feet away, the woman began to thrash, spreading her legs wider, driving her hand deeper into what he knew would be full, slick, pink folds. It took every ounce of his control not to stalk forward, remove her hand and replace it with his eager, raging erection.

What would it feel like to bury himself inside a woman again? To kiss and fondle and thrust his way to completion.

Of all the things he missed from his former life, he thought perhaps he missed fucking a willing lass most.

Her cries threatening to send him over the brink, he tightened his hold on himself, his fingers dancing and tugging on the rigid length. His own breathing grew ragged as he continued to watch the woman pleasuring herself, as his movements sped up and his legs turned weak with impending climax.

It was all he could do not to close his eyes in ecstasy, but he wanted to see her, wanted to watch the muscles in her thighs tighten, her back bow, her face contort as she reached her peak.

When she did, her shout echoed off the stone walls and through the keep, sending his blood past the boiling point. With it went the last of his control as he came in great, wracking spasms. If he'd ever had an orgasm such as that before in his misbegotten life, he certainly couldn't recall it. It made him almost glad the woman had come to his castle, encroaching upon his invisible but private boundaries.

It even made a part of him wish she might stay a while.

CHAPTER 2

LAURA AWOKE BRIGHT AND EARLY, FEELING RE-
laxed, loose-limbed, and happy, as she always did after one
of her erotic dreams about the mysterious Dougal MacKay.
As she dressed and gathered her things, she found herself
smiling for no particular reason and actually looking forward to the task ahead of exploring this intimidating,
run-down keep.

Also typical of the mornings after having one of her bizarre dreams about a man she'd never met, she wondered
how much of them might be true and how much was simply
her imagination running wild.

Did Dougal MacKay really exist? According to family stories and journals left behind by her great-grandmother Cosmina, he had at one time, but that didn't mean that the legends
of his continued existence were true. He could have died
years ago; many, many years ago, if his age at the time of her
great-grandmother Cosmina's curse was any indication. If the
curse had worked, however, he would still be alive and may
not have aged a day since the enthralling words were spoken.

She also wondered at the scales that covered his body in
her dreams, and the breath that was hot as lava. Were those,
too, a result of the hex her great-grandmother had thrust
upon him, or merely the way her subconscious chose to picture a man who would have been cursed in such a way.

She didn't know, but she prayed she would find out. After all, she hadn't made the trip all the way from the United States to Scotland for nothing.

Outside, the day was glorious, with the sun shining and a gentle breeze ruffling the tall green grass surrounding the castle. To document her search, she'd brought along a number of notebooks, as well as her camera.

She snapped several pictures inside the first initial room of the keep, then walked around outside to do the same. The landscape really was beautiful, and she could understand why someone, hundreds of years ago, had decided to build their castle here, overlooking both the ocean and the valley below.

But the longer she lingered outdoors, and the more she found to photograph, the more she realized she was stalling. Because as much as she wanted to find Dougal MacKay and discover the facts of the legend and her dreams, the truth was, she was afraid. Afraid of what she would find . . . and afraid of finding nothing. Afraid of learning that the images that had haunted her for years now weren't real . . . or that they were.

To further her procrastination, she considered going into town for breakfast, but then decided that was only avoiding the inevitable. She should get down to business and see what she could discover before she was faced with another long, lonely night inside this dreary castle.

Ignoring the tickle of anticipation that skated down her spine, she carried her camera back inside and gathered her other, more well-worn leather tote that contained some of the notes and clippings and research she'd gathered for this trek, as well as several cans of soda and the energy bars she'd brought along for situations just like this, when she might not have the time—or the inclination—to go into town for a bite to eat.

With her camera dangling in the crook of her elbow, she tossed the satchel strap over her shoulder and tore open the wrapper of one of the bars, biting into the yogurt-covered granola while she slowly made her way deeper into the keep.

Chewing worked as a bit of a distraction, but still her heart pounded inside her chest, and the muscles of her diaphragm contracted as she struggled to breathe normally.

Nothing will hurt you. Nothing will hurt you, she told herself over and over. She was here for a reason, and even if she was very afraid monsters—at least the storybook kind—really did exist, she was determined to see this quest through to the end.

Sunlight shone in narrow, muted beams through the door and tall windows of the main room, but past that, the structure was still fairly dark and dank. That didn't keep her from noticing a great number of cobwebs she hadn't the night before, though.

Her booted feet scuffed through the dirt covering the stone floor as she tiptoed deeper into the structure. It was beautiful, in a way. She could picture it one or two hundred years ago—a fire blazing in the hearth, tapestries covering the walls, a long trestle table crowded with people eating roasted boar and mutton stew.

She lifted her camera to snap a picture here or there as she moved along, but found nothing of exceptional interest. With the exception of an occasional broken-down table or chair, any furniture had been removed long ago.

To her right, a wide stone staircase led to the second level, where she imagined bedchambers and maybe a solar had been located. She was just turning to move in that direction when a noise from the other side of the keep, deep in the heart of the castle, startled her.

She stood frozen, pulse kicking as she slowly turned her head toward where she thought the sound had come from. Something had rattled, like glasses clinking together, only louder.

It was probably just one of those rats she'd envisioned sharing her space last night. But if it wasn't . . . well, she was looking for the castle's rumored inhabitant, so following the noise might be the way to go, whether she wanted to or not.

Taking a deep breath, she slowly spun on one foot and tiptoed across the earthen floor. Far at the back of the keep, to the left of one of the hearths, was the shadow of a doorway she hadn't noticed before. Stepping carefully and quietly, she entered the cavernous area, her hand tracing the rough stone of the wall to guide her path.

About six steps in, she hit a curved set of narrow stairs leading downwards. She'd left her flashlight behind, but her eyes adjusted to the light enough to keep from tripping and falling to her death.

At first there was pitch dark, but the closer she got to the bottom of the stairs, the lighter it became, a muted orange glow flickering at the base of the steps.

Her eyes narrowed as she considered how that was even possible. This had to be a basement or dungeon area, underground where there couldn't be any windows. And even if there were, she would expect the light from outside to be whiter, more like daylight than candle glow.

Rounding the corner, she sucked in a breath, realizing it *was* candlelight. There was a single, thick taper stuffed into the neck of a stout wine bottle in the center of a small, round wooden table, burning strongly enough to illuminate the center of the room and cast shadows farther out.

It didn't take long for her mind to shake off the sense of surprise she was feeling and make the logical conclusion that for a candle to be burning here, in the depths of the run-down, abandoned castle, there would have to be someone to light the candle.

She swallowed, concentrating on the soft, even rhythm of her breathing as she took in her surroundings. There was a build-up of melted wax running in thick rivulets down the sides of the bottle holding the candle, telling her it had been used for just that purpose many times before. She also noticed several more bottles strewn about . . . some empty, in a pile in the corner, others full or half-full, standing upright on the table or on the floor.

Along the far wall, there was a pallet—much like her own

upstairs—made up of blankets and a single, ratty-looking pillow. Books and old food wrappers littered the floor.

It didn't take a rocket scientist to figure out that someone was living here. *Living here,* in this old, abandoned keep, where there was no running water, no electricity, no anything but stone and dirt, spiders and vermin.

Until this moment, she didn't think she'd truly believe she'd find the person she sought. She'd hoped. She'd told herself she would just to bolster her own spirits. But deep down, she wasn't sure she'd actually expected to find the infamous Dougal MacKay.

Now, though . . . Someone was living here, exactly where all of her research had led her. And who else could it be but the man the villagers both feared and revered? The man her great-grandmother had cursed to a life of isolation.

A scuffling sound near the stairs had her spinning back around as a tall, dark figure stepped out of the shadows. He blocked the only exit, her only means of escape, and she was chagrined to realize that her brain was indeed urging her to run for her life.

She stayed where she was, though, even as her heart lurched and a scream worked its way involuntarily into her throat. She locked her lips, holding it back, and did the same with her knees, which had turned to rubber.

He loomed over her, making her feel like Jack after he'd climbed his beanstalk to confront the giant. He was covered from head to toe with some sort of cloak, the hood large enough to hide his face from view, and heat seemed to emanate from him in waves, the same as it did in her dreams.

Her fingers flexed at her sides and she shifted slightly, fighting the urge to lift her camera and immediately begin snapping pictures of the man who, until this moment, had been more legend to her than flesh-and-blood fact.

"Hi," she said cautiously, licking her dry lips. And then, because she couldn't think of a single other thing to say beyond what was bouncing around in her head, she blurted, "You're Dougal MacKay, aren't you?"

Even in the muted light of this underground room, she could sense his surprise and sudden wariness.

"It's all right," she continued when he seemed unwilling to answer the question. "I'm not here to hurt you, or expose you, or anything like that. My name is Laura Tomescu, and I believe you knew my great-grandmother. The woman who cursed you."

CHAPTER 3

DOUGAL STARED AT THE WOMAN IN FRONT OF HIM.
Everything about her screamed *danger!*, and it took every
ounce of bravery in his bones not to turn and make his escape.

Running did not come naturally to him. He had been no
coward during his mortal years. But after nearly a century
of being reviled and hunted, he'd learned well when to flee
and how to hide from those who would do him harm.

Last night, when this woman had first encroached upon
his sanctuary, he'd thought her dangerous only in the way
that all strangers could be dangerous to his safety. If discovered, they would be terrified of his appearance and perhaps
cost him his last refuge.

Now, however, he knew that she was a threat to him in
much more dire ways.

"Get out," he ordered, the words scalding his throat as
fury and alarm mingled in his gut.

"Excuse me?" Her dark brows rose, and instead of fear,
her expression conveyed only a whisper of shocked annoyance.

"You don't belong here." He took a menacing step forward, letting the full brunt of his rage sweep forward in his
words and the heat of his fiery breath. "Get out or face my
wrath."

If possible, her brows lifted even higher, but she stood her ground, not the least intimidated by either his size or his wrath. Crossing her arms beneath the full swell of her breasts, she cocked her head and tapped an impatient foot.

"If this is how you talked to my great-grandmother Cosmina, I can understand why she put a curse on you."

Because Dougal was used to people quaking in fear in his presence, he was unsure how to respond to this slip of a woman who not only didn't flee in horror, but had the nerve to return his ire with a sharp retort of her own.

Perhaps retreat was the best plan of action, after all, he thought, still somewhat taken aback by her behavior. With a huff, he turned for the stairs, intending to leave her here and find somewhere outside, deep in the woods, to hide until the wretched wench was gone. But just as his foot hit the first step, she reached out to grab his arm.

It wasn't her attempt to stop him that did so, but the fact that she was touching him. No one had touched him in a hundred years. Not even those who had run him off from his own home with torches and pitchforks, screaming that he was demon spawn and cursing him back to the devil. And certainly no woman, of her own free will.

But this one . . . this one *was* touching him, not by accident, but on purpose.

A ripple of something he was afraid came too close to abject gratitude and relief shuddered through him and he locked his knees to keep from sinking to the ground. Turning slowly back to face her, he found her staring at him, full in the face, and her expression was not one of disgust or terror, but of awe.

"Don't go," she said softly. "I'm sorry, I shouldn't have said that."

Perhaps not, but that didn't make her words any less true, did it? Had he learned nothing in the hundred years since he'd been transformed into a monster?

"I don't even know . . ." She paused, licked her lips, seemed to struggle to put voice to her thoughts. "I don't even know if the stories I've heard are true. If what the legends say my family did to you are fact or fiction."

"Fiction?" he snapped, anger once again pushing the boundaries of his self-control. Pulling back his hood, he threw his cloak to the ground. "Does this look to you like the work of an imaginary tale?"

He expected to see revulsion in her eyes, to hear the shrieks that had grown so familiar to his ears over the years. Instead, he saw a strange curiosity. Fascination, even.

Her gaze roamed over him, over every inch of exposed skin that even now flushed with the shame of his disfigurement. She looked her fill, taking in the reptilian slits of his eyes, the multi-colored patches marring his face, the rough scales that covered his hands and arms.

And then she reached out . . . reached out and touched him, flesh to flesh. He made a sound of protest and tried to shrug away, out of instinct and self-preservation. But she held fast, her grip tightening on his wrist, not the least aghast by the feel of his flawed skin.

He held himself rigid, still awaiting the moment when she would realize he was a fiend and she needed to run for her life, but as the seconds ticked by, eagerness began to pour through his blood like an elixir.

She was touching him, caressing him now, and she wasn't afraid. How long had it been since he'd experienced such a gift? Too long. A century, at least, since his last clear memory of human contact.

He swallowed, every muscle of his body growing tense as her fingers continued their exploration. His mind spun back to the evening before, when he'd watched her writhing in pleasure and imagined her touching more than his arm, stroking him with lust more than mere inquisitiveness.

"It really was you," she whispered, the words breathy and low as she lifted her head and met his gaze.

Her fingers continued to move in slow circles over the

roughened flesh of his forearm, sending streaks of longing straight to his groin.

"Last night. Every night. It really was you in my dreams."

Laura didn't think she imagined that they both stopped breathing at the same time. The entire situation was incredible to her. *He* was incredible to her.

He was real. The man who had been plaguing her . . . and pleasuring her . . . in her dreams for so long was real, and solid, and standing right in front of her.

Despite his appearance and the cruel reaction he seemed to expect from her, he was beautiful. Not something to be hidden away or scorned, but to be admired and celebrated.

The same colorful tattoo of scales that marked his arms circled his neck and fell in patches over his face. And his eyes . . . his eyes were like nothing she'd ever seen before. A bright, glowing green with black, almost serpentine pupils at their centers.

A shiver ran down her spine, but not from fear, from delight.

It *was* him. The man she'd been dreaming of for what felt like forever. The man who had touched her, held her, done unspeakably satisfying things to her body night after night.

She'd nearly convinced herself that he was some strange, erotic figment of her untamed imagination, but even she hadn't truly believed her subconscious could concoct someone with eyes and skin just like his.

He was even hot to the touch, the same as he'd been in the dream.

It was startling, amazing, and though he was standing directly in front of her, with her hands resting gently on his arms, she still had a hard time wrapping her mind around the fact that fantasy had just become reality, and she had finally found the man she'd been dreaming of, the one at the center of so many of the stories her family told and the legends passed down from generation to generation.

"You . . . dreamt about me?" he asked, no longer looking as though he was desperate to get away from her. His voice was low and deep, and tinged with the Scottish brogue she was just beginning to get used to.

"Last night," she responded with a small nod. "So many nights. I thought I was going crazy, but then . . . I remembered the stories I was told as a little girl, of the man my great-grandmother cursed to live as a beast, and I started to wonder. I've been looking for you."

Confiding that to anyone else would have made Laura feel like a fool. But with Dougal, she felt completely comfortable, as if she'd known him for years. And though they were only fantasies that came to her in the darkest hours of the night, she'd had him inside of her too many times to count. If that didn't build a certain level of familiarity, she didn't know what would.

His lips twisted into a snarl and the rough timbre of his voice grew even rougher. "Your grandmother did this to me?" he asked—the words part statement, part question, all accusation.

Beneath her fingers, his muscles tensed, growing rock hard and hot to the touch.

"I'm afraid so. Will you tell me why and how?"

She knew the stories, knew what her family said had happened, but she wanted to hear it from him, hear his opinion and his telling of the tale.

Momentarily releasing him, she moved to the small table in the center of the room and set down her camera and tote. Reaching into the bag, she pulled out a couple of energy bars and cans of soda.

"Here," she said, holding one of each out to him like a peace offering. "We can sit and have a bite to eat while you tell me what happened, why my grandmother felt the need to do this to you."

He made a sound low in his throat, but followed her when she moved to the far wall and sat amongst the blankets and rags that made up his sleeping pallet. Taking a spot beside her, close but not touching, he opened the bar she'd given him and began to chew, slowly and methodically.

The minutes ticked by while she did the same, throwing them into an eerie but relaxed silence. When she'd finished her bar and sipped half the soda, she shifted slightly in his direction, once again meeting his dark, intense gaze.

"Tell me," she pressed when he showed no signs of speaking, once again letting the tips of her fingers slide over the scaled flesh of his forearm. "Please, I really do need to know."

Dougal finished off the chunk of granola Laura had handed him and tossed the wrapper aside. His lips pursed as he considered how much to tell her.

She was a stranger, yet she claimed to be a descendant of the woman who had damned him to this unending life of hell on earth. He had spent the last hundred years alone, in hiding, with only himself for company, yet the pain of that isolation was quickly giving way to the desire to speak, to share, to take advantage of the opportunity to converse with another human being.

And if he understood her earlier remark correctly, at the same time he'd been watching her—watching her pleasure herself while he, in turn, pleasured himself—she'd been dreaming of him, as well.

She'd never seen him before, had certainly never seen his markings and disfigurement, yet her subconscious had apparently caused her to dream of him in a most erotic manner. Not once, but multiple times.

Like a match tip flaring to life, heat raced through his body, bringing his shaft to rock-hard attention. His blood boiled with want and need and memory, and a sense of possibility he hadn't experienced in a century.

Swallowing hard, he drew his attention back to her face, even as his mind lingered on thoughts of yanking down her trousers and having his way with her, pinning her to the wall and taking her until every ounce of pent-up passion and desire poured out of him.

"I was young," he began. "Young and arrogant and foolish. I was the firstborn son of the great Laird MacKay, and I thought I had the right." How wrong he had been. But then, with age came wisdom, and though his physical body showed no signs of the span of his life, he certainly had the years to claim great insight.

The wild yearning humming in his veins slowed to a low simmer as he spoke, and he expected the second, less pleasant memory he was being forced to recall to begin a sour roil in his gut and burn his tongue like acid. But a hundred years had apparently dulled the pain and degradation of that moment, for he felt himself relating the story as though it was just that—a story, an unfortunate incident that had occurred to someone else.

"It was a harsh winter that year, with little food to be found, and when I discovered a band of gypsies . . ." he cocked his head and met her eye, "your ancestors, I presume . . . hunting on my family's land, I tried to drive them off. One of the old women—your great-grandmother—was not impressed by my grandiose behavior or my threat to remove them bodily if they refused to leave of their own free will. She cursed me. Threw a bottle of some thick, amber liquid at my chest, which she claimed were dragon's tears. It soaked immediately through my clothes and onto my skin, not burning, but tingling. I could feel it seeping into my pores, spreading through my body.

"That was when she began to chant. A language I couldn't comprehend at first, followed by one that I could. She told me I would be forever hunted, trapped in a form between man and beast, the bodies of man and dragon becoming one until I learned the gifts of kindness and generosity, of putting others' needs before my own.

"Almost immediately, I began to change. I grew hot, nearly unbearably so. My flesh, my blood . . . I could barely breathe from the heat and the pain, but when I did, those breaths hissed with smoke and sometimes fire. I could feel my eyes changing. To this," he said, waving a hand in front of his face to encompass what he knew Laura saw when she looked at him.

"At some point, I lost consciousness. When I woke, the gypsies were gone, as though they'd never been there to begin with. I staggered home, thinking I'd imagined the whole thing, or perhaps that whatever the old crone had thrown at me had caused me to hallucinate. It wasn't until I arrived back at the keep—not this one, but one built later, where my family resided—that I came to understand it was all too real. By then, the scales had broken out to cover most of my body. As soon as the villagers and my family saw me, they began to scream, and cast me out for the demon I had become."

Story told, he fell silent, and for a moment, Laura remained so, too. Then her brow puckered and with censure clear in her tone, she said, "Your own family did that to you? Couldn't they understand? Didn't they at least want to know what had happened to you?"

He shook his head, once again stunned by her quick acceptance of both him and his accounting of past events, as well as the fact that she instantly jumped to the defense of the youth he'd once been.

"It was a different time. Things that today would be considered merely unfortunate were then thought to be the work of the devil. They ran me off with curses and prayers in the middle of the night. I came to this keep, which had been empty many years by then, to hide, and have been here ever since."

"Still . . ."

Laura didn't know what else to say after that, so she let her words trail off, her mind racing with the comparisons between her great-grandmother's version of the incident with Dougal MacKay and what he had just told her.

She'd listened to Dougal's deep, Scottish brogue with keen interest and more than a modicum of exhilaration, not doubting his claims for a second. Any other sane person might have, but she knew better. Though his tale had been flavored by his personal viewpoint, the details were too close to what she already knew of the legend not to believe and *know* that what she'd heard all of her life had really happened. That this man, cursed to life in the skin of a beast, really existed.

There was no denying that the markings on his body and the vertical slits of his eyes made him look like a dragon, which had been one of the hardest parts of her great-grandmother's story to believe. But if that could be true, then everything else could be, too.

"Can I see?" she asked, slowly climbing to her feet and drawing him up with her. Her palms gently explored every inch of bare skin she could find.

She found him fascinating, and handsome beyond belief. It didn't help, either, that she remembered every touch, every kiss, every moan and thrust from the many erotic dreams he'd starred in while she slept.

Dougal didn't move, didn't tell her she could or couldn't look her fill, so she continued to explore, loosening the ties at the front of his shirt.

Everywhere she glanced, there were scales. The flickering, orange-ish glow of the candle still burning in the middle of the room actually accentuated the colors, making the pale greens, blues, pinks, lavenders, and yellows glitter and glow. It was like staring into a bowl of precious gems or standing directly before a disco ball.

Wanting to see it all, she slipped her hands beneath the bottom hem of his shirt and peeled it slowly upwards. He raised his arms without prompting, letting her lift it up and over his head.

She bit back a gasp at the sight of him. He was glorious, a true masterpiece. And it was only moderately due to the dragonlike markings lining his chest and abdomen, wrapping around his waist to his back, spreading down beneath the waistband of his pants.

They were beautiful and fascinating, no doubt, but his body would have been a work of art even without them. He was sculpted and firm, each muscle smooth and well defined. He was the epitome of manliness, every woman's fantasy.

Her fantasy come to life.

Her hands trailed along his washboard abdomen, around his waist to his back, where the same rough texture of scales covered the skin there, as well. She let her fingertips drop lower, just inside the top of his pants.

His stomach muscles tightened as he inhaled sharply, and a thrill rolled through her own belly. She was being exceptionally bold, not at all like her usual self, but she simply didn't care.

She knew what she wanted . . . Dougal, again, just like last night.

"Laura . . ." His voice was a harsh whisper of sound through clenched teeth.

His hand clamped on her wrist, keeping her from dipping any lower, but she flexed her fingers, tugging against his hold in an attempt to delve deeper beneath his waistband.

"Laura," he growled again. "Don't. You don't know how long it's been . . . how much I want . . ."

His words trailed off as excitement skated through her veins. If he'd been hiding from humanity for a hundred years, then it was a pretty good guess that he hadn't had sex in that long, either. The thought of being the first woman he'd touched in a century turned her wet in an instant and made her ache.

He let her have her hand, and she immediately moved it to the clasp at the front of his pants.

"I do know," she told him softly. "And I want, too."

If she thought there would be any gentleness in a man who'd been celibate for a century, she was dead wrong. The minute she spoke and he realized she wouldn't try to stop him, he caught her under the arms and backed her against the nearest wall.

She gave a yelp of surprise, her fingers slipping from the front of his trousers. But it didn't matter. Holding her to the wall with his body, he reached between them to wrench open her own jeans and strip them down her legs.

In one swift motion, he had the pants, her underwear, and her boots completely off, leaving them in a pile on the ground. Then he moved back to his own zipper, shoving his pants down just enough to free his rigid erection.

She watched his every motion with a sense of awe and anticipation. Inside the cups of her bra, her nipples puckered painfully, and she licked her lips, eager for what was to come.

Rising out of a nest of tight black curls, his arousal was long and thick and covered with the same pattern of scales as the rest of his body. She didn't think she'd ever seen a man this hard, this enflamed, with each ridge and vein of his straining erection standing out in stark relief.

She reached for him, wanting to feel that heat and sturdiness, but he slapped her hand away. With any other man, she might have taken exception to that and walked away, but not with him, not during this particular encounter.

His hands clamped on her ass, lifting her off her feet while he pried her legs apart with one knee. She knew what he wanted. She wanted it, too.

Wrapping her arms around his neck, she crawled up the back of his calves and thighs until she was at just the right height for his entry. Ankles locked behind his back, breasts rubbing his chest through the thin cotton of her top, she held on tight and bit her bottom lip as he plunged inside, filling her to the hilt.

He started to thrust—no preliminaries, no tenderness, just pounding into her again and again. Her breath was coming in pants, her nails raking his sweaty back and scraping at the rows of scales there.

She moaned his name, arching even closer, her inner muscles squeezing and milking him, begging him to come. Instead, he stopped. His chest was heaving, his breaths blowing in and out in huffs of exertion.

Her own breathing was none too steady. "What's wrong?" she gasped out. "Why did you stop?"

He leaned forward, resting his brow on hers. "You made a noise. I didn't want to hurt you."

She tried to laugh, but it came out as nothing more than a strangled, oxygen-deprived wheeze. "You weren't hurting me," she told him without a hint of hesitation. Her fingers tunneled through his hair, clutching the back of his head as she gave a demanding little tug. "If you hurt me, I'll yell 'ouch,' otherwise, keep doing what you were doing."

One dark brow winged upwards. "You're sure? You want me to . . ."

"*Yes,*" she stressed, tightening her grip on his hair. "Fuck me, please."

It took a second for her words to sink in, but only a second. In the next instant, his eyes turned stormy and narrowed with erotic intent. Then his mouth swooped in to cover hers in a kiss so hot, it nearly singed her eyelashes.

His grip tightened on her butt and he was moving again, banging into her like he was drilling a hole through the stone wall at her back. She loved it, every pump, every flex, every grind. She thrust back, angling her hips and meeting him halfway.

Sliding his hands from the globes of her bottom, he let them skim her hips, her waist, up under the material of her fitted tee to her chest. His palms were rough and callused, heightening the sensations of his touch as he pushed her bra up and out of the way so he could cup her breasts.

He kneaded the soft mounds, pinching the nipples and scraping them with the side of his thumb and tip of his nail. The action sent rockets of ecstasy into every cell of her being. And where they were joined, each time he filled her, he hit her clitoris, making the sensations even stronger.

Pulling her mouth from his, she made sounds she'd never heard come from her own lips before, and she even thought she might have exhaled a puff of smoke, testament to the heat that pulsed through Dougal's entire system.

The muscles of her throat tightened as she threw her head back, cracking her skull into the stones at her back. She barely felt the sting, focused instead on the excruciating pleasure building in her veins, in her belly, deep in the engorged tissues of her feminine channel.

Her nails dug into the meat of his shoulders as his thrusts gained even more speed. "Yes," she groaned, spurring him on, wanting more, harder, deeper. Everything *now, now, now.*

He gripped her buttocks again, yanking her forward and back as he gritted words through his teeth in a language she didn't understand. And then she broke apart, coming hard enough to shake her to the core and make her scream.

Beneath her, Dougal pounded into her twice more before stiffening with a shout of completion and pouring his essence into her. She felt every burst, every tremor, the walls of her sex rippling with a second orgasm as it tried to suck up every drop.

For long minutes, they stayed as they were, propped against the wall like two marble statues. Struggling for breath, lacking the strength or energy to move so much as an inch.

When Dougal finally recovered enough to lift his head from the crook of her shoulder, it was to center his glowing, serpentine gaze directly on her face.

"Thank you," he whispered, and then he kissed her, a light, almost reverent brush of lips on lips.

CHAPTER 4

THEY ENDED UP COMPLETELY NAKED ON THE PILE of blankets in the corner through the rest of that day and into the next. Between bouts of incredible, combustible, mouthwatering sex, Dougal told Laura more about his life since being cursed . . . How he'd survived, how he'd remained hidden from the world for so long, how he'd tried in as many ways as he could think of to do selfless deeds and remove the magical enchantment her great-grandmother had forced upon him.

She found him fascinating. His struggle and subsistence; how intelligent he had to be to have remained invisible, yet find everything he needed, such as food and clothing.

And she told him a little of her life, of her family, of the dreams and compulsions that had brought her here to find him. To her amazement, he didn't hold her great-grandmother's actions against her or carry any animosity toward her family. He had, it seemed, learned his lesson about messing with gypsies.

At his request, she explained some of the details of the modern world, things he'd never had the opportunity to see or experience. She wanted to take him out and show him everything, introduce him to society and help him acclimate back into a normal existence. Not to mention find a way to help him remove her great-grandmother's curse.

Though he held no grudge against her for her ancestor's actions, she felt the guilt of it all the same. Yes, he'd been cruel to her people when they'd been desperate and starving, just trying to survive. But that had been more than a hundred years ago, and she thought that whatever his crime, he'd certainly paid enough of a price for it by now.

And if his version of events was accurate, they knew the key to removing the spell and returning him to his regular appearance—an act of selflessness, or becoming a more understanding, generous person. She wasn't sure exactly how to achieve that, but certainly there were things they could try.

Dougal, however, didn't seem nearly as interested in the idea of venturing out into the world as she'd hoped, and she supposed she understood why. The last time he'd revealed his markings to someone other than herself, he'd been threatened and ostracized.

She didn't want to believe the same thing would happen to him in this day and age, but she couldn't be certain. And it *was* possible that even if he weren't reviled for his affliction, he might be enough of an oddity for scientists and the media to turn his life into a nightmare of flashbulbs and needle pricks.

So maybe he was right. Maybe it was better that he stay here, at least for now. They could discuss other options later.

At the moment, his attention was focused on more important things, anyway . . . like making love to her as frequently and creatively as possible.

She'd had her share of lovers in the past, and would have thought that a few of those encounters qualified as being quite risqué. Now she realized that for all her experiences, before meeting Dougal, she might as well have been a nun.

He did things to her body that made her eyes roll back in her head, took her to heights she hadn't known existed, took her in *ways* she hadn't thought possible.

After reviving enough from their energetic bout against the wall to go at it again, he'd turned her over onto her hands and knees and taken her from behind until she was panting for release. He'd sunk between her legs and consumed her like a man dying of thirst who'd finally found an oasis. And when she recovered, she was only too happy to return the favor.

As much as she'd enjoyed every touch of his hands and mouth and body, and every earth-shattering orgasm he'd wrung from her, she thought she enjoyed having him in her mouth even more. She liked his taste and smell, the unique texture of his long, hot arousal against her tongue. She liked leaning over him, being able to explore his body with her hands while she watched his face contort with pleasure.

Her hands smoothed over his flat abdomen, narrow hips, and muscled thighs, slipping between to toy with the soft, twin globes of his testicles. The extra caress drove him crazy, causing his hips to cant off the floor in an effort to get deeper, closer to the pleasure she was bringing him.

Hiding a grin, she licked the plum-shaped tip like a lollipop, around and around in one direction, then back around and around in the other. His moans grew lower and more frequent, the thrust of his pelvis more powerful. And she moved with him, rolling, riding, never letting her concentration waver until she'd brought him off as thoroughly and violently as possible.

Crawling back up the length of his amazing body, she smiled and kissed his cheek before nestling close to his side. He tucked his arm around her, using his other hand to brush a stray strand of hair away from her face.

"*Mo gaol*," he murmured, pressing his lips to her forehead.

"What language is that?" she asked. The tips of her fingers drifted through the light sprinkling of hair covering his chest, circling his nipples and counting the lines of his rib cage while she rested her head on his shoulder. "You've used it before, but it's not one I recognize. Is it Scottish?"

"Aye," he answered in a low voice, his brogue slightly more pronounced than usual. "Scottish Gaelic. It's what my family spoke most often when I was growing up."

"And what does that mean—what you just said?"

He hesitated a moment, and she felt him tense beneath her. She was about to lift her head and look at him, to find out what the problem was, when he answered.

"My love," he told her, tone rough with emotion. "*Mo gaol* means my love."

A wide grin spread across her face while a blossom of happiness she'd never felt before unfurled in her chest. At any other time, with any other man, it might feel as though things were happening too fast. But here, now, she knew it was absolutely right. Thanks to the stories she'd heard about Dougal since childhood and the dreams she'd been having about him on a regular basis since adulthood, she felt as though she'd known him forever.

"Is that what I am?" she asked. "Your love?"

She held her breath, waiting for his reply, a thousand thoughts racing through her brain depending on his response.

"Yes," he said finally in a near whisper, "I think perhaps you are."

At that, she inhaled sharply, tipping her head back to meet his eyes. Her own felt suspiciously damp. "I think you are, too. *Mo gaol.*"

With a growl, he swooped in to capture her lips, kissing her with more than passion, more than desire . . . this kiss was filled with love.

A noise from the upper floor of the keep woke her some time later. From the second guttering candle on the small tabletop, she suspected hours had passed while she and Dougal had slept the sleep of the exhausted and thoroughly sated.

The sound came again, and she sat up, Dougal doing the same beside her as they both became aware that someone else was in the castle with them.

He rose, grabbing his clothes and quickly starting to dress. Scrambling across the dirt-covered floor, she found her own jeans and t-shirt and wiggled into them.

Dougal headed for the stairwell, but she stopped him with a hand on his arm.

"Wait," she said in a hushed whisper. "Let me go up and see who it is. I'll try to get rid of them so you won't be seen."

He hesitated, and she felt the rigid muscles of his forearm twitch beneath her fingers. But then he nodded, and she started forward.

She jogged silently up the stairs, wanting to catch whoever was snooping around before they reached the back of the keep and discovered Dougal's secret lair.

Near the front entrance of the castle, a man stood by her things, leaning on a gnarled walking stick as he surveyed her sleeping bag, camera bag, and the other assorted things she'd brought for her stay at Castle MacKay. He was older, with white hair and a full white beard. His worn and patched work pants were held up by a pair of red suspenders over a plaid flannel shirt.

The ball of dread that had been sitting so heavy in her stomach broke up and disappeared as she recognized him as one of the patrons of the small cafe in town where she'd stopped before making the rest of the trek to the keep. Mr. Abernethy, she thought was his name.

"Hello," she said, stepping forward, her fingers buried casually in the back pockets of her jeans.

Mr. Abernethy's head came up, and he smiled, backlit by the bright morning sunshine of another beautiful Scottish summer morning. As he turned, she noticed the walking stick wasn't the only thing he was holding. He also had a long, dangerous-looking shotgun tucked under his other arm.

She swallowed hard, stopping in her tracks.

"Hi, there," he said, his accent similar to Dougal's. "I came to see how you were doing up here in this place all alone."

"Oh, I'm fine," she told him. She forced her lips to curve, her shoulders to relax in an "I'm not hiding anything" pose. "Taking a lot of pictures, making a lot of notes. It's beautiful up here."

"Good, good."

When he started forward, still scanning the place with blatant curiosity, she quickly did the same, moving closer to the front of the keep to keep him from getting near the back. She had no doubt Dougal was standing at the top of the stairs, just on the other side of the opening that led to his underground room, and she wanted to keep Mr. Abernethy as far away from that spot as possible.

"They say this castle is haunted, did ye know that?"

Not haunted, she thought, *occupied.* There was a difference.

"Yes, so I'd heard," she responded, doing her best to nudge him back outside. But he seemed happy right where he was, and didn't move. "That's part of the reason I wanted to visit."

"Have you noticed anything, then? Anything . . . out of the ordinary?" he asked, his eyes moving all the time, scanning the surroundings.

Not unless he considered a man cursed to bear the traits of a mythical beast *out of the ordinary.*

"No, nothing. It's a great place, but I haven't seen or heard any signs of otherworldly inhabitation yet." She gave a light chuckle, trying to lighten the mood and emphasize again that there was nothing going on here that he needed to be concerned about . . . on her behalf, or his own.

"Well . . ." He scratched his chin through the thick hair of his beard. "I guess I'll be letting you get back to your work, then. If you need anything, just let us know."

"I will," she said, happy that he was finally leaving. "Thank you."

Abernethy started to turn, but before he was all the way around, he stopped, his head swinging back to stare over her right shoulder with a keen, sharp gaze.

"What was that?" he asked, his voice going cautious and alert.

"What?" she repeated, turning in the direction of his gaze, even though she was pretty sure she knew exactly what he'd seen. "I don't see anything."

And she didn't. But it was possible Dougal had peered around the corner just long enough for Abernethy to spot him. Dammit.

"There's someone back there." Abernethy took a single, dogged step forward, his boot crunching on the dirt of the floor.

"Mr. Abernethy, there's no one there," she told him firmly, moving directly into his path. "I've been here all day, exploring, taking pictures. If anyone else had come into the castle, I would know it. I knew you were here, didn't I?"

But her assurances didn't sway him one bit. His gaze never faltered from the dark doorway to the underground room.

"There's someone there," he said, lower this time, and with a distinct edge to his tone.

Bringing the barrel of his shotgun up and positioning it for easy firing, he stalked forward.

"No." She threw herself in front of him, shuffling back as he advanced. "Mr. Abernethy, no one's here, and I'd appreciate it if you would leave."

He didn't even acknowledge that she'd spoken, but continued as though he was hunting an elusive prey.

"Mr. Abernethy. Mr. Abernethy, please."

She pushed at his chest, pressed up against him, and used her body weight to try to halt his advance. Finally, he stopped, but it was only to raise the shotgun to his shoulder and aim it at the darkness that concealed Dougal's presence.

"Somebody's back there."

Her heart was racing, her stomach twisted in knots. But before she could deny his assertions again, Dougal stepped out from the doorway to tower at her back.

She stopped breathing, waiting to see what would happen, and she knew the exact moment Abernethy saw Dougal's reptilian gaze and the colored scales marring his face and neck.

Abernethy's eyes widened, his mouth going slack with fear. The barrel of the gun lifted slightly so that it bypassed her and pointed straight at Dougal's heart.

"Get out of the way," Abernethy ordered, both his voice and his hands shaking.

"No. Mr. Abernethy, it's not what you think. Dougal belongs here. This is his castle."

But her words were falling on deaf ears. She could see it on his face and in the twitch of his finger on the gun's trigger.

The rest happened so fast, her brain could barely register it all.

Dougal took a step toward her, his hands brushing her arms.

Abernethy took his actions as a threat, raised the shotgun a fraction higher, and fired.

Laura screamed, a high, drawn-out, frantic *"Nooooooooooo!"* and tried to throw herself in front of Dougal at the same time his hold on her arms tightened and he pushed her to the side, away from danger even as he walked directly into it.

It all happened in slow motion, only speeding up again after the boom of the shotgun blast finished echoing in her ears and through the stone walls of the keep.

Pushing herself up from the ground, she immediately turned to see what had happened to Dougal. She let out another shout when she saw him—lying on the ground, motionless, a splotch of bright red spreading sickeningly across his chest.

CHAPTER 5

"NO, NO, NO," SHE CHANTED OVER AND OVER,
tears streaming down her cheeks as she huddled over Dougal's prone body. She tore her t-shirt off and used it to staunch the flow of blood seeping from the wound in his chest. With her free hand, she brushed the hair back from his face, trying not to panic at the cool and clammy feel of his skin.

"Don't just stand there," she snapped at Abernethy, who had gone as pale as his beard, "go for help. Call 9-1-1 and get an ambulance up here. *Hurry.*"

Apparently realizing what he'd done, and as worried as she was that Dougal would die, he spun on his heel and raced from the castle.

Turning back to Dougal, she leaned even harder on his wound.

"Please don't die," she begged, throat clogging with emotion. "Please, Dougal, don't die. I don't want to live without you. I think I'm in love with you, and now that I've found you, I can't lose you. I'll stay here with you, I don't care, just please don't die."

His chest heaved with a ragged breath and he stirred, lashes fluttering as he fought to open his eyes. Lines of pain bracketed his mouth, his lips white with it.

"Oh, God." She didn't know if his regaining consciousness was good or bad, but his blood had already soaked through the material of her shirt, covering her hand in a warm, sticky layer of red.

"Hang on, Dougal. Help is coming, just hang on."

Though it cost him, he raised a hand to clutch her arm. "I love you, too. I waited . . . a hundred years for human contact . . . but don't regret . . . a single moment . . . because in the end, it brought you to me."

His voice was little more than a hitching rasp, but she heard every word as clear as day. She sucked in a breath, struggling not to break down even as her vision clouded and her heart took an unsteady dip.

Before she could respond, tell him again that she loved him desperately and didn't want him to die, his head rolled to the side and his body went slack.

"No. No, no, no." Pressing on his chest, she scrambled to feel for a pulse, for any indication that he was still alive, growing more and more terrified as the seconds ticked by and she couldn't find any signs of life. She slumped forward, her head resting on his unmoving chest as she sobbed out her overwhelming grief.

He couldn't be gone. He just couldn't.

Only moments ago, he'd been so vital and hot to the touch with his amazing life force. Now he was still and cool.

Shuddering with misery, she took a deep, stuttering breath only to let it out again in a wave of fresh tears.

She was ready to lie down beside him and die, too, when his lips suddenly parted to suck in great gulps of air. His eyes popped open and his chest heaved, bowing his body up and off the ground.

Laura jerked back, watching him writhe in agony, gasping for breath. Her eyes widened and her own heart nearly stopped beating as the scales on his face and neck began to lighten, the colors becoming paler, the bumpy texture becoming smoother. His pupils slowly rounded from slits to a more natural, human shape.

She was too stunned to say anything, too shocked to even

move. She simply sat there, legs folded beneath her, arms hanging limply at her side, mesmerized by the transformation taking place in front of her.

Seconds later, the spasms seeming to wrack Dougal's body stopped and he stilled again, his chest rising and falling slowly. Normally. His lashes fluttered as he blinked a few times, taking in his surroundings.

"Dougal?" She called his name softly, crawling forward to hover over him. Her fingers skimmed his face, coming to rest on the side of his throat where his pulse beat steady and strong. His skin was warmer than before, but not overly so, not burning the way it had when they'd made love.

Swallowing hard, she very carefully lifted the blood-soaked t-shirt she'd used to cover the bullet wound in his chest. The thought of what she might find underneath made her stomach clench, but though the area was red, the hole in his shirt jagged, there was no matching hole in his flesh. She reached out to touch him and was startled to find the spot totally intact.

"Oh, my God," she murmured.

Pushing up on his elbows, he looked down, then probed the area himself.

"Your eyes . . ." she told him. They were still a gorgeous, glorious shade of green, but the slits were gone, leaving them as human and normal as any she'd ever seen. "Your scales . . ."

He raised an arm, studying the back of his hand where the colorful markings used to be fully visible. Then he lifted that hand to his neck and face, feeling for signs of the scaling he'd lived with for the last hundred years.

"They're gone," he breathed, awe and disbelief evident in his tone.

All she could do was nod, her eyes turning damp again at the realization that he was alive and well . . . better than well, if his new appearance was anything to go by.

"So is the bullet wound," she said, voice shaky. "You're alive."

Pushing to his feet, he pulled her up with him. The bloody shirt fell to the ground and he quickly shrugged out of his own ruined garment, tossing it aside. His sculpted chest was smooth now, bare and clear, but no less attractive for its lack of iridescent scales.

"I guess throwing yourself in front of a panicked gunman to save my life counted as enough of a selfless act to lift the curse," she told him with a watery laugh, crossing her arms beneath her breasts, covered only by her white bra, which was now smeared in places with Dougal's blood. "We're going to have some explaining to do when Mr. Abernethy gets back with help, though."

"Let's clean up a bit, find something else to wear, and figure out what we'll tell them. My presence alone will make them wonder."

He turned toward the darkened doorway that led to the underground room, but stopped when Laura made a small sound of dismay she couldn't hold back.

"What is it?" he asked, cocking his head to look at her.

"Your back." She stepped forward to run her fingers over the beautiful rainbow of color there, rising out of the waistband of his pants to the right of his spine and curving upwards toward his shoulder blades. It was a peculiar shape, almost like one of those twisting Chinese dragons itself, but absolutely stunning to behold, and looked almost as though he'd had it tattooed there on purpose.

He twisted his body, trying to catch a glimpse of the new markings, which had apparently been left behind as a reminder of the years he'd spent living under the gypsy woman's curse. His brows crossed as he scowled, a low growl working its way up his throat.

"I like it," she said, moving close enough to wrap her arms around his waist and hug him tight. "It reminds me of the dragon I fell in love with. And it will certainly be easier to explain than the rest when I take you home with me."

His fingers feathered through the hair at her temples, tucking the jet-black strands behind her ears as he tipped her face up to his. "Take me home with you?" he asked, humor lacing his tone. "Like a stray cat?"

She shrugged one shoulder, holding his gaze even as her insides turned liquid with nerves. "Or like a lover. Or a husband."

His eyes, still the most gorgeous she'd ever seen, flashed with heat and desire. "Husband," he said, testing the word on his tongue. "I like the sound of that."

He lowered his head to capture her mouth, his kiss burning through her as hotly as it had while he was still cursed and breathing fire.

"So do I," she whispered when they came up for air. "So do I."

BROTHER'S KEEPER

Lilith Saintcrow

CHAPTER 1

A SHRILL SCREAM JERKED HER OUT OF THE DEEP well of sleep.

Selene fumbled for the phone, pushed her hair back, pressed the talk button. "Mrph." She managed the trick of rolling over and blinking at the alarm clock. *Oh, God, what now?* "This had better be good."

"Lena?" A familiar voice wheezed into the other end of the phone. He gasped again. "Lena, it's me."

Oh no. Not another panic attack. "Danny?" Selene sat straight up, her heart pounding. "Danny, what's wrong? Are you okay?" Sweat began to prickle under her arms, the covers turned to strangling fingers before she realized she was awake.

"Cold," he whispered, breath coming in staccato gasps. "Selene. Help. Help me. The book—the *book*—"

Another panic attack, it sounds like another one, oh God. They're getting worse. Selene swung her feet to the cold floor, switching the phone to her right ear, trapping it on her shoulder. "Where are you? Danny? Are you at home?" She grabbed her canvas bag the moment her feet hit the floor, craning her neck to read the Caller ID display. *Daniel Thompson,* his familiar number. He was at home.

Where else would he be? Danny hadn't left his apartment

for nearly five years. "Keep breathing. Deep breaths, down into your tummy. I'll be right there."

"No," Danny pleaded. His asthmatic wheeze was getting worse. "Cold . . . *Lena*. Don't. Don't. Danger—" The line went dead.

Selene slammed the phone back into the cradle, her breath hissing in. Her fingers tingled—a sure sign of something awful. *What was I dreaming? Something about the sea, again.* She raced for the bathroom, grabbing a handful of clothes from the dirty-laundry hamper by the bathroom door. *Just keep breathing, Danny. Don't let the panic get too big for you. I'm on my way.* She tripped, nearly fell face-first, banging her forehead on the door. "Shit!"

She yanked her jeans up with one hand and turned on the faucet with the other, splashed her face with cold water. She fastened her thick blond mane with an elastic band and raced for the door, ripping her sweater at the neck as she forced it over her head. She had to hop on one foot to yank her socks on, she jammed her feet into her boots and flung her bag over her head, catching the strap in her hair. *Just keep him calm enough to remember not to hurt himself, God. Please.*

She slowed down at the end of her block, searching for a cab. *One down, nine to go.* She sprinted across the street. Rain kissed her cheeks and made the sidewalk slick and slightly gritty under the orange wash of city light. Deep heaving gasps of chill air made her lungs burn. Her forehead smarted, making her eyes water.

She crossed Cliff Street, slowing down, pacing herself. *Can't run myself out on the first blocks or I'll be useless before I get halfway there. If this is another one of his practical jokes I am just going to kill him.*

Three down, seven to go. Selene's boots pounded into the sidewalk. Rain whispered on the deserted streets and along the length of her messy ponytail, dripped down her neck as she crossed Martin Street and cut across the intersection. There were more streetlamps here, she checked her watch as she ran.

Two-thirty. Santiago City held its breath under the mantle of chill night.

The back of Selene's neck prickled, uneasiness rippling just under her skin.

Why can't these things happen in the daylight? Or when I don't have lecture in the morning? This had better be something good, Danny, I swear to God if you're just throwing another snit-fit I will never *forgive you. Never, ever, ever.*

Something chill and panicked began to revolve under her breastbone. The back of Selene's neck crawled. *I'm getting a premonition.* Her breath came in miserable harsh sobs of effort. *Either that or I'm just spooked. Who wouldn't be at 2 A.M. in this busted-down part of town?* She set her teeth, grimly ignoring the stitch in her side. *Danny. Just breathe, please God, let him remember to breathe. Don't let him be in the kitchen, there are knives in there. This sounds like a doozy, he hasn't had a bad panic attack in at least six months, Christ don't let him hurt himself.*

"Hey, Selene."

Selene whirled. "Bruce!" she choked, her hand leaping instinctively to her throat. The silver medallion was still under her sweater, warm against her skin. She hadn't taken it off. "Good God, don't *do* that!" She clenched her hands at her side. *If only he was human, I could punch him.*

Bruce grinned down at her, canines glittering in the pallid orange light, his eyes glowing just like a small nocturnal animal's. Beneath his loud polyester sport jacket and eye-searing yellow tie, his narrow spotted chest was pale and hairless. "Don't worry so much, Lena. I wouldn't *dream* of taking a taste. His Highness wouldn't like that one little bit." His lips curled back even more, exposing more gleaming teeth.

Selene's heart slammed once against her ribs. Taking a long deep breath, she willed her pulse to slow. *Focus, goddammit! Danny needs you, you can't fight anyone or anything if you're busy screaming.*

"I don't have time, Bruce," she gasped. "Danny's in trouble."

"I'll go with you." Bruce shrugged and peeled his lanky frame away from the streetlamp. He had just been Turned, and still looked almost human.

Almost. The feral glow in his eyes and the quick jerking of his movements screamed "not-quite-normal."

Still, for a Nichtvren, Bruce was as close to human as possible. He'd just been Turned, so he didn't have the scary immobility of older suckheads. Small blessing, but she'd take it. "That's not neces—" she began.

Bruce folded his arms, the smile gone. "Danny's under Nikolai's protection too, Selene. If I let you go over there and get hurt, His Highness will peel off my skin in strips and salt me down." Bruce shivered, his long pink tongue wetting his lips. "Trust me. I'll go with you."

"Oh, for Christ's sweet sake." Selene wasn't about to argue with a dead lounge lizard. He fell into step beside her, long legs easily keeping pace as she trotted up the sidewalk. She glanced down. Black loafers and no socks. *All you're missing is a clutch of gold chains and chest hair.* She tried to keep her breathing quiet, pushing down a lunatic desire to giggle nervously. *Danny, Danny, I'm on my way. Don't hurt yourself.*

"I don't . . . know what . . . he's thinking," she gasped, speeding up. "I'm . . . perfectly . . . safe."

Bruce managed a high, thin giggle. "Oh, no you're not, chickadee. You should be glad His Highness took an interest in you." He didn't even sound winded.

I don't need Nikolai's protection. I did just fine on my own.

Okay, so she didn't *want* Nikolai's protection. She'd rather tap dance naked through a minefield singing "Petticoat Junction." Just because Nikolai was the prime paranormal Power in the city, responsible for keeping the peace among all the other factions of paranormal citizenry, didn't mean *she* would ever kowtow to him. His Highness Nikolai indeed. Just another suckhead come out from the shadows under the protection of the Paranormal Species Act.

Only this one had an interest in her.

Don't think about things like that. Danny, please be okay. Don't bite your tongue or cut yourself.

Her bag shifted, clinking when it banged against her shoulder. Steel and salt, the tools she needed to banish anything evil or unwanted; it didn't pay as well as teaching but God knew there was a need for her talents. She'd been so tired when she got home she hadn't unpacked, poltergeist infestations were like that. Not very difficult, but messy and draining. She pushed the strap higher. "I don't need his . . . protection or . . . yours, suckhead."

"That's what *you* think." Bruce grinned down at her, his words soft and even. "Want me to carry your bag?"

"Of . . . course . . . not." Selene sped up. *To hell with pacing myself. Danny needs me.*

Selene's medallion warmed against her skin, reacting to Bruce's presence—at least, she *hoped* that was what it was reacting to. By the time they reached Danny's building, the metal thrummed with Power. Gooseflesh raced down her body; she choked back a final gasp as she rounded the final corner.

Bruce smirked, letting out a soft little snort of laughter. Selene curled her hands into fists, resisting the urge to claw the smile from his face. *Jumping the Nichtvren won't get you anywhere, Selene. Just ignore him, and concentrate on what matters. Danny, my God, please be okay. Remember the visualizations I taught you.*

The tall black-clad shape rose from the shadows lying over the concrete steps. *Oh, no. Could this possibly get any worse?*

Of course not. Of course Nikolai would show up now. He always seemed to know when there was trouble.

Bruce dropped back behind Selene. *At least I won't have to see that fucking smirk on his face. Danny, please be okay, don't be banging your head on the wall again. I'm on my way, I'm coming.*

Her heart slammed once against the cage of her ribs and

her fingers curled into fists. Fire bloomed in her cheeks, spread down her neck, and merged with the growing heat of the medallion between her breasts. She fought for control, ribs flaring as she struggled against hyperventilation.

Hands in his coat pockets, chin tilted toward her, Nikolai's dark eyes catalogued her tangled blond hair, camel coat, scuffed boots. Her fingers itched to straighten her clothes, brush back her hair, check for loose threads. As usual, he was so contained she longed to see him roughed up a little.

I suppose you learn a little self-control when you're a Master powerful enough to rule Saint City. He's the Prime, after all. We all live our little lives in his long dark shadow.

A few strands of crow-black hair fell over his eyes as Selene, impelled by the medallion's growing heat, skidded to a stop inches from him. Her ponytail swung heavily, but he didn't reach out to grab her arm and "protect" her from falling headlong on the steps. Her heart actually *leapt* to see him again.

Stop that. He's not human, you know that, stop STARING at him!

Nikolai said nothing, the light stroking his high cheekbones. His mouth, usually curled into a half-smile, was compressed into a thin line. His dark, electric eyes flicked over Bruce, who cringed another three steps back.

Selene suppressed a burst of nasty satisfaction. *Serves you right.* She started up the stairs, pressing her left hand against the sudden stitch gripping her side. Her toe caught on the second step.

She fetched up short when Nikolai closed his hand around her left arm, steadied her before she could fall over, and let her go, all in the space of a moment. "Selene." The chill rain-soaked air shivered under the word, his voice soft and irresistible. At least he didn't have the scary gold-green sheen on his eyes tonight, Selene hated that. "Stirling."

"I was on watch." Bruce didn't sound half so smug now. Of course, he was an accident, Turned as a joke or mistake; Nichtvren didn't Turn ugly humans. It was an unwritten rule: only the pretty or the ruthless were given the gift of immortality, and Bruce was neither. Why Nikolai kept him around was anyone's guess, and Selene didn't want to ask. Bruce's doglike attachment and gratefulness for any crumb Nikolai threw his way was telling enough.

Besides, if she asked she had a sneaking suspicion Bruce might answer, and she wouldn't like the answer at all. Not to mention what she might have to pay for it.

Selene brushed past Nikolai. Her boots smacked against the cold, wet concrete of the steps. She reached the glassed-in front door and stopped short, digging in her coat pocket for her keys. *So Nikolai's having me watched.* She filed the information away.

Her fingers rooted fruitlessly around in her pocket and found nothing but an empty gum wrapper. "Oh, no." Her keys were on the table by the door at her apartment, she had *not* scooped them up on her way out. Just run right past them in her frantic dash. "Bloody *fucking* hell on a cheese-coated *stick*."

"You need to go in?" Nikolai's breath brushed her cheek, the faint smell of aftershave and male closing around her. He was *right* behind her, so far into her personal space it wasn't even funny.

A violent start nearly toppled her into the firmly-shut door. She hadn't heard or *sensed* him behind her, he just appeared out of thin air. *Dammit, does he have to do that all the time?* The only place she could go to escape him was through the glass. She stared at the door, taking in deep harsh breaths and willing it to open. There was a quick, light patter of footsteps—Bruce, making off into the night. "I left my keys at home. Danny called. I think it's a panic attack, and when he gets them he sometimes hurts himself. There's an intercom—"

Nikolai reached around her, his body molded to hers, and touched the lock. The gold and carnelian signet ring gleamed wetly in the uncertain light as his pale fingers brushed the metal. He went absolutely still. The medallion's metal cooled abruptly between Selene's breasts, responding to the controlled flare of energy Nikolai was using. She could almost See what he was doing, despite the stealthy camouflage of a Master Nichtvren's aura. The only thing scarier than their power was their creepy invisibility.

I really wish he'd quit crowding me. Her worry returned, sharp and acrid. Her lungs burned, the stitch knotting her left side again. *Please, Danny. Please be okay. I don't even care anymore if it's one of your midnight games, I hope you're all right.*

The lock clicked open with a muffled *thunk* and Selene grabbed the handle before it could close again. Nikolai's hand brushed hers, slid over the handle, he stepped aside and pulled the door open. She yanked her hand away. *He didn't have to touch me. He did that on purpose.*

"Thanks," she managed around the dry lump in her throat. *Stop it*, she thought desperately, biting the inside of her cheek. The pain helped her focus. *It's only Nikolai. You know what he is, and why he's doing this. You're here for Danny, remember?*

"My pleasure." His eyes dropped down to the medallion safely hidden under her sweater. The metal flushed with icy heat now.

He's looking at my chest like he sees dinner there. Heat sizzled along Selene's nerves. "Oh, stop that." She stepped through the door, sliding past him, suddenly grateful for someone else's presence. Her heart hammered thinly, the taste of burning in her mouth. *Danny. Just remember to breathe, kiddo. Little sister's almost there to take care of you.* "I suppose you want to come up."

"Of course." His voice stroked her cheek, slid down her neck. He leaned back against the open door, his dark eyes now fixed on her face. Selene gulped down another breath, her heartbeat evening out. The familiar bank of mailbox doors was on her right, and the peeling linoleum floor glared back at the dirty ceiling. "It is pleasant to see you, Selene."

Nikolai cat-stepped into the foyer, gracefully avoiding the closing door. Little droplets of rain glittered in his hair, sparked by the fluorescent lights. Under his coat, he wore a dark-blue silk t-shirt and a pair of designer jeans. The shirt moved slightly as muscle flickered in his chest.

Selene dropped her eyes, turned away from him. Oddly enough, he wore a high-end pair of black Nikes. *Vampire fashion just ain't what it used to be.* Selene had to stifle another mad giggle. *Where's the fangs and the black cape, not to mention the evening wear?* Her heart sped up, thundered in her ears. *God love me, I'm going to have a fucking cardiac arrest right here in the foyer.*

"Well, come on, then." She started up the orange-carpeted stairs, sidling away from him. Nikolai followed closely behind, but not too close, letting Selene take the lead. For once.

Given how he's always going on about how I need "protecting," it's a wonder he's letting me in the building at all. But dammit, if he showed up at the door he'd just scare Danny more. He's being tactful for once. Lucky me.

Her legs trembled and she rubbed at her eyes as she trooped up the stairs. Nikolai made no sound. "Would you make a little noise?" She immediately regretted asking. The silence behind her intensified. "Danny sometimes has panic attacks so he calls me. I just hope he's okay. He hasn't left the apartment for years." *Shut up, Selene, Nikolai knows. Danny'll be okay, it's probably nothing. He just stayed out of his body for too long and had trouble when he came back, another panic attack and the numbness. He's okay. Be okay, Danny, please?*

Nikolai's footsteps echoed hers as he climbed behind her. That was a relief, but Selene still felt the weight of his black eyes as they reached the fourth floor. Her thighs and ass burned. Climbing stairs after almost-running ten blocks without rest was a workout she could do without.

Nikolai's arm came over her shoulder again and held the heavy fire door open. The hall was dingy, most of the light fixtures missing bulbs, and a drift of fast food wrappers curled up from the far end. Selene's nose dripped from the chill. She rubbed at it with the back of her hand, tried not to sniff too loudly. Threadbare orange carpet whispered under her boots. The entire hall was so familiar she barely paid any attention. Down the hall a wedge of light speared through the gloom.

Danny's door was open.

CHAPTER 2

LONG JAGGED SPLINTERS POPPED OUT FROM THE frame, the door loosely hanging from its hinges. Lighter, unpainted wood peered through ragged vertical cracks. *Oh, Jesus. Oh no.*

"*Danny!*" Selene leapt forward just as Nikolai's hand closed around her arm and pulled her back, jerking her arm almost out of its socket. "Let *go* of me!"

"No," he said, quietly. "Let me."

"He's *my* brother." She struggled frantically, achieved exactly nothing.

Nikolai's fingers tightened, digging into her softer, human flesh. He pushed her back against the wall. "Stay here." He looked down at her, his lips a thin line and his dark eyes fathomless. No cat-shine in them now, either. *He must be worried.*

Selene's lungs labored to catch even a small breath. Her back and arms prickled. "Nikolai—" she began, but he laid a finger on her lips. The contact was electric. Her entire body went liquid, a moan starting in her chest. Selene strangled it before it reached her lips, making a thin dry sound instead. *Stop it, stop it, no time for this, stop it, God, what kind of a talent did you give me if it makes me feel like this? Goddammit, please, help me.*

Nikolai's skin was fever-warm. He must have fed, he was metabolizing whatever he'd taken that night—blood, or death, or pain, or sex. Was it wrong to be grateful it hadn't been her? Though God knew she'd done her share of feeding him. Being *fed* by him.

Danny. Selene tried to slip along the wall away from Nikolai, but he pinned her in place without even trying. He was being gentle, he could have broken her arm or put her *through* the wall if he'd wanted to. With hardly any effort.

He wasn't human, after all.

"Move again and I will force your compliance." Nikolai leaned closer, his lips a breath away from Selene's, inhaling. Tasting her breath. *Well, the dead do breathe, when they want to*, she thought in a lunatic singsong. *Just like the first night I met him.* She hastily shoved the thought away, freezing in place. It was a mark of *possession*, smelling her breath like that; a Nichtvren didn't get that close unless he or she intended to feed or mark you. If she struggled, his predatory instinct might come into play and he might well decide to sink his fangs in her throat right here.

So instead of looking at him, she stared over his shoulder. There was a spot of discolored, peeling paint on the opposite wall. Selene looked intently at it, her eyes hot and dry. She felt his eyes on her, waiting for her to speak, argue, something, Selene bit the inside of her cheek. *I'm not going to give you the fucking satisfaction. Something hacked his door down, oh God, oh God. Oh, Danny.*

The weight of Nikolai's gaze slowly lessened when she didn't struggle. It took everything Selene had not to move, to stay still and passive. *I will not give you the excuse. Danny, please be okay. Come on, Nikolai, you're so blasted interested in both of us*, help *him!* "Danny." The whisper escaped despite her. Nikolai took another long breath, leaning close, inhaling her scent deeply. Her knees went weak.

"Stay here." He disappeared. Selene felt the shimmer of Power in the close still air of the hallway. To a human it would feel like a chill walking up the spine, a tightness under the lungs, if they were sensitive. Someone without psychic sensitivity might feel a momentary breeze, a cold draft, a sudden flash of fear that would quickly be disregarded.

The shimmer slipped through the space between the door and the shattered frame. *God, please,* she prayed. *Please, God. Please.*

Always begging. They called witches like her— *tantraiiken*—the "beggars." Always moaning and pleasing. It was hard not to, when you had a talent that made your body betray you over and over again.

Stop it. Think about something useful. Why was Nikolai here? Or Bruce? Bruce's hunting ground wasn't around Selene's apartment building, at least, it hadn't been three weeks ago, when he'd turned up . . . well, Turned.

Nikolai must have set Bruce to watch her. Why *now* when she'd known Nikolai for all this time?

Known might be too strong a word. You can't know a Nichtvren. They're not human, no matter how charming they can occasionally be. You're food to them. That's all.

Selene's back prickled, her breath coming in shallow adrenaline-laden sips. *Danny, be okay. God, please, let him just be panicked. Let him just be upset but okay. Or even just a little hurt. Let him be alive.*

Caught between fear and excitement, Selene let out a slow sharp gasp. Her knees shook slightly, the outer edges of her shields thickening reflexively. The jeans she'd thrown on were damp at the ankles from the rain, and would be damp between her legs soon.

Oh, God. It was her cursed talent. A sexwitch didn't feel fear the way other people did. No, being afraid just turned into a different sensation entirely. One below the belt, thick and warm enough to make her heartbeat pound in her ears, a trickle of heat beginning way down low.

The agonized dread spiraled, kick-started a wave of desire that tipped her head back against the wall, forced her breath into another jagged half-gasp. Any more of this and she'd be a quivering ball of need and nerves by the time Nikolai reappeared.

Goddammit, Selene, focus! She shook out her trembling hands; if she had to throw Power she would need her fingers. Her heartbeat thundered in her ears. She repeated the mantra, as if it would help. *Please, God. Please let my brother be safe.*

Begging, again. Loathing crawled up her spine, mixed with the desire, and turned her stomach into a sudsing, bubbling washing machine.

The shimmer returned. Nikolai solidified right in front of her, a faint breeze blowing stray strands of hair back, her forehead cold as the moisture evaporated. Wisps of hair stirred at her nape. Her ponytail was loose.

He looked absolutely solid, *real*. Did his victims ever see him coming? It was like swimming with a shark and suddenly wondering if you'd cut yourself shaving that morning.

Selene met his eyes, tipping her head back. Nothing. She blinked, then looked at the shattered door again.

Nikolai caught her shoulders, pushed her back against the wall. "We will call the police."

Her body, traitor that it was, understood before she did. Her heart plummeted into her belly with a splash, and the stew of desire and horror faded under a wave of stark chemical adrenaline. "What's this *we*? What's wrong with Danny? What's *happened*?"

He smiled, and Selene backed up—or tried to, her shoulders hit the wall again. There were few things worse than Nikolai's lazy, genuinely good-humored grin. Especially his eyeteeth—*fangs*, she corrected herself, *the word is fangs, let's call it what it is, you're old enough to call things what they are.* She could all too well imagine what those teeth could do to her jugular.

It's not his teeth, though. It's the rest of him I have trouble with.

"You will disturb the evidence. We can't have that, can we? The police prefer to observe the formalities." Nikolai was calm, too calm, and that grin . . .

Danny, she thought, but it was merely a despairing moan.

Nikolai continued, softly and pitilessly. "We will go downstairs and call the police. *Verscht za?*"

She slid away toward the door, blindly. Nikolai pinned her to the wall, his body curving into hers. Heat slammed through her; she tasted copper adrenaline. Selene drew in a sharp breath and kicked, missing him somehow. He smiled, caught her wrists. He could hold her all night and struggling would only excite him—and her. *Stop it.* Then she said it out loud. "Stop it." Her voice broke, helplessly.

"You are being unwise." His tone was a mere murmur, so reasonable. "Do as I say, Selene. Help me."

Help you? Help you? "You bastard." The steel vise of his fingers strangled her wrists. A twisting wire of pain lanced up both arms. Jerking backward, she smacked her head against the wall, brief starry pain twinkling in front of her eyes. "Tell me what happened."

"Your brother is dead, Selene. Now we must call the police. Will you come with me or shall I drag you?" Nikolai smiled, his eyes twinkling. "I would enjoy carrying you. Particularly if you struggle."

"Let go of me. I'll go downstairs and call the police." *Like a good little girl.* Her teeth clenched together, her jaw aching. She'd have a goose-egg on the back of her head for sure. *Danny . . .*

"Very good," he breathed, and released her, finger by finger. Selene stared up into the lightless pools of his eyes. A kind of stunned calm slipped down over her body. Nikolai's eyes were so *dark.* So endlessly dark.

When he spoke next, it was in something approximating a normal voice. "I am sorry, Selene. I will help you, however I can."

Christ, does he have to sound like he means it? Any help

from you is help I can do without, Nikolai. "Leave me alone." Her lips were too numb to work properly. "If you won't let me see, just leave me alone."

"You do not want to see. It is . . . disturbing. Now come."

The metal box of the pay phone gleamed dully under the fluorescents. A four-year-old phone book scarred with permanent marker, dangled from a rust-pitted chain. Someone had tagged the plastic hood at the top of the box—an out-of-date gang sign, a phone number, a caricature of a donkey, other symbols much less pleasant. Selene picked up the receiver in nerveless fingers, staring at the graffiti-covered plastic.

"I suspect you will want to call your police friend first." Nikolai produced two quarters with a flick of his fingers, dropped them in. Selene's eyes burned dryly, the numbers on the square silver buttons blurring. Nikolai even dialed, his signet ring flashing dully, blood on gold. Somewhere in the numbness a thought surfaced. *How does Nikolai know Jack's number?*

The phone rang four times. "Urmph."

Selene couldn't get the words past the dust in her throat. Nikolai bumped against her, sending a rush of fire through her veins, kick-starting her brain. "Maureen?" she whispered, her voice coming from a deep screaming well of panic. "It's Selene Thompson. I need to talk to Jack. Now."

"What the . . ." Maureen's tone changed suddenly. Mother to the world, that was Maureen. She'd cooked Selene dinner more than once, during the cases Jack needed paranormal help on. "Sweetheart, are you okay? Jack, wake up."

Selene's knees nearly buckled, a moan bubbling up. The vision of the hacked and shattered door rose up in front of her. *Dear God what happened to his door . . . Danny . . .*

Nikolai's fingers slid under her ponytail, fever-hot. Fire spread from her nape, a deluge of sensation pooling in her belly. She hated the feeling, hated *him*, but the Power would help her. She was going into shock. Years of training kicked in, turning the desire into Power, shocking her back in control, her mind adding, subtracting, calculating. *What happened? He hasn't left here in five years. What went wrong?*

Danny was a Journeyman, an adept at etheric and astral travel. He didn't need to leave his apartment, and anyway couldn't bear to be away from the safety of the wards and defenses Selene erected around his three-room world. Nothing touched him inside his magickal cocoon, no thoughts or emotions that might compromise his body when he projected. Time had strengthened Danny's gifts, making him more sensitive to random buffetings, but also more sensitive to Selene's defenses and powers. He couldn't be with her all the time, so an apartment of his own with heavy shielding was the best—

She stiffened. *The wards!* They were a part of Danny now; he had taken over maintaining them since Selene had other problems. But they were originally *her* wards and would answer her call.

And they would have recorded what went on inside Danny's walls.

"Jack here." Detective Jack Pepper's cigarette-rough voice came over the line. "What the *hell*?"

Her voice almost refused to work. "It's Selene. Something's killed Danny. Jack, Nikolai's here." *I sound like I'm twelve years old again. And scared. I sound so scared.*

Selene heard Jack breathing. "Jesus, why is he there? Forget it; I don't want to know. Hang up and call 911. You got it?" The sound of cloth against cloth filtered through the phone. Jack was sitting up. Maureen's whispered questions, then . . . silence.

"I . . . He c-c-called me. Said he was c-c-cold and something about danger." Autopilot pushed the words out, she listened to her own ragged gasping breath. *Danny, oh God. Danny. Jesus Christ . . .*

"Selene, put Nikolai on the phone, honey. Now." Jack was fully awake. A click and a flare of a lighter, deep indrawn breath. *It must be bad if he's smoking in bed, Maureen won't like that.*

She handed the phone to Nikolai. He slid closer, pressing her into the phone booth, his fingers kneading heat into her neck.

I wonder what a gun would do to him? The thought surfaced, she pushed it hastily away. She wasn't sure if he could hear it; Nichtvren were psychic as well as physical predators. If he heard her, what would he do?

"Yes?" Nikolai paused. "Bad enough . . . No, not human . . . I did not. Nor did she. The door is shattered. She will of course not enter the apartment." Selene strained to listen. "Of course. I will stay out of sight. I would not want to cause trouble for my Selene."

Her neck muscles burned. *My Selene? Oh, boy. We're going to have to have a talk about that, suckhead.*

Selene's mind skittered sideways. *Danny. The door. What happened?* Nikolai brushed his thumb over her nape. Lightning shot down her spine and burst in the pit of her stomach. *Oh, God.*

"I will." Nikolai reached over her shoulder again, hung up. He gently turned her to face him, Selene didn't resist. Her head was full of a rushing, roaring noise, his voice came from very far away. "You must call the emergency services, Selene. You received a call from your brother. It was interrupted and you came to see if he was well. You noticed the door had been forced and decided to call 911. Do you understand?"

She stared up at him, his face suddenly oddly foreign. He looked more like a stranger than ever. Selene took a deep shuddering breath, fury crystallizing under the surface of her mind. "Why are you doing this, Nikolai? One dead human, more or less."

His fingers tightened. "One dead human under *my* protection, dear one. Whatever killed him is very dangerous. Now you will call the emergency services and you will be a very good girl for me." He touched his lips to her forehead, a gentle kiss that made her body burn, fire spilling through her veins. *How can I even think about that when Danny's upstairs?*

Hot acid guilt rose in the back of her throat. *I should have gone in there, I should have seen.*

Her eyes filled with tears. "I hate you," she whispered, looking up into Nikolai's dark eyes. "I *hate* you."

"Call them." The corner of his mouth quirked up, as if he found her amusing.

She turned back to the phone and blindly picked up the receiver. Punched the nine, the one, the one. A deep breath. Nikolai moved away suddenly, and she swayed, grabbing the metal edge of the booth to steady herself. One ring. Two. Three. Four. Five.

"911, what are you reporting?" A passionless, professional voice, possibly female.

For one awful moment Selene couldn't remember who she was or what she was doing. The metal bit into her fingers. Blood pounded in her ears and the hallway swirled beneath her. "My-my brother. He c-c-called me. I c-c-came to his apartment and the d-d-door is b-b-roken and I'm afraid t-t-to go inside."

How strange, she thought from inside the glass ball of hysterical calm descending upon her. *I sound like I'm scared to death.* It was her voice giving information, stammering out the story to the operator. Danny never left his apartment. The door was broken. She was afraid. Tiny diamond mice fleeing the huge black wolf running around in her brain made her voice jittery, made her hands tremble.

She glanced over her shoulder. The empty foyer glared under the fluorescents. There was no sign of Bruce or of Nikolai, though the medallion throbbed a heated beat between her breasts. A heartbeat. His heartbeat?

The urge to tear it off and throw it away made her shake. *Danny. Oh, Danny, please. Please, God.*

She slumped, trembling, against the phone box. Her nails drove into her palm. The terrified mice spun round and round inside her brain.

"Miss, please try to be calm. We have dispatched a unit to your location."

Try to be calm? Danny. Oh, God. How can I be calm if you're dead?

CHAPTER 3

THE FOURTH TIME THE OPERATOR TOLD HER TO BE calm, Selene jammed the phone back down. She looked across the mailboxes to the stairs, and the medallion tingled harshly against her skin. A warning. Her throat was full of something hard and slick, she swallowed several times, resting her forehead against cool cheap metal.

Don't go back, the operator had said. *Stay outside the building. Stay and wait for the police. It's safest to wait for the police, ma'am.*

Selene's hoarse inarticulate moan bounced off the stairwell walls. The stairs squeaked under her slow feet. Her legs burned numbly.

She only got halfway up to the first floor before Nikolai's hand closed over her elbow. She gave a startled, wounded little cry and found herself facing him, looking at his chest. He was somehow on the step above her, and his mouth moved, fangs flashing in something less than a good-natured grin. It was more like a smirk, or a warning.

"No," he said. Selene stared at him, and he gave her a little shake. Her head wobbled, the entire stairwell reeling. "Outside. This is not for you."

"He's my—" Her mouth was so dry the words were a croak.

"Your brother. Yes." He used his grip on her arm to pull

her down the stairs. Selene went limp, resisting him, but he simply dragged her as if she weighed nothing. Her boots dropped from stair to stair as if they weren't attached to the rest of her. "You cannot help him now. And I would not have you see this, *milaya*."

"I hate you." The fluorescents seared her wet eyes. "I wish I'd never met you."

He gave a gracious nod, as if she'd complimented him. "Thank you." They reached the bottom of the stairs. He half-carried her across the peeling linoleum. He shouldered the door to the building open, dragged her out and let the door go. The lock engaged.

Selene looked up at him. He set her down on the cold, wet sidewalk and brushed her hair back, settled her camel coat on her shoulders, stroked her sore damp forehead, she'd be lucky to escape a bruise from cracking her head against the wall.

His fingers were still warm. Too warm to be human, feverish, but oddly soothing.

She hated that comfort.

Distant sirens cracked the still air. *Breathe*, she repeated. *In through the nose, out through the mouth. Breathe.*

The mantra didn't help. "I mean it. I hate you." Her voice shook. "I *hate* you."

"And yet you need me." He smiled, an almost-tender expression that made her entire body go cold. Selene would have fallen over backward, but his fingers closed around her wrist, a loose bracelet. Sirens hammered at the roof of the night. "Selene, you do not wish to see what lies in that room. Remember your brother the way he was."

"I don't *need* you." Selene tore her wrist away. His fingers tightened slightly, just to let her know he could hold her, before he let her go and she stumbled. There was something hard and small and spiny in her hand, cold metal.

A police cruiser materialized around the corner, whooping and braying. She opened her hand to find her key ring. *He must have had Bruce sneak into my house and get my keys. The little thief. Always creeping around, peeping in windows and doing Nikolai's bidding. No wonder His Highness keeps him around.*

She looked up. Except for the police car—siren, flashing lights—the street was deserted. Nikolai had vanished. She saw the blurring in the air, the shimmer that might have been him or just the tears filling her eyes. She fumbled on the ring for the key to the front of Danny's building.

Numb, her cheeks wet with rain and tears, she raised her hand to flag the cops down. Thankfully, they cut the siren as soon as they pulled to a stop. Selene waved, her bag bumping at her hip. *No poltergeist here, no curse to be broken, no client looking down their nose at me. No, this time the person needing help is me.*

Two cops, a rookie and a graying veteran who looked at her as if he recognized her. Selene hoped he didn't. If he recognized her, he might ask questions. *Hey, aren't you that freak who hangs around with Jack Pepper?*

"My brother." Her teeth chattered. "He's a shut-in. He doesn't leave the apartment. He called me—his doorjamb's all busted up—it's not normal—"

They barked questions at her, who was her brother, what apartment, who was she, was anyone armed, what did she see? The mice scurrying in Selene's head supplied answers. "4C, apartment 4C, Danny Thompson, I'm Selene, I'm his sister—no, nothing, just the door, that's all I saw, it's busted all to hell—"

Before she unlocked the building door for them, the medallion scorched against her skin. Warning her.

Fuck you, Nikolai.

She followed the cops up the stairs, sliding the medallion's chain up over her head. She pulled it out of her sweater. Light flared sharply from the silver disc before she tossed it into a dark corner of the second-floor landing. The cops didn't notice—they were too busy looking up the stairs and speaking back and forth in cryptic cop-talk. Both had their guns out. "Fourth floor. Apartment 4C," she repeated, and took a deep breath, choking on tears.

"Go back downstairs," the older cop told her. "Go back downstairs!"

Fourth floor. They saw the shattered door, the wedge of light slicing through the dim hall. The older cop radioed for backup.

They edged forward and cautiously pushed the splintered door open. Told her again to go downstairs. Selene told them she would and stood where she was, hot tears spilling down her cheeks.

Now that she wasn't standing next to Nikolai, the wards vibrated with Selene's nearness, lines of light bleeding out from the hole torn where the door used to be. Something had blasted right through the careful layers of defense she'd painstakingly applied to the walls. What could do that?

She took two steps, and the rookie backed up out of the apartment. He was paper-white and trembling, freckles standing out on his fair face, his blond mustache quivering.

After glancing past him once, Selene could see why.

She clamped her right hand over her mouth, staring past the rookie, who stumbled to the side and vomited onto the hall rug. Selene didn't blame him. She could only see a short distance down the entry hall and into the studio room. The kitchen was to the left, bathroom to the right, and she had a clear view almost to the night-dark window, with the orange streetlamps glowing outside.

A moment later her eyes tracked a shimmer up over the streetlamp, a shimmer that resolved into a dark shape balancing atop the streetlamp's arm. A tall shape, crouched down, hands wrapped around the bar, eyes reflecting the light with the green-gold sheen of a cat's eyes at night.

I wish he wouldn't do that, perch up there like some kind of vulture.

Selene looked down again, and her hand tightened over her mouth. Her throat burned with bile. The shapes she was seeing refused to snap into a coherent picture. Blood painted the white walls, soaked into the thin beige carpeting, and the . . . the *pieces* . . .

Footsteps echoed in the hall, shouts, radios squawking. Four more cops. Selene stepped back against the wall, her hand still clamped over her mouth, fingernails digging into her cheek. She struggled to swallow the hot acid bile instead of puking like the rookie.

Detective Jack Pepper, his graying buzz-cut and familiar rumpled gray wool coat steaming in the hall's heat, came striding from the other end. She stumbled back, hitting her head against the wall. Jack gave her a look that could have peeled paint. "Aw, Christ. Get her downstairs," he said as one of the cops took a look past Selene and into the apartment, swearing viciously.

Selene couldn't help herself. She began to giggle into her hand, her eyes streaming. The shrill sound echoed under the crackle of radio talk and more sirens outside.

After wiping his mouth, the blond rookie was finally delegated to take her downstairs. Selene had to steady him, her fingers against the creaking leather of his jacket. The queasy flickers of fear coming off the young man were enough to make her flush, her stomach tightening. Her mental shields were as transparent and brittle as crystal, he was hyped enough to broadcast all over the mental spectrum.

Lawrence, his name is Lawrence. He's an open door right now, and I don't have enough control to shut him out. Knowledge burned through her, the fear turning into a wash of heat that made her nipples peak and her entire body tighten. Her jeans were definitely damp between her legs.

I wish I'd stopped to put my panties on. The sanity of that thought saved her, slapped her back into herself. *Focus, Selene. In through the nose, out through the mouth. Breathe.*

She filled her lungs and tapped in, the rush of Power sparking along her nerves. *I hope he puts me in a car, I can use this and yank the wards off the apartment. A killing like that leaves a mark on the air, the wards will be vibrating with it. I'll be able to track whoever did this to him.* Selene made a slight crooning noise, patted the rookie's shoulder when they reached the foyer. He was looking a little green again, his cheeks pooching out and his lips wet. Selene smelled fear, the sharp tang of human vomit, and her own smell, rich floral musk. *Tantraiiken* musk, the smell of a sexwitch.

Put me in a police car. She patted the rookie's back as he heaved near the stairs. A loose ring of cop cars sat in the wet street. More sirens cut the distant darkness. *I don't want to work magick right here on the street. God alone knows what sort of notice it will attract if I pass out, too.*

"It's okay, Lawrence." She looked up in time to see another cop come flying out of the door—some thoughtful soul had braced it open with a chunk of pavement. This man—tall, stocky, brown hair combed over a bald head Selene could see because he'd lost his hat—made it to the bottom of the stairs before he puked, too, vomit spraying out onto the street.

Selene's gorge rose. She swallowed against it. "Nice boy," she said softly, stroking Lawrence's back. "It's okay. You okay?" *Quit retching and put me somewhere quiet where I can Work, you waste.* The coldness of the thought almost surprised her. He was just the type of ordinary civilian to come running to Selene for her help in dealing with something extraordinary—and then decide she was less than a used Kleenex when everything was said and done.

They were all alike, every one of them. Except Danny, and Danny was gone. Selene's jaw clenched, her teeth grinding together.

Come on. Quit puking so I can work.

He did put her in a police car, mumbling something about her safety and a report, and she closed her eyes, settling back into the cracked vinyl seat. *Finally. What did you eat for dinner, anyway, it certainly stank . . . oh, God, what am I going to do now? Danny.*

Tears pricked behind Selene's eyes. *Quit it! Focus!* She

pictured the hallway leading into Danny's living space, the foldout bed and salvaged wooden shelves of books and curios and the blood—

Her concentration guttered, came back; her ability to visualize under stress had plenty of practice. *Don't fail me now,* she thought, and dropped through the floor of her own consciousness, into the place where she truly lived. Her breathing stilled, her heartbeat paused. An onlooker would have thought she was sleeping, or just sitting with her eyes closed, head tilted back, mouth slackly open. In shock.

She dove into a black blood-warm sea, her concentration narrowing to a single point. Pulled on the threads of the Power she'd spent warding Danny's apartment. The defenses recognized her, left the place in the world where they had been bleeding free, and leapt for her.

Selene "caught" the energy, folded it deftly. The resultant mass shrank, a small bright star to her mental vision, taking on more mass as she compressed it. Selene's body arched upward, gasping for air. The energy she'd taken from the hyped-up rookie drained away. Her skin was prickling and her lips wet, her hips rocking forward slightly, tensing, tighter, tighter, aching for release.

She couldn't afford to let it spend. She had to find something physical to hold the Power until she could take a closer look. Her fingers dipped into her black canvas shoulder-bag and found smooth wood.

My athame. Christ. Here I am in the back of a police car with an illegal-to-carry eight-inch ritual knife. Why did I have to be born a tantraiiken?

Training brought her focus back and the star of Power drained into the knife, leaving her sick and shaking, her entire body aching for completion. The pain was low between her legs, and it would torture her all night unless she found some way to bleed off the pressure.

The whole event had taken less than five minutes. The rookie was gesturing to an ambulance crew. Lurid light from the cop cars and stuttering flashes from the ambulance painted the street in gaudy flickers. The entire street was now swarming with cops and emergency personnel. Selene slumped down against the cracked vinyl and peered out the window, her senses dilated, looking for a dark blot or a breath of anything that didn't belong. Nothing. Not even a shimmer in the air.

Was Nikolai gone? She couldn't be that lucky.

Danny. The numbness was still there. Whatever was locked inside her athame would give her a direction, somewhere to go . . . hopefully. At the very least, she would see how her brother died.

The *how* might tell her *who,* and once she knew she could start planning. There weren't many things she could take on as a *tantraiiken,* she was worse than useless in a fight since pain and fear turned to desire and swallowed her whole.

But she could give it a try, couldn't she? Nikolai wouldn't help, he would be too interested in getting leverage on her. One more dead human wouldn't matter, even if it was the brother of his semi-pet sexwitch.

I hate you, Nikolai. The hate was a bright red slash across the middle of her mind. She closed her eyes, set her jaw. Her fingers itched to unzip her jeans, slide down, touch the slick heat between her legs. *Hate you. Hate you.* She felt her face contort into a screaming mask, tears spilling down her cheeks.

The door creaked open, letting in a burst of chill rainy air. "Hi, princess," Jack said. "Get your ass out. We got a hot date with some paperwork."

Selene blinked, her fists curled at her sides. She let out the breath she'd been holding. Her cheeks hurt, so did her lower belly; her eyes were hot and dry.

Jack didn't mean to be cruel, he was just used to treating her like one of the boys. If she had been waiting to join another investigation, he would have acted the same way. Selene would have had an equally brisk response for him. She searched for something sharp and hard as a shield to say.

Instead, her throat swelled with grief. "Danny?" she whis-

pered. It was stupid, she knew it, Nikolai would not have
lied and her own eyes had told her the truth. But still, she
had hoped. Hope, that great human drug.

Jack's face turned milk-pale. He was thin and stooped,
except for his potbelly straining at his dingy white shirt. His
lean hound-dog face under its gray buzzcut was almost always mournful, now it was actively sad. "Lena . . . Jesus,
I'm sorry. Nikolai was supposed to keep you from seeing . . .
any of that."

I have a right to see what happened to my brother, Jack.
Selene slid her legs out of the car. She had to catch her
breath as the material of her jeans rasped against swollen
tissues. She *needed*, and there was no way to fill that need
tonight.

"Nikolai can go to hell," she rasped around the obstruc-
tion in her throat. That helped—it sounded like the old Selene, the tough Selene. "I'm sure it's where he's bound sooner
or later."

She twisted her hands together. Her palms slid against
each other, damp with sweat. The image of Danny's apartment, framed by a shattered blood-painted doorway, rose up
again. Numb disbelief rose with it.

Her jeans were uncomfortably wet, and she was starting
to sweat under her arms. Her neck prickled, and she was
suddenly aware of empty hunger. She was starving.

How can I think of food at a time like this? Jesus.

"I'll do your report up for you. Come by, sign it in the
morning. Look, Selene—" He offered her his hand and she
took it, nervous sweat slicking her palm. He pulled her to
her feet. The car's windows were frosted with vapor. *How
long was I in there?*

He also firmly took his hand away from her, tearing her
fingers free.

Selene would have kept his hand, run her thumb along the
crease on the inside of his wrist, wet her lips with her tongue.
Her eyes met his. She *needed*, and he was male. Women were
also good for what she needed, but there weren't any around.

God. Look at me. Look at what I almost did. I'm a whore, and my brother is dead.

"I'm sorry," Jack continued awkwardly. He was starting to sweat now, too, looking down until he realized he was looking at her chest, then staring up over her shoulder at the circus of lights and people in uniforms milling around. "Christ, I'm sorry. Lena . . . I'm so sorry."

Selene crossed her arms, cupped her elbows in her hands. Jack took her upper arm, kicked the cruiser's door shut, and steered her away from the hive of activity the street had become. People were starting to peek through their windows, lights were coming on. The cops were too busy to pay much attention to one lone woman being led away by Detective Pepper—especially when some of them recognized her as his tame spook, the woman that had broken the Bowan case last month. Just how she did it nobody knew—but then again, nobody wanted to know. The girl was just too weird. And Pepper was starting to look a little weird himself. The joke was that he'd apply for the new Spook Squad soon, just as soon as he could get his head out of a bottle and quit working hopeless freezer-cold homicide cases.

Selene shivered, hugging herself, their easy dismissal of her roaring through the open wound she was becoming. *I've got to get home before I start to scream. I'm in bad shape.*

"You're pretty worn out," Jack said, diffidently. "Look, go home. I'm sorry, Lena. I'm glad you called me. I wish you wouldn't have gone up there." He stopped near a pool of convenient shadow, and Selene looked up.

Of course.

Nikolai was there. Part of the darkness itself, his long black coat melding with the gloom that filled an alley's entrance.

Jack faced her. Here, numb and shocked, with her shields thin and the aftermath of the Power she'd jacked and the magick she'd worked pounding in her pulse with insistent need, she drowned in what *he* was feeling.

Agonizing pain. Nausea. Sick aching in his chest, the

heartburn that wouldn't go away—*she shouldn't have to see this, shouldn't have seen it.*

Jack sighed, his shoulders slumping. "It's bad, Selene. Something I ain't never seen before. And Nikolai says it's not human. Which means . . ." His brown eyes were almost black in the uncertain light. "Christ," he finished, when she just stared at him, her mouth slightly open. Her breath rasped in the chill rainwashed air. "Just go home. Come by the station tomorrow to sign your statement. I'm sorry."

Selene shrugged. "Great. Just go home, he says." She heard the funny breathless tone in her own voice. She was close to the edge, so close—did Jack think she was numb and grieving? Or did he guess that she wouldn't be able to grieve until the need pounding in her blood was blotted out?

Grieve, hell. There was something sharp as a broken bone in her chest. *I'm going to get whoever did this.*

Nikolai stepped forward. His eyes were depthless. "I will take her, Jack. Thank you."

Jack nodded. "Go with—"

"Like a good little girl, right?" Her voice sounded shrill even to herself, it bounced off the alley's walls and came back to her through a layer of cotton wool. "What I'm hearing is that you're not going to work too hard, because it's a P-fucking-C. Right?"

Jack's shoulders hunched as if she'd hit him. "Paranormal cases are technically not the jurisdiction of the Saint City police force, until the new laws go into effect. They're the jurisdiction of—"

"Of the reigning prime paranormal Power in the city." She stepped away from Jack and his hand fell down to his side, releasing her. "Which means Nikolai. Which means I can kiss any hope of finding out who did this to my brother goodbye."

"Not necessarily." Nikolai's eyes never left her. He moved closer, not precisely crowding her, but stepping past Jack without so much as glancing at the detective. "Cooperate with me, Selene, and I will see the killer brought to you, for your revenge. Will you take that bargain?"

Jack coughed, uncomfortably. "I've got to go. Sorry, Selene."

You son of a bitch. Both of you. "Are you really," she said, flatly, and turned on her heel. She put her head down, started to walk. At least she wasn't staggering. *Oh, God. Danny. What happened to you? Who did this to you?*

Nikolai murmured something behind her—no doubt talking to Jack, something along the lines of *women, irrational, what can you do, she'll see reason in the morning.*

It was too much. Rage and something like a sob made flesh draw tighter and tighter under her breastbone, and the tension snapped.

Selene ran.

CHAPTER 4

BY THE TIME SHE REACHED CLIFF STREET, SHE WAS stumbling. She'd fallen once, scraping her palms on pavement, and scrambled to her feet, looking up to see a shadow flitting over a rooftop above her. He didn't even have the decency to try and conceal himself.

Her hands jittered. Her keys jangled, her scraped palms singing in pain. Her heart threatened to burst out of her chest. Sweat rolled down her spine, soaked into the waistband of her jeans.

She checked the street behind her, deserted under the orange streetlamps. It took her three tries to unlock the door to her apartment building, her breath coming high and harsh and fast, expecting to feel a hand closing on her shoulder at any moment.

The run up her own stairs took on a nightmarish quality, moving too slowly while something chased her from behind. Those had been the worst dreams when she was little, running through syrup while the monster snarled behind, gaining on her.

Doors. Her *own* door. She fumbled out her keys, tried to unlock it, made a short sound of agonized frustration when her fingers slipped.

Finally the key slid into the lock.

She twisted it, opened her door, yanked the key out,

kicked the door shut with a resounding slam. She threw the deadbolt, then turned around and hurled her keys down her dark hall.

Nikolai plucked the keyring out of the air, his signet ring glittering. One moment her pretty, spacious one-bedroom apartment was empty—the next moment, a slight breeze brushed Selene's cheek and she let out a strangled scream. The protections placed in the walls of her apartment and the whole building shuddered with a sound like a crystal wine-glass ringing, stroked just right. *Don't worry, nobody will hear it, I'm the only Talent in the building. A merry little party, just Nikolai and me.*

And whatever he's going to do to me.

Selene whirled and started trying to unbolt the door. Her sweat-slick fingers slipped against cold metal. *Christ why can't he leave me ALONE?*

"Stop." He was suddenly *there,* laying the keys down on the small table by the front door. His fingers bit into her shoulder and he yanked her back, locked the second dead-bolt with his other hand. The sound of the lock going home was the clang of a prison cell closing.

Selene heard her own harsh sobs, the low moaning sound of a strangled scream.

Nikolai slid the coat off her shoulders while he dragged her along. Tossed it over the back of the couch as he pulled her into the living room. Then he grabbed the canvas strap of her bag, wrapped it around his fist, and jerked it up over her head. Selene let out a short cry, cut off midway when he clamped his free hand over her mouth. He dropped the bag on the couch as well, and looked down at her.

Silence, except for the muffled sounds slipping past his fingers. Fire raced up her side, tearing through her ribs—the stitch in her side, getting worse. Her calves were burning too. Her lower back ached, and her palms were scraped raw.

Worse than that was the miserable, hot, prickling need slamming through her. The low, relentless burn between her legs, spreading through her entire body. Now that she wasn't running, it returned. When would she start to beg?

He considered her, cocking his head to one side. A few soft strands of black hair fell over his forehead. "I told you not to look." There was no inflection to his voice, it was a passionless murmur. "But look you must. Are you happy? Are you *satisfied?*"

Selene's shoulders slumped. *I could bite him. What would he do if I bit him? Would he hold me down and . . .*

Nikolai let out a low pent breath. It was for effect—he didn't need to breathe, did he? He only did it when he *wanted* to.

He slid one hand around her waist, flattened it against the small of her back. His fingers scorched through her sweater. "I forgive you much." His hand exerted a little pressure, enough that she shifted back away from him, resisting. "I forgive you because you are young, and because you are unique, and because you amuse me." A ghost of a smile touched his lips. "Sometimes you even surprise me, which is rare. But sometimes, my Selene, I wonder if I forgive *too* much."

She tried to twist free, but he had her, one hand on the small of her back, the other over her mouth. Tears trickled down her cheeks. He pulled her close to him, closer, until she could feel something very definitely alive pressing against her belly, through his jeans and her sweater. *I could give a lecture on this,* she thought hysterically. *Vampire Anatomy: Dead or Alive? I never even knew a Nichtvren could* get *a hard-on—they didn't cover that in the textbooks.*

It was her effect on him—her effect on any man. Maybe it was pheromones, maybe it was only her cursed power making sure it could complete itself. Nikolai had known what she was the first time he smelled her.

Or so he said.

"Now," he said, leaning down just a little, whispering in her ear. "You disobeyed me. You tossed my last gift to you away like a piece of trash. You also acted as a complete fool, dropping your defenses and working the Art while you sat in the back of a police car. And I saw where you found the Power for that trick, my sweet." He was murmuring, and Selene shut her eyes. Her entire body shook now, straining against his, recognizing that here was something it *needed*. Something that could take the ache away. "I wonder how you're feeling."

He took a step, and let her move too, back toward the bedroom. Only the nightlight in the hall broke the darkness of her apartment, but that would present no difficulty to him. Not to a Nichtvren, who could see in complete dark.

"Well?" He moved, his legs bumping hers.

Selene's body betrayed her. Her hips jerked forward and her hands came up, sliding along his arms to find his shoulders and clenching, trying to pull him forward. Her lips parted, and she sobbed in a breath behind his hand. Two.

I hate myself. It was the only clear thought in the straining welter of sensation she'd become, her curse awake and alive under her skin. *I hate him and I hate myself.* She tasted salt, and kissed his palm, her lips softening, unable to help herself.

"I see," he continued, pitilessly. "The succubus needs her food."

That's not what I am! She wanted to scream, but his hand was still over her mouth.

"You are the only *tantraiiken* of adult age to walk the earth freely for five hundred years, and you do so because of my protection." He moved her back a step at a time, toward the bedroom. "If I were cruel, dear one, sweet Selene, I'd chain you in a stone cell and let you suffer. Let you burn for a little while, until you better appreciated me and the liberty I allow you." Then he gave a bitter little laugh, and Selene went liquid against him, relieved. She knew that sound.

He would give her what she needed. He would make it *stop*.

Then she could do what she had to do. Find out who had done . . . *that* . . . to Danny.

"Please," she mouthed against his palm, before she could stop herself. "Nikolai."

I am such a whore. Loathing filled her mouth like spilled wine, added another complex layer to the straining need pounding in her blood:

"Hush." He pushed her through the bedroom door, kicked it shut. She flinched, shaking so hard she couldn't walk, and he pushed her down on the bed. She landed hard, her head flung back, her back arching. The covers were still thrown back.

Danny, the part of her that wasn't crazed with need sobbed. *Danny. Oh, my God. My brother is dead, and what am I doing? God help me.*

He stood there, watching her shake against the cotton sheets. Selene bit her lower lip. That was a mistake—the pain now fed the loop of sensation, fear and pain and lust driving in a circle that wrung shuddering little sounds from her.

Finally, he shed his coat, draping it over the chair set by the closet. Selene closed her eyes, twisting, her hips rising, falling back down. Her clothes were impossibly hot, confining, scraping against suddenly sensitive skin.

He knelt down, and worked her damp boots off, and her socks. Touched the inside of her ankle with a fingertip, under the damp cuff of her jeans. The touch sent a spark racing up her leg, through her entire body. "Selene." Why did he have to sound so *human*, so soft and reasonable? "I wanted to save you that sight."

"My *brother*," she whispered, then moaned as the bed accepted Nikolai's weight next to her. He propped himself up on one elbow and used the other hand to pop the button on her waistband. *I'm going to kill whoever did that to him. Just get this over with so I can go on.* She drew in a sobbing breath, her hips lifting helplessly.

"I would rather have you remember him alive." Nikolai slowly unzipped her jeans. The sound of the zipper was loud in the dark stillness of her bedroom. Tears leaked out between Selene's eyelids, and her sweater was drenched with sweat.

Addicted to this, but I have no choice. I never have a choice. The need would get worse and worse, a *tantraiiken*'s curse burning through her bones, until she was little more than an animal. She'd gone that far sometimes, when she was young and thought she could rule her own body, at least.

Before she'd learned how to use the curse for her own benefit. And before she'd met *him*. Since she'd come to Nikolai's notice, she hadn't needed to feed her curse in alleys or cheap hotel rooms. Even if she *could* forget it, he reminded her often enough. She owed him.

Owed, and was owned by. There wasn't much of a difference where Nichtvren were concerned.

"Nikolai . . ." It was a long despairing moan. It wouldn't take long before she started to beg. She'd drained her batteries and worked herself into a frenzy.

He slid his hand into her jeans, settling the heel of his palm against her mound. His fingers slipped down, and made a slight beckoning motion. Selene arched, her breath hissing in. But then, torture of tortures, he stopped.

"Why disobey me?" His breath was warm against her cheek. "Why, Selene? You leave me no choice."

"Nikolai—" It was all she had left, the pleading. He would give her what she needed, and then she could think again, ponder, consider, plan. But how much would he make her suffer first, and how much of the suffering would she enjoy because of her traitorous body?

He took pity on her then, and made another little beckoning motion with his fingers, and another. He knew exactly what to do. It was all Selene needed, and she cried out, arching, her head tipped back and her entire body shuddering. It was like being dipped in fire, and the relief was instant.

Relief—and fresh need. She would need more. Much more. But now she could think, the first edge of her curse was blunted.

"Nikolai," she said, when she could speak again. "You were in there, what did you see?" *Give me something, you*

*fucking suckhead. Get it, Selene? Fucking suckhead? You're
such a whore.*

The image of Danny's apartment rose in front of her eyes
again, and she struggled away from Nikolai's hand, curling
into a ball, pulling her knees up while she hugged herself,
making small sobbing sounds like an animal in a trap. Her
wet clothes rasped uncomfortably against her skin.

Nikolai sighed again. He sounded frustrated. Good for him.

"Later, dear one. Right now you are in pain." He sliced
her sweater up the back—his claws, extended delicately, not
even brushing her skin beneath the wool. Chill air met her
wet skin. Then his fingers, skating down the muscles on either side of her spine. His claws were retracted, but she
could still feel the strength in his hands. He pushed her hair
aside—the elastic band holding her ponytail snapped—and
his mouth met her nape. She shivered, curling even more
tightly into herself. He stroked her shoulder, touched the two
dimples down low at the small of her back.

The first edge of pain was gone, and the burning settled
back into a low dull agony. Her Talent wasn't like others, she
had to fuel it with sex. It was the only thing that worked.

*But Christ, do I have to let him touch me like this? He's
not human. Can't he just fuck me and get it over with, leave
me alone so I can do what I need to do?*

The rest of her ruined sweater was discarded over the side
of the bed. He worked her jeans free and tossed them away
too, then took her in his arms. His own clothes were
gone—how he did that she couldn't guess, but it probably
had something to do with his claws, and the fact that she was
too busy trying to gulp down air and fight her body's need to
really pay attention to him.

She was paying for the magick she'd done earlier. No
preparation, no patterning—she'd simply dropped her defenses and gone for it, performed a major Work without any
thought of the consequences. No wonder she was shaking
with need.

Everything has to be paid for. She realized she'd said it

out loud. "Everything has to be paid for in magick, Nikolai, *everything*."

"Do you think I do not know?" He pushed her onto her back, slid his hand between her legs. She was slick and feverish, damp with need. "Hush. Lie still."

It took a massive effort to do what he said. It would be quicker if she just let him—if she submitted, if she gave in.

Selene erupted into wild motion, trying to fight him off. He caught her wrists, stretching them above her head, and pinned her to the mattress. She would have been screaming, but his mouth was on hers, catching the scream, killing it. She tried to kick him, straining, but he slid a knee between hers. Then all of his weight, and Selene felt the edges of his hips against the soft insides of her thighs. He was much warmer now, his skin almost scorching hers.

The energetic discharge of sex would feed him, too. That was why a *tantraiiken* was such a valuable paranormal pet.

Pet? *Slave.* It was frowned upon, of course, but paranormals and Talents weren't that tightly policed, even though the laws were almost in effect to give them some protection and codify them. The higher echelons of the human world—the powerbrokers and politicians—knew about the slavery, of course, it was an open secret in some circles. But no newspaper would ever report on it, and no television anchor would ever talk about the things that went on under the blanket of normality. How sometimes, people born with certain Talents were lost to the night side of life.

He found the entrance to her body, thrust in, and his hands tightened around her wrists, the small bones grinding together. Selene gulped back another useless scream, relief spilling through her. His fingers gentled, threaded through hers. He murmured something—maybe it was Russian, she didn't know, didn't care, the only thing she cared about was that the agony had stopped. He was in her to the hilt, stretching her, her hips slamming up, silently begging.

He moved, again, and Selene closed her eyes. Pleasure tore through her, a dark screaming pleasure wrapped in barbed wire and dragging hot velvet laceration through tender flesh. Soon enough she would be able to think about grieving.

"Get . . . it . . . over . . . with." She set her teeth together, even as her hips rocked and her ankles linked together at the small of his back. Her body betrayed her over and over again, that was the worst. Her body was an enemy, a traitor, it didn't care who he was as long as he had what she needed.

"Oh, no," he whispered into her ear, then caught her earlobe in his teeth, gently, delicately. A slight nip of razor teeth, and she sucked in a breath. He laughed, a low harsh breath against her cheek. "There are a few hours until morning."

"I hate you," she whispered back, even as her body shook and the blind fire took her again. And again.

CHAPTER 5

IN THE END, EXHAUSTED, SHE LAY LIMP AGAINST the bed, hugging a pillow rescued from the floor. Nikolai curled against her back, sweat slicking his skin so it slid against hers. Her entire body sparked pleasantly, and her shields were back up, thick enough to protect her again.

If Danny had been able to shield himself, would he have died? If he'd been able to run away from whatever had battered his door down, maybe he would have survived.

Don't worry, Danny. Little sister's on the job. I'll get whoever did this to you. I promise. The words were a lump behind her breastbone, steel closing around her beating heart. *I swear to you, Danny. I'm going to find who did this to you. I'll do whatever I have to do.*

That was one thing being a whore was good for. It let her contemplate doing just about anything to get what she wanted. What she needed.

Nikolai's hand polished the curve of her hip, something cool and metallic sliding against her skin. He drew it up over her ribs, under her breast, until the medallion lay where it used to, half the chain spilling down to pool on the sheet. He fastened it at the back of her neck, one-handed, and flattened his other palm against the silver lying between her breasts. "There. This is important, Selene. Without it, you're at risk. This gives you *protection*. You cannot throw it away. Understood?"

Shut up, suckhead. "Someone killed my brother." Her throat rasped from choking back screams. "What happened? What was it?"

"If I tell you what I know, it would be nothing. If I tell you what I suspect, it will be confusing, because I suspect many things." He yawned, burying his face in her hair, then spread one hand against her belly. He was warm enough to pass for a feverish human, metabolizing the jolt of sex into fuel. "If I tell you what I expect, we will be here for many hours, since I have learned to expect everything. It is too soon to tell."

"My brother," she said, tonelessly. His knees were behind hers, one arm under her head, the other holding her to him. A huge exhausted yawn took her unaware, threatened to crack her jaw. "Someone killed my *brother*, Nikolai." *If you won't help me . . .*

"Cooperate with me, and I will find whatever killed your brother," He sighed again, relaxing against her back the way a cat might. A very big, very warm cat. "Dawn is approaching. Will you come with me?"

She should have known. The same offer as always, delivered as if she should be grateful for it. Leave it to Nikolai to use even her brother's murder to try and get what he wanted out of her. "I have work tomorrow." She watched the edge of her pillowcase, breathing shallowly. *Leave me alone. You got what you wanted, now go away.*

"Already attended to. You are not expected there for another two weeks."

Jesus. "I can't afford—"

"With pay."

"I don't want your money." *I don't want to fuck you, either. See how well that works out?*

"Mh. It is not mine; it is from the college. You may call it a gift. For my Selene."

She closed her eyes. *If he was human, what would I do?*

I'd ask him to help me and he might even do it without turning it into a power play. "Don't call me that. I'm not yours."

"You must belong somewhere," he said softly.

"I belonged with my brother." Poor Danny. Locked in his apartment except for those times he slipped the chain of his own body and went Journeying. How many times had Selene climbed the steps to his apartment to ask his help for the cases Jack Pepper brought her? How many times had she brought him meals, or little things he needed because he couldn't stand to leave the wards Selene had made for him?

Danny had been immune to her pheromones, immune to her curse. He had been the only man capable of seeing her without her goddamn body complicating things.

I belonged with him plenty, you undead jerk. Now he's gone, and you wouldn't have even let me look at his body.

I hate you.

And he was so easy to hate, wasn't he? A Nichtvren. Inhuman, for all that he'd been mortal once, however long ago. How old *was* he, anyway?

"He was under my protection too," Nikolai said. "Come with me, Selene. You will be safer."

Like hell I will. "No."

"One day you will." He didn't push the issue, for once. "Jorge will come to offer you use of a car."

"And to keep an eye on me? No thanks, Nikolai." Selene bit her lower lip. It was bruised already. She tasted blood. She would ache tomorrow. It had been too long, she'd built up a heavy debt, and her body had exacted its toll with a vengeance. Not only had she cleared a poltergeist infestation and pulled the wards from Danny's apartment, but there had also been the work for that witch over on Seventeenth Street.

She'd needed the money. She always needed the money. Lecturing didn't pay nearly enough for both her rent and Danny's. And by God, Selene never wanted to be poor again. She agreed with Scarlett O'Hara on *that* count, thank you very much.

Nikolai paused, and his hand tensed against her belly. She held her breath, but he didn't move, just tightened his arm around her.

"This is not a request. Jorge will come, and if you leave this place it will be with him. If you do anything foolish I will be vexed." Even his breath was warm against her hair. *Does he breathe because he knows it makes me a little more comfortable? I suppose he has to breathe to talk, doesn't he? I should ask.*

Exhaustion crept in. If she fell asleep now she might be able to get a few hours of rest before . . . no. The fatigue blurred everything, made it difficult to think.

"Vex all you want, Nik," she said, and his fingers tapped against her belly once, twice. Then he stopped. "I'm not your servant. I don't take your orders."

Yeah, Selene. If you lie often enough, you might even be able to halfway believe it.

He made a low sound against her hair, and Selene's entire body leapt. The medallion gave one scorching burst of heat. "Of course, if Jorge is incompetent enough to lose you, I suppose he will need punishment."

You bastard. I should have known. "You wouldn't."

"I would, Selene. I would also make you watch." He sounded calm as if he was discussing a grocery list. "I dislike the thought of damage to you. I will take steps to avoid it."

Everyone knows I'm your little pet. Nobody messes with me anymore, you jerk. I might even be able to use that to find out who killed Danny. "Nothing's going to happen to me."

"Especially not with Jorge watching over you." He sounded pleased to have painted her into a logical corner.

"Fine," she said. "I'll wait for him. I'll be a good little girl. Now go away and leave me alone." *So I can cry in peace. Leave me that, at least. Just leave me alone so I can cry.*

Nikolai rolled away from her, his arm sliding out from beneath her head. She heard him moving, getting into his clothes. She could imagine him getting dressed, pulling his jeans up, pulling his t-shirt back over his head, running his fingers back through his hair to push it back out of his face. Then his coat. She heard the sound of the heavy wool moving.

Best of both worlds. He has to go home before dawn. *Can't stay to make things sticky. And he's so fucking careful not to damage me. Though I can take it, can't I? It's hard to kill me. With sex, at least.*

He leaned over the bed to pull the sheet and the blankets up, tucking her in gently and efficiently. Finally, when the covers were smoothed, he settled on the side of the bed and touched her hair. Ran his fingers through the heavy mass, lifting it slightly, and gathering it all up, pulling it back from her face. He stroked her cheek with his fingertips, delicately. His claws didn't prickle, but she knew they were there.

Go away. I have to cry first, then I will figure out what to do. Oh, God. Danny. Selene kept her eyes shut. Her breathing evened out. She hugged the pillow. Her right hand was under the covers, and she made a fist, her nails biting into her palm. Squeezed. Tighter. *Tighter.*

Finally, Nikolai touched the corner of her mouth with a fingertip. Selene didn't open her eyes—but she did peek out through her lashes. Under the bedroom window shade, a faint grayness showed. Dawn was coming.

There was a slight sound—a breath of air. A cold breeze touched Selene's cheek.

Nikolai was gone.

Selene drove her fingernails into her palms and took in a shuddering breath.

Now, at last, she could cry.

(LIKE A)
VIRGIN OF THE SPRING

Susan Sizemore
and Denise Little

GINGER WAS CERTAIN THAT THERE HAD BEEN A time in her life when she found public fornication shocking. That time was long behind her. Now, crossing the courtyard between the baths and the sanctuary of the sacred spring, she barely glanced at the naked couple coupling on the altar at the center.

What the pair was doing was a sacred rite meant to please the gods. She did take a moment to glance their way, and observed that the lad had a truly fine ass. The way his broad back narrowed down to his waist was a work of art. But the offering to the gods being shared out there with such energy was business, not pleasure—for her, at least.

It was spring, festival time, and people were crowding in to the stronghold from all over the countryside of southern Britain. It was a joyful season for most people, one that embraced relief at surviving the winter, appreciation of the new life emerging in field and flock, and enthusiastic participation in the fertility rites so important to the gods.

Ginger normally would have been overseeing the celebrations. But her knowledge of the darkness moving ever closer toward them overwhelmed her interest in this seasonal festival.

As priestess of the spring, she had responsibilities that ran far beyond the rites taking place on the altar. She already knew that the next few days were going to be hard on her, and she was certain that her talent as a seeress was going to be called upon on this day when she was supposed to be resting up for the festival.

The future was hers to see and to interpret for others. And now it seemed the gathering storm had managed to alarm even the highest power in this land. The Lord of Ched had called for his senior advisors to gather before him at the sanctuary. Lord Ched was there when she arrived, a big man going to fat, his grizzled gray hair cut short in the Roman manner. Despite being near to fifty, a great age, he was still handsome. It was obvious where his daughter Morga got her beauty.

Morga was chosen of the Mother and she and the Year King should have been here with her father, bracing for the coming storm, instead of outside worshiping on the altar. Ginger wondered at the exclusion, but it wasn't just a warning from her extrasensory perception that twisted her belly with apprehension. She hadn't always been the priestess of the well. At one time she'd been a student of history, a collector of the great stories from the past. She'd studied the manipulation of power by men strong enough to seize and keep it. Their names lived on in tales long after they died—Phillip of Macedonia, his son Alexander the Great, Caesar Augustus, Claudius, Constantius, even the cursed Vortigern, whose ill-fated dealings with the Saxons had torn Britannia apart less than a century ago.

The machinations of power and politics were as much a part of her original world as science and psychic research. But that world had changed forever when she'd decided to put her knowledge to good use. Traveling back in time hadn't made her life any simpler. Of course, back home she'd been more of an observer than a player. She was well aware of the irony that the disaster of a time transfer gone wrong had turned her from the observer she was supposed to be into a person of importance in this time and place.

Not much importance, thank goodness. She wasn't trying to change history—she wasn't even sure what history was supposed to look like here. The sixth century in Britain was notorious for its lack of reliable documentation. Sources like the monks Gildas and Venerable Bede were great tellers of tales, but short on reliable details.

So now she was trying to survive in a dangerous, alien world where her psychic gift gave her a small edge. Or, to be more precise, a job. The seeress gig put a roof over her head and two meals a day in her belly, and gave her the protection of the most powerful person in the region. But all that could change soon if the invaders, who she knew were coming thanks to both her studies of history and her gift, moved inland from their raids on the coast. Not today. Not even tomorrow. But one day soon, death would be beating a path to the walls of this sanctuary.

It could only mean war.

War seemed a certainty, really. Her existence could be hanging by a thread—along with that of every person in this room. She needed to know which side to foster, which army to influence, if she was to survive. Her recent visions had shown her fire and death, but no clear images of who the victors would be.

The steward of the manor followed Ginger into the sanctuary. After him came the harried-looking commander of the guard. The bishop visiting from Wales came inside as well. It was not a large space, though the entrance was wide and open to the courtyard. The four of them gathered around the tiled basin into which the waters of the sacred spring trickled from the back of the sanctuary. Ginger made up a quick prayer to the goddess of the water and to the new God of the cross and when she was done with the blessing they got down to business.

The guardsman did not wait for his Lord to speak. "Can we make this quick? With the crowds coming in—"

"We need a new war leader," Lord Ched cut him off. He

looked around the gathering, his expression hard, daring them to argue. "Right now. This very day would be good. Do you want the job?" he demanded of the guardsman.

A scar ran over the empty socket of the guard's left eye. He glanced toward the courtyard with his one good eye. They all followed his gaze. The couple was still busy on the altar. Morga's thighs were wrapped tightly around the Year King's slender waist and the beautiful young man was pistoning away with hard, swift strokes. He was covered with a glowing sheen of sweat, his muscles bulging.

Damn, but that boy had stamina!

"He's perfect," the guard said. "How could I take his place?"

"He's not perfect," Lord Ched said. "He's an idiot, a fool, and a braggart. He pleases my daughter and her belly's already swelling with a second brat, but he's useless for anything else."

"In normal times that would be enough," the steward spoke up. He rubbed his jaw, the tough stubble on his cheeks making scratching sounds. "I suppose we could go back to the old ways. We could sacrifice him come the Planting Ceremony instead of just letting the lads wrestle for rights to Morga this year. The gods might like that. The crowd certainly would."

"Morga would not," Ginger said.

"Nor would I," added the bishop.

They were both ignored.

"Even if we return to the old ways," the lord said. "We need someone to replace the Year King first. Someone who can fight. Someone who can lead. I'm too old. Morga's son is still with the wetnurse. Tradition dictates that the Year King lead us into battle. A battle is coming, and that boy out there isn't up to the job."

All Ginger had wanted when she took on this role was a little peace and quiet while she tried to find a way home, but the invaders marching up from the coast weren't likely to leave anyone in peace. Or even alive, if the rumors they'd been hearing proved to be true. The whole point of returning to the Dark Ages was to find out what happened, to fill in the holes left by Bede and Gildas. Her simple research project had instead left her stuck in the very Dark Ages where she didn't know what happened.

At least on a grand, historical scale. Here and now, in this little corner of the world, she knew too much. She was a board-certified psychic. She knew trouble was coming soon, marching here as fast as the old Roman roads would allow. But her gift only went so far, in certain directions, and after that she was as on her own as anyone else here.

Her worried musings were interrupted by Lord Ched. "What shall we do, priestess? Look into the water and tell us what the gods say."

So her Sight was supposed to save them.

As she had suspected would be the case. She always tried to tell the truth of what she saw in the water, but divination was one thing and politics was another.

What she Saw might not be enough to help them.

Ginger sighed, but didn't argue about her duty. She owed the Lord of the manor her life, and she understood his concerns. His world was threatening to fall apart, and the people he was sworn to protect were in danger. As one of those people, she applauded his take-charge attitude.

She gestured for the men to stand back. They moved fast, obviously delighted the decision was in her hands and not theirs. If things turned out wrong later they could always claim that the priestess read the signs incorrectly.

Pin the blame on the psychic—it was a game that never went out of style. She had no doubt that back in the lab she'd come from in the distant future, they were playing it still. Somehow, they'd undoubtedly decided her team's failure to return from the past was all her fault.

She knelt by the pool.

Ginger brushed away the bitterness she felt at their willingness to let her be the savior or the scapegoat. In fact, she put the men out of her mind altogether. She'd had years of practice honing her abilities, learning to ignore every possible kind of distraction. She looked into the crystal clear water, her awareness going far deeper than the eight-inch depth of the pool. As always, she was amazed at how quickly her perceptions attuned to the energies present at this energy nexus.

From a long way away she heard herself ask, "Question?"

From even farther away the Lord's voice came to her in an echoing whisper, "Who shall lead my people to war?"

Almost instantly a face appeared on the surface of the pool, though Ginger was the only one who could see it. A pair of piercing green eyes caught hers and she gasped, for she was certain that he could see her as clearly as she saw him. Nothing like this had ever happened to her before.

"I see visions, I don't make contact," she told the face.

"That's not my fault, is it?" His rough, deep voice answered. "Who are you? Where are you?" he demanded.

His gaze enveloped her, but all she could do was continue to stare. She wanted to fall into the vision, into him, wanted him to fall into her. She wanted him the way a woman wanted a man. That had never happened before, either.

She shook off the desire that threatened to swamp her and concentrated on the task at hand. He was as handsome as any Year King should be, but for a small scar on one cheek. He couldn't be the man the lord wanted, then, for a Year King must be perfect.

A crowd of men suddenly appeared in the water behind the stranger's wide shoulders. They were a rough and dangerous-looking lot, with travel-stained clothes and heavy packs.

"Mercenaries," she said, understanding at last what they were. He had to be their leader, the alpha among a pack of hungry wolves.

"Wolves mate for life," he said, clearly keying into her thoughts. He shook his head hard. It seemed his words made no more sense to him than they did to her.

"What do you see?" Ched's anxious voice came to her.

The question drew her away from the vision, but a sense of urgency drew her to her feet. "He's here," she said. "Now. At the gate."

"What did you say, sir?"

Bern felt the weight of Sergeant Kaye's hand on his shoulder as the world came back into focus. "I hate when that happens," he muttered. He frowned, and the sergeant stepped back. "Was I just talking to somebody, Kaye?"

"You spoke," Kaye answered. He glanced at the rest of the team, who were spread out across the road. "But you weren't talking to any of us."

"I was afraid of that."

Bern's rating on the psychic scale was a lowly little three, enough to get him transferred into the TTP's security force but not high enough to really interfere with his leading a normal, sane life. Except—sometimes he heard voices, or had a flash of intuition. He'd learned to listen to the voices and trust his gut feelings. He'd just had one of those flashes, though he couldn't remember all the details. Of course, some details demanded he pay attention to them. He loosened his belt and adjusted his tunic.

"Something's up," he said. And in more ways than one.

He studied the lay of the land while he got his reaction to the woman he'd heard in his mind under control. It was spring, very close to the major seasonal fertility festival, and the road they were on led to one of the holy sites scattered all over the southern part of the island. This particular temple to the local mother goddess was located on private property, and the pilgrims were camping out in cow pastures on either side of the road. The manor at the top of the hill had been built by a wealthy Roman colonist, but the local chieftain had taken over after the Romans abandoned all their foreign outposts a generation ago. Bern didn't care about the festival, but it made a good cover for checking out the place.

The locals were expecting travelers to congregate here.

His holomap pinpointed this site as one of the nexus locations, and despite growing doubts that any of the sites they surveyed were going to provide enough energy to get them all home, it was his duty to check it out. Finding the right door back to the future was only the second half of his assignment. His first duty was to find and rescue the science team that had disappeared six months before his unit got the order to go back and look for them.

In his opinion it had been stupid to send the eggheads back in time without a whole team of sensible people to keep them out of trouble. The mission had been fucked from the get-go. This was the farthest back anyone had tried to travel. The lost team had been sent without proper backup to a time period very little was known about. It was no wonder everything had gone wrong—twice.

He and his men were now stuck here, too.

He gestured toward the crudely built wooden palisade surrounding the estate buildings. "Let's go see if we can get a look at what's inside."

Ginger was used to the world around her going fuzzy and faded, but she realized the moment before she fainted that this time it was because she'd been holding her breath while standing behind the men waiting at the gate.

When the gate opened, she simply blacked out, just as the man from her vision walked in. Their gazes met for a moment, and then everything went dark.

It was ridiculous, and she was so embarrassed that she scrunched her eyes tightly closed when she woke up, not wanting the person holding her to know that she'd come around. Those strong arms were his, weren't they? Her head rested against a broad, hard male chest. Warmth and the scent of him engulfed her. Awareness of him pooled deep in her belly. Her nipples stiffened, scraping against the cloth of her dress, and her breasts grew heavy.

"Oh, my," she whispered. Without making any conscious decision to move, her hand came up to stroke his strong, stubbly jaw.

She could hear his heart rate pick up when she spoke, and the deep sound of his laugh rumbled through his chest. For a moment the arms around her tightened, pressing her body harder against him.

Bern liked the weight of the woman in his arms. The touch of the bare skin of her arms and the feel of the rest of her beneath her dress made him ache, made him remember how long it had been since he'd had a woman. It also made him thankful that women didn't wear underwear in the dark ages. And this woman was a perfect fit against him. He liked the softness of her curly red hair where it tickled his neck and cheek. He wanted to bury his face in her thick hair, then follow the line of her throat all the way down to snuggle between—

Bern gave his head a stern shake. As stimulating as holding her was, he didn't know why he'd rushed into the courtyard and scooped her up off the ground when she fell. This wasn't an age of chivalry yet. In fact, in these days they typically saved the cattle before they saved the women.

Calling attention to himself and his men was stupid. Keeping a low profile was a matter of policy and survival among TTP teams. So why was he holding this lady? He had no idea who this woman was or what she meant to all the locals who were staring at him. Though she did look familiar.

When she woke and spoke, he couldn't help but laugh. It was good to know that she was as aware of him as he was of her.

Then Bern realized that the words he'd heard hadn't been filtered through his translator implant: she'd spoken in English instead of the local lilting Celtic dialect.

He knew exactly who she was!

Her name was Virginia White, and though he'd never met

her in the flesh he'd studied her holo image. Hers, and all of the others on the missing team. He had his hands on one of their primary targets. Since he already held her, he was tempted to call for his men to cover his withdrawal. They could run out the gate and make tracks, anything to ensure her safety now that he'd found her.

Since that wasn't the smart way to play it, he put her down. Her body slid slowly down his until her feet touched the ground. She was tall and willowy, her height another clue that she wasn't from this time.

"You—" he began.

But before he could speak or she could answer, a hand landed on his shoulder.

Bern whirled around, his hand on his sword. Over the last six months, that had become second nature.

"What?" he demanded of the potbellied graybeard before him. The stranger wore a threadbare silk tunic. Since silk was a luxury rare in these parts since the Roman withdrawal, Bern guessed he was looking at the local chieftain. "My lord," he continued, with a polite nod.

The chieftain's frown turned into an effusive smile. "You're quick, I see. Good. Good." He glanced toward the hand Bern still rested on the pommel of his sword. "Welcome to Ched," he went on. "Come to worship at the well, have you? For the festival?"

Bern nodded. He was aware that Virginia White had moved back into the shadow of an arched doorway. He wanted nothing more than to follow her, but he had to stay in character and deal with the local potentate first.

Bern brought out a small leather pouch, heavy with gold, and handed it over. "Please accept this small gift, in honor of the goddess and your hospitality."

The chieftain tossed the little purse to feel its weight, glanced inside, and beamed.

He looked at Bern's people—an obvious unit of soldiers— waiting by the gate, alert for Bern's orders. "Those are fine-looking lads you lead."

"We come in peace for the festival," Bern reassured the chieftain. Then he saw the speculative look in Ched's eyes. He smiled. "But afterwards, our swords are for hire if you are interested."

He hoped that made him sound like a friendly and useful fellow to the chieftain, just in case his unit needed an excuse to stay on after the festival. Though he hoped he could find out what Virginia White was up to before then.

Lord Ched's grin widened. He put his arm around Bern. "Join me for some wine. What's your name, lad?" he asked as he led Bern into the main hall.

Ginger considered going back to her duties at the spring, but curiosity got the better of her. That, and an irresistible craving not to let the man who named himself Bern out of her sight made her follow the men into the hall. For some reason being close to Bern made her feel as if she was not alone anymore, and she needed that nearness after all these months. She knew very well that any attraction to a man was foolish, and not even because intimacy with an indigenous resident was against Project rules.

If the gleam in Lord Ched's eye was any indication, this dangerous stranger would soon be the Year King sharing the bed of his daughter Morga. Jealousy ripped through Ginger at the thought, but she knew it would be for the best. They needed a warrior hero right now and Bern looked to have all the qualifications for the job.

He was tall, dark, and handsome, with broad shoulders and big hands and the brightest, most beautiful eyes she'd ever seen. There was an aura of steely danger around him that should have scared her to death, but instead it sent fireworks shooting through her. He wore a knee-length tunic that left his legs bare. Over it was metal-studded leather body armor buckled and strapped into place and a light woolen cape. Her fingers itched to pull off all those layers and thoroughly explore what she found underneath.

But they were in public. Even by the debased Roman

standards still observed here, it was unseemly for a woman to jump a man in the middle of a meeting—unless she'd been purchased or hired for that purpose, of course.

Ched sent for his daughter and settled down to explain his plan to Bern over cups of strong wine, unwatered, as was the local custom. Effete Romans might drink their spirits diluted, but not Ched. Here business was usually conducted once the menfolk were well on the way to being drunk.

So Ginger stayed in the background to listen and watch. She took a seat at the side of the public space among a group of women working on spinning and embroidery. The men were barely into their second libation to the goddess when Morga came flouncing in. *At least she's dressed,* Ginger thought. Morga was beautiful, knew it, and had no qualms about showing it even if she wasn't lying naked on her back on the holy altar.

I live like a nun, Ginger thought, *and she gets to whoop it up anywhere, any time.*

Until a few minutes ago this hadn't bothered Ginger a bit. Now she very nearly snarled as Morga caught sight of Bern, licked her perfect lips in appreciation, and made a beeline to sit beside him.

"Daughter," Lord Ched announced once the girl was snuggled up against Bern's side, "meet your new husband."

Morga bounded to her feet, looking appalled. So did Bern.

"What?" Morga screamed.

"What?" Bern echoed.

His voice was firm, but anger crackled off him.

Morga gave Bern another once over, and her lips curled in disdain at the lack of signs of rank or fortune. "I don't mind giving him a toss, but I like the husband I've got," she told her father.

Lord Ched banged a fist on the table. "You'll take the man I choose."

"The goddess chose for me already."

"Your Year King has already reigned too long. When this

warrior challenges, the younger man will lose. Be prepared for
it—be prepared to do your duty by your father, your goddess,
and your people." He gestured toward Bern. "Now, be a proper
priestess and take this fine bear of a man off to the bath."

"You sound like a Roman," the girl complained. "But this
land is Celt again. And I'll do no such thing as bathe a
stranger." She looked around haughtily, and pointed to Ginger. "There's a priestess who obeys you. Let her service this
great bear of yours."

And, with that pronouncement, she flounced back out
again, leaving everyone staring at Ginger.

Bern's initial impulse was to protest all this nonsense about
marriage, and bathing with buxom young women, but he let
it go when the girl suggested Virginia White as her replace-
ment. That situation had possibilities. It would be a good
way to get White alone.

"Perfect!" he exclaimed, and stepped forward to drag the
stunned Virginia out of the crowd, his hand tight around her
slender wrist. She looked at him with astonishment, and he
had to fight off laughter as he caught an impression of her
thinking about having a barbarian in her bathtub. He also
noticed that she wasn't completely opposed to the idea.

Warmth spread wherever they touched.

Hmmm . . . maybe they could turn this ridiculous situation into a bit of mutual fun.

"What are you waiting for, priestess?" the chieftain said.
"Show the man the hospitality he deserves!"

"Come along," Bern said. He pulled White along with
him out of the hall.

Once out in the courtyard she got her voice back. "You're
in for a treat, warrior, for the Roman hypocaust is still working and the pool is deep, and hot. The baths draw as many
visitors as the sacred spring, increasing the lord's prestige
and—"

"I'm not interested in a hot bath."

She sniffed and wrinkled her pretty nose. "You should be."

He laughed. "I guess I am a bit ripe from a few days on the road. My tunic could probably use burning, besides."

"Where I come from that would be breaking a law against polluting the air."

For a moment he'd let attraction get in the way of professionalism. This reminder that she was no local priestess brought Bern back to his duty. "Lead on to this bathhouse," he growled.

He watched her walk ahead of him to the baths. She wasn't a local, or even native to this time. *I could have her,* he thought. Then he reminded himself to concentrate on the mission. But he feared his body was going to overwhelm his brain at any moment.

Ginger was aware of the rough soldier's gaze. She'd never been so instantly and dangerously attracted to a man before. All the rules about indigenous relations were being overruled by the demands of her body. She didn't think she'd be able to keep her hands off this guy.

Conveniently, to keep up her cover as a priestess intact, she didn't have any choice but to scrape his naked body down with scented oil and rinse him off.

Her job description was getting more attractive by the day.

She grinned with anticipation as they entered the bath. But her grin was wiped away and replaced with a surge of fear an instant after they stepped into the room.

He grabbed her shoulders and spun her to face him. At the same time he growled, "Out!" to the pair of waiting bath attendants. She heard the slap of their bare feet on the stone mosaic as they hurried out.

"What the hell do you think you're doing?" he demanded the moment they were alone.

"Only what my lord ordered—" Then she realized why her senses were in shock. "You're speaking English!"

On a burst of sheer relief she grabbed him and kissed him.

What was a man to do when a woman flung herself against him and her soft lips pressed against his own? Then Bern didn't care what anyone else might do. Her hips ground enticingly against his. Her mouth was delicious, and his tongue delved possessively into the sweet warmth. Her breasts pushed against his chest and he brought a hand up to cup the soft roundness, stroked a thumb across the hard nipple he could feel beneath her dress. He'd never wanted anyone so much or so quickly. He picked her up and tossed her into the water, took a moment to unfasten his sword belt and toss off his armor, then jumped in after her.

Though she was fully clothed, the wet dress clung to her body and outlined her breasts and hips in a way Bern found irresistible.

"People generally get undressed before bathing," she said.

"And before sex, too."

She laughed, and reached below the water to grab onto her soaked skirt. "Wet wool," she muttered. "Now I smell like a sheep." She gave him a once-over.

"Does that make me a ram?"

She was holding the dress up around her thighs. He caught a glimpse of pale skin through the steaming water. "Don't stop now," he urged. He wanted her naked.

She inched up the skirt some more.

"Oh, lord," he groaned. He splashed through the waist-deep pool and grabbed her. "Don't tease me, woman."

She threw back her head and laughed, and he took the opportunity to kiss the base of her throat.

"Help me," she said. "This thing weighs a ton."

It took him a moment to realize that she was talking about her wet dress, but once he caught on he grabbed a double handful of soaking wool and yanked while she pulled and squirmed.

Soon he had her as naked as he wanted her. The water gave her skin a translucent sheen.

"You look like milk in moonlight," he said. Then he remembered her name. White. "You look like your name, Dr. Virginia White."

"Ginger," she answered instantly. "No one calls me Virgin—of course around here no one calls me Ginger, either."

"What do they call you?" he asked, while his hands got very busy.

She drew back. "Priestess," she answered. "Or the Lady of the White Bird Spring when they're being formal." She ran her hands down his chest, admiring the rippling muscle beneath his damp tunic. "Who are you?"

He needed to know how she'd gotten separated from her team, how she'd gotten here, and why she was part of the indigenous power structure. But he needed something else even more right now.

"Later, he said. "We can get to it much later . . ." He pressed his hips against her. "Touch me," he demanded. He circled her nipples with his thumbs.

She found the hem of his tunic, and pulled it above his hips. Once his cock was free she stroked him slowly from his balls to the throbbing tip. Ginger loved the heat of him, the weight and thickness, the velvet over steel feel of him in her hand.

But she wanted him inside her even more.

She backed up a few steps to the edge of pool, pulling him with her.

When they reached the side of the bath, he cupped her ass and lifted her onto the mosaic edge. She leaned backwards on her arms and spread her legs.

He filled her in one hard thrust.

Then both of them forgot everything else.

He collapsed on top of her for a long time afterwards, unwilling to move away from her warmth. He reveled in the feel of her soft breasts and the scent of her skin. He didn't know why, but the sound of her heartbeat against his ear made him feel like he was home.

Then she laughed and the sound brought Bern back into the here and now. He lifted his head to look at her.

"What?"

"Lord Ched sent me in here with you to make Morga jealous." She grinned at him. "She'd really be jealous if she knew what we've been doing."

"What's with the chieftain wanting me to marry his daughter?" Bern asked.

"I suppose that's my fault. It's a local custom. He needs somebody to rally the troops," she answered. "He's looking for a warrior to replace the Year King, and I saw you in the well when he asked who could lead his army. So—"

"I think we've both been in the past too long," he said. "Because what you just said seems to make sense to you, and it almost makes sense to me."

Tears suddenly welled in her big blue eyes. "You're really from my time." The relief in her voice bordered on worship.

He kissed her cheeks, tasting the salt from her tears.

"Happy to be of service," he said.

"You're not from my team," she said. "I would have remembered you. How do you know my name? What are you doing here?"

He should have explained all that to her already. He should have gotten a debriefing from her. Duty should have come before sex.

But he found it difficult to regret the last few moments.

"You couldn't tell what I was doing? I guess I'll just have to do it again . . ." He kissed her again. "I can't seem to stop wanting you."

"In the vision, maybe I communicated my lust through the psychic link with you," she explained. "My gift is for scrying with water energy."

"Right," he answered. He knew that about her. He'd read it in the file. It hadn't been something he'd been happy about.

Frankly, he wasn't all that comfortable with a scientific/military Project that used psychics, despite the fact that he was a bit of a psychic himself. He was a soldier first, and the mission certainly needed soldiers. But the nature of time travel had required psychics for the Project to be successful. No matter how much data time travelers collected on jaunts into the past, it was only the travelers with psychic gifts who were able to remember their actual experiences from the journey. So, Project teams took back all sorts of recording equipment. But they also took along a psychic to serve as a living, subjective memory of the events from their voyages into the past.

Psychics also came along to study the energy nexuses, the doors, as it were, where time travelers could enter and leave the eras they were visiting. The scientists in charge of the TTP didn't always feel comfortable with all this use of psychic talent, it just wasn't scientific enough for them, but the people in charge of funding the project insisted on using every available research tool. Besides, as far as anyone could explain the process of time travel, it still seemed a hell of a lot more like magic than it did science.

"We ought to put on our game faces and get down to business," he said. He got up and adjusted his tunic, then helped Ginger to her feet. The woman looked good naked.

"Sorry about soaking your dress." He reached down, grabbed, and offered her the mass of wet wool.

"It needed a spring wash anyway," she answered. She picked up the sodden lump of cloth and began wringing it out into the bath water. "Give me a hand," she said, and together they managed to wind the dress tight enough to squeeze out most of the water. The whole time they worked Bern tried to keep his eyes off her. He couldn't.

"You've got great tits," he told her. They were large and round and just as pale as the rest of her, but for the lovely dark circles of her nipples. Nipples that grew peaked and hard when she noticed him looking at her. He grinned as a flush spread across her chest and throat. It wasn't only a smile that rose as he watched her.

"Ginger White, you may be the death of me," he said.

She snatched her dress out of his hands. "I think maybe you better help me on with this."

"Pity. I like this view so much better." He stepped close

and ran his hands over her in the pretext of helping her maneuver the wet dress. She was cool to the touch, but she went warm where he touched.

"You feel like satin," he told her.

"Back off, soldier," she said. He did.

When she was finally dressed, she seemed to remember what was at stake here. She had more questions for him than he could answer. "Is your name really Bern? When are you from? Do you know what happened to the rest of my team? How did you find me? Where's the nexus? When can we go home?"

Bern held up his hands to halt her rush of words. "I'll answer yours if you'll answer mine." He spotted a stone bench against the wall and led her over to it.

They sat together in the warm air of the bath, and he tried to sum up what he knew. "My team was sent out six months after yours. Our mission was specifically to search for your team—not a single member made it back. When we came in through the Tintagel nexus, it crashed behind us. We couldn't get back."

"So now your team is missing as well?"

He nodded. "At least my team all came through together. It didn't look like your team made it here intact. The theory is that some kind of hiccup in the time/dimensional energy field scattered your team in transit—"

"I noticed. So we all came through at different nexus points?" she asked.

He nodded.

"I'm no physicist, but I managed to figure that out on my own." She gave his hands a sympathetic squeeze. "So your team's as lost here as we are."

"Yeah. But we still had our mission. Along with hunting for you people we've been searching for a working exit point. No luck yet with that. It hasn't been easy, since the energy hiccup shorted out most of your team's ID transponders. So far you're only the second team member we've found alive."

"Who else have you found?"

"Sergeant Kaye."

"Thank goodness! I've been so worried about him." Then she blanched. "You've found others—dead?"

"Yeah. Sorry. We found Dr. Bohrs's grave outside a village near Aqua Sulus. Gwayne had been enslaved on a Saxon farmstead on the coast. We got him out of the place alive, but he caught an arrow in the throat when we ran into a raiding party the next day."

"Damned Saxon invaders," she muttered.

"You've been hanging with the indigenous folks too long. Remember, the Saxons are *supposed* to take over the island after the Romans left."

"Yes, but not like this. The incursion seems to be happening far quicker than the archeology I've seen would indicate. The Roman influences that overlaid the Celtic base culture should have time to fade. If the Saxons aren't halted soon, the world we come from won't get a chance to develop. I've been starting to believe that maybe I'd transported into one of those alternate worlds the theorists worry about."

"I didn't think you were your team historian."

"They brought me along for my visions. History's just a hobby. I'm an Anglophile."

"Me, I go where I'm sent and do what I'm told to do. Speaking of that, how did you end up as the local priestess?"

She glanced down sheepishly, before looking him in the eye again. "I know direct involvement with the locals is against the rules, but I was stuck here and I wanted to survive. I'm lucky that the holy spring's point of origin is in the woods behind the shrine and that's the nexus where I came through. The Romans channeled the spring into the sanctuary pool when they built the villa. So it was easier for the inhabitants to believe that I was the only survivor of a band of pilgrims attacked by bandits when I wandered bloody and burned out of the woods than it would have been if I'd appeared out of a blaze of light in the fountain."

"So, you decided to save yourself instead of searching for the rest of your team?"

She pulled her hands from his. "How would I look for the

others? I don't have any computer equipment. I'm too high level on the psi chart for any implant but the wrist chip."

"Right. Sorry."

"I've tried scrying to hunt for them, but I've never seen them, much less their locations."

"Makes sense. Seers don't see things connected with themselves."

"At least not often. I thought about striking out on my own to hunt for them after the locals nursed me back to health, but it was the dead of winter. This isn't the best of times for a woman to play tourist, between the bandits and barbarians massing outside Lord Ched's rather flimsy walls. Since this was the only safe place I knew about, I set about proving my usefulness so I could stay. The sanctuary hadn't had a resident seer for a long time. I used my scrying abilities and got the job. Having a real fortune teller at the holy spring increases the prestige and fame of the place. Which means a larger gathering of pilgrims bringing rich offerings for the goddess, and greater wealth for Lord Ched, at this year's fertility festival. Unfortunately, he's decided that the fertility part of the festivities needs a bit of rearranging, and that's where you come in."

Bern thought about what he knew of the local customs, politics, and religious practices, and concluded, "The chieftain wants a warrior to challenge the Year King at tonight's ceremony."

She nodded.

He grimaced. "Ah, crap, he wants me to kill some kid for the right to screw his daughter."

"Exactly. And become the local war leader. He wants you to stop the Saxons." Ginger cleared her throat. "This is my fault, really—I told him I saw you in the water when he asked who would be the next Year King."

Bern shot to his feet. "Oh, for crying out loud, woman!"

She jumped up to face him. "Hey, I just report what the water shows me. How was I supposed to know you were a time traveler sent to rescue me?"

"You couldn't lie sometimes?"

"It's not like I knew who you were when I saw you. It's not my fault the water says you're fated to be king! And sleep with Morga," she added.

He heard the jealousy in her voice, and he liked it. He noticed that they'd moved close together while they argued, and that arguing with her was arousing him all over again. The attraction between them was strong and hot, and driving him crazy. Being crazy was no way to run an op. Knowing that didn't stop him from putting his hands on her hips.

"There you are!" Lord Ched's voice boomed out behind them before he could pull Ginger into his arms.

They turned to face the chieftain, and the trio of men that followed him into the bathhouse. Ched had a smile plastered on his face, but there was anger in his eyes. His hand was on the pommel of a dagger on his belt. Bern had been prepared to tell the man he had no interest in his game of kings and priestesses, but decided this might not be the right time to assert his opinion.

"What's wrong?" he asked instead. He put his arm protectively around Ginger's shoulders. He was aware of the way she leaned into him all down the length of his body.

"You're a clever one," Ched said, nodding approvingly.

"I know trouble when I see it. And it's in your eyes right now."

His impulse was to gather his squad and see what was going on for himself, but he waited for an explanation. Even if the Saxons were attacking the gates it wasn't his problem unless the team he'd been sent to save was in immediate danger. He was not in charge of the indigenous situation here, and wasn't going to interfere with the locals despite the chieftain's plans or Ginger's visions.

Ched cleared his throat, and Bern realized he was embarrassed. "It's something to do with your daughter, isn't it?"

"Morga's run off," Ched said. "And the Year King ran with her." He sighed.

"But she's the Mother's priestess!" Ginger gasped. "And he's—"

"You've been spending too much time with the locals," Bern whispered to her in English. "A pair of runaways is not your problem."

"But—the ceremony is tonight." She, too, spoke English.

Ched might not have understood what Ginger said, but he recognized the desperation in her tone. "You see the problem, don't you, Lady of the Spring? Oh, we could go after those foolish children. But if we drag them back I'll have to execute my own daughter to appease the crowd gathered for the festival. And you'll have to kill that stripling she's bonded with."

"But what about the ceremony?" a one-eyed man asked. "Tradition—"

"We've changed tradition before," Ched cut him off. He looked at one of the other men, a wizened, white-bearded fellow in rough brown robes. "Haven't we, Bishop Myrdyn?"

The old man was carrying a gnarled staff, and reminded Bern of Gandalf.

"You're not thinking of giving up your heathen fertility festival, are you?" the old man asked.

"Of course not!" Ched answered. "The people would riot for sure if we changed custom that far."

"There you go again—you promise to change your pagan ways, but you always find a way out of your promises."

"Didn't I say I'd let you baptize as many folk as you wanted tomorrow morning? And in our own sacred pool?"

"That you did," the Christian cleric conceded. He tugged thoughtfully on his earlobe. "Once the people are sated and sore from the sex, and their heads are splitting from too much drink, I'll preach a sermon that will lure them to save their souls from the great sins they're going to commit this night. It will be a fine harvest of souls. They'll be crying for forgiveness. You'll make a fine Year King," he added, looking Bern over. "I'll give my blessing to that."

"But we need a priestess for the king to mate with," the one-eyed man insisted. "The crops will wither without the spring mating."

"Well, if I'm going to turn the pool into a baptismal fount, it won't need a priestess anymore, will it?" the bishop said, eyeing Ginger critically. He pointed at her. "Use this priestess instead of the one that's run off."

"That'll work," Lord Ched said, clapping Myrdyn on the shoulder. "One priestess is as good as another in the eyes of the goddess."

"But—I'm not a virgin," Ginger blurted. "The priestess of the Mother must be a virgin when she lies with her first Year King."

"Don't encourage them," Bern complained. Then he realized where she was going with this and spoke loudly. "We can't offend the goddess. I'm no virgin, either."

Ched waved his hand dismissively. "You were both virgins once, after all. It's virility and fertility that matter most. You'll both do. I'm glad that's settled." He began to turn away.

"But I don't want to be king," Bern said.

"What man doesn't want to be king?" Ched asked, turning back. "Especially when the choice is between becoming Year King or going to the goddess with the priestess and all of your men sacrificed inside the burning belly of the wicker man?" His smile had more than a touch of threat in it.

"Sex or death," Myrdyn said. "Either way, the crowd will be entertained."

They weren't making hollow promises. Bern had seen the piles of kindling and a crudely woven straw statue in a field on his way into the stockade. He knew that criminals were often burned alive inside such structures during the spring festival. Lord Ched could probably get the mob angry enough at missing out on the orgy to attack his team. The ensuing massacre wouldn't look good on Bern's record. And there was the chance that some of his people could get hurt. He wasn't ready to risk any of them, especially Ginger.

All he had to do was be the Year King.

It wasn't like he minded having sex with Ginger White.

"King it is then," Bern said.

"Good," Lord Ched said, and he and his people marched away.

When they were gone, Ginger asked, "Now what are we going to do?"

Bern was still grinning as he took her in his arms. "Why, rehearse for the fertility ceremony, of course."

"You'll have to wear a pair of stag horns, you know."

He grimaced. "And what will you be wearing?"

"Not a damn thing."

The grimace turned into a grin. "I can live with that."

"Yes, but—"

"My name's Andrew." He picked her up and carried her toward the narrow bed. "Colonel Andrew Bern. Just Bern to almost everybody." He kissed her before adding. "Under the circumstances, I thought we ought to be formally introduced."

She twined her arms around his neck. "Nice name. Kiss me again."

"All over," he promised.

Night had fallen, sacred fires were lit, and hundreds of pilgrims were waiting within their glow just outside the front of the estate. The ceremony was ready to begin.

"I wasn't this nervous at my wedding," Bern confided. "Or my divorce hearing."

Ginger rounded on him. "You're married? I do not have sex with married men."

"Then you're in luck, because I'm not married."

"Oh. Right. Divorced. Sorry." She rested her forehead against his bare chest. "I am *so* nervous that I don't know what I'm saying or doing. I've never done anything like this my whole life."

"Just enjoy the moment. Don't think about anything but me. I promise, I won't be thinking about anything but you.

You look beautiful," he told her. "Like the bride of the summer god ought to look."

They had braided spring flowers into her thick red curls, and she was wearing Morga's most diaphanous white silk dress. He was wearing a doe-skin loincloth. He had to claim the Summer King's sword, then be acclaimed by the people. After that they'd get naked and down to business.

They made their way through the watching crowd to where Lord Ched stood between two widely spaced bonfires. Ginger was deeply aware of the expectant mood of the hundreds of watching people. She told herself that Bern was the only thing that was real here, that everything else was a dream. She concentrated on the feel of him where his skin touched hers. Being near him truly did make her body ripe with need.

When they reached the chieftain, Ched held up a richly decorated sword and shouted, "Behold your priestess and her new Summer King!" While the crowd cheered, Ched plunged the tip of the sword into the soft, spring earth.

"Now what?" Bern whispered to Ginger.

"You say something about accepting the kingship for the love of the Mother and the fertility of the land, and pull the sword from the ground."

"Okay, then." He began to step forward, hand out to take the hilt of the sacred blade.

"Wait!" a man shouted from the crowd before Bern could touch the sword.

"Now what?" Bern said, turning toward the man who came rushing forward.

"I challenge!" the man shouted, coming up to glare at Bern.

"Oh, crap," Ginger muttered. "I forgot about Lanc."

"Who the hell is Lanc?" Bern demanded.

She pointed at the broad-shoulder, dark-haired man. "He's this druid from Brittany that's been trying to get me to run off with him."

Bern rounded on her. "What? You weren't going to mention that there's this other guy who wants to skewer me tonight?"

"You're jealous."

"Yes!"

She grinned. "Oh, that's so cute. Don't worry. You're more than a match for him."

"I challenge!" Lanc shouted again. "Fight me for your kingship!"

Bern gestured at the challenger. "Hold on, I'll be right with you. What is this guy to you?" he demanded of Ginger.

"Nothing. He's one of a group of druids going around trying to recruit psychics to come back to Brittany. They're trying to keep the old religion alive back home."

"So, he doesn't want to have sex with you?"

"Not as far as I—"

"Yes, I do!" Lanc cut her off.

"Oh, stop it," Ginger told him.

"Fight me for her!" Lanc insisted. The crowd was beginning to shout for the battle to begin as well.

"Okay," Bern said. Without even stopping to take a breath, he turned around and hit the man in the jaw.

Lanc went down, but was up again almost instantly.

Bern took a step back and smiled, glad that the opposition had some fight in him. It was strange, almost as strange as being in another place and time than the one he'd been born to, but he was glad to have some competition. He wanted Ginger, wanted to properly claim the woman as his. Fighting for her hand felt, in some atavistic way, right. Deep in his gut, deep in his heart, he knew Ginger was a woman worth fighting for.

The druid was a big, fit guy with some hand-to-hand skills. They circled, then sparred against each other, flesh and muscle straining, moving through firelight and shadow while the crowd cheered and shouted. Sweat stung Bern's eyes, and he tasted blood when Lanc got past his guard once to strike him in the face. Excitement built deep in Bern's gut and the clarity that only came with combat focused his whole attention on the struggle.

For a while he almost forgot the purpose of the challenge

while he concentrated on the fight. Then he caught sight of Ginger. She was flushed and her eyes were bright with excitement that sent a zing of lust straight to Bern's groin. But her arms were tensely crossed, and she also looked annoyed.

"Enjoying yourself?" she called sarcastically when she had his attention.

The momentary distraction almost cost him, but he caught Lanc's sudden kick out of the corner of his eye and quickly countered. He ended up with a hard foot grazing his thigh as he turned. He returned the favor with a hard kick to Lanc's solar plexus that brought the man down.

Enough of this toying with his prey.

When Lanc tried to struggle up again, Bern knocked him unconscious.

Ginger rushed up to him "Are you all right?"

"Oh, yeah." He grinned, and kissed her, pulling her tightly against him. "Never better." The loincloth left nothing to her imagination about how he was feeling. The cheering crowd faded away from his attention as he concentrated only on the woman in his arms.

Her hand brushed against the erection straining against the soft leather. Then she pried herself out of his tight embrace. "Not yet."

"Oh, come on!" he complained. But he understood when she pointed toward the sword buried in the ground. He laughed. "Right. Well, at least I don't have to pull it out of a stone."

"Uh . . ."

"What?"

She looked at him strangely, and asked, "Doesn't Bern mean 'bear'?"

"Yeah . . ." He crossed to the sword. Bits of earth clung to the blade as he pulled it out and held it up for all to see. He waited for the cheering to die down, then shouted, "For Britain and the White Lady!"

The roar this time was deafening.

"Must have sounded good," he murmured.

Ched came up to him, taking both him and Ginger by the

hand. A trio of young women accompanied him. One of the girls held a stag-horn headdress. The other girls made quick work of stripping off his and Ginger's clothes.

After fastening the headdress on Bern, Ched turned to the crowd and proclaimed, "Behold the queen and king of summer. This mating will bring fertility to the land! Let the festival begin!"

"You know, I'm beginning to think—" Ginger started.

"Don't." Bern grabbed her and kissed her.

He swung his naked lover up into his arms and covered her mouth with his. While his tongue probed inside that sweet, responsive warmth he carried her to the cloth-covered mound of grass and flowers that was to serve as both bed and altar for them to mate upon.

"Put me down!" she demanded.

"Don't chicken out on me now," he pleaded.

Ginger laughed wickedly. "Not a chance." She remembered his directions to just look at him, but the crowd was the last thing on her mind at the moment. She wanted to taste him, and that was what she did.

The crowd cheered. A wave of raw sexual energy washed over her. The lust channeled by the masses shot through her, and she projected it back to the people around them. In that moment the goddess filled her, and she worshipped the god of summer and king of the land with all the fervor and passion due him.

Bern pushed her gently onto her back on the soft, fragrant altar. He knelt over her, poised at the moist opening of her vagina. He waited while her hips rose pleadingly.

"Now!" she demanded.

But he didn't move until her gaze finally met his. "The night is just beginning," he told her.

Then he entered her, and his worship of the goddess began in earnest.

"Ahem."

The embarrassed throat-clearing, followed by a second

voice demanding, "Cover your shame, woman!" was the last thing Ginger expected to hear after the night she'd enjoyed.

Besides, she wasn't sure how shame was supposed to be covered, especially when what she felt was marvelous. All right, she was sore and tender in places, and rather hung over, though not in the having-drunk-too-much-alcohol way. Who knew too much great sex could make you groggy?

Could you have too much great sex?

If it could be done, she'd done it tonight.

"Colonel, sir," the embarrassed voice whispered. "Excuse me for waking you up, but—"

"Rouse yourself, man!" the other voice boomed.

Ginger giggled. "Please don't," she murmured. "Not on my account. Not just yet, anyway."

"Wha? What?" Bern muttered.

She felt his breath brush her cheek when he spoke, and realized that he was the warm weight lying half on top of her. The cool morning breeze skimmed across the rest of her, teasing one bare nipple to a hard peak. Maybe that was the shame the guy was talking about. Was that any way to talk to the goddess's own—

That voice . . . There was something familiar about it . . .

"Is that you, Dr. White?"

Ginger's eyes flew open and she caught sight of a familiar, concerned face.

"Sergeant Kaye?" Oh, good Lord, she was naked in front of a colleague! She didn't recognize the man standing next to him, but the stranger was frowning down at her with utter disgust written all over his face.

"His name's Percy Perkins, and he's a jerk," Bern whispered. He sat up and said, "I hope you brought us some clothes, Kaye."

The sergeant held out the dress Ginger had worn last night, and a long tunic for Bern.

"Of course you realize that I intend to report this infraction," Percy said.

"Infraction of what?" Bern asked. "There's no rule against team members fraternizing."

"You led an orgy! Your disgusting behavior roused the indigenous population to—"

"He didn't get any, sir," Kaye put in.

Bern scratched his jaw. "I can see how that might make him cranky."

"Not to mention being named Percy," Ginger added. "That alone probably put the guy into years of therapy. Could you sue your parents for giving you a name like that?" she asked Bern.

He shrugged. "Ask Percy."

"Well?" she said.

Percy declined to respond. But his posture, though it seemed impossible, became even more tense.

"I could use a shave," Bern said. "And a bath." He sprang to his feet and helped Ginger up. "How about you, sweetheart?"

"Definitely."

"Have the team meet us at the bath, Kaye. But give us a few minutes, will you?"

They could hear Percy spluttering as they walked away.

She slipped the white dress over her head, and they walked arm in arm across the field toward the villa, frequently stepping over and around still-sleeping revelers.

The spring ceremony had apparently been a great success.

Kaye went off to his assignment, and Percy followed behind them, making the occasional disapproving sound. The morning sun shone down, the sky was blue, the earth was green, birds sang, and Ginger was happier than she'd ever been before. They had the blessing of the goddess, she supposed.

They passed the old bishop preaching to a small group of revelers who looked thoroughly hangdog and hung over. Myrdyn gave them a pleasant nod when he saw them pass him by.

"We must be good for business," Bern said.

"If he baptizes all those people, the energy in the pool is going to be whacked out for days," Ginger said.

"That is hardly a scientific explanation of a temporal malfunction, Dr. White," Percy complained.

They both ignored him.

Once they reached the bathhouse, Ginger led them into the preparation room where oils scented the bathers' bodies before they got into the hot water of the bathing pool. Benches lined the walls, and the floor was tiled in a beautiful leaf-patterned mosaic.

"This is where I meant to bring you yesterday," she told Bern.

He pulled her close. They looked into each other's eyes. "It was worth the detour."

"You two are being disgusting," Percy said.

Bern sighed. "You know, this time I think I agree with him." He let her go. "We do need to make plans."

"We have work to do," she said.

"Do I detect some professionalism at last?" Percy whined.

"Shut up, Percy," Ginger and Bern said together.

"And that's an order," Bern added.

Ginger took a seat on a bench against the back wall. Within a few minutes Kaye and the rest of the team joined them. Bern allowed his people a few minutes of teasing him before the introductions.

"This is Gareth and Lamorak."

Ginger smiled. "Of course they are."

He didn't understand what amused her, and didn't ask. "Let's get down to business."

"Now that we have recovered Dr. White, it's time to continue surveying the nexus points," Percy said immediately.

"Percy's a douser," Bern explained to Ginger. "He's working on a new nexus map. But he hasn't yet found a spot with enough energy to get us home."

"It's hardly my fault that this island is swamped with

more energy points than anywhere else on the planet, especially in this area. It was a mistake to send a team this far back, and especially to this geographic location."

"Yeah, I think we're all aware of that," Gareth said. "We noticed the problems. And that's before you started telling us every five minutes."

"We have one more man to find," Lamorak said. "That'll round out our mission."

"Finding the exit point is far more important for our own survival," Percy said. "We should cut our losses and concentrate on finding a functioning nexus. Perhaps Dr. White could conjure up a vision of where we should go," he added. But not as though he meant it.

"What'd I ever do to you?" was Ginger's response to this rudeness. "See if I tell you if I find it!"

Bern liked that she refused to be intimidated by the jerk. "No one gets left behind," he reminded Percy. "We're still looking for Owens."

"But his transpond—" Percy started.

"What does your gut tell you, sir?" Kaye jumped in. "You found me—"

"Your transponder was working—" Percy cut him off.

"Intermittently. It was Colonel Bern's instincts that really found me."

"Balderdash," Percy scoffed.

"Does anyone really say balderdash?" Ginger asked.

"Just Percy," Bern replied.

"The colonel's gut led us here and we found Dr. White," Gareth said. "So what do you think about Owens, sir?"

Bern considered for a moment, sensing more than thinking. Finally, he said, "I think that most of the population in the area is camped out around this stronghold. If I was Owens, I'd be here too." He swept his gaze around his team. "Break up. Go look for him. Reconvene here at noon."

There were nods, and people turned to leave.

Before he left, Percy just had to ask, "And what will you be doing while we're searching?"

Bern put his arm around Ginger's shoulders. "I'm going to be standing at the Lady of the White Bird Spring's side while she seeks a vision to help us find a way home."

"Good, Bishop Myrdyn hasn't used the place yet," Ginger said as they entered the empty shrine.

Now she didn't have to regret insisting that they get cleaned up before coming to the spring. Her skin felt fresh and tingly, and all the aches from strenuous bouts of sex were soothed. Her hair hung in a damp braid down her back, and Bern had shaved.

"If only we had coffee, I could face anything," she said.

"Find us the right nexus and I'll buy you your own Starbucks," he replied.

He wouldn't be able to do any such thing, of course, even if she could somehow pull the right vision out of the sacred pool. It saddened her to know that she would return to her point of origin, and he would return to his, which was six months further along the main timeline than hers. She would remember what happened, and six months later he'd read a report filed by her, and learn what he'd done in the past. It wouldn't be proper to record their sexual encounters in the official record, even if the dry bureaucratic tone of reports could use spicing up a bit.

He'd probably never even know who she was.

But she'd remember forever.

"What are you smiling about?" he asked.

"Nothing." She turned her smile briefly on him, and then dropped to her knees. "I doubt this will work," she warned. "I don't normally see anything dealing with my own future."

"You saw me, didn't you?"

"I saw you in response to Lord Ched asking who the next king would be. By the way, there's something important you should know about that," she added.

"Not now. As soon as we conclude the search for Owen, I'm taking you and the rest of my people out of here."

"But—"

"You'll find me a nexus. I know it. Look into the water. Calm yourself. Concentrate."

"I know how to summon the visions, Andrew."

He put his hands on her shoulders and gently began to massage them. He communicated his faith in her through his touch. Damn, but she was going to hate losing this man! She appreciated the moment, refused to feel sorry for herself, and set about doing her duty.

At first, of course, all she saw was a pool of water as still and clear as a looking glass. But the calm, peaceful water changed quickly.

Bern grew worried when Ginger's muscles went suddenly tense. "What?" he asked. "What do you see?"

"Fire," she answered, her voice distant and dull. "Fire on the hill."

"What hill? What's burning?"

"There's a battle," she said. "You have to defeat them. It's your destiny."

A battle? He didn't like the sound of that. "What does any of that have to do with getting us all safely home?"

Lord Ched came running into the sanctuary before she could respond. "They're coming!" he shouted. "The Saxons are coming." A guard followed him in, pushing a woman ahead of him. Ched looked at the woman. "Tell him," he commanded.

The woman was crying. "Mercy, my lord! I did come back to warn you."

"Yes, yes," the chieftain said. He pointed to Bern. "Tell the king what you told me."

Everybody looked at him. Bern wanted to yell at them to cut out calling him king, but even Ginger had come out of her trance and was looking at him like he was the hero of the hour. And, damn it, the thought of disappointing her made him feel like a jerk. He gritted his teeth, and nodded for the woman to go on.

"It's true I helped my lady Morga and her man escape. I've taken care of the girl all her life, and I understood how she'd been with the last Year King long enough to think of him as her husband and not to want to bed a new man." She looked Bern over. "Though I think she would have gotten the better part of the bargain had she stayed and done her duty."

"Get on to the important part," the chieftain urged.

"The pair of them were angry and affronted at being forced to run from their home. After we made camp last night they talked about how they would betray the secrets of the stronghold's defenses to the Saxons."

Ched rubbed the back of his neck. "But that is the secret—we have no defenses."

"But the invaders aren't aware of how weak we are," the guard said. "They'll march straight for us now."

"They will be arriving soon," the woman said. "I had to come back to warn my people that their doom approaches."

Bern wished she hadn't put it like that. It made him feel sorry for the indigenous population. Even worse, the way they all looked to him to take command made him feel responsible for them. These people were going to be easy pickings without some help. Bern thought of all the defense-less people camped out around the stronghold. They'd come here for a religious celebration, not to be slaughtered.

"How will you defend us?" Lord Ched asked him.

Ginger came forward and put her hand on his arm. "I was studying the pool for advice on that very subject when you arrived. If you would let us continue with the divination, the king will meet with you afterwards, better prepared to save your people."

The chieftain and his people left without another word.

When they were alone, Ginger grabbed the front of Bern's tunic, held on tight, and talked fast. "You listen to me, Colo-nel Bern. I will not have you quoting rules and regs about noninterference and the possibility of changing history. We don't have any solid history from this era to go on. But we do have myths and legends, and, hon, I think I know what's going on here. You have to fight the invaders. You. You are the element necessary to slow down the incursions and give the native culture more time to recover from Roman rule. That way, when the Saxons do take over it'll be overlaying a British-based culture rather than a Roman one. In our time we'll have England the way we know it. If you duck this battle we won't. It's your duty take on the invaders here and now. You were meant to do this."

Bern gaped at her. "What the hell are you talking about?"

"You said it yourself, last night, *'at least I don't have to pull it out of a stone.'* You pulled the sword from the soil of Britain and claimed the kingship. You are—"

"Don't you dare put that on me." He'd finally figured out where this was going.

"Bern means 'bear,'" she went on. "One of the translations of—"

"No."

"And then there's your men's names. There's Kaye and—"

"You've been drinking that spring water too long, as well as looking into it, haven't you?" His tone was doubtful, but his instincts were shouting at him that she was right.

He knew he'd hurt her feelings, but they were interrupted once again before he could apologize. This time it was the rest of the team that came into the sanctuary.

"Look who we found, boss!" Kaye crowed. "Your gut was right again."

"Stop looking smug," he ordered Ginger. "Welcome to your rescue, Professor Owen," he said to the newcomer.

"I'm grateful the Project sent a team for us." Owen gave Ginger a nod and smile. She smiled back. "And if rumor is correct, you've come to the rescue just in the nick of time."

"We've heard that the Saxons are heading this way," Kaye told him. "Time for us to bug out, right?"

Bern waited for Ginger to protest, but she crossed her arms and bit her lower lip instead of nagging him. Damn it! That made it even harder for him to say no to her.

"I took an oath to protect these people last night," he told the team. "The least we can do is give the locals a chance at getting away."

"What precisely to you mean by 'we'?" Percy spoke up. "At no point do I recall having signed a social contract with these people. Going native is not one of our options."

"What's wrong with helping people?" Owen demanded. "The locals have helped me survive for months. I owe them."

"So do I," Ginger said.

"Very touching, but irrelevant," Percy responded.

"You are such a wuss," Gareth said. "Come on, fighting a bunch of barbarians will be fun."

"No, it won't," Bern said sternly. "And don't make the assumption that I'm asking for a consensus, or volunteers. This is a military operation, and I'm in command. We're all going into this fight."

His soldiers immediately snapped to attention, and he nodded to them. Percy didn't look happy, but at least this finally shut him up. Bern glanced at Ginger. She was looking at him with enough pride in her eyes to set his heart on fire. She made him feel like a hero. This wasn't the time to kiss her all over the way he wanted to, but he did put his arm around her waist and draw her close.

As they stood, hip to hip, he said, "Remember the hillside we crossed on the way here?" There were nods. "We're going to set up our perimeter there. It's time to break out the claymores, boys."

Ginger gave him a puzzled look, but her expression cleared before he could explain. "Oh, you're not talking about big Scottish swords, are you?"

"No, hon, I'm talking about shaped charges that blow up."

"Fire in the sky," she said. "Just what the vision showed me."

This had better work, Ginger thought. She hugged herself tightly. *Please, God, let it work. And don't let anything happen to Bern—or any of the good guys—while you're at it.*

Please, Lady, she added, since she was officially a priestess of the goddess.

Well, maybe not officially anymore since soon she'd be leaving Lord Ched's villa forever. She was standing in the woods at the source of the spring with a bundle of provisions at her feet, waiting for the rest of the team to join her. The plan was for her to wait safely out of the way while the men carried out the op. Bern had insisted she stay out of harm's way, and she hadn't argued. She was no warrior.

Besides, securing their nexus was probably the most important part of this op.

Some of the other women had taken up arms to fight alongside their men after Bern gave a rousing speech to the gathered pilgrims. This was the ancient way of the Celts, and more proof as far as Ginger was concerned that this battle was going to slow the tide of invasion. The people were eager to follow Bern into battle. Their willingness to defend their homeland was a good sign, too. Right?

Please, Horned God and Lady of the Spring, don't let me have started something that's going to get a lot of people killed. Especially not Bern.

She reminded herself that he was a competent professional soldier. He had a good strategy. He had trained subordinates. He had explosives. He was going to win the day.

The plan for the TTP team was that after the battle was joined, and the good guys were winning, they'd withdraw and join Ginger in the woods. With their obligation to help the people fulfilled, the team could then continue their search for a working nexus that would take them home.

Home. Away from Bern. She dashed away tears. It had to be. If she went home with a broken heart and a deep ache for the way he made her body sing, she still had the memories to appreciate. At least they'd spent as much time as they could over the last three days making love while waiting for the Saxons. And now the Saxons were here.

Ginger paced nervously. What if it didn't work? Was there something she could do to help?

She hated the quiet here in the woods. Maybe she was safer here, but the sudden need to know what was going on got the better of her. She cut through the woods rather than take the path that led toward the villa.

The perfect spring weather of the festival had been replaced by a pewter sky that threatened rain, and a wind that blew cooler than it should for this time of year. It was a grim day, fit for a battle, she supposed.

When she reached the south edge of the woods she got a good view down the valley to the hill beyond. Half of the British fighters were spread out below the hill, waiting there instead of occupying the high ground. She caught sight of chainmail and swordblades as gray as the day and the energy—a mixture of fear and anticipation—hit her like a blow. She put herself behind a tree and waited, and watched.

The atmosphere grew even more tense. Thunder rumbled in the distance. Soon a large band of Saxon warriors appeared on the crest of the hill. They saw the Britons waiting for them and drew to a halt. More of the invaders came up behind them, and more, until there was an army of several hundred fierce barbarians looking down upon the several dozen not-quite-so-fierce barbarians below. The Saxons formed into a long line that stretched out along the top of the hill, but since they held the high ground they didn't seem to be in any hurry to rush the people below.

Which was what Bern had counted on.

A line of claymore mines had been set right where the Saxons were now standing. When the mines went off there was indeed fire bursting up toward the sky. And screaming, and blood, and flying body parts.

What was left of the Saxon invaders turned to flee, but that could not be allowed. Bern's team and the other half of the British force came out of hiding in the woods on the far side of the hill and drove the remainder of the Saxons down the hill onto the swords of those waiting for them.

The reality was so much worse than her vision, but she never doubted the necessity of this battle. Ginger watched the carnage long enough to be assured that everything was going to turn out as planned. There would be a victory here today at Camlan Hill. Legend would speak of magic making the very soil of Britain gape wide to send the enemy to the fires of hell.

Only witnessing it upset her more than she realized, because she got lost in the thick woods making her way back to the spring. By the time she found her way to the rendez-vous point it had started to rain. Bern and the team were waiting for her. They'd brought horses with them.

"You scared me half mad, woman!" Bern stopped pacing and pulled her roughly to him by the elbows. "Where have you been?"

She was so happy to see him that she kissed him. She began to cry with relief, and was glad to have the rain to cover this excess of emotion.

Except she knew it didn't work when he kissed her cheeks and said, "You taste salty."

"And you smell sweaty," she said. "Let's get out of here."

He kept his arms around her when she would have gone for her pack. "But where do we go from here?" He glanced toward Percy.

The subject had been under discussion for days. The problem with this area was an overabundance of sites where energy concentrated. Ginger had stayed out of it, because she didn't want to be dismissed out of hand as a total loon. Now she had to speak up. She had the answer they needed.

"We need to go to the Isle of Apples," she told them.

"Where's that?" Bern asked.

Gareth laughed. "So, I'm not the only one who's seen the parallels."

Kaye nodded thoughtfully.

Maybe she should have spoken up sooner.

Percy pulled a handheld computer out of a leather pouch on his belt. He checked a map screen and then frowned at her. "I've worked out the search grid very carefully. There's no reason to deviate from—"

"Where is this Apple Island?" Bern asked.

"Isle of Apples," Ginger corrected. She cleared her throat, took a deep breath, and made herself publicly say, "Avalon."

"Oh, for crying out loud!" Percy yelled in disgust.

She didn't blame him. "I admit it might seem a little far-fetched."

"A little?" He sneered "Living among these people has made you as superstitious as they are. You've come to accept their mythology as—"

"It's not one of the local myths," Gareth spoke. "Not yet, anyway. It *is* one of *our* myths. Following it might lead us home."

"Gambling on what *might* happen is not a scientific or logical basis for finding the correct nexus," Percy argued.

Bern rubbed his jaw and chuckled. "Might doesn't always make right. I just remembered where that came from. But where is Avalon? Hasn't that always been a mystery?"

"It doesn't exist. You're not going along with this, are you, Colonel?" Percy demanded. He pointed accusingly at Ginger. "Why? Because she's good in bed?"

Ginger was rather pleased that several team members stepped forward, but Bern got to Percy first, and punched him in the jaw. Percy hit the wet ground, and was wise enough to stay down. He sat in the mud, rubbed his jaw, and kept his mouth shut.

"So, where do we go?" Bern asked her.

"Tradition points to Glastonbury," she answered.

"There's a nexus on top of that big hill that's there?" he asked.

She shook her head, and glanced at Percy. "Not on top of the tor, right?" He grimaced, but nodded. "There's a sacred spring called Chalice Well at the foot of Glastonbury Tor. I think that's where we have to go."

"Let's do it. Mount up," Bern ordered the team. "We need to get out of here before the locals come looking for us so they can throw a feast in our honor."

As the men moved to mount their animals, he snatched

Ginger around the waist and put her up on the horse in front of him. She snuggled back against him, and he wrapped his cape around both of them. In this warm, intimate position he leaned forward to whisper, "Being like this with you almost makes me like riding a horse."

She tilted her head against his shoulder, determined to draw every bit of nearness to him she could in the time they had left. "Then let's enjoy the ride."

"I don't believe it," Percy said. He double-checked his equipment as the water of the Glastonbury spring bubbled up at his feet. Then he gave Ginger a sour look. "She's right."

"The energy reading is right?" Kaye asked.

"It's off the scale," Percy answered.

"Enough to take all of us home?" Owen asked.

"Jump in and find out," Percy invited. He glanced around the green and lovely glade. "Before the priestesses we chased off come back."

"With an angry mob," Kaye added.

If at all possible, TTP operatives were supposed to appear and vanish without any witnesses around. Scaring the locals with the sound and light show that accompanied time travel was considered not only impolite, but possibly dangerous to the primary timeline TTP visits wove in and out of. And the problem with places like sacred springs as nexus points was that they tended to be occupied with priests and pilgrims and such like. So, Bern had had his people approach this one with swords drawn and chase everyone away. Percy was right about their not having much time for goodbyes.

"Form up into teams," he said. He took Ginger's hand before she could join the people she'd traveled with into the past. He drew her away from the spring and tilted her chin up with his fingers. "You are so beautiful," he told her.

"In a pale, freckled sort of way," she answered. She tried to sound light, but her voice came out tight and strained.

"I'll miss you, Dr. Virginia White." Words couldn't begin to describe what having to separate was doing to him.

"Have I thanked you for rescuing me yet?" she asked. She gave him a brief, hard embrace. "It's been a pleasure knowing you, Colonel Andrew Bern."

He kissed her then. It was fierce and quick, and not enough. He ran the back of his hand across her cheek. "Hey, we made history."

"Or something like it."

He nodded, and his throat was too tight for him to manage to say more than, "Go."

She gave him a sad smile, and went over to join Kaye and Owen who were already standing in the spring's shallow pool. They each placed their left thumbs over the inside of their right wrists. Ginger's gaze didn't leave his.

"On my mark," Kaye said. "Activate."

Everyone pressed down hard on the retrieval implant.

The column of light that sprang from the water blinded him. The roar of the shock wave was deafening. Bern refused to look away. The last thing he saw was Ginger's face as she whispered, "Goodbye."

Ginger looked up from the photo before her on the desk, and sighed. A copper bowl filled with water sat on the desk, but she wasn't interested in looking into it. Being a psychic wasn't as much fun for her as it used to be. It had been six months since she'd gotten back to her own time. Six months and three days to be precise, not that she was counting. She'd done the debriefing and written up her report, and been sent back to her regular life until such time as the TTP deemed her special skills necessary again. For now her regular life consisted of working with law enforcement on cold-case files, and being alone.

She sighed again, and stood up. It wasn't that she didn't appreciate being back. She loved her house and garden. She loved central heating and modern medicine and interactive holographic entertainment and regular meals of anything she wanted. She hadn't realized how much she'd missed shopping for shoes until she'd entered her first mall. She loved being home. It was just that—

She missed Bern.

Her body ached for him when she was alone in her bed at night, but the notion of taking another lover was anathema. Even trying a holo lover hadn't worked for her.

She got up and began to pace around her office. She was well aware that Bern had returned to the present three days before, and even more aware that it didn't matter. Maybe there was some way that she could introduce herself to him, but how fair would it be to him when she knew their past and he didn't? There was no way for them to pick up where they'd left off. There was a good chance he wouldn't even be interested in her under normal circumstances. Maybe she wouldn't be interested in him.

She laughed hollowly, still conscious of the ecstasy he brought her when his body joined with hers. "Yeah, right, sure I'm going to forget that."

Then again, she really wanted the man, why shouldn't she fight for what she wanted? She should find a way to introduce herself and see what—

"There is someone at the door," the house's security system announced. It was an old house with a very basic system, so it wasn't about to be more informative than that. So, unless the water in the scrying bowl suddenly showed her who it was—which it wasn't likely to do—she had to answer the door herself. Entertaining a visitor, even someone looking to get their future read without an appointment, was better than pacing around feeling sorry for herself.

The man standing at the door was the last person she expected to be there. And the one person in all of space and time she wanted to see.

"Bern!"

He kissed her before she could say anything else. The fire that had been between them from the first moment sparked to flames. She clung to him with all her might, her body molded against his. If he'd taken her there on the front porch she wouldn't have minded. Instead he swung her around into the house, and kicked the door closed behind them. They fell together onto the entryway carpet and clothes were quickly shed and pushed aside.

He was thrusting inside her, hard and strong and fast, before she managed to breathlessly say, "You remembered me!" Then she came for the first time and forgot about words for a long time afterwards.

"Of course I remembered," he said later, when they were lying together in a sweaty tangled heap. "You're unforgettable."

She stroked his cheek. "Oh, that's sweet . . . wait a minute . . . that means you're psychic." He nodded. "I thought Percy was your team psychic."

"He was, on the civilian side. The military side always tries to have someone who'll remember the op on a TTP team."

"Really? I didn't know that."

"That's because that information is shared on a need-to-know basis. This seems like a good time for you to need to know."

"Now I understand why Kaye kept talking about your gut feelings. I should have guessed he meant your psychic intuition."

"You should have guessed when we went for each other like we were in heat instantly right after we met. That kind of lust only comes when like meets like."

"So I've heard. Hey, the lust had me pretty distracted. That and starring in orgies and fighting the Saxons and that whole Matter of Britain thing we had going."

He sighed. "Matter of Britain, my ass."

She stroked it. "It's a very nice ass. I have a nice big bed it might fit in upstairs," she told him.

He helped her to her feet, even though she groaned in protest when he stopped touching her breasts. "I'd be delighted to spend as much time as possible in your nice big bed."

"Good."

"But first," he added, "I did come here to ask if you'd like to go on a date this evening. I've got tickets for a revival of an old musical I think you'll enjoy."

Curiosity nibbled away some of her lust. "What would that be?"

He grinned. "*Spamalot.*"

She hooted, and they held each other tight, shaking with laughter. What other production could possibly be more perfect for their first date?

LIFE IS THE TEACHER

Carrie Vaughn

EMMA SLID UNDER THE SURFACE OF THE WATER and stayed there. She lay in the tub, on her back, and stared up at a world made soft, blurred with faint ripples. An unreal world viewed through a distorted filter. For minutes—four, six, ten—she stayed under water and didn't drown, because she didn't breathe. Would never breathe again.

The world looked different through these undead eyes. Thicker, somehow. And also, strangely, clearer.

Survival seemed like such a curious thing once you'd already been killed.

This was her life now. She didn't have to stay here. She could end it any time she wanted just by opening the curtains at dawn. But she didn't.

Sitting up, she pushed back her soaking hair and rained water all around her with the noise of a rushing stream. Outside the blood-warm bath, her skin chilled in the air. She felt every little thing, every little current—from the vent, from a draft from the window, coolness eddying along the floor, striking the walls. She shivered. Put the fingers of one hand on the wrist of the other and felt no pulse.

After spreading a towel on the floor, she stepped from the bath.

She looked at herself: she didn't look any different. Same

slim body, smooth skin, young breasts the right size to cup in her hands, nipples the color of a bruised peach. Her skin was paler than she remembered. So pale it was almost translucent. Bloodless.

Not for long.

She dried her brown hair so it hung straight to her shoulders and dressed with more care than she ever had before. Not that the clothes she put on were by any means fancy, or new, or anything other than what she'd already had in her closet: a tailored silk shirt over a black lace camisole, jeans, black leather pumps, and a few choice pieces of jewelry, a couple of thin silver chains and dangling silver earrings. Every piece, every seam, every fold of fabric, produced an effect, and she wanted to be sure she produced the right effect: young, confident, alluring. Without, of course, looking like she was *trying* to produce such an effect. It must seem casual, thrown together, effortless. She switched the earrings from one ear to the other because they didn't seem to lay right the other way.

This must be what a prostitute felt like.

Dissatisfied, she went upstairs to see Alette.

The older woman was in the parlor, waiting in a wingback chair. The room was decorated in tasteful antiques, Persian rugs, and velvet-upholstered furniture, with thick rich curtains hanging over the windows. Books crammed into shelves and a silver tea service ornamented the mantel. For all its opulent decoration, the room had a comfortable, natural feel to it. Its owner had come by the decor honestly. The Victorian atmosphere was genuine.

Alette spoke with a refined British accent. "You don't have to do this."

Alette was the most regal, elegant woman Emma knew. An apparent thirty years old, she was poised, dressed in a silk skirt and jacket, her brunette hair tied in a bun, her face like porcelain. She was over four hundred years old.

Emma was part of her clan, her Family, by many ties,

from many directions. By blood, Alette was Emma's ancestor, a many-greats grandmother. Closer, Alette had made the one who in turn had made Emma.

That had been unplanned. Emma hadn't wanted it. The man in question had been punished. He was gone now, and Alette had taken care of her: mother, mentor, mistress.

"You can't bottle feed me forever," Emma replied. In this existence, that meant needles, IV tubes, and a willing donor. It was so clinical.

"I can try," Alette said, her smile wry.

If Emma let her, Alette would take care of her forever. Literally forever. But that felt wrong, somehow. If Emma was going to live like this, then she ought to live. Not cower like a child.

"Thank you for looking after me. I'm not trying to sound ungrateful, but—"

"But you want to be able to look after yourself."

Emma nodded, and again the wry smile touched Alette's lips. "Our family has always had the most awful streak of independence."

Emma's laugh startled her. She didn't know she still could.

"Remember what I've taught you," Alette said, rising from her chair and moving to stand with Emma. "How to choose. How to lure him. How to leave him. Remember how I've taught you to see, and to feel. And remember to only take a little. If you take it all, you'll kill him. Or risk condemning him to this life."

"I remember." The lessons had been difficult. She'd had to learn to see the world with new eyes.

Alette smoothed Emma's hair back from her face and arranged it over her shoulders—an uncharacteristic bit of fidgeting. "I know you do. And I know you'll be fine. But if you need anything, please—"

"I'll call," Emma finished. "You won't send anyone to follow me, will you?"

"No," she said. "I won't."

"Thank you."

Alette kissed her cheek and sent her to hunt alone for the first time.

Alette had given her advice: go somewhere new, in an unfamiliar neighborhood where she wasn't likely to meet someone from her old life, therefore making her less likely to encounter complications of emotion or circumstance.

Emma didn't take this advice.

She'd been a student at George Washington University. Officially, she'd taken a leave of absence, but she wasn't sure she'd ever be able to continue her studies and finish her degree. There were always night classes, sure . . . but it was almost a joke, and like most anything worth doing, easier said than done.

There was a place, a bar where she and her friends used to go sometimes when classes got out. They'd arrive just in time for happy hour, when they could buy two-dollar hamburgers and cheap pitchers of beer. They'd eat supper, play a few rounds of pool, bitch about classes and papers they hadn't written yet. On weekends they'd come late and play pool until last call. A completely normal life.

That was what Emma found herself missing, a few months into this new life. Laughing with her friends. Maybe she should have gone someplace else for this, found new territory. But she wanted to see the familiar.

She came in through the front and paused, blinked a couple of times, took a deep breath through her nose to taste the air. And the world slowed down. Noise fell to a low hum, the lights seemed to brighten, and just by turning her head a little she could see it all. Thirty-four people packed into the first floor of this converted townhouse. Twelve sat at the bar, two worked behind the bar, splashing their way through the fumes of a dozen different kinds of alcohol. Their sweat mixed with those fumes, two kinds of heat blending with the third ashy odor of cigarette smoke. This place was hot with bodies. Five beating hearts played pool around two tables in the back, three more watched—these were female. Girl-friends. The smell of competing testosterone was ripe. All the rest crammed around tables or stood in empty spaces, putting alcohol into their bodies, their blood—Emma could smell it through their pores. She caught all this in a glance, in a second.

She could feel the clear paths by the way the air moved. Incredibly, she could feel the whole room, all of it pressing gently against her skin. As if she looked down on it from above. As if she commanded it. There—that couple at the table in the corner was fighting. The woman stared into her tumbler of gin and tonic while her foot tapped a nervous beat on the floor. Her boyfriend stared at her, frowning hard, his arms crossed, his scotch forgotten.

Emma could have him if she wanted. His blood was sing-ing with need. He would be easy to persuade, to lure away from his difficulty. A chance meeting by the bathrooms, an unseen exit out the back—

No. Not like that.

A quartet of boisterous, drunken men burst into laughter in front of her. Raucous business-school types, celebrating some exam or finished project. She knew how to get to them, too. Stumble perhaps. Lean an accidental arm on a shoulder, gasp an apology—and the one who met her gaze first would be the one to follow her.

Instead, she went to the bar, and despite the crowd, the press of bodies jostling for space, her path there was clear, and a space opened for her just as she arrived because she knew it would be there.

She wanted to miss the taste of alcohol. She could remember the taste of wine, the tang on the tongue, the warmth passing down her throat. She remembered great dinners, her favorite Mexican food, overstuffed burritos with sour cream and chile verde, with a big, salty margarita. She wanted to miss it with a deep and painful longing. But the memories turned her stomach. The thought of consuming anything made her feel sick. Anything except blood.

The glass of wine before her remained untouched. It was only for show.

She never would have done this in the old days. Sitting alone at the bar like this, staring into her drink—she looked like she was trying to get picked up.

Well, wasn't she?

When the door opened and a laughing crowd of friends entered, Emma turned and smiled in greeting. Even before the door had opened, she'd known somehow. She'd sensed the sound of a voice, the tone of a footstep, the scent of skin, a ripple in the air. She couldn't have remembered such fine details from her old life. But somehow, she'd known. She knew *them*.

"Emma!"

"Hey, Chris." Finally, her smile felt like her old smile. Her old friends gathered around, leaned in for hugs, and she obliged them. But the one who spoke to her, the one she focused on, was Chris.

He was six feet tall, with wavy blond hair and a clean-shaven, handsome face, still boyish but filling out nicely. He had a shy smile and laughing eyes.

"Where've you been? I haven't seen you in weeks. The registrar's office said you took a leave of absence."

She had her story all figured out. It wasn't even a lie, really.

"I've been sick," she said.

"You couldn't even call?"

"Really sick." She pressed her lips in a thin smile, hoping she sounded sad.

"Yeah, I guess." He took the cue not to press the question further. He brightened. "But you look great now. Really great."

There it was, a spark in his eye, a flush in his cheek. She'd always wondered if he liked her. She'd never been sure. Now, she had tools. She had senses. And she looked great. It wasn't her, a bitter voice sounded inside her. It was this thing riding her, this creature inside her. It was a lure, a trap.

Looking great made men like Chris blush. Now, she could use it. She knew how to respond. She'd always been uncertain before.

She lowered her gaze, smiled, then looked at him warmly, searching. "Thanks."

"I—I guess you already have a drink."

The others had moved off to claim one of the pool tables. Chris remained, leaning on the bar beside her, nervously tapping his foot.

Compared to him, Emma had no trouble radiating calm. She was in control here.

"Let me get you something," she said.

For a moment—for a long, lingering, blissful moment—it felt like old times. They only talked, but the conversation was long and heartfelt. He really listened to her. So she kept talking—so much so that she almost got to the truth.

"I've had to reassess everything. What am I going to do with my life, what's the point of it all." She shrugged, letting the implications settle.

"You must have been really sick," he said, his gaze intent.

"I thought I was going to die," she said, and it wasn't a lie. She didn't remember much of it—the man, the monster's hand on her face, on her arms, pinning her to the bed. She wanted to scream, but the sound caught in her throat. And however frightened she was, her body responded to his touch, flushed, shuddered toward him, and this made her ashamed. She hoped that he would kill her rather than turn her. But she awoke again and the world was different.

"You make it sound like you're not coming back."

"Hm?" she murmured, startled out of her memory.

"To school. You aren't coming back, are you?"

"I don't know," she said, wanting to be honest, knowing she couldn't tell him everything. "It'd be hard, after what's happened. I just don't know." This felt so casual, so normal, that she almost forgot she had a purpose here. That she was supposed to be guiding this conversation. She surprised herself by knowing what to say next. "This is going to sound really cliché, but when you think you aren't going to make it like that, it really does change how you look at things. You really do try to live for the moment. You don't have time to screw around anymore."

Which was ironic, because really, she had all the time in the world.

Chris hung on her words. "No, it doesn't sound cliché at all. It sounds real."

"I just don't think I have time anymore for school. I'd rather, you know—live."

This sounded awful—so false and ironic. *Don't listen to me, I'm immortal,* part of her almost yelled. But she didn't, because another part of her was hungry.

When he spoke, he sounded uncertain. "Do—do you want to get out of here? Go to my place maybe?"

Her shy smile widened. She'd wanted him to say that. She wanted him to think this was his idea. She rounded her shoulders, aware of her posture, her body language, wanting to send a message that she was open, willing, and ready.

"Yeah," she said, touching his hand as she stood.

His skin felt like fire.

Chris took her back to his place. He lived within walking distance, in a garden-level unit in a block of apartments. A nice place, small but functional, and very student. It felt like a foreign country.

Emma watched Chris unlock the door and felt some trepidation. Nerves, that was all. Anticipation. Unknown territory—to be expected, going home with a new guy for the first time.

Chris fumbled with the key.

There was more to this than the unknown, or the thrill of anticipation. She stood on the threshold, literally, and felt something: a force outside of herself. Nothing solid, rather a feeling that made her want to turn away. Like a voice whispering, *go, you are not welcome, this is not your place, your blood does not dwell here.*

She couldn't ignore it. The voice fogged her senses. If she turned away, even just a little—stepped back, tilted her head away—her mind cleared. She didn't notice when Chris finally unlocked the door and pushed his way inside.

She didn't know how long he'd been standing on the other side of the threshold, looking back at her expectantly. She simply couldn't move forward.

"Come on in," he said, giving a reassuring smile.

The feeling, fog, and voice disappeared. The unseen resistance fell away, the barrier was gone. She'd been invited.

Returning his smile, she went in.

Inside was what she'd expected from a male college student: the front room had a ripe, well-lived in smell of dirty laundry and pizza boxes. Mostly, though, it smelled like him. In a moment, she took it all in, the walls and the carpet. Despite how many times the former had been repainted and the latter replaced, the sense that generations of college students had passed through here lingered.

The years of life pressed against her skin, and she closed her eyes to take it all in, to feel it eddy around her. It tingled against her like static.

"Do you want something to drink?" Chris was sweating, just a little.

Yes. "No, I'm okay."

Seduction wasn't a quick thing. Though she supposed, if she wanted, she could just take him. She could feel in her bones and muscles that she could. He wouldn't know what hit him. It would be easy, use the currents of the room, slow down the world, move in the blink of an eye—

No. No speed, no fear, no mess. Better to do it cleanly. Nicer, for everyone. Now that they were alone, away from the crowd, her purpose became so very clear. Her need became crystalline. She planned it out: a brief touch on his arm, press her body close, and let him do the rest.

Fake. It was fake, manipulative ... She liked him. She really did. She wished she'd done this months ago, she wished she'd had the nerve to say something, to touch his hand—before she'd been attacked and turned. Then, she hadn't had the courage, and now she wanted something else from him. It felt like deception.

This was why Alette had wanted her to find a stranger. She wouldn't be wishing that it had all turned out different. Maybe she wouldn't care. She wanted to like Chris—she didn't want to need him like this. Didn't want to hurt him. And she didn't know if she'd have been so happy to go home with anyone else. That was why she was here. That was why she'd gone to that particular bar and waited for him.

That doesn't matter, her instincts—new instincts, like static across her skin, like the heat of blood drawing her—told her. The emotion is a by-product of need. He is yours because you've won him. You've already won him, you have only to claim him.

She reached out—she could feel him without looking, by sensing the way the air folded around his body—and brushed her fingers across the back of his hand. He reacted instantly, curling his hand around hers, squeezing, pulling himself toward her, and kissing her—half on cheek, half on lip.

He pulled back, waiting for a reaction, his breath coming fast and brushing her cheek. She didn't breathe at all—would he notice? Should she gasp, to fool him into thinking she breathed, so he wouldn't notice that she didn't? Another deception.

Rather than debating the question, she lunged for him, her lips seeking his, kissing forcefully. Distract him. In a minute he wouldn't notice anything. She devoured him, and he was off balance, lagging behind as she sucked his lips and sought his tongue. She'd never been this hungry for someone before. The taste of his skin, his sweat, his mouth, burst inside her and fired her brain. He tasted so good on the outside, she couldn't wait to discover what the inside of him tasted like, that warm blood flushing just under the surface. Her nails dug into his arm, wanting to pull off the sleeves of his shirt, all his clothes, to be closer to his living skin. She wanted nothing more than to close her teeth, bite into him—

She pulled back, almost ripping herself away. Broke all contact and took a step back, so that she was surrounded by cool air and not flesh. She could hear the blood rushing in his neck.

This wasn't her. This wasn't her doing this. She couldn't do this.

Chris gave a nervous chuckle. "Wow. That was . . . Emma, what's wrong?"

She closed her eyes, took a moment to gather herself, drew breath to speak. It would look like a deep sigh to him.

"I'm sorry," she said. "I can't do this."

She couldn't look at him. If he saw her eyes, saw the way she looked at him, he'd know about the thing inside her, he'd know she only wanted to rip him open. How could she explain to him, without explaining?

"I had a really nice time . . . but I'm sorry."

Holding the collar of her jacket closed, she fled before he could say a word in argument.

Alette had had to force her to drink blood the first time. Emma hadn't wanted to become this thing. She'd threatened to leave the house at dawn and die in the sunlight. But Alette persuaded her to stay. A haunted need inside her listened to that, wanted to survive, and stayed inside, in the dark. Still, she gagged when the mistress showed her the glass tumbler full of viscous red. "It's only your first night in this life," she said. "You're too new to hunt. But you still need this." Alette had then stood behind her, embraced Emma and locked her arms tight with one hand while tipping the glass to her mouth with the other. Emma had struggled, fought to pull out of her grasp, but Alette was deceptively powerful, and Emma was still sick and weak.

Emma had recognized the scent of the blood even before it reached her lips: tangy, metallic, like a butcher's shop. Even as she rebelled, even as her mind quailed, part of her reached toward it. Her mouth salivated. This contradiction was what had caused her to break down, screaming that she didn't want this, that she couldn't do this, kicking and thrashing in Alette's grip. But Alette had been ready for it, and very calmly held her still, forced the glass between her lips, and made her drink. As much spilled out of her mouth and down her chin as slid down her throat. Then, she'd fallen still. Helpless, she'd surrendered, even as that single sip returned her strength to her.

Eventually, she could hold the glass herself and drain it. She even realized she should learn to find the blood herself. She thought she'd been ready.

Alette found her in the parlor, sitting curled up on one of the sofas. "What happened?"

Emma hugged her knees and stared into space. She'd spent hours here, almost until dawn, watching dust motes, watching time move. This was fascinating—the idea that she could see time move. Almost, if she concentrated, she could reach out and touch it. Twist it. Cross the room in a second. She would look like she was flying. She'd almost done it, earlier tonight. She'd have taken him so quickly he wouldn't have known . . .

Alette waited patiently for her to answer. Like she could also spend all night watching time move.

"I don't know." Even after all that had happened, her voice sounded like a little girl's. She still felt like a child. "I liked him. It was . . . it felt good. I thought . . ." She shook her head. The memory was a distant thing. She didn't want to revisit it. "I got scared. I had him in the palm of my hand. He was mine. I was strong. And this *thing* rose up in me, this amazing power—I could do anything. But it wasn't me. So I got scared and ran."

Poised and regal, Alette sat, hands crossed in her lap, the elegant noblewoman of an old painting. Nothing shook her, nothing shattered her.

"That's the creature. That's what you are now. How you control it will determine what your life will look like from now on."

It was a pronouncement, a judgment, a knell of doom.

Alette continued. "Some of our kind give free rein to it. They revel in it. It makes them strong, but often leaves them vulnerable. If you try to ignore it, it will consume you. You'll lose that part of yourself that is yours."

In her bones, in the tracks of her bloodless veins, Emma knew Alette was right, and this was what she feared: that she wasn't strong, that she wouldn't control it. That she would lose her self, her soul to the thing. Her eyes ached with tears that didn't fall.

How did Alette control it? How did she manage to sit so calm and dignified, with the creature writhing inside of her, desperate for power? Emma felt sure she wouldn't last long enough to develop that beautiful self-possession.

"Oh my dear, hush there." Alette moved to her side and gathered her in her arms. She'd seen Emma's anguish and now sought to wrap her in comfort. Emma clung to her, pressing her face against the cool silk of her jacket, holding tight to her arms. For just a moment, she let herself be a child, protected within the older woman's embrace. "I can't teach you everything. Some steps you must take alone. I can take care of you if you like—keep you here, watch you always, hold the creature at bay and bring you cups of blood. But I don't think you'd be happy."

"I don't know that I'll ever be happy. I don't think I can do this."

"The power is a tool you use to get what you need. It should not control you."

Not much of the night remained. Emma felt dawn tugging at her nerves—another new sensation to catalog with the rest. The promise of sunlight was a weariness that settled over her and drove her underground, to a bed in a sealed, windowless room. At least she didn't need a coffin. Small comfort.

"Come," Alette said, urging her to her feet. "Sleep for now. Vanquish this beast another night."

Her mind was still her own, and she still dreamed. The fluttering, disjointed scenes took place in daylight. Already, the sunlit world of her dreaming memories had begun to look odd to her, unreal and uncertain, as if these things could never really have happened.

At dusk, she woke and told herself all kinds of platitudes: she had to get back on the horse, if at first you don't succeed . . . But it came down to wanting to see Chris again. She wanted to apologize.

She found his phone number and called him, half hoping he wouldn't answer, so she could leave a message and not have to face him.

But he picked up. "Hi."

"Hi, Chris?"

"Emma?" He sounded surprised. And why wouldn't he be? "Hey. Are you okay?"

Her anxiety vanished, and she was glad that she'd called. "I'm okay. I just wanted to say I'm so sorry about last night. I got scared. I freaked. I know you'll probably laugh in my face, but I want to see you again."

I'd like to try again, an unspoken desire she couldn't quite give voice to.

"I wouldn't laugh. I was just worried about you. I thought maybe I'd done something wrong."

"No, no, of course you didn't. It's just . . . I guess since this was my first time out since I was sick, my first time being with anyone since then . . . I got scared, like I said."

"I don't know. It seemed like you were really into it." He chuckled nervously. "You were really hot."

"I was into it." She wasn't sure this was going to sound awkward-endearing or just awkward. She tried to put that lust, that power that she'd felt last night, into her voice. Like maybe she could touch him over the phone. She held that image in her mind. "I'd like to see you again."

The meaning behind the words said, *I need you.*

Somehow, he heard that. She could tell by the catch in his breath, an added huskiness in his voice. "Okay. Why don't you come over."

"I'll be right there." She shut the phone off, not giving him a chance to change his mind, not letting herself doubt.

Emma could screw this up again. There was a gnawing in her belly, an anxious thought that kept saying, *this isn't right.* I'm using him, and he doesn't deserve that. She was starting to think of that voice as the old Emma. The Emma who could walk in daylight and never would again.

The new Emma, the voice she had to listen to now, felt like she was about to win a race. She had the power here, and she was buzzed on it. Almost drunk. The new Emma didn't miss alcohol because she didn't need it.

It felt good. Everything she moved toward felt so physically, fundamentally good. All she had to do was let go of doubt and revel in it.

That near-ecstasy shone in her eyes when Chris opened the door. For a moment, they only looked at each other. He was tentative—expecting her to flee again. She caught his gaze, and he saw nothing but her. She could see him, see through him, everything about him. He wanted her—had watched her for a long time, dreaming of a moment like this, not thinking it would happen. Not brave enough to make it happen. Assuming she wasn't the kind of girl who would let him in.

Yet here she was. She saw all of this play behind his eyes.

She touched his cheek and gave him a shy smile. "Thanks for letting me come over."

Gazing at him through lowered lids, she pushed him over the edge.

He grabbed her hand and pulled her against him, bringing her lips to his, hungry, and she was ready for him, opening her mouth to him, letting him devour her with kisses and sending his passion back to him. He clutched at her, wrinkling the back of her shirt as if he were trying to rip through it to get to her skin, kneading, moving his hand low to pin her against him. These weren't the tender, careful, assured movements he might have used if he were attempting to seduce her—if he'd had to persuade her, if she had shown some hesitation. These were the clumsy, desperate gropings of a man who couldn't control himself. She made him lose control. If she could now pick up those reins that he had dropped—

She pulled back her head to look at him; kissed him lightly, then slowly—staying slow, forcing him to match her pace. She controlled his movements now. She unbuttoned his shirt, drawing out every motion, brushing the bare skin underneath with fleeting touches. Lingering. Teasing. Heightening his need, feeding his desire. Driving him mad. He was melting in her arms. She could feel his muscles tremble.

Taking hold of his hands—she practically had to peel them off her backside—she guided them to her breasts and pressed them there. His eyes widened, like he'd just won a prize, and she smiled, letting her head fall back, feeling the weight of her hair pull her back, rolling her shoulders and putting her chest even more firmly into his grasp. Quickly, he undid the buttons of her shirt, tugged aside her bra, and bent to kiss her, tracing her right breast with his tongue, taking her nipple between his teeth. For all that had happened, for all that she'd become, her nerves, her senses, still worked, still shuddered at a lover's touch. Her hands clenched on his shoulders, then tightened in his hair. She gasped with pleasure. She wanted this. She wanted this badly.

She pulled him toward the bedroom. Didn't stop looking at him; held his gaze, would not let him break it. Her own veins were fire—controlled fire, in a very strong furnace, directed to some great purpose, a driving machine. She needed him, the blood that flushed along his skin. His very capillaries opened for her. She did not have a heartbeat, but something in her breast cried out in triumph. He was hers, to do with as she pleased.

She ran her tongue along her top row of teeth, scraping it on needle-sharp fangs.

He tugged at her shirt, searching for more bare skin. She shivered at his touch on the small of her back. His hands were hot, burning up, and for all her desire, her skin felt cold, bloodless.

She would revel in his heat instead.

She pushed his shirt off his shoulders and let it drop to the floor, then wrapped herself around him, pulling as much of that skin and heat to her as she could.

"You're so warm," she murmured, not meaning to speak at all. But she was amazed at the heat of him. She hadn't felt so much heat since before . . . before she became this thing.

He kept his mouth against her, lips working around her neck, pressing up to her ear, tasting every inch. Her nerves flared at the touch.

And suddenly, finally, she understood. It wasn't just the blood that drew her kind to living humans. It was the heat, the life itself. They were bright sunlight to creatures who lived in darkness. They held the energy that kept her kind alive and immortal—for there would always be people, an endless supply of people, to draw that energy from. She was a parasite and the host would never die.

Neither, then, would she.

With new reverence, she eased him to the bed, made him lay back, and finished stripping him, tugging down his jeans and boxers, touching him at every opportunity, fingertips around his hips, along his thighs. She paused to regard him, stretched out on his back, naked before her, member erect, whole body flush and almost trembling with need. She had brought him to this moment, with desire burning in his eyes. He would do anything she asked, now. She found herself wanting to be kind—to reward him for the role he'd played in her education, in bringing about the epiphany that so clarified her place in the world.

This exchange would be fair. She would not simply take from him. He would have pleasure as well.

She rubbed her hands down his chest, down his belly. He moaned, shivered under her touch but did not interfere. She traced every curve of his body: down his ribs, his hips. Stretched out on the bed beside him, she took his penis in her hand. Again, their mouths met. His kissing was urgent, fevered, and she kept pace with him. He was growing slick with sweat and smelled of musk.

She laughed. The sound just bubbled out of her. Lips apart, eyes gleaming, she found joy in this. She would live, she would not open the curtains on the dawn. She had power in this existence and she would learn to use it.

"Oh my God," Chris murmured. He froze, his eyes wide, his blood suddenly cooled. In only a second, she felt the sweat on his body start to chill as fear struck him. He wouldn't even notice it yet.

He was staring at her, her open, laughing mouth, the pointed canine teeth she'd been so careful to disguise until this moment, when euphoria overcame her.

In a moment of panic like this, it might all fall apart. An impulse to run struck her, but she'd come too far, she was too close to success. If she fled now she might never regain the nerve to try again.

"Shh, shh, it's all right," she whispered, stroking his hair, nuzzling his cheek, breathing comfort against him. "It's fine, it'll be fine."

She brought all her nascent power to bear: seduction, persuasion. The creature's allure. The ability to fog his mind, to erase all else from his thoughts but his desire for her, to fill his sight only with her.

"It's all right, Chris. I'll take care of you. I'll take good care of you."

The fear in his eyes ebbed, replaced by puzzlement—some part of his mind asking what was happening, who was she, what was she, and why was she doing this to him. She willed him to forget those questions. All that mattered were her, him, their joint passion that would feed them both: his desire, and her life.

He was still hard against her hand, and she used that. Gently, carefully, she urged him back to his heat, brought him again to that point of need. She stroked him, first with fingertips, then with her whole hand, and his groan of pleasure gratified her. When he tipped back his head, his eyes rolling back a little, she knew he had returned to her.

The next time she kissed him, his whole body surged against her.

She twined her leg around his; he moved against her, insistent. But she held him, pinned him, and closed her mouth over his neck. There she kissed, sucked—felt the hot river of his blood so close to his skin, just under her tongue. She almost lost control, in her need to take that river into herself.

Oh so carefully, slowly, to make sure she did this right and made no mistakes, she bit. Let her needle teeth tear just a little of his skin.

The flow of blood hit her tongue with a shock and instantly translated to a delicious rush that shuddered through her body. Blood slipped down her throat like honey, burning with richness. Clenching all her muscles, groaning at the flood of it, she drank. Her hand closed tight around his erection, moved with him, and his body responded, his own wave of pleasure bringing him to climax a moment later.

She held him while he rocked against her, and she drank a dozen swallows of his blood. No more than that. Do not kill, Alette's first lesson. But a dozen mouthfuls would barely weaken him. He wouldn't even notice.

She licked the wound she'd made to hasten its healing. He might notice the marks and believe them to be insect bites. He would never know she'd been here.

His body radiated the heat of spent desire. She lay close to him, gathering as much of it as she could into herself. She now felt hot—vivid and alive. She could feel his blood traveling through her, keeping her alive.

Stroking his hair, admiring the lazy smile he wore, she whispered to him. "You won't remember me. You won't remember what happened tonight. You had a nice dream, that's all. A vivid dream."

"Emma," he murmured, flexing toward her for more.

Almost, her resolve broke. Almost, she saw that pulsing artery in his neck and went to drink again.

But she continued, "If you see me again, you won't know me. Your life will go on as if you never knew me. Go to sleep. You'll sleep very well tonight."

She brushed his hair with her fingers, and a moment later he was snoring gently. She pulled a blanket over him. Kissed his forehead.

Straightening her bra, buttoning her blouse, she left the room. Made sure all the lights were off. Locked the door on her way out.

She walked home. It was the deepest, stillest hour of night, or early morning. Streetlights turned colors but no cars waited at intersections. No voices drifted from bars and all the storefronts were dark. A cold mist hung in the air, ghostlike. Emma felt that she swam through it.

The stillest part of night, and she had never felt more awake, more alive. Every pore felt the touch of air around her. Warm blood flowed in her veins, firing her heart. She walked without fear along dark streets, secure in the feeling that the world had paused to notice her passage through it.

She entered Alette's town home through the kitchen door in back rather than through the front door, because she'd always come in through the back in her student days when she studied in Alette's library and paid for school by being Alette's part-time housekeeper. That had all changed. Those days—nights—were finished. But she'd never stop using the back door.

"Emma?" Alette called from the parlor.

Self-conscious, Emma followed the voice and found Alette in her favorite chair in the corner, reading a book. Emma tried not to feel like a kid sneaking home after a night of mischief.

Alette replaced a bookmark and set the book aside. "Well?"

Her unnecessary coat wrapped around her, hands folded before her, Emma stood before the mistress of the house.

Almost, she reverted to the teenager's response: "Fine, okay, whatever." Monosyllables and a fast exit.

But she felt herself smile broadly, happily. "It was good."

"And the gentleman?"

"He won't remember me."

"Good," Alette said, and smiled. "Welcome to the Family, my dear."

She went back to the bar once more, a week later. Sitting at the bar, she traced condensation on the outside of a glass of gin and tonic on the rocks. She hadn't sipped, only tasted, drawing a lone breath so she could take in the scent of it.

The door opened, bringing with it a cold draft and a crowd of college students. Chris was among them, laughing at someone's joke, blond hair tousled. He walked right by her on his way to the pool tables. Flashed her a hurried smile when he caught her watching him. Didn't spare her another glance, in the way of two strangers passing in a crowded bar.

Smiling wryly to herself, Emma left her drink at the bar and went out to walk in the night.

MOONLIGHT BECOMES YOU

Linda Winstead Jones

CLAIRE PRESSED HER BACK TO THE WALL AND
listened to the footsteps. When she was certain her prey was
moving away from her, not toward her, she leaned forward
to peek around the corner and watch him walk down the
dimly lit hallway. Watching her neighbor walk away was not
exactly a chore. Not in those jeans.

Too bad he was a vampire.

When he turned the corner and was out of sight she
stepped into the hallway proper and silently followed in his
footsteps. It sounded crazy, she knew that, but there were
too many coincidences to ignore. He never went out in the
daytime. He was much too pale, as if he had never seen the
sun. He always wore black. Even those jeans he seemed to
favor were a faded shade of black. She never saw him bring
home groceries of any kind. Yes, he was lean, but the man
had to eat *something*. He was definitely mysterious, and the
one time he'd caught her eye she'd been sure he was hypnotizing her, even though the glance had lasted only a few
seconds. Or maybe one full second.

Just last week she'd found an inexplicable dusting of dirt
in the hallway outside his door. Dirt! This apartment building was surrounded by concrete, and the amount of dirt
she'd seen was small but more than what would've been

brought in on someone's shoe. Maybe it was some of the dirt that lined his coffin, or—gross—the remains of a dusted enemy vamp. When she'd gone back to check the dirt more closely to see if it looked like potting soil or bone dust, it had been gone. Someone had disposed of the evidence.

One night not so long ago she'd been awakened by an absolutely unearthly howl that had sent chills down her spine. She wasn't sure if it had been a victim's plea or a monster's cry of victory, but the sound had been memorable and unnatural.

There was yet another telling clue that all was not as it should be. Marlie James from the second floor had a new cat. The feline Houdini was tough to contain and very often ended up wandering throughout the building. Fluffy wouldn't come to the third floor. Marlie had walked up once with the cat in her arms, but before she'd reached her destination Fluffy had screeched and escaped her owner's arms and run down the stairs. Animals knew. Animals sensed danger when humans did not, and Fluffy obviously sensed danger on the third floor.

Claire's apartment shared a common wall with the newest resident of the complex, here on the third floor of this less-than-magnificent but relatively trendy apartment building in downtown Atlanta. He played music often. Apparently he didn't care for popular tunes, but was stuck in the forties. Claire recognized some of the songs he played as those her grandparents had favored. Obviously her neighbor had been turned into a vampire in the forties, and he was still drawn to the music of the era in which he'd been human. What other explanation made sense?

Claire didn't jump to conclusions without checking as many facts as possible. She'd done an extensive search on the Internet and found almost nothing about her neighbor. Simon Darrow, that was his name, had lived in four places in the past three years. Before that, nothing—that she could find, at least. That in itself was odd. The man hadn't popped out of thin air! True, she wasn't a detective and she didn't have access to every useful Internet site, but still, she should've been able to find more.

It didn't help Darrow's case that he'd moved into the building right before people from the neighborhood started to disappear. Charlie on the first floor, who everyone knew hit his wife when he drank too much. The often-obscene panhandler who'd been a regular on the southeast corner for as long as Claire could remember. That punk who'd robbed old Mrs. Bernard and gotten off with a slap on the wrist. All of them gone in a mere six weeks. Just *gone*. The people who'd disappeared would not exactly be missed, but she couldn't allow that to cloud her judgment.

Add the insignificant detail that Claire had been reading quite a few vampire novels lately, and it all made perfect sense.

The common belief was that vampires didn't exist, but Claire knew to the pit of her soul that there was more to the world than most people realized. Granny Eileen had spoken often of ghosts and were-beasts, of vampires and curses. There had been a time, a span of several years in fact, when Claire had chosen not to believe the tales her grandmother had spun so effortlessly, but in the past few years it seemed that her eyes and ears had been opened. Legends had to be based in fact, and it wasn't her fault that most people had to deny that fact in order to survive from one day to the next.

Her overactive imagination didn't hurt matters at all.

It was obvious that *something* was going on with her neighbor, and like it or not, *vampire* made sense. The dirt, the howl, Fluffy, the missing people . . . yes, it made perfect sense. No one would believe her if she didn't collect proof.

Claire walked down the hallway on quick tiptoes, hoping that when she glanced around the next corner she'd catch a glimpse of her neighbor as he made his way to the stairwell. The elevator was out of order once again—no surprise there—and to reach the stairs she and everyone else on her end of the floor had to walk two and a half short hallways. Down the hallway, right, and then right again before reaching the stairs.

She wouldn't follow her subject outside, she hadn't *entirely* lost her mind, but she had decided to keep a detailed record of his comings and goings as best she could. One never knew what small detail might be helpful.

When she reached the corner she flattened her back to the wall as she had before, and she listened. She heard nothing, but then her neighbor did have an easy step, even in those heavy black boots he usually wore. Another vampire trait, she supposed. The easy step, not the boots. Maybe he was floating an inch or so above the floor, since he didn't know anyone was watching. She leaned slowly forward to take a glimpse down the hallway . . .

And found herself nose to chest with her vampire neighbor.

Claire caught and held her breath, as her heart threatened to break free of her chest. There was no way she could outrun him, whether he was a vampire or not. That meant she'd have to wing it. First, she had to regain the ability to breathe.

"Are you stalking me?" he asked, a touch of humor in his deep voice.

"I . . . you . . . of course not." Claire managed a tight smile. "I lost an earring. I thought maybe I dropped it earlier this evening, on my way in after work."

"Too bad. I was rather hoping I had a pretty stalker."

Yes, there was something unnaturally hypnotic about his eyes, which were such a dark brown they were almost black. She could feel herself being sucked in by those eyes. That had to be a vampire trick.

He thought she was pretty?

The man, who was taller up close than she'd imagined he would be, offered his hand. "Simon Darrow. I live next door to you."

After a moment of paralyzing fear, she put her hand in his

and shook. "Claire Murphy. I know." His hand was oddly warm, for someone who was possibly undead.

He released his grip and leaned casually against the wall. "So, what does this earring look like?"

"What earring?"

"The one you lost," he said, that hint of good humor remaining in his hypnotic voice.

"Oh, yes." This was the perfect opportunity for her first real test. Since arriving at her suspicions about her neighbor she'd been wearing a small gold cross all the time. She slept in it, showered in it, wore it when she went to the gym on Tuesdays and Thursdays. She grabbed the cross between her fingers and held it up so he could see. "It matches this. A tiny little cross with a teeny diamond chip in the center."

Simon—quite an old-fashioned name, eh?—didn't touch the cross, but he didn't recoil, either. She had to judge that test as inconclusive, since she wasn't quite ready to leap forward and press the cross against his forehead to see if he began to smoke or howl in pain. He turned away from her and searched the dingy carpeting, his eyes scanning the faded fibers. Claire pretended to do the same, though her eyes often flitted to her neighbor. Oh, he really was studly, more so up close than from a distance. His dark hair was shaggy and a tad too long but was not completely neglected, and he had a very finely sculpted masculine jawline. The body, as she had already noted, was not bad at all. She took it all in, appreciatively and as surreptitiously as possible.

"I don't mean to hold you up," she said after watching him bend over to examine what turned out to be a piece of lint. "I imagine you have somewhere to be."

"I'm not working tonight."

"You work at night?"

"Not much call for jazz musicians during the day. The club's closed until the weekend. Some sort of plumbing issue."

Her head crept up slowly so she could once more check out his face, which was much more interesting than the old carpet. Simon Darrow wasn't pretty—his features were too masculine to be called pretty—but his face was definitely fine. "You're a musician?"

"Piano. I have a small electric keyboard at my place, but I practice while you're at work so I won't disturb you."

A *considerate* vampire. "I'm sure I wouldn't mind hearing you practice," she said, determined to be no less considerate as she took a couple of unnecessary steps and her eyes scanned the floor for a nonexistent earring. This was an opportunity she could not let slip by. "So, if you're not playing tonight, where are you headed?"

"Just out to grab a bite," he answered.

Interesting choice of words. "Oh, really?"

"I thought I'd check out that sandwich shop down the street."

"They close at seven so you've already missed them, and to be honest their food is better at lunch."

"I'll find someplace else, then."

This was a golden opportunity that might never come again. She had her neighbor right where she wanted him, and he had no idea that she suspected his secret. "Maybe you can . . ." she swallowed hard and gathered her courage, "have dinner with me."

"I knew it," he said in a lowered voice touched with gentle wit. "You are stalking me."

"I am not," she protested. "You're new to the building. I'm simply adhering to the Southern Women's Code, Section One, Paragraph Three. Feed Thy Neighbor. I could make spaghetti," she said before he could argue again that she was stalking him. "And garlic bread."

He didn't sneer at the garlic bread any more than he'd sneered at her cross. Hmm. Maybe she was wrong about him. Even though she was drawn to Simon Darrow in a way that had to be unnatural, and there were a number of unanswered questions about him and his life, and Claire knew to the pit of her soul that there was more to the night than what made the newspapers and the evening news, her neighbor might be exactly what he appeared to be. A man with a mysterious past who'd had the misfortune to move into the building just when people in the general area started disappearing and someone spilled dirt in the hallway.

"I love spaghetti," he said. "But I'm meeting some people later so I really should get going."

Her heart sank a little. "Okay. Maybe another time. I don't want to be in violation of the Southern Women's Code."

"Heaven forbid." He smiled, and it was very nice.

Claire decided to take a chance, one more time. "How about tomorrow night? About seven?" Normally on Tuesdays she went to the gym after work, but it would really be no chore to skip a workout. Wouldn't be the first time. She held her breath and waited for another refusal, another excuse.

"Sure." Simon glanced down at the carpet one last time. "I'm sorry to say I don't think we're going to find your earring."

"Yeah," Claire sighed. "Me neither."

Claire didn't expect Simon for about an hour. Her homemade spaghetti sauce was simmering, and the garlic bread was ready to be popped into the oven. The pasta would go on at the last minute. After changing her clothes three times, she'd settled on an outfit that made her look at least three pounds lighter. The slightly snug black shirt showed off her boobs—the advantage of carrying a few extra pounds—and the knee-length skirt was flattering and comfortable. It was pretty without being an obvious date outfit. There were very cute open-toed shoes with high heels that made her legs look better than they really were waiting close by, but she'd save those for the last minute, like the pasta.

Giving in to her curiosity, she opened the door to her apartment and slipped into the hallway, tiptoeing on bare feet to Simon Darrow's door to press her ear to the wood.

Was he in there? She knew he wasn't working, and since she was feeding him in less than an hour he couldn't be out looking for supper. Unless he needed supper of a different sort . . .

If he was in there he was being very quiet. Why didn't she hear him practicing on his portable piano or showering or just moving about in his apartment? She held her breath and closed her eyes, listening for signs of life. Maybe he wasn't in at all. Oh, if he stood her up she would never forgive him! Not that this was a date, or anything like it.

"I knew you were a stalker."

Claire's head popped up and she found her vampire neighbor standing in the hallway, one hand behind his back, that smug and yet undeniably appealing smile on his pale face. Why did he continue to hold his hand behind his back? Was he carrying a knife, or maybe even a short sword? Not that vampires needed such weapons.

She had to think fast. Again. "I heard an odd noise," she said. "I thought maybe you'd fallen and . . . and . . . couldn't get up."

His smile faded very quickly. "Do you think someone's in there?" The hidden left hand popped around as he reached into his pocket with the right. Instead of a knife or a sword, he held a very pretty bouquet of mixed flowers. "These are for you," he said absently, all but thrusting them at her.

Claire took the flowers . . . not that she had any choice considering the way they were shoved at her chest . . . and carried them to her nose while Simon opened the door to his apartment and stepped inside, worried about a burglar he wouldn't find. Vampires were known to be very romantic, at least in the books she read, but she would've expected the flowers to be blood red or starkly exotic. Instead they were springy and bright and very much *not* reminiscent of the undead. It had been a very long time since any man—or whatever—had given her flowers.

"What kind of sound was it?" Simon called from inside his apartment.

Flowers in hand, Claire stepped into his apartment through the door he'd left wide open. When Mrs. Tillman from across the hall opened her door to peek out—nosy old woman—Claire closed the door to Simon's apartment. She didn't miss the disapproving glare from her stodgy neighbor.

Claire's eyes scanned the main room, which was laid out much like hers but was decorated very differently. Simon had a state-of-the-art CD player, but no television, at least not in this room. A couple of comfortable chairs, but no sofa. Blinds instead of curtains. Framed antique album covers instead of family pictures or art. The lines were stark and clean, and he used little color in his decorating scheme. There were no mirrors, not that many men would hang mirrors anywhere but the bathroom.

There was no coffin in sight, but of course he'd keep that in the bedroom, if he had one.

"What kind of noise?" he asked again.

Claire rose up on her bare toes and dropped down again. "It was just kind of a thud. You know, now that I think about it the sound probably came from upstairs or downstairs. My mistake. Sorry."

Simon glanced into the bedroom and the bathroom, and then returned to her with a very skeptical expression on his face. "Everything appears to be fine."

Claire shrugged her shoulders and glanced back to the kitchen, which like hers was open to the main room. It was clean and uncluttered and probably for the most part unused.

"You are so odd," he said as he walked toward her.

"I'm not odd," she said defensively.

"You're definitely odd," he argued. "Don't get me wrong, I like odd girls. Ordinary girls are boring and predictable. I have a feeling you're neither."

Her life was both predictable and boring, but she wasn't about to share that information with Simon. Not *now*.

"Thanks for the flowers," she said, trying desperately to change the subject.

He took the bouquet from her hand and tossed it onto the closest chair. The blooms looked so out of place there, so wonderfully bright against the black leather. "No more games, Claire. What do you really want from me?"

She opened her mouth, but did not get a chance to speak.

"No more lies about lost earrings or noise from the apartment, no more quotes from the Southern Women's Code. What do you really want?"

She could defend herself and swear she had not lied, but those eyes of his . . . they would see. Somehow he would *know*. "Honestly?"

"Please."

She licked her lips and listened to one thud of her heart before answering, "I don't know what I want."

Simon moved in closer, hovering in her personal space, stealing her breath and making her heart pound even harder. He leaned toward her, his mouth heading directly for her throat. Something in her wanted to back away and clap her hand over her vulnerable artery, but another part, a deeper part, wanted to lean into him, to meet him halfway.

Maybe she was hypnotized and didn't know it. Maybe she was moments away from calling her studly neighbor "master" and begging him to bite her.

Deep down Claire considered the possibility that Simon wasn't a vampire at all. She'd allowed her imagination to run away from her, that's all. He was just a man like any other. Well, not like any other but still . . . he *might* be just a man. She closed her eyes as he placed his mouth on her throat and kissed. He didn't bite, he kissed. Her reaction was immediate and intense. It was no wonder she read and fantasized about vampires. There was no place on her body as sensitive as her neck. Well, one, but other than that . . . When it came to erogenous body parts that were not located between her legs, she'd prefer a man at her neck over her breasts any day. Simon knew exactly how to kiss her neck.

One fine, strong hand gripped the back of her head while he kissed her throat gently. Claire felt that kiss everywhere. Her knees went weak, her insides tightened, she grew wet . . . just like that.

Why had she suspected him of being a vampire? It was easy to rely on imagination when reality sucked. Well, usually reality sucked, but at this moment it did not. Not at all. Simon kissed her throat and her body responded with an unexpected fierceness. Her body was pressed against his, and so she knew she wasn't the only one affected.

"What do you want?" he whispered against her throat.

"Don't you have another question?" she asked breathlessly. Men could be so single minded. Why did he feel the need to *talk* at all?

"No," he said briskly.

Claire could hardly speak at all when she answered. "I want more."

Simon sighed. "Finally, an honest answer."

His hand slipped beneath her skirt. She was shocked at first, but then . . . not so much. It was a natural if rather quick progression, and she would not pretend to be demure or hesitant when she was neither. Simon's hand, large and warm, caressed her inner thigh and then moved up with agonizing slowness. The higher that slow hand moved, the more intensely Claire felt the caress. She held her breath and waited for contact. Almost there . . . almost . . . bingo.

Simon touched her through silk panties and she shuddered. All the while he kissed her neck. If he was a vampire, if he really did drink blood, he could have every drop of hers as long as he didn't stop.

He didn't stop, and Claire felt herself spiraling out of control. Control. Did she have any? Had she ever? Her head tilted back, and as Simon took full advantage of the new position by kissing a portion of her throat he had missed, his hand slipped into her panties to touch bare, damp flesh. He did not hesitate, he did not falter. It was as if he knew her body well, as if he had touched her this way before and knew exactly where and how. His hands were warm and large and foreign . . . and yet somehow not so foreign. Claire wriggled a little, her panties slipped, and she spread her legs slightly. Simon took advantage of that new position just as he had when she'd offered him a better shot at her throat. His touch changed, it shifted, and then he slipped one finger inside her.

It had been a long time since any man had touched her, and she came hard and fast, convulsing, gasping, holding onto Simon so she wouldn't fall to the floor. The orgasm itself didn't take her by surprise—good heavens, she'd been rushing toward orgasm since he'd placed his mouth on her throat—but the intensity did. She came, and she came, and she grasped Simon hard as the waves washed over her.

"Oh, my," she whispered when she was able.

Simon held her up, thank goodness, but he took his hand away and he no longer gave his attentions to her throat. After a moment he released her and backed away. Claire straightened her clothes and smoothed her hair. She must look a mess, and Simon . . . Simon, looked as calm and collected as he had before he'd touched her.

A quick glance down proved what the press of his body to hers had told her, that he had not been unaffected. Well, didn't this change everything? She'd started out determined to prove that he was a vampire, and had ended up here, shaking from an unexpected orgasm and shamelessly wondering when there would be more.

She tried to be logical, for once. If vampires had no heartbeat then there was no blood flow, and without remarkable blood flow what she saw straining his jeans would be impossible.

"I've always had a thing for odd girls." Simon collected her bouquet from the chair where he'd deposited it so indifferently. With greater care, he handed the flowers to her once again. She took them.

"I'm really not . . . well, maybe I am a little odd."

Surely vampires didn't smile that way. This look was definitely not evil. Then again, maybe she was quick to judge Simon not a vampire because he'd just had his very talented hand in her panties.

Claire twitched and then jumped. "My sauce!"

"You left it on the stove?"

"Yes!" Claire ran to the door. "When I . . . when I heard that noise I had just put it on to simmer."

"It's probably fine." Simon followed her, and while they were in the hallway Mrs. Tillman's door opened a crack once again. Even though Claire couldn't see the old woman, she heard a decided scoff from behind that door. Talk about *odd*.

At the doorway to her apartment, Simon hesitated. Without thinking, Claire gave a wave of her free hand and said, "Come on in." So much for that test. She'd invited him in, and that was one of the vampire rules that seemed to be unbreakable. A vampire could not enter a home unless it was invited, and she'd invited Simon into her apartment without so much as a second thought. Darn. Too late to do anything about it now.

Simon studied her apartment as she had studied his, as she rushed to the stove and turned down the heat, then fetched a vase from beneath the sink and filled it with water. As in his apartment, there was a low, open bar between the kitchen and the living area. Simon could sit on the couch and watch her, and she could keep a close eye on him, as well. She had a small shaker of garlic salt close at hand, just in case he tried to move too close too fast. Besides, he wouldn't be so foolish as to eat his next-door neighbor. Everyone would be looking at him for the crime if that happened. Mrs. Tillman had seen them together. No, she was as safe as she could be, given the circumstances.

If he'd intended to do her harm, he'd had his chance.

She had to admit, there was an inexplicable animal attraction about Simon Darrow that really got under her skin. Maybe it was because she hadn't had sex in such a long time. Maybe it was because she hadn't had really good sex for years. She didn't count what had just happened as sex because, well, she'd come alone. That wasn't the same, and of course, the evening was young.

Simon was extremely attractive, pale skin aside. At the moment he looked more beautiful than ever, but of course her vision had been temporarily affected. In truth he wasn't horribly pale, just untanned. It was clear he preferred the night to the daytime, moonlight to sunshine. Maybe it was a musician thing, not a vampire thing. The same could be true of the black wardrobe and the odd hours he kept.

He turned his head to look at the stack of books on her end table. *"Bite Me,"* he read aloud, as he perused the titles. *"The Return of Dracula. Night of the Undead. The Vampire Stan."*

"That one's kinda funny," she said, wondering how he would react to the collection of vampire novels. "It's a spoofy thing."

"Intriguing reading material." He looked at her again, and somehow those almost-black eyes darkened. "Do you have an interest in vampires?"

Just as she'd been ready to dismiss her suspicions and simply embrace the man, he asked that question in a voice that was less than casual. *Do you have an interest in vampires?*

"I suppose I do," she confessed. "Particularly vampire romance." She shivered a little. It was the neck thing, she imagined. Her hand rose up and touched her neck, there where Simon had kissed her and brought her to the edge of paradise with his mouth alone.

Simon sighed. Claire tried to ignore his reaction as she put on water to boil and preheated the oven for the garlic bread, but in truth the fact that he asked the question made her wonder . . . why did he care if she read about vampires or not? Obviously he *did* care. He was actually annoyed by the books she'd left sitting out, and that put her right back where she'd started.

Still, he hadn't bitten her when he'd had the chance. Maybe sometimes vampires needed sex, too—lack of blood flow aside.

"You know," Simon said after an uncomfortable bout of silence, "I'm really not very hungry. I should go."

"No!" Claire left her not-yet-boiling water behind as Simon stood, unfolding his body with that unexpected grace that seemed only slightly unnatural. There was a mirror in her bathroom, another in the bedroom. If she could just get him to stand in front of one of those mirrors . . . if she could just be *sure* . . . "You need to eat something," she said softly.

"I'm not going to starve," he responded.

"What do you have at your place if you get hungry later?" she asked logically. "Frozen dinners? Soup and crackers? I make very good spaghetti."

"I wish you would be honest with me," he said, a touch of anger coloring his voice. There was a pleasant melodiousness to his voice, she decided, even when he was mad. "Something strange is going on here. There was never any earring in the hallway, there was no noise from my apartment, and I've never heard of any Southern Women's Code. I think yesterday you were following me, and tonight you were snooping."

"I'm not . . ."

He moved in very close and placed one finger over her lips. "I talk, you listen. You're much more transparent than you intend to be."

Claire couldn't move. Somehow he held her in place with that one finger on her mouth, and with his eyes. His magical, mesmerizing, unbelievably dark eyes. Her heart beat too hard. He knew that she'd discovered his secret, and now he was going to kill her. This time when he lowered his head he was going to bite down on her neck and feed and that would be the end of everything for her.

Claire Murphy was found dead in her apartment. The body was discovered by a nosy neighbor, Mrs. Iris Tillman, who was bothered by the gross smell. Miss Murphy has no family and she will not be missed by anyone. Oh, and by the way, it seems someone had taken all her blood, but who cares?

"Maybe I am transparent," she whispered, angry at the knowledge that she could die here and now and no one would care. "You didn't seem to mind a few minutes ago."

"No, I didn't mind at all. I've been dreaming about getting you in that particular position for weeks. I've been dreaming about more, Claire. To be honest, I've been watching you since I moved in," he said in a lowered voice. "There's no boyfriend, and you're in bed every night very early and very alone."

"If you work at night how do you . . ."

"Shhh," he ordered gently. "I know. I've also known all along that if I touched you just right you'd come apart, and you did. Before tonight, when was the last time you came, Claire Murphy?"

She swallowed hard before answering half-heartedly, "Does it count if I was alone at the time?"

"No. That most definitely doesn't count."

"Hey, wait," she said indignantly. "*You've* been stalking *me!*"

"Just a little."

Claire was frozen in place as Simon lowered his head to her neck. His lips pressed there at the place where neck became shoulder, and a rush of sensation shot through her. She shouldn't be so easy, what had happened in his apartment aside. Her insides clenched and her knees went weak, and all he had done was lay his mouth on her throat. The kiss was gentle, and yet it made her feel as if she were melting.

"I know what you want, Claire Murphy," he whispered

against her flesh, "and it isn't spaghetti or a fictional ear-ring." His hand slipped beneath her shirt and raked against her back until he found her bra clasp and very easily un-hooked it. "I want the same thing you do. I have since I first saw you in the hallway, more than a month ago. Does that surprise you? It surprises me. I don't normally want things I shouldn't have. I learned better long ago."

How long?

Claire wanted to believe that what had driven her to sus-pect her neighbor of horrible crimes and unnatural abilities was nothing more complicated than her overactive imagina-tion combined with the need to be touched and an undeni-able attraction, which was apparently reciprocated. Her reasons for suspecting Simon of being an unnatural being were lone-liness, boredom, and the craving for what he was offering her at this very moment, as he removed her tangled blouse and bra and tossed them to the floor.

He lowered her to the sofa. This time there would be more than a heated sexual moment that came and went too quickly. This time they would be naked and he would be inside her, and . . . oh, my. His mouth was warm on her breasts, and vampires were not warm. They were dead and cold. *Unless they'd just fed and he'd picked up something besides flowers while he was out.* Simon was not at all cold. In fact, his skin was hot, and she was almost certain she could hear the beat of his heart against her belly, where his chest rested as he sucked her nipple deep into his mouth. She wanted him at her neck again, but certainly didn't complain. He would return there soon enough, she imagined.

He didn't move back to her neck, not right away. Instead he unfastened her skirt and began to shimmy it down.

"Not so fast," she whispered. "Not this time."

"Trust me, this won't be fast."

She found comfort in those words, comfort from this man she had suspected of being a vampire moments earlier. What silly thoughts, thoughts she easily dismissed as he kissed his way down her body, which was naked but for the gold cross she'd taken to wearing. He didn't seem to mind that tiny piece of gold, which was another point in his favor.

It was not the only point in his favor. Simon Darrow had a fine, sensuous mouth that was determined to explore every inch of her body. Where she was ticklish, where she was sensitive, where she had never been kissed before, he tasted her. He even lifted her leg and kissed her behind the knees, introducing her to an unexpected burst of joy. She felt that surge of joy everywhere, and yes, if he'd touched her where she was wet for him she would've come. She would've screamed. Again.

It occurred to her, as Simon trailed that lovely mouth very slowly up her inner thigh, that he was still completely dressed. That was so wrong.

"Take off your clothes," she whispered, her voice raspy and demanding.

He laughed lightly, and his breath was warm against her skin. "Not yet." He spread her thighs and touched her intimately with his tongue. He flicked his tongue, he teased her with light strokes and flickers, and then he moved in and rasped against her harder, fiercer. Claire came so hard she screamed and her back arched up off the couch. She grabbed Simon's head and pulled him closer, and he did not fight her but pressed harder and deeper, slipping his tongue inside her as she shook.

And he hadn't bitten her once.

"You said it would not be fast," she said breathlessly, delirious and sad, shaking and satisfied, needy and happy.

"It's not over, Claire," he promised as he crept up and over her body and finally, once again, placed his mouth at her throat and sucked against that sensitive skin. "Women are wondrous creatures who can come again and again and again in a very short period of time."

"I've heard that's true," she said as she turned her head more to the side to allow him the greatest possible access.

He nipped at her skin, but just a little. Naked, entirely vulnerable and recently satisfied, her mind began to work somewhat properly. What if she only imagined that Simon was warm and that his heart beat? That could be part of the spell he had cast on her. Why else would she be so, well, easy? Not that she was complaining. Far from it. In all the books she read vampires were sensuous creatures who wallowed in intense sexual encounters. She certainly felt as if she were wallowing, at the moment.

She no longer thought Simon was a vampire. Not conclusively. There was one other test she could try tonight, just to be certain. The sun had already set so she couldn't study what happened to him in the daylight, but there was a mirror in her bedroom and if she could just see his reflection in it she'd be satisfied.

Claire took Simon's head in her hands and drew his wonderful mouth away from her neck. "You have to be at least six foot two, and this sofa isn't more than five feet long."

"I can manage."

"I have a perfectly good bed."

"Beds are boring and ordinary. Everyone has sex in a bed." His eyebrows lifted slightly. "What about the kitchen counter? The balcony? The elevator." He grinned quite wickedly.

"I know you prefer odd, but I really am boring and ordinary," she said as she reached down to fiddle with and then unfasten his belt buckle. He strained the denim with his erection, and she could not wait to have him in her hands, to touch him, to arouse him the way he'd aroused her. She gently forced him up and back, and placed her mouth on his neck. Yes, he was most definitely warm. His heart pounded. He shuddered, and she was glad.

"You're neither boring nor ordinary," he said. "You just haven't discovered that for yourself yet. I see it, even if you don't."

Claire knew the truth about herself. She was nothing if not pragmatic. She was average looking, and her hair was an ordinary dark blond that rarely did what she wanted it to do. She was usually between ten and fifteen pounds overweight, and there were a variety of clothes in three different sizes in her closet. Fat clothes, ordinary clothes, and a handful of very nice *I have a dream* clothes.

She was a failure where men were concerned. More rightly, they had always failed her, which was why she now satisfied herself with reading on weekends instead of dating or painting her toenails or shaving her legs for some man who in the end . . .

But now was not the time for that old tirade. A very handsome man who was hard for her had just promised her again, and again and again. And maybe another again. She'd lost count. If she could just prove to herself decisively that he wasn't a vampire, he might be the perfect man. At least for a while. No man was perfect forever.

"But you want the bed anyway, don't you," Simon whispered.

"Yes."

"Fine." Unsnapped and partially unzipped, still more dressed than not, Simon left the couch. He offered her his hand and she took it. He pulled her up and headed for the bedroom. It wasn't as if he had to search. The apartment was laid out just like his own, in a mirror image.

Speaking of mirrors . . .

She led Simon toward the bed, and when they were in the center of the small room she stopped and turned to face the mirror above her dresser. There he was, gorgeous and black-clad and somehow animalistic. He definitely had a wild magnetism. She was so happy to see him there, reflected in all his human glory, that she smiled . . . until she realized that she was there too, in all her fifteen-pounds-overweight glory.

"Yikes." She turned away and headed very quickly for the bed and the safety of a coverlet where she could hide. She jumped into the bed and pulled the lilac comforter across the plumpest parts of her exposed body.

Simon followed her at a slower pace, laughing. Not at her, at least she didn't think so. When he peeled back the comforter that she'd grabbed to protect herself from his gaze, his smile disappeared and his eyes narrowed. "Don't hide. You're gorgeous."

Claire knew she was anything but, but she didn't argue. At this moment, so turned on he was probably not seeing straight, Simon believed it to be true. That was enough for her. At this moment she didn't even care if he was a vampire or not. He'd brought her flowers and thought she was gorgeous and made her come so hard her head was still spinning. Nothing else mattered.

He quickly shed his clothes, and she was not disappointed by the body he revealed. Lean and perfectly sculpted, he had a runner's body. And an impressive erection she could not look away from. If he was shy at all, she'd never seen any evidence of that shyness. If he had a single second thought or an ounce of hesitation, he hid it well.

Even if it was their first time together, there would be no awkwardness, no uncomfortable moments where she wondered what was expected of her or they bumped foreheads. No, this was an extraordinary night, and Claire felt as if she were caught in a wonderful dream, as Simon joined her on the bed.

The sensation of his bare body against hers was breathtaking, and when he kissed her on the mouth she held his head in her hands and gave that kiss all she had, because she could give him no less. Instinctively she wrapped her legs around him, pulling him close, pulling him toward what she craved.

"Oh!" She twitched and pulled away slightly. "I'm such an idiot! Do you have protection? A condom?" *Anything?*

"I can't have children, and I carry no disease." The words were pragmatic, simply spoken.

"Why should I take your word on that?" she asked, certain that many a woman had been fooled by similar promises.

"I will never lie to you, Claire."

She shivered to the bone. Those were important words, and he spoke them as if they were truth. Of course, she wasn't sure any man was capable of *never* lying. Still, the expression in his eyes was one of honesty as well as passion. Maybe she was a fool, but she believed him.

Yesterday she'd been stalking him down the hallway, convinced he was a vampire. Tonight he was in her bed, and she didn't care *what* he was.

He understood that she liked his attentions at her neck, and while he didn't neglect the rest of her body he spent many wonderful minutes there. Claire touched the hard curves and planes of his body, and discovered he was particularly sensitive just below the belly button, especially if she touched him there with the tip of her tongue. As she had suspected, there was no awkwardness, no hesitation.

Her curtains were open, so moonlight lit Simon's face as he spread her thighs and guided himself into her. Making love with him was like dancing with a lifelong partner, like waltzing without conscious thought—and maybe an inch or two above the dance floor. She didn't think at all with him inside her, not about vampires, not about being odd or boring, not about mirrors or crosses or garlic. There was just his body and hers and the way they came together.

It did cross her mind once, briefly, that the water on the stove was probably boiling by now, but it was a thought that did not last long.

Simon looked at her face, he held her eyes with his as he rocked above and inside her, pushing deeper and deeper with each thrust. The way he looked at her . . . he saw her, in a way no one else ever had. He knew her. He wanted her.

He held himself deep, and for a half second it seemed that his dark eyes were touched with streaks of red. Flashes of fire lit the depths. Claire came again, and with Simon inside her it was more powerful than before, more important. Her body convulsed around his, and he came, too. They were so incredibly connected, so very much together, that she wondered why she'd ever been satisfied with anything less.

And to top it all off, like the cherry on top of a hot fudge sundae, he drifted down and kissed her neck.

Claire's job was undeniably tedious, and on Wednesday her mind was elsewhere as she mindlessly entered data into her computer. She yawned a time or two, and fielded the questions from her coworkers who were sequestered in nearby cubicles. Do you feel OK? Are you coming down with something? You look like you didn't get enough sleep last night, what happened? You're a little pale, someone said.

She finally decided to tell them that a noisy neighbor had kept her up half the night. That was close enough, though in truth she was much noisier than Simon.

Maybe if she'd felt closer to any one of them she might've said more, but while they were friendly coworkers they weren't exactly friends. Most of her good friends were now married and had kids, so she didn't see any of them on a regular basis, not like in the old days. Oh, they got together and had lunch now and then, but the talk always turned to potty training and which kid had learned the alphabet at the earliest age and which schools in the area were the most acceptable. There were occasional weekend barbecues or infrequent and horrific blind dates that made conversations about three-year-olds seem scintillating. No, her friends had changed, and so had she. Claire didn't feel like she could call even them to share what had happened.

Besides, what had happened with Simon last night had felt so very, very personal. More intimate than sex, more important than the laughing and the touching and the orgasms.

This morning was still a blur. Simon had given her a fabulous kiss that had led to more, and then he'd gone home—a conveniently short trip. Claire had been left with no time to get ready for work. She'd showered quickly and grabbed clothes from her closet. The long blue skirt and blouse were comfortable. If the blues didn't exactly match and she'd forgotten to put in earrings, well, if anyone noticed the lack was excused since she hadn't gotten much sleep.

She never had gotten around to putting on those sexy shoes that made her legs look good. Maybe tonight—if there was a tonight.

More than once during the day she'd remembered that moment when it had seemed she saw fire in Simon's eyes. She hadn't been herself at the time, and there *was* a red neon light across the street. Maybe his head had been in just the right position at that moment to catch a glare. That had to be it.

There were logical explanations for all the clues that had led her to believe he was a vampire. The dirt might've come from a potted plant, even though he didn't have any living plants—or fake ones, for that matter—in his apartment. The howl might've been an overly excited Fluffy or—considering some of the sounds she'd made last night—a *very* happy woman somewhere on the third floor. The hypnotizing eyes . . . Simon just had great eyes, and that was enough of an explanation to suit her.

So she didn't tell anyone that she'd suspected her neighbor of being a vampire, or that she'd decided she was wrong and last night they'd eaten spaghetti in her kitchen—both of them starving from marvelously vigorous and unrestrained sex—she wearing nothing but her bathrobe, he in nothing but those incredibly sexy black jeans. She didn't tell them that for the first time in a very long time, she was happy. Tired, but happy.

Happy as she was, she tried not to get her hopes too high. She'd been burned before, after all. A man who wanted a woman in bed might say or do anything to get her there, and then . . . then there were phone calls that never came, an old girlfriend who just happened to make an appearance, or that horrible "It's not you, it's me." For all she knew she'd get home and find out that her neighbor had moved during the day just to get away from her, or else he had a wife who'd show up out of nowhere, or else—worst of all—he'd ignore her and pretend that nothing had happened.

Claire was thinking about Simon so intently her fingers quit moving across the keyboard. She simply stared at the screen, imagining the worst. The worst, at this moment, had nothing to do with vampires.

She jumped when the phone on her desk rang, and answered it quickly with a too-curt, "Claire Murphy."

"Hello, Claire Murphy."

She smiled. No one else had a voice like that. No one else could make her shudder simply by saying her name. "Hi, Simon."

"What are you doing?"

"Working." Trying to, anyway. Her heart lurched. "How did you get this number?"

"I asked the building manager where you worked, and then I used all my detective skills to thumb through a phone book."

Would he go to so much trouble just to inform her over the phone that it wasn't going to work? That he was already tired of her? That he was married?

"What time do you get off work?" he asked, and when he did the connection faltered a little. Apparently he was calling from his cell phone.

"Four-thirty."

"That's too long. Ever leave work early?"

"Sometimes."

"Leave now," he said, his voice low and commanding and sexy as hell. "Right now."

Claire's heart fluttered. "I really shouldn't . . ."

"To hell with shouldn't. I need you."

Her mouth went dry, while between her legs she was anything but. "I suppose I can take half a sick day."

"Do it."

With that, he ended the call. No "See you later," no "Bye, now," No "I can't wait." Just a command and a click and a dial tone.

Claire closed down her computer program and picked up her purse. Her hands were trembling, and she couldn't wait to get home. Usually on pretty days she walked home, but maybe today she'd grab a taxi. She informed her boss that she was going home, and since she'd been yawning and droopy-eyed all day he didn't give her the third degree. In fact, he told her that she looked a little flushed and should stay home until she was sure she didn't have anything contagious.

Claire agreed and headed for the elevator with a decidedly un-sick spring in her step. Simon needed her. All the way down, she had one thought in her mind. Please, don't let him be a vampire or a jerk. Let him be just a guy. Maybe even *the* guy.

Less than a minute later she stepped off the elevator intent on grabbing a taxi and quickly making her way home, but she hadn't taken two steps before a hand fell on her shoulder. She almost screamed she was so startled, but when she spun around she smiled widely and her heart . . . her heart did something odd and unexpected.

"I told you I couldn't wait," Simon said. He took her hand and they headed for the front door. "I can't get you out of my head," he mumbled, and he didn't sound entirely happy about the fact.

"I thought about you today, a time or two," Claire said, hefting her purse on her shoulder and picking up the pace. Simon's steps were longer than hers.

"I went to bed after you left for work, and I woke up thinking about you," he said.

"Only good thoughts, I hope."

"What do you think?" He looked at her, and his step instantly altered. For her, he took shorter, slower steps.

At that moment Claire realized that her life had changed in a matter of hours. She realized that she had found the perfect man. She realized that if Simon was a vampire . . . she didn't care. Not that she could tell him any of that. Not yet.

They exited through the front doors and into the afternoon sunlight. Simon's eyes narrowed as the sun's rays caught him full in the face, but he didn't explode or catch on fire or recoil. That was good. He gripped her hand in his and it felt very right. That was even better.

Claire had fallen in love before—many times, if teenage crushes counted—but she'd never fallen in so far so fast. Simon was a wonderful lover, an *incredible* lover, and when they weren't in bed he introduced her to his musical passion. Jazz. Maybe she would never love the music the way he did, but she did quickly find a few favorite tunes in his collection.

Simon was passionate about his music, almost as passionate as he was about her. He made her laugh, again and again. They danced. Naked. With her head resting on his chest she heard his heartbeat and it always made her smile. How could she have ever suspected him of being a vampire?

Mrs. Tillman kept close watch on their comings and goings as the days passed, and her disapproval was obvious. Once they even heard the whispered words, "foolish girl" drifting from the old lady's slightly opened door. Claire didn't have time to worry about one sour old woman. Not when her life was going so wonderfully well.

She felt incredibly silly when Charlie from downstairs, one of the three neighborhood lowlifes she'd believed had disappeared thanks to a bloodsucking vampire, showed up one evening in his usual classless manner, screaming at his wife and making loud, unintelligible excuses for his long absence. If Charlie wasn't a vampire's victim, odds were the other two were either in jail or had simply moved on to harass some other neighborhood.

Simon had removed her collection of vampire books from the end table in the main room and stored them on the bookshelf with other novels. She wasn't sure why they bothered him but they did. Again, she didn't care. Lately she hadn't had any time for reading, in any case. Why escape into fiction when reality was so wonderful?

He kissed her neck frequently, but he didn't bite. Much.

On Friday night, the club where Simon played reopened and he insisted on taking her with him. He didn't have to insist very hard; she was anxious to go. She'd heard him play on his portable piano, and they'd listened to numerous recordings, but she wanted to see him on stage with a band, lost in the music she knew he loved.

And he did love it. At the small but crowded nightclub Claire sat at a small table near the raised stage. She sipped wine and watched as Simon and the other three musicians made beautiful, fast, and furious music. They all loved what they did, not just playing their instruments but creating *this* music. Simon's face lit up when he performed. Claire had always known he had remarkable hands, but to see them fly over the piano keys and make such music, that was magic. It was a different kind of magic than that which her grandmother had told her about, but still, it was magic. Until tonight she had only seen Simon look this happy in bed, and yes, she was a little jealous.

But more than that, she was happy for him. Everyone should have something or someone in their life that they loved so much.

When the evening was over, at an hour much later than Claire had ever been out even on a Friday night, they walked from the club heading toward the apartment. It was a trip of just a few blocks, which was one of the reasons Simon had chosen her apartment building. The evening was a bit cool, but with Simon beside her she didn't feel too chilly. He was very warm, very much alive, and she smiled contentedly as she remembered that she'd once believed he might be a vampire.

She was still convinced that such creatures were real. She knew in her heart that there was more to the world than most people ever saw. But Simon, Simon was just a man. The perfect man, perhaps, but still . . . a man. He was warm-blooded, his heart beat well, he didn't mind going out in the late afternoon sun.

. . . and he ate her garlic bread.

They held hands very easily, as they walked toward home. Claire couldn't remember when she'd ever felt so close to a person, when she'd ever felt so much a part of someone's life. This relationship which had begun so very oddly was important, and if she had her way it would only become more important in days and weeks and years to come. Only one small detail kept her from perfection.

"There's something I should tell you," she said as they reached the front entrance to the building. She sensed there were possibilities with Simon, possibilities that went beyond sex and shared laughter. Such a connection couldn't be built on a lie, no matter how small.

And this lie wasn't particularly small, to be honest.

As they walked up the stairs, she gathered the strength to begin. "Do you remember when you accused me of stalking you?" she asked.

"Four days ago?" he responded lightly. "Yes, my memory works well enough to remember that."

"Well, you weren't *entirely* off the mark."

They continued to climb. "You wanted my body," he teased.

"No! Well, yes I suppose I did, but that's not why I was following you."

A small line appeared between his eyes, a hint of a frown. "What, then?"

Claire licked her lips as they entered the third floor hall-way, where a few days ago she had attempted to gather proof that Simon was not what he appeared to be. "I thought you might be a vampire."

She expected an outburst of laughter, and was prepared

to order him to be quiet so he wouldn't wake the neighbors. He continued to walk steadily, and there was no laughter. He didn't so much as smile. "Why would you think such a thing?"

It seemed like a long way to the section of the third floor where their apartments were located. Maybe this conversation would be best finished in her apartment or his, since he wasn't taking the news as well as she'd expected he would. Maybe it was too soon. Maybe she should've kept the truth to herself for a while longer.

It was a little too late for *that* particular revelation.

"Why?" he prompted.

Claire ticked off her reasons. "I never saw you during the daytime, for one thing, and I never saw you bring in food, and you listen to that old music . . . which I understand now, really I do, but I didn't before I knew you . . . and I could swear that when you looked at me you were looking right through me, looking into my soul in a way that was not at all human. And, ok, I Googled you and you've moved a lot in the past few years. A man who doesn't want his immortality to be discovered might . . ." she hesitated after her breathless rush of words, realizing how ridiculous it all sounded ". . . move frequently," she finished in a lowered voice.

Finally they reached her apartment, and she grabbed her keys from her purse. Simon said nothing as she fumbled with unlocking the door, and she was terrified that she'd ruined the best relationship she'd ever had simply by telling the truth.

"What about now?" he asked as they stepped into her apartment. "Do you still think I'm a vampire?"

"No!" she insisted. Here, alone, the door closed behind them, she could take Simon's face in her hands to look him in the eye. Yes, there was power in those eyes but it was perfectly ordinary power, right? Maybe what she saw, what touched her, was a power only she could see.

"Because I didn't gag on garlic bread or explode in the sun?"

"Because I love you!" she insisted.

Once again Simon went very quiet, and Claire cursed herself. It was too soon for those words that sent some men running. Simon was a man, just a man, and he would run like hell from those words delivered too soon. But it was too late to take them back, and in truth she didn't want to take them back. "I love you," she said again. "It happened too fast and it took me by surprise but that's the truth. I don't want any kind of lie between us and that's why I wanted to tell you about my ridiculous notions."

He seemed to relax a little. "Did you tell anyone about your theory?"

"No. Who would I tell? My girlfriends would never believe me. Co-workers? I'm pretty sure that would get me fired, or sent to counseling at the very least. There's really no one else to tell." Except Granny Eileen, and she'd been gone five years.

"That's good." More relaxed than he had been as they'd entered the apartment, Simon began to undress her. As always he took his time, caressing skin as it was revealed, kissing her mouth and her throat, raking his talented hands across her body. He played her as well as he played his piano, and they did make music.

Simon removed his clothes, with her help, as they walked into the bedroom. Once there, he did not rush to the bed as he sometimes did, but held her so that she was facing the mirror while he stood behind her. They were both naked, both entirely bare, but for the small gold cross that caught a glimmer of light from the other room. Simon's hands covered her breasts. His fingers rocked back and forth, very gently, and she found herself leaning into him, reveling in the sensation of her skin against his. There had been a time when Claire had been embarrassed to look at herself this way, but Simon thought she was beautiful and he'd said so so many times she was beginning to believe him. He bent his head and kissed her shoulder.

"Do you really love me?" he whispered.

"Yes."

"Just for today because you like the way I make you feel, or for forever? Think before you answer," he added quickly. "Forever is a very long time."

She did think, but in truth she'd known the answer before he'd even finished asking the question. "Forever," she said.

"For better or for worse?"

She nodded, and his hands slipped lower, where he aroused her with a deliberate slowness while his eyes held hers in the mirror. She saw a flash of fire there, and this time she knew the fire was real, not a reflection of neon.

"I was bitten in 1941," he said.

Claire gasped, but did not move.

"It was hard at first, adapting to a new way of life. I had no one to help me, no one to teach me. I was bitten and abandoned to find my own way in a new world."

Claire's heart pounded as Simon spoke calmly and his hands caressed.

"It's the immortality that's hardest to take, I must admit. You'd think it would be wonderful, a gift instead of a curse, but friends always grow old and die and it's impossible to stay in any one place for very long before people start asking questions about why I don't grow older. Immortality is lonely. Very lonely."

"Are you saying . . ."

"I'm not a killer," he interrupted. "At least, not an indiscriminate one. Since '41 I've killed three people. Two were trying to kill me. The other was a mistake."

"A mistake?"

"I did not know my own strength." His hands continued to arouse her, and his eyes held hers in the mirror. The flame there had died, but she did not fool herself into thinking it had never existed. "You have a choice to make. If you'd like I can pack my bags, change my name once again, and go somewhere so far away no one will ever find me. Say the word, and I'm gone."

"I don't want you to go!" she whispered, horrified at the idea that he might disappear from her life. "What's the other choice?"

Simon lowered his head and nipped at her bare shoulder. "You know, Claire. You know. Come with me, if you dare. It's your choice."

"I don't want you to go," she said again. She didn't want to go back to the life she'd lived before Simon had come into it.

"That's not an answer," he protested.

"There must be another way!" But she knew there was not. *When I was bitten. I'm not a killer. Come with me.*

Claire slowly tipped her head to one side. That was her answer. She would not lose Simon. Not now, not ever.

"Look," he whispered.

His hands now rested against her bare stomach, and as she watched they began to change. Long nails grew in the blink of an eye, and hair sprang up on his arms, his hands, his face. What had been lean, pale muscle grew larger and was almost instantly covered with dark fur. The shape of his face changed from the handsome face she had come to love to one that was caught between man and wolf. The teeth that grew long and sharp were fierce, but the eyes were Simon's. She knew those eyes.

He raked his fingers, his claws, across her belly. Sharp talons did not break the skin, but they did leave fine red marks in their wake. She looked so pale, so vulnerable, with those powerful claws moving against her flesh. And yet, she was not afraid.

"I'm no vampire," Simon said, the voice his and yet not his. It was throatier. Deeper. Colored with the force of an animal even though he touched her with the gentleness of the man she loved. "Whiny bastards," he added beneath his breath. "Look at me without flinching, without being filled with horror. Look at me and understand that if you choose me we will never have children. We will never make a home that will last more than a few years. For an eternity, we will only have one another. Still love me, Claire? Still want to come with me?"

Because she knew those eyes so well she saw the pain there. Simon thought she would say no, that she would be terrified by what he had become . . . what she would become if she joined him. She should be terrified, but she was not. In fact, she remained amazingly calm. The face of her lover was no longer beautiful, but it was still his face. He was a werewolf—a shapeshifter, a Jekyll and Hyde—a monster to the minds of most just as a vampire was a monster.

But in spite of his current appearance, Simon was the best man she had ever known. She loved him. He was hers.

She reached up and touched his head, surprised by the softness of the fur that met her hand. She gently but surely drew him down until his mouth touched her neck. That was all the answer she had to give.

It didn't hurt much when he bit her, when his sharp teeth broke through the flesh at her neck. A heartbeat later she felt the power of the animal that was inside him enter her blood, rushing through her veins with a burning sensation that traveled quickly throughout her body, changing her. Feeding her. Making her stronger. Simon held her with tenderness, though his limbs looked as if they could not offer tenderness.

There was pain, as the burning increased, but Claire welcomed the pain as she welcomed the rush of energy and strength. A new element was added to her body, and it shook her to the core. She and Simon were completely joined, much as they had been during sex, and she dismissed everything but the way it felt to be held in this way, to be joined. To be bitten.

The teeth were withdrawn from her neck, and Simon became a man once again, quickly, smoothly, and completely. Again, he met her eye in the mirror.

"When?" she asked. "When will I change?" For a moment she felt a tickle of panic, but the panic did not take root. It did not last.

"Some changes will come to you immediately. Others will arrive with the rise of the next full moon."

"Hey, wait a minute," she blurted. "You changed and there's no full moon tonight. I thought . . ."

"Don't believe everything you read, love," Simon said with that touch of humor she adored. "You'll learn all you need to know, in time. I'll teach you. I'll teach you everything."

He led her onto the balcony that overlooked downtown Atlanta. Already Claire felt stronger, more alive. In addition she felt something she had not expected . . . an increased pull to Simon, who was, in a way she had never expected anyone to be, hers. Forever hers. He was in her blood, now, and she was in his.

"I was so sure there was a vampire in the building." She laughed lightly and easily.

"There is." Simon said. "When you come into your full abilities you'll sense when a vampire is near."

"I knew it," Claire whispered. "Is there like a club or something? Monthly meetings?"

"Vamps and Weres don't get along, but we refrain from fighting openly so we won't bring undue attention to ourselves. Existing in a world that doesn't believe in us is tough. Keeping it that way is even tougher."

"Who is it?" she asked, searching her mind for the most logical answer. The young guy from the first floor, Charlie, the handyman . . .

"Mrs. Tillman. Don't let the doddering old lady act fool you. She can be a nasty bitch when she feels like it."

"But she's *old*."

"Only because it suits her at this moment in time to be old."

Claire pictured Mrs. Tillman's sour but unthreatening face in her mind, and imagined that mouth coming down on her neck. She shuddered, and Simon wrapped his arms around her in response. "At least now I understand why you were so upset at my teeny obsession with vampires."

"Teeny?" he teased.

"Miniscule."

The moon was not full, and still Claire drank in its power. The moon was a living thing that fed her, that called to her like a drug she needed in order to survive, in order to be strong. The moon's rays washed over her much as Simon's hands did, and she knew she had made the right decision in offering him her neck. No wonder he was so often out at night. To be bathed in the moonlight was magical.

"When did you know . . ." she began and then faltered. "When did you see that I . . ."

"That you were meant to be mine?"

"Yes." The words sounded so right, so true to her heart. *Meant to be mine.*

"The day I moved in I saw you come in from work, and . . ."

"The day you moved in?" she interrupted. "Why did you wait so long?"

"I knew if I was right and you were the one then you would come to me, in time. You did so, in your own unique way. You were drawn to me, Claire. That's why you became obsessed. From that first glance, we were united." With his fingertip, he touched the gold cross she wore. "I'm just glad this isn't silver."

Claire turned and leaned over the balcony railing, face lifted to the moon. A cool night breeze washed over her bare body and she opened her arms to drink it in. Even the brush of the wind on her skin felt finer, sharper, more beautiful.

Simon kissed the wound on her neck, a wound she knew would quickly disappear. "You are remarkably gorgeous tonight," he whispered in her ear. "Gorgeous and powerful and mine in a thousand ways." His body was molded to hers, and she felt as if she not only absorbed power from him but also gave back, in some way she could not yet explain. The night was at their feet, waiting to be claimed and conquered. Her life had just begun.

Again, Simon kissed her neck. "Moonlight becomes you, love," he whispered against the sensitive skin. "Moonlight becomes you."

DIRTY MAGIC

Kim Harrison

MIA WALKED DOWN THE DAMP, RAIN-DESERTED sidewalk, her seventy-five-dollar heels clicking faintly from fatigue on the wet cement. She was tired, but she could still maintain her elegant, upright posture if she moved slowly. Her dress-length overcoat and matching umbrella of midnight blue kept her dry, and it was rainy enough that she didn't need to wear her sunglasses to protect her pale, nearly albino eyes.

With a small toss of her head, she shifted her black hair, cut short as she liked it. Traffic was light, but she didn't want to risk being splashed, so she shifted closer to the classy, well-maintained narrow buildings that lined the street. The paper sack of groceries on her hip wasn't heavy, but her daughter's needs were telling. It wasn't the usual fatigue brought on by an energetic newborn. Holly was the first banshee born in Cincinnati in over forty years, and if Mia couldn't keep her in an emotion-rich environment, the child took what she needed from her mother. It wasn't as if Holly could draw upon her father for her emotional needs. Not now anyway.

Frowning, Mia brushed her hair from her eyes and wondered if having a child at this particular time had been a good idea. But when Remus—psychopath, murderer, and gentle lover—had fallen into her lap by way of a bungled rape attempt, the chance to use his anger and frustration to engender a child in her had been too great. A smile curved Mia's delicate mouth up. Remus had quickly learned the difference between his unreasonable rage at the world and her true hunger, becoming pliant and gentle. Respectful. The perfect husband, the model father.

And at the thought of Holly, happy, inquisitive Holly, so pretty and soft, looking like a younger, mirror image of her mother, babbling innocently as she sat on her mother's lap and basked in the love for her, Mia knew she'd have it no other way. She would do anything for her daughter. As her mother had done for her.

The soft whoosh of a passing car brought Mia's head up, and she blinked at the rain heavy on her eyelashes despite the umbrella. It was cool and damp, and she was weary. Seeing a rain-abandoned table outside a cafe, she slowed, brushing once at the wrought-iron chair before sitting with her groceries on her lap and trusting her coat to keep her dry. The awning helped shield the rain and she closed her umbrella. She was just a casually sophisticated young woman waiting for a cab that would never come.

People passed, and slowly her pulse eased and her fatigue lessoned as she soaked in the emotions of the pedestrians, taking in flashes of feeling like water eddying around a rock in a streambed. It was all the law would allow now, this passive sipping of emotions. If she fed well, people noticed.

Mia straightened when a couple arguing over whether they should have taken a cab walked by, sensation rolling over her like a sunbeam. Almost she rose to fall into step behind them, to linger and drink it in, but she didn't, and the warmth faded as the couple continued on.

One might think that a predator existing on emotions might have an easy life living in a city that measured its population in the hundreds of thousands, but since humanity had learned banshees were not the stuff of story but living among them, humans had armed themselves with knowledge, and their numbers had dwindled.

The image of a mysterious weeping woman foretelling death had given way to the reality of a sophisticated predator: a predator who could feed well upon office arguments started between co-workers with a careful word or two, gorge upon the death-energy a person released when dying, but barely survive upon the ambient emotions around her that the law allowed.

As in most fairy tales, there was a kernel of truth in the myth of a banshee's tears. Created to serve as a conduit of emotions, they let a banshee feed from a safe distance or simply store the emotion for later consumption. For though banshees were predators thriving on death, they were also fragile. Much like a rattlesnake, they left their poison, then sat back to feed in safety while others fought, loved, or killed each other. Psychic vampires was what the psychology texts called them, a definition that Mia could not find fault with.

Her subconscious had brought her down this street for a reason, and as she fingered the tarnished coin draped around her neck on a tattered purple ribbon, her gaze traveled to the apartment building across from her, rising up through the misty rain, all the way to the topmost floor. The light was on, golden and hazy in the afternoon's rain. Tom was in. But Tom was always in now. He was too tired to go to work. Not like when she first met him.

Nervous, Mia spun the wedding ring on her finger. Tom hadn't given it to her. Tom hadn't given Mia her beautiful daughter either. Remus had. There had been so much raw anger in him that she could have used it to create two children. But Remus could no longer give Holly the emotion she needed.

Glancing at the window hazy with rain, Mia hesitated. She had to be so careful never to permanently harm anyone. There were old ways to track her down and new, excruciating techniques to punish a species that lived on the emotions of another. Mia was a good girl, and now she had a daughter to think of.

I shouldn't be doing this, Mia thought in worry. *It's too soon.* Someone might see her. Someone might remember she'd been here. But she was tired, and the thought of Tom holding her, filling her with the strength of his love, was too strong a pull. He loved her. He loved her even knowing that she was why he was ill. He loved her knowing she was a banshee and unable to keep from stripping his emotions and strength from him. She needed to feel his arms around her, for just a moment.

With a soft quiver of anticipation to set her skin tingling, Mia stood, gathered her grocery bag onto her hip, and pushed herself into motion. Not bothering with the umbrella, she crossed the street with a false confidence, pacing to the unattended common door with a single-minded intensity, looking neither left nor right, praying no one would notice her.

Fear a dim substitute for strength, she pulled the glass door open and slipped inside. In the small space where the mailboxes were, she lifted her chin and ran a hand over her wet hair, feeling more sure now that she was off the street and out from so many potential eyes. The shiny front of the mailboxes threw back a blurry image—color mostly: dark hair, pale skin, and an almost-black coat.

Leaving the umbrella in a corner, she ascended the stairs so as to keep the cameras in the elevator from getting a good look at her. The open stairway taking up the middle of the building wasn't monitored, and anyone looking out here would only notice an usually petite woman with a bag of groceries, cold from the rain. Worry someone might actually see her trickled back, and her pace quickened, gaining strength as she rose instead of fatigue.

Around her was the flow of life, slipping under the doors and into the hallway like the scent of baking bread or someone's too-strong cologne. It eddied about her feet and puddled on the stairs, and she waded through it like surf, able to see the energy the people living behind the doors sloughed off, kicking up anger here, and frustration there, her pace slowing to take in the softer, harder-to-find emotions of love, a mere whisper lingering outside a door like perfume.

She paused, pretending to be tired outside a door where the soft sounds of music and laughter were a muted hush. Love and desire carried the headiest amount of energy, but they were hard to find, not because they were scarce, but because people directed the emotions to a specific person, holding the feeling close to themselves as if knowing how powerful they were. Love seldom ventured past a person's aura unless it flowed into another. Not like the wild bitterness of anger, which people threw away from them like the refuse it was.

Mia closed her eyes, swallowing up the ambient love the couple had left in the hall as they had fumbled for their keys. It had only been a few hours ago, and though it bolstered her, it caused her pain. It had been too long since she had felt the full, unshielded warmth of another's aura. She was tired of filling herself on garbage and stolen wisps of love.

With a sudden resolve, she took off her ring. Slipping it into a pocket, she guiltily patted it to see if it made a telltale shape against her coat. Head high, she continued up until she reached the top floor.

Tom's door was unadorned, and with her pulse fast in tension, she tapped softly, hoping he heard. She didn't want a neighbor remembering a knock in the hall. Tom had promised her he wouldn't tell anyone he knew a banshee, afraid they would see him failing and convince him to never see her again. She shouldn't be here this soon, but the memory of his love was like the scent of flowers, begging to be inhaled and irresistible.

The door opened with a quickness that sent her back a step, and she stared at Tom, her eyes wide and her breath held. He looked good. Better than the last time she'd seen him, the lines of fatigue only lightly etching his mid-thirties face. Standing tall, he had once had a beautifully vigorous, if slight, body, but since meeting her in the grocery store a year ago, nearly all the substance had been stripped away to leave him looking as if he was recovering from a long illness. His short brown hair was clean but untidy from his shower, and he wore jeans and a comfortable flannel top against the damp chill.

Seeing her, he smiled, pleasure coming over his long, somewhat sallow face. His skin was pale from a lack of sun, and his muscles had lost their tone months ago. His fingers, long enough to facilitate a high amount of proficiency with his instrument, looked thin as he reached to pull her into a hug.

Mia felt his arms go around her and almost walked away. Breathing in his initial delight, she realized it was too soon. She should not be here, even if she *was* pining for him. Someone might have seen her, and he hadn't recovered fully from her last visit. But she was so tired, and even a wisp of his love would renew her.

"I saw you on the sidewalk," Tom said as he felt her shoulders tense and his hands dropped from her. "I'm glad you came up. It's been lonely here by myself. Come on in. Just for a moment."

Her pulse raced, and she stepped into his apartment with a guilty quickness. "I can't stay," she said, her voice high. "Tom, I promised I'd only stop by to say hi, and then I have to go."

She sounded frantic even to herself, and she bit her lower lip, wishing things were otherwise. The click of the door closing mixed with the soft sound of talk radio. The warmth of his apartment soaked into her, and she felt herself relax at the emotion-rich air his apartment had. He'd been practicing his music, and that always filled his rooms with life. It was what had attracted her to him in the first place, as he had strolled past the grapes, trailing joy like the wisps of the symphony he'd been humming. Slowly her jaw unclenched, and the worry and guilt slid into nothing. She couldn't help herself. This was what she was.

"Let me take those," he said, reaching for her groceries, and she let him, following him soundlessly down the short hall to the kitchen as she untied her coat. The kitchen opened to the living room where Tom usually practiced his music now that he was too tired to make the trip to the university's hall. Down the corridor at the back was the single bedroom and bath. Everything was tidy and clean, done in soothing tones of brown and taupe. The furnishings were simple and clearly masculine, and Mia loved the contrast from her own home, filled with the primary-colored clutter and untidy life of a new baby.

"I won't stay long," she said, noting his thin, trembling hands. "I was passing by, and . . . I missed you."

"Oh, Mia," he said, his deep voice swirling over her like his aura was as he took her in his arms. "I know how the rain depresses you."

Depresses her wasn't exactly it. It depressed everyone else, and in turn, lowered the amount of ambient emotion they gave off. She was hungry, and she lowered her gaze before he saw the rising need in their pale blue depths.

"I missed you, too," she whispered, eyes closing in bliss as his love soaked into her, his arms gentling her to him, forgiving her for what she did to him, knowing she had no choice. The scent of his soap was sharp, and she drew away when she heard his pulse quicken. She was pulling his strength from him as she soaked in his aura, rich with emotion. That was why he was weak. A person could replace a surprising amount of their aura, but take too much too fast, and the person died when their soul was left bare to the world and unprotected.

"I'm sorry," she said, blinking to keep her emotions in check. "I shouldn't have come."

"I'm fine," he said, smiling wearily down at her.

"Fine?" she said bitterly as she pulled away. "Look at you. Look what I did to you. I hardly walked in the door, and you're shaking already."

"Mia."

"No!" she exclaimed, pushing him away when he tried to hold her. "I hate who I am. I can't love anyone. Damn it, Tom, this isn't fair!"

"Shhhh," he soothed, and this time, Mia let him take her in his embrace, laying her head against his chest as he swayed her gently as if she was a child. "Mia, I don't mind giving my strength to you. It comes back."

Mia couldn't breathe from the wave of pure love rolling off of him, carrying the delicate beauty of wind chimes tinkling forgotten in the sun. His love was so heady, so sweet. But she shouldn't take it. She had to resist. If she could keep from drinking it in, it would eventually flow back into him, keeping him strong and untouched.

"But not fast enough," she mumbled into his flannel shirt, hardening herself to his emotion if not his words. "I came back too soon. You're not well. I should go."

But his arms didn't release her. "Please stay," he whispered. "Just a little while? I want to see you smile."

She pulled back, gazing into his earnest eyes. It was too soon, but she would make it be okay. She could do this. "I'll make you coffee," she said as if in concession, and he let her go.

"I'd like that. Thank you."

Motions unsure, Mia took off her overcoat and slipped off her shoes. Barefoot and in a soft dress of pale blue and gray, she busied herself in the kitchen, taking a moment to arrange her hair in the reflection in the microwave. Guilt stared back at her, with a rising black of hunger in her pale eyes. The pierced coin on the purple ribbon about her neck dangled like a guilty accusation, and her pale fingers held it for a moment as she thought. She would not take anything more from this man. She could do this. She had wanted to find love, and she had. It was worth the risk.

Tom's sigh as he sat at the table between the kitchen and the living room was weary but happy. Past the tasteful furniture and his scattered music was a large plate-glass window overlooking the street. The drapes were open, but the rain was like a sheet, gray and soothing to create a soft, hidden world.

Her silk dress was a gentle hush as Mia sat two empty cups on the table. She watched Tom's long fingers curve about his, though the cup was dry and cold. Concerned, she sat beside him and took his hand in her own, drawing his attention to her. Behind them, the coffeemaker warmed. "How are you doing?"

He smiled at the worry in her voice. "Better now that you're here."

Mia smiled back, unable to keep from soaking in his love like a sponge. Overcome by the purity of it, she dropped her gaze, only to have them fall upon the coin. Her mood tarnished.

"Work going okay?" she asked, hoping he would practice, but Tom gave her hand an apologetic squeeze in a gentle refusal. When he played, he expended a huge amount of emotion when he became lost in his music, as if tapping into the universe still ringing from its creation. If she were here to soak it up, it would leave him weak for days. If she wasn't, the expended emotion would linger in his rooms, bathing his soul in what was akin to an extended aura. Not exactly feng shui, but more of a lingering footprint of emotion that could alter moods even days later.

It was what had attracted her to him from the first.

"Work's going great," he said, leaning back and away to look at the coffeepot. "There's a concert next month, and it looks like I'll be ready."

As long as you don't take my strength, Mia could almost hear him finish in his mind.

"I'm sorry," she breathed, starting to lose her upright posture and her eyes beginning to swim as they looked at his instrument propped lovingly in a corner. She could feel a puddle of intensity on the couch from earlier this morning, and she hardened herself to ignore it. If she went to sit in it, it would warm her like a sunbeam.

"I don't mean to take so much from you," she said. A single tear slipped down, and Tom moved his chair to hers. His long arms enfolded her, and her pulse raced from the love swirling through her aura, seeping into her despite her trying to stop it.

"Mia," he crooned, and she held her breath, stiff and resolved to not take it, but it was hard. So hard.

"Don't cry," he soothed. "I know you can't help it. It must be hell to be a banshee."

"Everyone I love dies," she said bitterly into the soft depth of his shirt as the guilt of three hundred years of existence rose anew. "I can't come back here. I'm making you ill. I have to leave and never come back."

With an abrupt motion, she broke from him. She stood, panic an unusual showing on her usually collected, proud face. *What if he told her to leave?* Tom stood with her, and as she reached for her coat, he pulled her back.

"Mia," he said, giving her a little shake. "Mia, wait!"

Head lowered, she stopped, allowing his fear to coat her in a soothing sheen like fragrant lemon oil, and she felt her hunger jealously claim it. It was bitter after the exquisite airy lightness of love, but she took it. Stronger in body and resolve, she pulled her head up to see him through a haze of unshed tears.

"You are so beautiful," he said, wiping a tear away with a thumb. "We will find a way to make this work. I recover faster every time."

He didn't, and Mia dropped her gaze at the wishful lie.

"There has to be a way," he said, holding her close.

Head tucked under his chin, Mia felt a quiver start in the deepest part of her soul. *Again. It was going to happen again.* She had to be strong. Need would not rule her. "There is . . ." she said, her hand creeping up between them to hold the coin about her neck.

Tom pushed her back, his long face showing his shock. "There's a way? Why didn't you tell me before?"

"Because . . . because it won't work," she said, not wanting to deal with a false hope. "It's too cruel. It's a lie. If it doesn't work, you might die."

"Mia." His grip on her upper arms pinched. "Tell me!"

In a quandary, she refused to look at him. From the living room, the talk radio turned to a classical guitar, the intensity rising with her tension. "I have a wish . . ." she breathed, hand clenched about the pierced coin on its purple ribbon. It was how wishes were stored, and she had had it for years.

Braver now for having admitted it, she looked up, feeling his excitement roll off of him in a wave. It washed into her, and she forced herself to keep from taking it. The room grew richer with subtle shades of want and desire, purple and green, shifting about her feet like silk.

"Where . . . where did you get it? Are you sure it's real?"

Mia nodded miserably, opening her hand and showing him. "I got it from a vampire. I don't know why she gave it to me, except perhaps that I shamed her into trying to become who she wanted to be. But that was years ago. I was so bad that day, making her angry so that I could drink in her guilt. I shamed her, but I shamed myself more for telling her I couldn't love anyone without killing them, giving her my pain in return for her strength. Perhaps she wanted to thank me. Or perhaps she pitied me and wanted to give me the chance . . . to find love myself."

Steadying herself, Mia took a breath, refusing to let his hope warm her like the sun. She wouldn't take any more. She had to be strong. "I've had it all this time," she finished faintly.

Together they looked at it, small and innocuous in her palm.

"You waited?" he said in wonder, taking it up and running his fingertips over the detailed relief engraved on it. "Why?"

Mia blinked to keep from crying as she gazed up at him. "I wanted to fall in love first," she said, almost bewildered he didn't understand.

Tom's expression turned to one of pure, honest love, and Mia choked, muscles trembling from the effort to keep from taking it in. He gathered her to him, and she shook in the effort. Thinking it was tears, Tom shushed her, making things worse. It was almost too much, and Mia forced herself to stay, feeling the emotions in the room build and grow like a sheltering fog. It was like spreading a feast before a starving man, and she held back by her will alone. She would take no more from Tom.

"Use your wish," he said, and hope leapt in her. "Use it so we can be together."

"I'm afraid," she said, trembling. "Wishes don't always come true. Some things you simply can't have. If it doesn't work, then I not only lose you, but I lose my hope to ever have anyone." Vision swimming, she gazed at him. "I can't live without hope. It's all I have when I'm alone."

But Tom was shaking his head as if she was a child. "This is love, Mia," he said, both their hands holding the coin between them. "All things are possible. It's a wish. It has to work! You have to have faith."

A single tear slipped from Mia to make a cold trail down to her chin.

"Make the wish," he said, drying her cheek. "Wish that I can love you."

"What if it doesn't work?" she whispered, feeling the weight of the emotions in the room pressing on her skin in a deepening tingle.

His eyes full of his love for her, he timorously smiled with a raw hope. "What if it does?"

"Tom—" she protested, and he leaned over the space between them and covered her mouth with his.

Fear flashed through her, and she tried to pull back. It was too much. She wouldn't be able to stop herself. If he gave so freely, she had no way to stop it, and he would die!

But his lips were so soft on hers, and her breath caught at the depth of his feeling, his love, all for her, as encompassing and dark as a moonless night. *I was right,* she thought as she curved her arms around his neck and stretched to reach him. She couldn't stop herself, not when he was trying to give his love to her, and she soaked in the strength he had put in his kiss, almost crying at the sensation filling her. It was going to happen again. There was nothing that could stop it.

Tom broke their kiss, and she stumbled back, afraid.

"Please," he said, shaking from the energy he had given to her. "For us. I want to love you," he pleaded. "All of you in every way."

Mia leaned against the cheerful yellow wall of the kitchen, her pulse fast and her chin high. This was the best she had felt in weeks. She could take on the world, do anything. To have this every day would be the fulfillment of her deepest wish. Humans were so ignorant, taking for granted what they received from each other, never knowing the energy they passed between themselves. But the only reason she could see it was because it was what she needed to survive. She could drain the love from Tom like scooping water from a well, but it would kill him.

"I'm afraid," she whispered, though she stood powerful and strong.

Trembling, he stepped forward and took her hands. "Me too. I want you to be happy. Make the wish."

Mia's eyes filled, but they didn't spill over. "I wish," she said, her voice shaking, "that this man be protected from the pull of a banshee, that love will protect him and keep him safe, that no harm should come to him through my love for him." She held her breath, forcing herself to keep from taking even a wisp of emotion as a single tear fell to splash on their fingers, joined about the wish.

For a moment, they did nothing, waiting. The guitar on the radio changed to a full orchestra, and Tom looked at her, wide-eyed with his hope radiating to fill the room. Mia almost swooned at the effort to leave it untouched, to keep him strong. "Did it work?" he asked.

A lump in her throat, Mia steadied herself. "Kiss me?"

She tilted her head up as Tom leaned in, his long hands holding her shoulders. Dropping the coin to fall between them, she tentatively put her hands about his waist, unsure at how they felt there. She had never kissed him back. With a gentle sigh, Tom met her lips, and Mia went dizzy from the will needed to keep from soaking him in.

A wall, she thought, strengthening her own aura to keep them separate, gradually making it opaque, and then solid. She thickened her aura so that nothing could penetrate, nothing would come to her. He would fill the room with his love, and if she left it there, he would remain strong. His emotion would wash against her like water on a beach, and like a wave, it would ebb back to the ocean, undiminished.

And though it left her shaking in hunger, it worked.

Hope replaced her aching need in a rush, and somehow Tom felt it. Perhaps having been pulled upon so often by a banshee he had become sensitive to the emotions in a room. Perhaps because of his love for music he could read them easier. Whatever the reason, he knew she was taking nothing from him even as they shared their first passionate kiss.

Breaking from her, he stammered breathlessly, "Mia, I think it worked."

She smiled at him, a real one, and tamped down her excitement lest it break her control. "Do you?"

In answer, he pulled her to him, and with a tenderness born in the fragile beginnings of love, he cupped her face and kissed her again. Mia felt his lips on hers, but walled herself off, not allowing any of his emotion to stir her, even as his hands left her face and began to search, his beautiful long fingers tentatively seeking her skin beneath the shoulder of her dress. It had been in his eyes a long time and Mia welcomed it, even as she struggled to stay passive, to withhold her instincts to drive him into a deeper state of vulnerability. She wanted this. She wanted this so badly.

"Be careful . . ." she whispered, her heart pounding as his one hand found the buttons of the back of her dress, and she gasped at the wave of heat that his fingers, slipping the buttons free with a soft pop, made along her spine.

"I love you," he said, his voice husky and standing too close to see his face. "You can't hurt me. It worked, Mia. I can feel it. It worked."

He gently slid her dress from her shoulders, and the patterned silk fell softly to her waist to leave her shivering in the chill of the kitchen. She looked deeply at him, seeing her hope reflected in his eyes, feeling it pool about them like a heady wine. A tremble took her, but if it was from the new coolness on her skin or the effort she was exerting to let his love continue to build in the room, she didn't know. Maybe she didn't care.

He believed, and that was enough to soothe her fear.

She closed her eyes, and with that as an invitation, Tom pulled her to the living room. He sat on the edge of the couch amid the pooled emotion of his music, bringing her bare middle to his face as she stood before him, breathing her scent, his hands at her back. Her hands were among his hair, holding him there so he knew his touch was welcome.

"Mia," he whispered, and at the sensation of his words on her skin, she threw her head back to the ceiling. Desire cascaded from him, and she caught her breath, wire-tight as she refused to taste its strength, made doubly hard as it was directed to her. Her hands clenched once, and mistaking it for desire, he brought her to sit atop one knee.

He nestled his head between her small breasts, holding her to him with one arm as he nuzzled her, promising more. A wave of sexual heat hit Mia, and dizzy with her conflicting emotions, a slip of his need cracked the barrier she had made of her aura. Groaning, she went limp, basking in the depth of it. He responded by taking her in his mouth, pulling, tugging, not aware that she was growing tense with a hunger older than his religion.

"Tom, stop," she breathed, but he didn't. It was too late. He was filling the room with his desire. It would be up to her to keep from killing him outright, to take everything he was giving her. She could do this. It would end well.

His breath grew heavy, falling into a deliberate pace. Mouth never leaving her, he fumbled with the rest of her dress. It slipped to the floor at her feet when she leaned into him, pushing him back into the couch. Shifting his weight, he moved her, settling her light weight into the cushions and holding himself above her.

He pulled back, strong and dangerous with the heat of his emotions falling from his hands to warm her. She gazed at him in a bewildered haze, struggling to keep even the smallest bit from getting through to her again. She loved seeing him like this, strong and alive, and she reached up to undo the buttons of his shirt.

It was a bold move for her, for despite her confidence, she had little experience with men. Usually they were dead by this point.

Tom's smile grew gentle as he saw her fingers tremble, and as she got the last of the buttons free, he worked his pants from himself, easing down beside her. The rain was a hush against the glass, insulating them from the world.

Softer, more gently now as if knowing how rare this was, Tom caressed her middle with all the skill of a musician pulling a gentle note into life. She sighed, feeling his touch crack her aura. Everywhere his fingers alighted, every stroke he made, melted through the barrier she had made to give her jolts of his passion and desire, filing her with an almost never-tasted depth of feeling.

She moaned, and he lowered his head to take her breast again. A flash of need struck through her, and blood pounding, her hands darted into his hair, pressing him into her. Spurred on, he became aggressive. The pinch of teeth was like knives in her, slicing through her defenses to lay her bare to his lust. There was no love anymore. This was raw, animal hunger, and she relished it even as she strove to mend the tears in her aura he was making. She had to keep from taking it all. She shouldn't take anything. Even this little bit would show.

But his weight atop her was delicious, and the heat from his body drove everything else out. Mia shifted under him, tracing her hands down his back, feeling the muscle and bone, running lower as his mouth broke from her to rise and find her lips.

Her need quickened, and panting from effort, she met his

eyes once, reading her desperation in her reflection in her gaze. And then he kissed her.

Once more he broke through her aura, and she moaned, clutching him and arching her back as he drove his tongue into her with an animalistic fervor. Wave after wave of strength flooded her. She simply couldn't shield herself from this intimate contact that reached far past her aura and into her soul. She was alive, alive and scintillating. But she was taking too much, and she felt it in his faltering heartbeat.

"No," she whispered, groaning in despair. "Tom, stop."

He wouldn't, sending a pulse of heat through her when his hands grew stronger on her, demanding. Fear that she couldn't do this, fear she couldn't wall herself from him and it would all be for naught, was a sharp goad, and with a sudden realization, she knew what she had to do.

Desperate to regain control and keep from draining him of his life force, she took his face in her hands and turned his mouth to hers. Panting from a desperate need, she held him to her, and forced a kiss. Again, his desire broke through her aura, flooding her with an almost unbearable emotion, but this time, she pushed her own desire into him—redoubled.

He gasped, his entire body shaking as it rested atop her.

Mia felt the heat of tears under her closed lids. It was hard, so hard to push what he had given her back into him. It went against every instinct she had, but clearly he felt it, and his kiss and his hands upon her grew rough, savage. He hadn't several centuries to learn how to control such an influx of power and strength as she had.

His grip upon her waist hurt, and she did nothing as he forced her legs apart. She wanted this. Exalting in the savage response she could invoke, she gave him more, feeling it leave her in a scintillating sensation of sparkles.

A guttural sound came from him, and Mia gasped in an exquisite pain as he entered her, pushing to fill all of her in one move. She groaned, arching into him, wanting this.

Wanting it so badly that she gave him even more of herself.

Wave after wave of emotion drenched her, running off her to pool in the room as if to drown her in lust. He moved against her, dominating and aggressive. Every motion was like knives in her aura, breaking it, destroying what she had built to protect him. But she gave back more than she took, and he grew wilder, more demanding. He forgot all as he sweated above her, and she moaned with every breath, feeling an end coming, the wait an exquisite pain.

And in a sudden pulse, it broke upon them. A twisted groan eased from him, and he clenched her to him as wave after wave of ecstasy fell on them. Mia's barrier shattered. Gasping, she clutched at him, feeling his entire soul empty into her as she reached fulfillment, her body wracked with tremors as they hung unmoving in a haze of bliss.

Emotion shook the room in silent thunder only she could feel, and she almost passed out, taking breath after heaving breath until the sensation gave a final pulse and vanished.

"Tom," she panted, feeling his breath in her hair as he lay atop her, too spent to move. "Tom, are you okay?"

He didn't answer, and she pushed on his shoulder. "Tom?"

"I love you, Mia," he whispered, and he sighed, his full weight coming to rest against her.

"Tom!" she exclaimed, shoving him to the back of the couch and wiggling out from under him. The air felt thick, like sunshine pooled at the bottom of a valley, eddying about her feet with the heaviness of honey. She hadn't kept any of the emotion from the room. It was all here, cloying and thick, making her dizzy with a repressed need. But Tom . . .

Clutching her discarded dress, she stared as his aura went wispy and thin. An unbearable brightness began to emanate from him, and seeing it, a single tear trickled from her. Her hand trembling, she reached to touch him, shaking at the taste of his aura. It was fading, spreading out, becoming silver and thin to fill the room with unseen sparkles. Any other banshee would take it, gorge on the last life energy and dance in exaltation—but she didn't. Mia walled herself off, and a tear slipped down as she watched his life fill the room in a bright, ever so bright, light.

"Tom . . ." she whispered, weary even as her body still sang with the ecstasy he had filled her with. She had seen this before. He was dead. He was dead, and there was nothing that would bring him back. In that single moment of fulfillment, his emotion-rich aura had washed over her, laying his soul bare. She hadn't taken it, and it lay pooled about her feet to rise like a slow fog shifting from gold to purple. But she hadn't given him anything back, either, not like a human would have, protecting his soul until he gathered it back unto himself again.

Mia fell to her knees before him, still touching his shoulder warm with the last of his life. Misery twisted her delicate features, and then a sob broke free, harsh and pain-filled. It was followed by another, and she knelt beside him, her hand trembling as she gripped the wish that had caused his death. The tears falling into her lap turned from salt water to black crystal, the mark of a banshee's pain, and they fell soundlessly as she wept.

The glow from Tom's soul filled the room, and she closed her eyes, the light too painful for her pale eyes. The doors were shut, the windows locked, and though his soul was gone, the energy of his death lingered.

And Mia cried. She had killed him, sure as if she had driven a knife into his lungs. Sob after sob filled the apartment, her crystalline tears soaking up the energy of the room until the brightness dimmed to a memory, and then, even that vanished and the air was pure. The love was gone, the fear, the comfort, everything was gone, as if no one had loved, lived, and died sheltered by these walls. She kept none of his energy for herself. It had been hard, but to take it into herself had never been her intention.

Slowly, Mia's tears abated until her breathing steadied and her breath no longer came in racking gasps. The tears falling from her had eased from black to gray and were now perfectly clear, reflecting the dim sun from the ended rain. The emotions of the room were condensed and pooled in them. There would be nothing to link her to the death of this man, nothing to indicate that he had died in anything other than peaceful sleep.

Tom's body lay facedown on the couch, an arm trailing to brush the floor. Not looking at him, Mia slowly got dressed, drained and tired. She looked once at the wish about her neck, then left it to hang. The tears she gathered like photos of lost children, love and pain mixed in equal parts. If she didn't, someone would find them, recognize them, and she would be pulled in for questioning. The law knew what a banshee was capable of, and she would not allow herself to be jailed for this.

Fingers slow and clumsy, Mia felt the back of her dress to be sure the buttons were done up properly. The coffeepot was steaming, and she carefully put her empty cup away in the cupboard before unplugging the pot and setting his filled cup on the coffee table beside him. She turned the music down, and guilt prompted her to drape an afghan over him as if he was sleeping. His clothes went into the hamper.

Silent, she stood above him in her coat. "Goodbye, Tom," she whispered before gathering her groceries and quietly leaving.

Fatigue hit her anew when she found the sidewalk. The rain had stopped, and the sun was peeking past the heavy clouds. Fumbling, Mia put her sunglasses on. Traffic hissed wetly, and she breathed deep when a couple passed her, hotly discussing the amount of the tip one of them had left. It was a sour taste after Tom's love, and she let it eddy behind her unsipped.

She glanced at her watch and picked up the pace. Digging in a pocket, she found her wedding ring and put it back on. With a shamed slowness, her fingers slipped back into the pocket, running through Tom's life force, pooled and condensed.

Delicate features pulling into a grimace, Mia took out a

handful of tears, slipping the lightest one between her lips and sucking guiltily on it. His strength poured into her, and her pace quickened, heels clicking smartly against the concrete shining with the new sun.

Stupid man, she thought as she waved and jogged to catch the bus. The wish did work. Well, perhaps it would be more fair to say it *had* worked. It had worked very well when she met Remus—savage, angry Remus whose psychotic rage had been strong enough to bring Holly into existence. The love had come later, until now, she, Holly, and Remus were a real family. Like any family on the street, and Mia was proud of it.

Holly was the first banshee child to know her father, plying him with innocent love and devotion. It had been watching father and daughter that Mia learned it was possible to force emotion back into a person, lulling them into thinking they were safe while making themselves more vulnerable. The child had, in her innocence, returned to her species all the cunning and power human laws had taken from them, and for that alone Holly was going to be revered among her own. Once she learned how to walk and talk, that is.

Breathless, Mia smiled at the bus driver as she just made it to the door, fumbling for her bus pass. Tom, dead in his apartment, was hardly a glimmer of memory as she settled beside a young man smelling of cologne and shedding lust Mia knew to be from a new girlfriend. Easing back, she soaked it in, sated.

Her lids fluttered as they rumbled over the railroad tracks, and she looked at her watch, mildly concerned. Remus would likely throw a bloody-hell tantrum that she was running late, being unable to go to work until she got home to watch Holly. But they would both enjoy her kissing him into a calm state, and he'd get over it.

Besides, little Holly was hungry, and it wasn't as if *he* could do the shopping.

LIST OF CONTRIBUTORS

TANYA HUFF lives and writes in rural Ontario with her partner Fiona Patton, six cats and an unintentional chihuahua. Her third novel in the Confederacy of Valor series, *Heart of Valor*, was published from DAW Books in the summer of '07 and she is currently working on book four, *Valor's Trial*. When she's not writing, she's keeping an eye on the production of *Blood Ties,* her Vicki Nelson books adapted for televison. She's recently become addicted to homemade chai latte and thinks life would be pretty much perfect if the crawlspace would just quit flooding.

MARJORIE M. LIU is an attorney who has lived and worked throughout Asia. She hails from both coasts, but currently resides in the Midwest, where she writes full time. For more information about her books, which include the bestselling *Dirk & Steele* series, as well as her upcoming urban fantasy, *The Iron Hunt*, please visit her website at www.marjoriemliu.com.

New York Times and *USA Today* bestselling author **CHEYENNE McCRAY** has been writing ever since she can remember. She always knew one day she would write novels, hoping her readers would get lost in the worlds she created, as she did in her favorites.

For St. Martin's Press, Chey writes the bestselling "Magic" series, most recently *Shadow Magic* and the upcoming *Dark Magic.* She also writes romantic suspense novels, including the high-octane thriller *Moving Target* and the soon-to-be-released *Armed and Dangerous: Zack.* Cheyenne is married to her college sweetheart, has three sons, three dogs, a messy house, and will do anything to get out of cleaning, which may be why she writes so much. Visit Cheyenne's website at www.cheyennemccray.com.

L.A. BANKS, (aka, Leslie Esdaile Banks) is a native of Philadelphia and graduate of the University of Pennsylvania Wharton undergraduate program, as well as holds a masters in fine arts from Temple University's School of Film and Media Arts. After a ten-year career as a corporate marketing executive for several Fortune 100 high-tech firms, Banks changed careers in 1991 to pursue a private consulting career—which ultimately led to fiction and film writing. Now, with over twenty-seven novels plus ten anthology contributions in an extraordinary breadth of genres, and many awards to her credit, Banks writes full time and resides in Philadelphia. Look for her Vampire Huntress Legends series and a full listing of her published works at www.vampire-huntress.com or www.LeslieEsdaileBanks.com.

Born in the San Francisco Bay Area, **SUSAN KRINARD** received a BFA from the California College of Arts and Crafts and "fell" into writing after her dream of becoming a SF/fantasy cover artist fell through. The author of fifteen novels and several short stories and novellas, Susan focuses on the combination of fantasy and romance in her work. Her most recent novel, *Lord of the Beasts,* reached the *New York Times* bestseller list. She now lives in Albuquerque, New Mexico, with her husband Serge, a cat named Jefferson, and her dogs Freya, Nahla, and Cagney. You can reach her at susankrinard@comcast.net.

KERI ARTHUR was born and bred in Melbourne, Australia, and grew up sharing her life with dragons, elves, vampires, werewolves, shapeshifters, and the occasional talking horse. Which worried her family to no end. Of course, now that she actually makes a living sharing her life with the above-mentioned creatures, they no longer contemplate calling the men with the little white coats. When not at her keyboard, she can be found with her hubby in front of the TV, or taking her two dogs for a walk. For more information about all her books, head on over to www.keriarthur.com.

Bestselling, award-winning author **HEIDI BETTS** combines believable characters with compelling plotlines to create stories that focus on the commitment of one man and one woman to each other. She has written more than a dozen historical and contemporary romances, with several more projects in the works. Her first book for Silhouette Desire hit number one on the Waldenbooks Series Romance Bestseller List, where her books have continued to make an appearance ever since. Heidi loves to read, write, watch movies (and just a little too much television), and surround herself with furry, four-legged friends in her home in the beautiful hills of Central Pennsylvania. You can visit her website at www.heidibetts.com.

LILITH SAINTCROW was born in New Mexico and transplanted to England at an early age, where she imbibed some very odd notions about tea and language before being violently uprooted and returned to the U.S. She is the author of the Dante Valentine series as well as other interconnected books about Santiago City, which exists only in her head—despite what you may have heard. You can learn more about both the city and the books at her website, www.lilithsaintcrow.com.

Bestselling author **SUSAN SIZEMORE** lives in the Midwest. She loves canines, basketball, and coffee. When she isn't writing she's knitting, or wasting time on a couple of blogspots. These blogs can be reached through her website http://susansizemore.com.

DENISE LITTLE is a writer, editor, anthologist, and former bookseller. Her recent and forthcoming releases include *The Official Nora Roberts Companion, The Valdemar Companion* (with John Helfers), and the anthologies *Mystery Date* and *Front Lines*. She lives in Green Bay, Wisconsin.

CARRIE VAUGHN is the author of a series of novels about a werewolf named Kitty who hosts a talk radio show. The most recent is *Kitty and the Silver Bullet.* She's also published over thirty short stories in magazines such as *Weird Tales* and *Realms of Fantasy.* She has masters in English literature and lives in Boulder, Colorado, where she seems to be collecting hobbies. For more information about Carrie see www.carrievaughn.com.

USA Today bestselling author **LINDA WINSTEAD JONES** has written more than fifty romance books in several subgenres, including historical and fairy tale romance as well as romantic suspense. In the paranormal genre, she's written both contemporary and historical stories of ghosts and ghost-hunters, time travel, psychic phenomena, and fantasy set in alternate historical worlds. She's an award-winning author and three-time RITA® finalist. Writing as Linda Fallon, she won the 2004 RITA® for paranormal romance. Her recent releases include her popular Columbyana-set fantasy stories for Berkley Sensation and the contemporary paranormal romance *Raintree: Haunted.* You can find occasionally updated news about Linda at www.lindawinsteadjones.com.

New York Times bestselling author **KIM HARRISON** is presently living in the more sultry climates of the Southeast, where she can enjoy missing the snow of her childhood more efficiently. She has been known to venture into the kitchen when her taste for chocolate becomes unbearable, but her favorite pastime is shopping for good music, good food, and sexy boots—in that order. Kim has been hanging out with the same guy in leather for about twenty years, and since the publication of her latest, *For a Few Demons More,* has been working steady on the next Hollows novel and "loving every minute of it."

PROWL THE NIGHT WITH
NEW YORK TIMES BESTSELLING AUTHOR
KIM HARRISON

DEAD WITCH WALKING

978-0-06-057296-9 • $7.99 US/$10.99 Can

When the creatures of the night gather, whether to
hide, to hunt, or to feed, it's Rachel Morgan's job to keep things
civilized. A bounty hunter and witch with serious sex appeal and
attitude, she'll bring them back alive, dead . . . or undead.

THE GOOD, THE BAD, AND THE UNDEAD

978-0-06-057297-6 • $7.99 US/$10.99 Can

Rachel Morgan can handle the leather-clad vamps and even tangle
with a cunning demon or two. But a serial killer who feeds on the
experts in the most dangerous kind of black magic is
definitely pressing the limits.

EVERY WHICH WAY BUT DEAD

978-0-06-057299-0 • $7.99 US/$10.99 Can

Rachel must take a stand in the raging war to control Cincinnati's
underworld because the demon who helped her put away its former
vampire kingpin is coming to collect his due.

A FISTFUL OF CHARMS

978-0-06-078819-3 • $7.99 US/$10.99 Can

A mortal lover who abandoned Rachel has returned, haunted by his
secret past. And there are those willing to destroy the Hollows to get
what Nick possesses.

FOR A FEW DEMONS MORE

978-0-06-114981-8 • $7.99 US/$10.99 Can

An ancient artifact may be the key to stopping a fiendish killer.

Visit www.AuthorTracker.com for exclusive
information on your favorite HarperCollins authors.

Available wherever books are sold or please call 1-800-331-3761 to order.

HAR 0907

At Avon Books, we know your passion for romance—once you finish one of our novels, you find yourself wanting more.

May we tempt you with . . .

- **Excerpts** from our upcoming releases.

- Entertaining **extras**, including authors' personal photo albums and book lists.

- Behind-the-scenes **scoop** on your favorite characters and series.

- **Sweepstakes** for the chance to win free books, romantic getaways, and other fun prizes.

- Writing **tips** from our authors and editors.

- **Blog** with our authors and find out why they love to write romance.

- **Exclusive content** that's not contained within the pages of our novels.

Join us at
www.avonbooks.com

AVON

An Imprint of HarperCollins*Publishers*
www.avonromance.com

Available wherever books are sold or please call 1-800-331-3761 to order.

FTH 0708